ANGEL FIRE

ANGEL FIRE, BOOK 1

MARIE JOHNSTON

LE PUBLISHING

He doesn't have to like his new mate, even if she is the *only* angel to accept him.

Bryant should've behaved himself. Now he's been ordered to find a mate. Easier said than done when a bloke like him looks the way he does in a realm full of angels. He'd rather be fighting the good fight in the human realm. But mating the ravishing female that claims him shouldn't be a hardship. If only her father wasn't the reason for his scars.

Perhaps mating the surly, scowling warrior wasn't Odessa's best idea. But she's committed, and he's…frustrating. Enticing. Carrying a grudge she knows nothing about. Yet when her boss winds up dead and she's attacked, he's there to save her.

Digging into the danger Odessa's facing uncovers an ambitious plot against the realm. Good thing Bryant's a persistent guy. He'll stick to Odessa's side and keep her safe, all so he can let her go in the end. Because one thing he's learned about the down-to-earth angel is that she deserves better than him.

Except Odessa doesn't want to be rid of the loyal warrior. But that's an argument for a day when someone's not trying to kill them.

CHAPTER 1

*H*umiliating.

      Bryant Vale scanned the crowd of angels milling through the ornate, marbled ballroom. Groups of the not-quite-divine angelic creatures murmured and laughed with their heads thrown back. Some sipped white wine made from the sweet grapes of this realm that had been dispensed into delicate crystal goblets. All wore white, elegant robes, their wings of varying shades of gray, held high as they mingled and flirted with one another. All were having a fabulous time—at his expense.

Beside Bryant, Director Richter frowned at the haughty party-goers, "I can't believe it."

"What did you expect, Director?" Bryant kept his gravelly voice low. "Numen angels aren't like divine angels in attitude, just beauty. They take one look at my ugly mug and decide to wait an eternity for their sync mate rather than settle with me."

"It'd help if you didn't look like you were going to murder whomever you looked at."

Bryant lifted his wings in a shrug. The scar tissue on his

face made it hard to smile. So did the director's earlier words. You did this to yourself. A mate will mellow you, and more importantly, be there to aid in your healing when needed.

He didn't expect the director to understand. Like Bryant, Director Richter had been gravely injured in a demon battle on Earth when his sync brand appeared, and he'd made it to his destined mate in hopes to properly bond and heal. Their paths differed drastically from there.

Director Richter had settled here in Numen, the realm between Heaven and Earth, with his new love. Bryant had watched his destined mate die horribly before they were bonded. Rather, *instead* of being bonded.

Standing on display like a human's prized stallion at auction was salt on his wound, almost literally because he hadn't healed properly without a mate's energy. Unlike a nice-looking horse, Bryant received no bids.

No female accepted his offer to mate. None met his gaze. He mentally rolled his eyes when a couple of them approached from his right side, only to catch a full view of his old wounds when he faced them. They veered off to the punch bowl.

The females didn't leave, though. Interest in whether or not he'd land a mate was too great now. Who would take the damaged male home?

Bryant's wings twitched in irritation. He was a warrior. A protector of humankind against the demons that sought to control them. His life was work and more work, thankfully not in his own realm of Numen among these wankers, but down on Earth, among those souls he fought for. His steady absence isolated him from the reactions of his own people to the way he looked. The injuries he'd endured were garish at best. Even with his gunmetal gray wings splayed wide and his best white dressing gown—or *robes* as most Numen called them—draped over his muscular frame, no one saw beyond his mangled face.

Check it out, ladies. This is the best I'm going to get.

He gazed at the ballroom floor where angels mingled, enjoying the free entertainment. Mating galas attracted more than just the lonely. Old angels looked for a life partner and young angels sought an exciting mate instead of risking who destiny paired them with. Galas were a damn good reason to party. Bryant studied the conversations, the flagrant flirtation, the way females and males alike sashayed toward his fellow warriors. Many would find a mate for the night. Maybe two.

Bryant snorted. *At least some bloke would be getting lucky.*

"All right. Time to wrap this ceremony up." Director Richter set down his punch and nodded to a member of Bryant's warrior team. Urban banged the ceremonial gong. The sound reverberated through the room. Conversations hushed and attention focused on the dais—and Bryant.

Bryant clasped his hands behind his back, his shoulders tight. What would the director do now? Hopefully, stop this foolish pursuit and put him back in the field. The director accused him of being careless. Bryant considered himself fearless. Perhaps he was meant to die in battle. It was far better than enduring another night like this. Bryant's destined mate had the right idea. He'd throw himself in front of a bus, too, if the director scheduled another such event.

Director Richter flared his downy wings to signal he was ready to speak. The room sank into stillness, the guests probably wondering *what now?*

"Honored guests," the director intoned, "it is time to close this ceremony with one final opportunity to claim acceptance of Bryant Vale, honored warrior team leader."

The silence was astounding. Many females suddenly had

3

to inspect the corners for cobwebs. The rest searched the room for the poor soul who would offer herself up to Bryant.

A few more tense moments almost had Bryant squirming in his dressing gown, but he refused to give the audience the satisfaction. He'd been sliced by demon blades, burned by angel fire, yet this night ranked as one of the worst in his life. *Wrap it up, already.*

Director Richter opened his mouth to speak when the ten-foot high doors at the end of the ballroom swung open.

Every head turned to watch a tall, graceful female glide in. Bodies automatically parted, clearing a path. Her long legs carried her confidently through the crowd without slowing. Bryant absorbed the vision marching in his direction.

Long locks of glossy hair cascaded from the elegant style atop her head. Mahogany curls caressed a strong face with stunning teal eyes framed by dark lashes. Her lips formed a perfect red bow.

She carried her wings high and proud with a subtle flare, hinting at the rank of her family. They were the lightest gray, the feathers reflecting the light and complementing her dark hair and vibrant eyes. His gaze drifted down until the silky, tanned flesh of her legs snagged his attention. Her confident stride swirled her white dressing gowns, allowing the slit in each side to tease any male with a heartbeat.

His perusal eventually made it back up to her face. A jolt of awareness hit him in the gut. She had been placidly assessing him the entire time. She spent more time on his face than all the other females in the ballroom combined. Why? He cursed the first emotion that surfaced. Hope. That this ethereal creature might find him attractive. He was too old for fairy tales.

He met her dauntless stare boldly, giving her the full force of his scrutiny.

Tearing her unsettling gaze away only to seek out

Director Richter, her rich voice sent electrical shocks through Bryant's body.

"Director, I accept this male."

ODESSA'S HEART beat so loudly she swore the imposing male on the stage could hear it. He was everything she had hoped for and, oh, so much more. Bryant Vale radiated power, danger, and virility.

One of the first things she had noticed about him, other than his height and a shoulder width that suggested his robe was hiding ropes of muscle, were his amber eyes. They practically glowed with the emotion he buried deep inside. She'd noted with satisfaction how his gaze had trailed from her wings to her legs—her best asset. They were bronze and toned, and she didn't mind showing them off. Some angels abandoned the robes for human fashion, but she rarely did unless she was among humans and needed to blend in.

Odessa forced herself to maintain eye contact with the stunned director.

Was she too late? Had the warrior already accepted another?

Gulping her anxiety down, Odessa concentrated on exuding strength and confidence. Some called her arrogant.

If only they knew.

Director Richter snapped his mouth shut and rushed on as if he was afraid she might change her mind. "Absolutely. Yes, yes. Come, my lady."

He stepped to the edge of the stage to offer her a hand as she climbed the few stairs. When she reached the top, she headed straight to Bryant. She buried her hands into the folds of her robe lest she betray her nerves by wringing them.

A few hours ago, she had worried her decision was rash,

impulsive. She'd read the missive announcing the gala and, well, she had needs. After rushing home to clean up and change, she was here, accepting a mating offer with a stranger. Standing next to him confirmed the description of her feelings as rash and impulsive was inadequate. This was insane.

She peered up at him from the corner of her eye. No emotion registered on his face. His whiskey gaze bored into the far wall. Intense was how she would've described his picture. He was formidable in person, like a stone wall stood next to her.

The crowd stood motionless, spellbound to watch the scene play out. She imagined it was more drama than they all could've hoped for, and she was loath to give it to them. She preferred a quiet life, but any quieter and no one would notice if she suddenly disappeared.

Hence why she was here, in front of angels she'd known all her life, or had never cared to meet. The energy of the crowd pushed against the stage. She nearly frowned, but that'd give them the wrong impression. The anticipatory glee on their faces, as if they waited for her to run, aghast at his appearance.

Too bad. Wasn't happening. Her sanity was invested in this decision. Bryant Vale's fierce vibe didn't scare her as badly as the males who'd attacked her all those years ago—who were still at large.

Were they the ones who were following her? Would they stop once she mated? Bryant Vale was an honored warrior for their people; he protected humans from the demons sneaking into their realm. If he'd had fewer accolades, she wouldn't have gone through with this.

Resolute, Odessa faced Bryant as he pivoted toward her. Did he intentionally keep his damaged side away from the crowd? Her gaze roamed over his features. His scarring wasn't atrocious. It gave him quite the thuggish appeal, especially with the twisted ear, but it didn't overpower his masculine features. His dark hair was trimmed down to the scalp. At a distance, he'd looked bald, and he was, sort of. She didn't think much of his left side could grow hair any longer. He had broad cheekbones and a square jaw, a straight nose and high forehead. From wingtip to toe, he oozed power.

Bryant's brows drew in as if he waited for her repulsion, and when she didn't express any, he didn't trust why. In a realm of beautiful immortals, she doubted he'd been entirely accepted since he'd earned those scars. She could sympathize. Not all scars were external.

The director moved beside them to face the audience and preside over the ceremony. He leaned in. "May I have your name?"

"Odessa Montclaire." She smiled, predicting his reaction to her name.

Bryant's eyes widened. The director stammered over the introductions. Hushed conversation rippled through the audience. Most recognized her last name, but Odessa didn't know many in attendance. She'd only been back a few years since her analyst training, and she hadn't grown up in this section of Numen.

The Montclaires had been pivotal in top branches of Numen government. Her father liked to pretend he still was. She'd grown up in a privileged, spoiled house. At least until *that* night.

The ceremony continued. Since they weren't destined mates, Director Richter used the power of his station to bestow the sync mark upon them. She had no time to wait around for her brand to organically appear like it did when a Numen finally had a destined mate somewhere in the world. Her inner left wrist tingled. She ignored the urge to glance down to see the outline of a single wing, one half of a pair.

7

When it came time for their vows, Odessa's spine tingled as Bryant's rough voice bit off her name in a clipped British accent.

He must've either lived in England for several years or had a parent from there. It wasn't unusual for Numen to live on Earth before they settled into their angelic duties. Some chose to remain on Earth, conceal their true nature, and provide aid to those in need. Was it his mother or father? Or both? Odessa couldn't wait to learn about him.

A shiver of anticipation flitted through her. They were getting *mated*. They would intimately learn about each other tonight. Her breath caught as the subject she'd been solidly ignoring in case it caused her to abort her mission crowded foremost in her mind.

Could she lie with a male she just met?

Would he be gentle? Or rough?

Either way, from the power radiating off him, it would be quite an experience. And probably not a bad one. At all.

It was time to clasp their wrists so their marks touched. Odessa willed her palms to stop sweating, but she couldn't quit thinking about where else he'd be touching her later that night.

His skin was on fire. Warmth seeped in, soothing her fears and chasing her personal demons into the shadows. He had a strong grip and didn't loosen it for her. She glanced up. Bryant's expression was indiscernible. If she had to label it, she'd say he looked suspicious, and definitely not pleased. Was he not attracted to her?

No matter. As long as he slept under her roof, then she could finally sleep, too. Wouldn't dread the memories her empty house dredged up or hide in her closet at every noise.

Director Richter completed the ceremony and presented them to the crowd. Her hand slid out of Bryant's much larger one. She was caught off guard by enthusiastic clapping and whistling from a section toward the back, near the table with the drinks.

From the way Bryant scowled at them, and the information from his gala announcement, Odessa guessed that was his team, six fellow warriors who trusted him with their lives. Maybe they could convince him this sync was a good thing.

The rest of the night was a whirlwind; they didn't have time to say a word to each other. Strangers shook their hands and offered congratulations. His fellow warriors swarmed, but not even their exuberance cracked a smile on Bryant. She smiled enough for both of them, ever the dignitary's daughter.

Finally, the gala wound down and angels filtered away. Bryant faced her and said the first sentence she'd heard him utter other than his vows.

"Lead me to your place, Odessa." His tone snapped on her name. Without waiting for a response, he stalked toward the exit and disappeared through the tall, wooden doors.

Odessa inhaled a shaky breath. This was it. It was for real. She followed him out.

Her heart thumped and she was grateful her robe hid the flush creeping up her torso. The thought of him claiming her certainly wasn't unwelcome, just...so soon. She wasn't the one-night-stand type—she wasn't her sister. Bryant was an imposing male, exuding an intoxicating scent that induced a rush of pheromones, but he was obviously not happy with being forced to sync. He actually seemed less pleased that it was *her* he had mated with.

It hadn't occurred to her that the willingness to mate would be one-sided. Had the gala not been his idea? Why would he have been forced into mating? Regardless, he had been, and she had accepted.

Lifting her chin and gathering her courage, she lifted off,

her wings whispering into the night. Bryant's looming presence stayed behind her. She touched down outside her front door and waited for him to land before tapping the security panel of the door. He was a wall behind her. She wanted to run, but there was nowhere to go except into her own house that was now his, or smack against his wide, hard chest. Once they stepped into her foyer, she nervously peeked at him from under her lashes. Determination darkened his gaze.

"Tell me the truth." He rounded on her, drowning her in his bright gaze. "Why did you sync with me?"

CHAPTER 2

*B*ryant vibrated with fury. His anger had begun to grow when she spoke her name, but now that he found himself in the mansion of an upper-crust Numen… He tightened his wings lest he thrust them out in the universal sign that an angel was pissed.

Why would a *Montclaire* sync with his sorry arse? What could possibly be her motive for not waiting to be awarded with a proper mate, likely a proper *upper*-level angel? Did her father put her up to it? He refused to be a pawn in that haughty senator's game again.

Her deep blue-green eyes flared with incertitude at both his demeanor and his abrupt demand that she answer with her reason for syncing with him. *Good luck with that, gorgeous.* He wasn't going to be the plaything of a bored socialite looking to get Daddy's attention.

"What do you mean?"

And she was stalling.

"You know what I mean. Look at me. Look at this." He gestured around them, indicating the white marble columns and posh tiled floor. A world apart from the stone barracks he still slept in.

Odessa set her shoulders, those pouty lips of hers flattening.

He admired her for that but pressed on. "What would make you sync before your time? You're all of what, twenty-two?"

Crossing her arms, a movement that pushed her ample cleavage higher, she continued to square off with him. "I'm twenty-five, and my birthday is in two months."

"I'm ninety-two and was supposed to sync fourteen years ago, but she stopped dead in traffic when she saw my face." Bryant raised a hand and slapped it with his other hand to demonstrate the moment that continually haunted him. Odessa flinched. "Not even her Numen heritage could save her from that level of trauma. So tell me, why did you throw yourself at me when my first mate dove in front of a bus?"

She was mortified over the description. Her kind was immortal, but if the injury was great enough, they could die. Especially in the human realm and if the female refused to mate. But then Bryant's last statement sunk in. Her jaw dropped open with indignation. "I did not *throw* myself at you. I'm not your prior sync mate so don't hold me accountable for her actions. And it doesn't sound like she dove, but was too stunned to move."

The statement caught him off guard. He'd expected her pity, had dreaded it.

She recovered her serenity. "As for my reasons, I have my own, as I'm sure you do."

"I had *one* reason. It was either endure that public humiliation or remain off duty until I synced." *You're getting too impulsive, Bryant.* Director Richter's words spiked his blood pressure. *Irresponsible. Find a mate to settle you down.* "I live for my work. So here I am, and I have to work bloody early in the morning. Where's the sofa?"

At this point, Bryant wondered if Odessa could understand him. When he was emotional, his accent became stronger. He snapped off his T's, rolled his R's, and his I's sounded like "oi." His mother preferred to reside in England as much as possible, and she'd hauled them all out of Numen for months at a time to go do her goodwill projects. Bryant still kept a flat in London for his time off, while his parents, like many other Numen who weren't assigned specialty positions, carried out relief work all over the world.

Confusion furrowed her brow and the fight in her eyes died. He hated to see it go. She was radiant in her indignation.

"Are you…? Aren't we going to…?"

He caught the intention of her question. His normally quiet libido roared to life, but he stomped it back down by mentally repeating her father's name.

Did she know what her father had done to him? Would she care?

"No, Odessa, we aren't. Not until you tell me why I'm here. Until then, I'm not your toy."

"Toy?" Her offended tone matched her expression. "I assure you, Bryant Vale, I'm not the type to bring home *toys*. I desired a strong sync mate."

His name on her lips excited a part of his anatomy that should best ignore how unearthly gorgeous she was. Instead, he barked out a laugh. "I see. You didn't have faith your destined mate would have a decent pair of bollocks. No doubt he would've been some winged hothead that built his life breaking other's backs instead of his own." *Like your father.*

Odessa peered at him a long moment before she spoke,

her brow furrowed like she was working out math in her head. "What do you have against me?"

"That fact that you don't know just shows how young and naïve you are." Bryant stalked away to search for the sofa. "I'm going to sleep. Tell your servants to leave me the hell alone."

"I have no servants."

The soft words sounded forlorn. Maybe she was still getting settled or something. It didn't look like anyone lived in this place. Pristine columns rose to connect with an elegant arched ceiling. A curved staircase appeared to be more decoration than useful with its cold and uninviting marble. The whole mansion lacked hominess. It had more of an atmosphere of being suspended in museum-quality preservation.

He discovered a sofa that sported minimal padding. Tucking his wings against his body, he flopped down on it. His dressing gown would keep him warm enough for a few hours of sleep and then he'd be back out in the field.

WHAT AN— What did her human friend Harper say?

Asshat.

That's it. What an asshat!

Odessa granted him leeway after hearing the quick description of his destined sync mate. That would give anyone a hit to their self-worth. Mates were supposed to be their perfect partner, but his hadn't had a chance to prove it. Run down by a bus. Tragic.

But Odessa couldn't understand why Bryant hated her because of her rank in Numen society. Yes, her father was a senator and active in the Numen government. So much so, everyone seemed to forget about his wife and daughters, and that was for the best.

Odessa had been concerned her move back to the heart of Numen would reignite gossip. So far it had not, and she planned to stay out of the limelight and at her desk while she worked, aiding in human and Numen protection alike. The demons of Daemon were a constant threat. They infiltrated the human realm like worms and if left unchecked, they could storm the figurative gates of Numen.

With a sigh, Odessa allowed her wings to droop. Bryant had indeed claimed the couch instead of her. She trudged up the curved staircase to her suite. It took up the entire right wing of the second level and after three years back, it was finally starting to feel...not homey. Familiar. Sometimes she remembered the good days, of running through this wing when it was her parents', before she'd been shipped off to boarding school. Laughter had been constant in those days.

Her eyes filled with tears. Had her family done the right thing? Regardless, her mother was gone, Odessa was estranged from her sister, and she rarely visited her father. She could only preserve the memory of happier times, the ones before *that* night.

That horrible night was the reason Odessa stayed out of the left wing where she and her sister used to share a room. Most days, she never entered her old room. Part of dealing with her fear was to quit running from it and protect herself from another night like that again. Living somewhere else would be avoidance, though tempting...

Which was where Bryant came in. At least he was under her roof. Maybe that would be enough.

CHAPTER 3

*S*unlight blazed through the crack in the cream-colored drapes in Odessa's bedroom. She blinked herself awake, allowing her eyes a moment to adjust. For the first time since she'd been back living in the mansion, she felt rested. It'd been a late night, though not for the reason it should have been. Disappointment curled in Odessa's belly. She had been looking forward to getting to know Bryant. Until he'd announced he wanted nothing to do with her.

But he was hers now. She could eventually break down his barriers and kill his misconceptions. They had eternity together. Too long for resentments and grudges. They came from opposite ends of the realm, something he proved sensitive about, but they didn't have to live on opposite ends of the mansion.

Odessa stretched and shook out her wings. With her looks, she had never lacked for attention. While she chose boyfriends wisely, she was afraid her immaturity and the trauma she had faced as a kid made her a little, well, *clingy*.

No need to worry about that any longer. She had a mate. A distinguished warrior that would live under her roof. And with him here, those shadows she swore were stalking her wouldn't enter.

Odessa rushed to clean up, hoping Bryant would be more amiable over breakfast. She threw on a casual white robe, a toga style that wasn't as long as her formal robes. With one last peek in the mirror, she straightened her outfit and fluffed her hair. She hopped down the stairs to check on Bryant.

The couch was empty.

"Bryant?" Was he eating already?

Her kitchen was empty.

She drew in a shaky breath. He had to be here.

The bathroom? Nothing.

He was gone.

Odessa chewed her lip, her panic rising. How long had she slept blissfully unaware—*and alone?*

How could he have left her? She twisted her hands into her robe's soft material. She refused to be the weak, clingy girl again, but years of fear didn't vanish overnight.

Maybe he had to go to work early and hadn't wanted to wake her. He didn't know she had a deep-seated fear of the dark.

Coaxing her alarm down, she reframed her thoughts—something much easier to do in the light of day. Her Saturday was now free.

She dug her cellphone out of her underwear drawer. No one was allowed in her house, and who knew when Bryant would come into the bedroom, but she preferred the privacy. Phones were one of the human devices Numen had adopted to maintain their connections in the human realm. The phone could be powered by angelic energy and used to converse without changing realms. Pretty darn handy until a human asked what service plan she used.

But she had no good reason to be in another realm. The phone stayed hidden.

Harper answered after the first ring. "'Sup?"

Odessa smiled at her adorably human friend. Working with Harper highlighted how stifling Numen life could be. Humans were so much freer with their words and actions. Maybe it was their shorter life spans—they didn't take emotions for granted as often as angels.

She had no good reason to be granted ascension abilities —to descend into the human realm and transcend to her own. It was one of the few benefits of being a senator's child. Senators ruled the realm. They were power and authority, and they often came from wealth and a long line of senators. She could move freely between realms and no one questioned why.

"Do you still need help this weekend? I'm free after all." *Please, please, please.* Finding a weekend retail job in the human realm had helped Odessa heal more than anything. Her parents had done nothing but ship her off to boarding school when the night terrors got to be too much. *You'll be around plenty of others, dear. You'll sleep in dorms and not be alone.*

"Whaaaat? I thought you were getting married."

Rats. Why hadn't Odessa lied when Harper texted her asking her to pick up a shift at the store?

Because she was an angel and, while not divine, angels were not supposed to lie.

"Well." Odessa cleared her throat. "You remember I told you it was more of an arranged marriage?"

"Uh-huh." Harper's tone implied she wanted all the juicy details.

"He's a little resistant to the idea. So, yeah, he decided to work this weekend." Odessa's cheeks burned at the humiliation of her admission. As far as describing the situation in human terms, that summed it up.

"What an asshat. But, like, you're actually married?" Her curiosity was obvious.

"Yes. A quick ceremony."

"Aaaaand?"

"Resistant."

Harper blew out a breath. "Whoa. I don't know whether to be happy for you or disappointed. Take care of yourself. We found someone to cover, so don't worry. Next weekend, remember, we're going out with our boots on."

"I'm a maybe, just in case he comes around."

"Odessa." Harper's tone was stern. "You are making plans with friends, and your man can sit at home and wait for you. If he doesn't like it—tough. If he decides you're the hottest thing since volcanoes and wants to pleasure you all weekend —tough. He needs to wait. You're going out."

Odessa gave in to her grin. During their time together, talk sometimes ended up on men, and Odessa had discussed her failed relationships with her friend. Harper's goal was to make sure Odessa didn't resort to the simpering female again.

"Fine. Code Boots On," Odessa affirmed using the saying her friends used when they wanted to hit the town for dancing.

"Woo-hoo!" Harper triumphed. "So…what's he like?"

Amber eyes and an accent that made her insides melt came to mind. "Intense," Odessa sighed. "He's soooo male."

"I likey that description. Don't worry, he'll come around. If he doesn't realize how lucky he is to be married to your insanely hot self, then there's no saving him."

Friends were awesome. Harper and her coworkers were worth those first few terrifying trips to the human realm to learn their ways. The human connections Odessa had formed made life worth living, not just surviving. When Numen became too stifling, too terrifying, Odessa hung with the humans.

"You're the best," Odessa told her.

"I know."

Chuckling, Odessa ended the call and hid her phone in her underwear drawer. Her smile died with the connection. She was back to being alone.

ODESSA WORKED AROUND HER HOUSE, cleaning into late evening. Fresh air from the open windows lightened her spirits. Birds chirped, but unlike the human realm, there were no sounds of traffic. Numen had many of the same materials, built similar structures, and had angels dedicated to handcrafting clothing, but was blissfully quiet when it came to the sound of motors and engines.

Though there were days when she missed the noise that drowned out her insecurities.

When daylight wiped the shadows from every corner, she could almost pretend the place wasn't holding a part of her hostage. Perhaps her expectations of Bryant's presence and protection was unfair to him, but it wasn't like she had her family around to help her.

Odessa couldn't bring herself to trust servants in and around her living quarters. She lived with no staff at all. Only she was responsible for the upkeep, but that was okay. Busy hands, healthy mind.

Nightfall approached, and Odessa's anxiety built. Darkness invited flashbacks and nightmares. Odessa endured most nights locked in her room with a carving knife under her pillow. Every sound, every whisper of wind, she'd flinch and fight back tears.

Where was Bryant? Warriors often took night shifts as it was demons' favorite time to orchestrate chaos in the human realm. All angels who chose specialty work for the realm were free to adapt their schedule.

For her work as an analyst, she was a transcriber of the reports of angelic watchers, those who followed humans and reported on their activity. Half the notes she transcribed were of human nightlife. The other half were from the daytime when her kind discreetly waged battles away from human detection. She could read about the wild side of life and the dangerous parts all from the safety of her office, and all while she worked what humans called "banker's hours."

Unlike those angels, whose tasks took them out of the realm at all hours of the day and night, she could be safely tucked away in her mansion when night fell. Demons were weaker and human hosts were stronger during daylight hours. Since Bryant had been gone all day, he had to be coming back soon.

Odessa dusted around her home, flitting through the lower level, her hand trembling as daylight faded. It was always summer in Numen, with weather almost as glorious as Heaven. Sure, it rained, sometimes even stormed, but the sun stayed out a good sixteen hours a day. She'd used up fifteen and a half hours on housework.

She'd taken for granted that Bryant would be around when the sun dropped below the horizon. She hadn't mentally prepped herself for the night to come. Maybe she should call Harper again.

No. She'd already bothered her today.

Shadows grew around the room. Amid her panic, a spark of anger smoldered. Her new mate wasn't coming home.

Unless...what if he got hurt at work? Bryant would need the aid of her healing power. Angels were only immortal in that they didn't die from old age and illness. But like his former assigned mate, he could get killed if injuries in the human realm were severe enough. Or—

Her heart seized. What if he was in a fight and got wounded by a weapon crafted in their own realm—or worse the Daemon realm? She shuddered. Daemon steel was cursed with evil that festered, making healing difficult to impossible without a mate's aid.

But no, if Bryant was too injured to get ahold of her, surely Director Richter would have contacted her.

The anger returned.

She could stay home and wait, or she could utilize the last rays of light to find her wayward mate. The warrior barracks would be her first stop. She stepped out on the dais off the back of her house and took flight. Her wings flared out, catching air to keep her adrift. With the setting sun, a few Numen were floating around in the sky. Many were couples out for the angelic version of a moonlight stroll, flying hand in hand. She shoved back twinges of longing and replaced them with determination.

Odessa flew past the manors as large as her own, over smaller housing structures situated in blocks, each with a tidy lawn surrounding it. A faint glow dusted the horizon. Its source was the angel fire fountain the rest of the realm was constructed around. Angel fire. She shuddered. It'd stolen so much from her while at the same time keeping their entire realm safe. The ethereal plasma was a tried and true weapon against demons and its origination was a gift from the Almighty.

She was happy to put her back to it and fly in the opposite direction. Her realm was beautiful. Manicured. Pristine. There was no garage spilling over bins, no smog, no pollution. Angel fire burned clean. The energy required came from the realm itself. The borders knew no bounds. Numen was as large as it needed to be.

Finally, she located the large, square buildings that comprised the training center. She drifted down in front of the most ornate one. Her gaze flicked to the sign: Numen Warrior Training Center. She was at a loss for where to go from there.

A familiar male spoke from behind her. "Miss Montclaire?"

She spun to face Director Richter. Humiliation nearly lifted her wings for a flight home versus having to tell him she didn't know where her mate was. What she wouldn't give to be able to ascend or descend in her own realm, but ascension was only for travel from earth to Numan, and vice versa was called descending. Besides, that'd smack too much of desperation. Pride was in short supply. She'd seize it when she could.

"Can I help you with something, Miss—I'm sorry, Lady Vale?"

Pleasure warmed her at the use of her new name. At least something about her mate gave her satisfaction.

She plastered on a false smile. "I'm looking for Bryant, Director. I haven't seen him all day." She winced at her own confession.

Surprise, then irritation highlighted his eyes and was quickly replaced by a competent, professional demeanor. No wonder Director Richter garnered so much respect.

"Come. I know where he might be." His mouth was set in a determined line. He inclined his head in an invitation to follow.

They passed several gray stone buildings, each a uniform three stories tall, until they arrived at the end of the line of barracks.

"Wait here, please." He disappeared inside.

She did as he asked, clasping her hands in front of her. What was the best way to loiter outside of warrior barracks? And why barracks? Why didn't Bryant have his own home?

Male warriors drifted in and out, throwing curious glances her way. She avoided eye contact, didn't want to acknowledge that they may know who she was, or give them any indication she was hunting down her mate.

"Odessa." The clipped accent brought her head up.

Her heart fluttered. Damn her nerves. He was even more imposing in the twilight. The shadows that tormented her only increased the span of his shoulders. His wings blended into the fading light, his expression obscured so she couldn't gauge the strength of his emotions. Director Richter was nowhere to be found.

"You didn't come home." She crushed her hands together to keep from fidgeting.

"This is where I live."

She studied the gray building and then him. His resolute expression and solid stance screamed that he wasn't leaving with her. Hurt flared, hot and bright in her chest.

She tilted her gaze skyward and took to the air, not trusting herself to keep her tears at bay. Staying any longer would have resulted in a bout of ugly crying, or worse, begging. She'd had enough semi-public disgrace today.

But landing outside her home was akin to diving into the middle of shark-infested waters. Her skin prickled like danger swarmed around her. With an unsteady breath, she faced her door but didn't open it. It was dark. So dark and quiet. She usually left a light on but had forgotten since she'd left so quickly. She reached for the doorknob. Her fingers trembled. She snatched them back, cursing her weakness then cursing Bryant.

How could he treat her like that? If he was all about duty, wasn't his mate his duty?

An owl hooted and she jumped, expecting hands to reach

out and grab her any moment. Terror threatened to override common sense as she imagined being pinned down, helpless —again.

Desperate, her mind spun, searching for a way to calm herself down. An idea formed.

No. She couldn't.

Or could she? It would be embarrassing, but she survived the wait of shame outside the barracks. Plenty of angels had witnessed Bryant avoiding her. Good gossip stopped nosy angels in their tracks. She and her mate would be the hot topic at the angel fire fountain by morning. So what if she added more fuel to speculation? The only thing to lose was her pride, but she'd make, in Harper's words, a helluva point.

Raising her wings with determination, she fought off her fear. Odessa stalked over to her bed and chose a pillow and a blanket. She stormed back to the dais with her bundle and flew to the barracks.

BRYANT TOSSED and turned in his bunk in the bay he shared with his team. They could have separate apartments, but then they might as well live in the heart of the realm. It was easier for unmated warriors to reside in barracks. It was just as easy to live in a house and walk or fly here, but no one mentioned that. Sometimes, the horrors they witnessed in the field stayed in the shadows when surrounded by other warriors who understood.

Director Richter's ass chewing still rang in Bryant's ears. *Be the male I know you can be, Vale. Don't act a fool.*

Easy for a happily synced guy to say. His sync happened the way it should for a warrior. The male had earned himself a fine mate, one who made brownies divine angels would fall for.

Bryant had gotten himself synced to the daughter of the most devious, corrupt, and heartless politician he'd ever dealt with. The one and only conversation Bryant had ever had with Odessa's father was more than memorable. His blood boiled and his scars throbbed thinking about it. One conversation, one order from the senator, and Bryant had found himself burning alive, with over half his team already dead.

Now the despicable senator was linked to him through that frustrating, unearthly beautiful daughter of his. Had it been Daddy's idea, or his daughter's?

Movement outside the door caught Bryant's attention. He rose on his elbow to see what was going on through the bay window. A head with long, dark hair bobbed through the hall.

He clenched his jaw, grinding his teeth. The audacity. He'd underestimated his unwanted mate.

Odessa stopped to ask a young warrior a question. Bryant wanted to throttle the male when he blushed and grinned broadly before pointing in Bryant's direction. He grew even more pissed at the sweet smile the male earned from her.

Bryant glanced at his teammates. He'd choke them as well. All six were eyeballing his woman with shit-eating grins they pointed in his direction before they settled back on their bunks to watch the show. *Bloody tossers.*

Glaring at the female striding toward him with mile-long legs, Bryant's gaze kept drifting to her one bare golden shoulder. Shite. Was she carrying a pillow and blanket?

Bryant sat up, scowling. "Odessa?"

"Unlike you," she said coolly, "I take my sync seriously." Flipping her pillow down between his bunk and his teammate Urban's bunk, she folded her blanket in half and laid it down. She crawled between the fold like a makeshift sleeping bag.

"You've got to be joking," he said for her ears only. The

floor was marble and awfully cold in the morning.

She rolled onto her side, her back toward him, her wings tucked into the blanket. "Good night, Bryant."

Urban peered down at her, the dim lights of the bay reflecting off his dark hair. He smirked up at Bryant. "Good night, Bryant."

Bryant glared at his friend.

Sierra, one of the females on his team called, "Good night, Bryant," in a sweet tone.

"Good night, Bryant," echoed the other two females, Harlowe and Dionna.

"Good night, Bryant," cooed Bronx.

"Good night, Bryant." This from Jagger, who had the bollocks to blow him a kiss.

They were his closest friends, and right now, he loathed them all.

With a huff, Bryant rolled off the bed, snatched the pillow and Odessa's arm. She didn't say a word as he pulled her up and hauled her out of the bay and down the hall. He refused to look at anyone, his gaze plastered to the wooden exit door at the end of the corridor. As soon as fresh air hit his face, he released her and flew to that damn mansion, praying she'd follow.

He snapped his wings closed as she landed. Startled, she faltered and was mid-stumble when he caught her around the waist. The mystery of how good her body felt should have remained just that.

When she regained her equilibrium, he gently pushed her inside, handing her the pillow. "Go to bed. You've won. I'll sleep here from now on."

Hurt wiped out the hopefulness in her expression.

"I made a point. I didn't win anything." She hugged her pillow and trudged toward the stairs to her suite, leaving him to feel like he'd kicked a defenseless puppy.

CHAPTER 4

*B*ryant stayed on Odessa's sofa for three days before he decided it was time to move his stuff over. He was only around long to catch a few winks and he was gone again. The arrangement provided little contact with his mate.

What contact he did have was excruciating. She was a beautiful female. Achingly so. Her long gown did nothing to conceal her curves, or the slope of her neck, or the radiance of her wings. He caught himself staring too long when she wasn't looking. But each time she attempted conversation, he cut her off with an "I gotta get to work" and rushed out before he tented his own gown like a randy boy veering into puberty.

Like it or not, this cold, stale mansion was his new home. He couldn't risk her coming to the barracks again. He'd lose his credibility as a proper leader if it appeared he couldn't care for his own mate. As obstinate as he wanted to be, he couldn't sleep in a bed while she took the floor. Having her in the tiny bunk with him wasn't an option, either. He grew irritatingly hot at the thought alone.

His workday done, he changed out of his black tactical demon fighting clothes and into a standard gown in the barracks before packing his meager belongings. He loaded the rest of his clothing into a bag. The trunk at the foot of the bed would haul his equipment. He opened it and dumped his weapons inside—knives, throwing stars, vials of holy water, and small bottles of angel fire. Many thought he'd be too edgy to carry angel fire, having been marked by it already. He wasn't. It was a weapon, nothing more.

And also a wicked fast way to maim or kill an angel.

Shoving his weapons into his bag, he slammed gear around to make it all fit, releasing his irritation with each satisfying *thunk*. He stewed over those who vexed him—the director for trying to get him to settle down; Odessa for being Kreger Montclaire's daughter—and so damn beautiful; himself for being too risky in the field and allowing this union to happen.

Bryant's job was to kill demons. Because of his work in the human realm, naïve angels never felt the true destruction of demon malevolence. He also kept those festering parasites from latching onto humans and destroying the poor mortal's life. He *lived* for killing demons. He didn't want a female who might interfere with all that.

He protected humans from all the creatures spawned in the demon realm of Daemon. He hunted archmasters out to possess souls. He tracked and killed the slightly weaker symasters that influenced morally weak humans into dirty deeds. Then there were sylphs. It was his life's work to kill those nuisance sylphs as they disrupted the daily life of people.

He couldn't deny that Daemon tactics were organized. Sylphs created the bad day that turned into a human's bad week. As their mental status deteriorated, symasters took their turn, the evil fiends. Once the soul was vulnerable, archmasters swooped in to claim it. Bryant protected humans. It was all he ever wanted to do. His work came first. His mate second.

But it was getting harder and harder to keep his mind from straying to the alluring female that claimed him.

His packing was done, but he wasn't ready to move out. The barracks had been his main home since he'd started training as a warrior. It was the only place he stayed unless he was pressured to take time off. This was…home. He stood over a duffel bag and the trunk full of everything he owned lost in thought until he heard someone approaching.

"Director wants to see you." Harlowe eyeballed his stuff with shrewd lavender eyes. "You're really moving?"

"Aye." He hated his gruff tone. Moving out of the barracks shouldn't bother him like it did, but he'd lived here for decades. It was like the teammates he'd lost never left when he lived among their memories.

His inner turmoil went unnoticed by the tall, blond warrior. "Good. Don't fuck it up." As usual, she was brutally honest. Usually—not today—it was why he liked her.

"Did he say why?" Did it matter? It prolonged the inevitable move to under Odessa's roof.

"Does he ever?"

Urban strolled in. His coffee-colored eyes read the luggage like Harlowe's had. "About time."

Urban was a male of few words and much honor. Bryant missed living here already. They were his family and, apparently, they all thought he was being a plonker in how he was treating Odessa. But they didn't know his history with her father. Not even Urban or Dionna knew and they were part of his team when it happened.

Harlowe stopped him before he charged to the director's office. "Oh, FYI, there's some political hotheads in the office. You know, the ones who are young and drunk on power."

Bloody perfect. Once outside the director's office, he knocked. Maybe they'd be gone already.

He entered at the command. Harlowe had been spot on. Three young senators stood around the director's desk, wings flared in a display of power. Director Richter appeared unruffled, but that didn't mean anything with the bloke's admirable poker face.

After introductions, the director cut right to the chase. "Vale, the senators want us to hunt an archmaster demon suspected of targeting angels living in the human realm."

Obviously. That was his job. He didn't spend his time hunting demons that only preyed upon humans. He meticulously hunted demons that stalked angels who dwelled in the human realm to perform service. Was this a case of young senators demonstrating their power? Lord knew it wouldn't be the first time. Bryant pitied the director for having to waste his time.

Bryant's face must've said so. The director rushed on like he was afraid Bryant would speak his thoughts out loud. "So far, the demon has been sporadic. In one country, then another the next day, making it appear as if there's no rhyme or reason. One of the angels is the relative of a senator. We can get more data from an analyst like your mate to narrow your search. We'll get a specific region."

Wait—Odessa was an analyst? Foolishness threatened to flood his cheeks with color. He didn't know what his own mate did for work. He'd assumed she lived off of her daddy's coattails and strolled through Numen networking and looking pretty. Analysts were angelic nerds and that wasn't a description he'd pin on Odessa.

"Given the sensitivity of the target..." Director Richter leveled his gaze on Bryant.

Bryant read between the lines. *Given it's a relative of a senator who could make life hell for us...*

"I'd like you and one of your team to look into it," the director continued. "Find the demon, yank it out of the human host into the Mist, and kill it."

The Mist, the misty realm that separated Numen and the human realm, was Bryant's battleground. It was where they did their dirty work outside of the human realm, to protect both their existence and innocents from happening upon the battle.

"Give me the details and we'll find the demon." Bryant never lost a demon. Not even the one that used his fallen teammate's angel fire on him. That bastard had died violently.

Director Richter rattled off data and the cockiest of the young senators interrupted sporadically to fill in more information. He was being redundant and undermining the director, who calmly paused at each interception, then continued his report.

The restraint the director showed increased Bryant's respect. Bryant's fist would've connected with the senator's nose before he interrupted a second time.

Armed with the information he needed, and more than eager to leave, Bryant marched out. He would walk back to the barracks to prolong the move. Hauling his gear would take his mind off the task. Every time he faced Odessa, his body threatened to override common sense.

The senators trailed him out of the office. Once the director's door shut, the cocky one caught up with him. "The analyst who's your sync mate—is that Odessa Montclaire?"

The gleam in the male's eyes ratcheted Bryant's ire up a notch. He had luggage waiting for a move he wasn't looking forward to and an exotic angel that he somehow had to try to ignore. But he didn't quite like another male inquiring about his mate, either. Especially not this posh wanker who represented everything Bryant wasn't—polished, handsome, and affluent.

"Aye. Why?" If Bryant's team had heard his tone, they would've known better than to pursue the line of questioning.

The senator slapped him on the shoulder. "I heard she claimed some unfortunate soul who doesn't know the load of crazy she brings to the table."

Bryant glared at where the senator thumped him on the shoulder as if they were human fraternity brothers. Had the senator called Odessa crazy? Protectiveness surged, his wings puffed, ready for a fight.

A male had his pride, and no one insulted his mate.

And Odessa wasn't crazy. She was… Bollocks, he didn't know her that well, but she wasn't deserving of this senator's treatment.

Clueless, the young male continued. "Needy, am I correct? I bet you can't even shower without her there asking where you're at. I wouldn't have hung around so long, but she was so good in bed. I kept tapping that a—"

His knuckles pounded the senator's nose. Bone crunched, and the male cried out, falling to his knees. The other two senators backed up a few steps, unwilling to confront Bryant.

No honor among spoiled brats. Bryant snorted with derision. If he'd gotten decked, his team would've made sure the other guy was toast before finding out if Bryant had deserved it or not.

Blood welled through the senator's fingers. He'd heal quickly, like their kind did. Bryant reckoned the damage to his ego was worse than a broken nose.

Bryant squatted down with his scarred side closest to the wounded senator, an intimidation tactic he never failed to use when appropriate. "Don't ever talk about Odessa like that again." His calm tone bordered on menacing.

33

He glared at the other two males until they nodded in understanding for their downed friend. Bryant clapped the bleeding senator on the shoulder before he stood and strode away, his flared wings as good as a middle finger.

~

LOVELY, firm breasts bounced in Jameson Haddock's face as his latest catch ground down on him. She was as sexy as they came, a black rose tattooed around each dusky rose nipple. The ink was the reason she'd made sure to take her miniscule top off before crawling on top of his dick and making his eyes cross. No complaints from him. She showed her dedication to his cause in several ways. The tattoos always pleased him, but this was oh, so much better.

"You like this, baby?" she said with a throaty purr.

Christy? Misty? Busty, that's what he'd refer to her as until he knew for sure. Busty panted, gripping his shoulders as she rode him fast and hard. His preferred method of getting laid. Along with no chitchat.

He grunted his reply hoping Busty would get the message of no talky-talky. She flashed him a sultry grin, swiveled her hips, and leaned back to give him a clear view of where they were joined while still being able to see, and feel, those luscious breasts.

He was cupping the bountiful orbs when a sharp knock sounded on the door. To Busty's credit, she didn't slow her pace.

"Boss! I need to talk to you." His assistant, Andy, was responsible for the interruption. If he wasn't such an asset to Jameson's team, he'd have a few teeth missing for interrupting a good lay.

Busty leaned forward, nibbling and licking his ear, as if

the prospect of Andy walking in on them turned her on more.

"Boss?" Andy tried one more time.

"Wait!" Jameson yelled. Must be serious, but he was going to get his happy ending with the hot chick. And so was she. He had a reputation to protect.

Grabbing her waist, he took over. Lifting and smashing her down on him so he could arch his hips and thrust into her wet heat, hitting just the right spot to push Busty into orgasm. She moaned and writhed, loving how he took control. He wondered if she'd be a screamer, a gasper, or one of those that sounded like a dying moose in the middle of winter.

She let out a long keen right before she tightened and pulsated around his cock. Then the screams of *yes, yes, yes!* started and those lifted, gorgeous double-Ds shook and quivered in front of him. He was addicted to that shit—women's bodies, the way they lost control, how they gripped him tight, giving him everything he wanted.

He was about to finish his ride over the cliff of climax when she reached behind her, grabbing him by the ball sac.

Fucking yes.

Throwing his head back with a roar, he gave in to his powerful release.

Who was the wounded moose now?

When he could finally see straight, he gazed into her clear aqua irises—a real color, unlike her bottle blond hair. She sensuously licked her bottom lip. "Want me to wait here until you're done?"

Hell. Yes.

"Don't get dressed," Jameson growled, lifting her off.

He pulled up his slacks after throwing his condom in the trash. One never knew with these club girls. Some thought getting into the owner's bed wasn't enough, that a baby would be a direct line to the bank account. Jameson was religious about protection, and that was the *only* thing he was religious about these days. He was 99.9 percent sure he couldn't impregnate a human female, but the tricky part would be explaining *why* to her—or her lawyer.

Once he was finished stuffing his ruby-red shirt back into his waistband and straightening his ink-black tie, he opted against throwing his suit coat on. After Andy updated him on whatever crisis had cropped up, he planned to come right back and bang Busty until she was too hoarse to scream. Then do her a few more times before he got some sleep.

Turning to watch his new woman of the week climb into his king-size bed, he admired the rounded curves of her ass and sleek muscles of her legs. She could be worth keeping around for a month or two if she had more sexual tricks to surprise him with. He might even endure the repeated questions that his scarred back inevitably incited just to strip down and spend the night dominating a woman's body like he preferred.

He touched up with a dash of cologne that would cover the stench of sex and ran his hand through the brown hair that fell to his ears. Usually, he kept it slicked back to aid in the aura of power and authority his tailored suits, Italian shoes, and sports car suggested. Tonight, it hung loose, keeping his startling chartreuse eyes camouflaged. He had no need to throw his power around, at least for now. His little plan was in motion and gaining in momentum. All was well.

Unless Andy had news otherwise.

He strode down the expansive hallway a short distance to the main area of the penthouse over his club. Faint bass reverberated, the vibrations rippling under his feet. He could've paid for more insulation for the penthouse, but the beat soothed his nerves.

Turning into the meeting room, his gaze landed on his

human assistant perched on the end of the table. The man's trusty laptop was open in front of him, and the dull glow from the screen wasn't doing any favors to his pale complexion.

"Mr. Haddock, I'm sorry to disturb you and Miss Sampson," Andy started, but Jameson waved him off. Get to the point, and maybe drop Busty's first name, too. Throw a guy a bone. "Our Numen contact brought me this."

He turned a laptop toward Jameson, who didn't bother to look at it, pinning Andy with his sharp gaze.

"It's data," Andy rushed on. "Written up by a Numen analyst. She's not only onto how we recruit humans to do our bidding, but worse, she is investigating our signaling system, suspecting ties to Daemon. She notified her supervisor, and he approached our contact with the observations."

Jameson drew in a deep, cleansing breath. Analysts. They were too smart for their own good. The fucking librarians of the angelic realm. If she was on to them, then the watcher whose notes the analyst combed through knew too much. Watchers did nothing but monitor humans all day.

His signaling system was simple. With humans, it didn't need to be complex. All he needed to know was what they were willing to do with demons for him. The whys were never explained and most of his disciples didn't care. The parties, the club, the sense of belonging—gullible. All of them.

But he was only in the early stages of his grand plans. His personal army wasn't strong enough yet to go against Numen. Not the warriors they'd send if they found out about his club. They couldn't discover anything yet. "Who else knows?"

"Besides the two analysts? The notes name a specific watcher female that requested a thorough investigation of her observations."

Jameson headed to the bar to pour himself a Macallan on the rocks. He liked his whiskey like he liked his women. Mature and expensive. "Are the analysts synced?"

"The supervisor is not. The female just got mated, sir." Andy cleared his throat. "To a warrior."

Well, fuck.

Jameson took a drink, letting the smooth liquor burn its way down. "Take care of the supervisor. Make it look…" He let Andy fill in the blanks. "Dig up some dirt on the female analyst and get the watcher's route here in Vegas. Who she's following, where her subjects live, everything. If they land in the human realm, we can get them there."

"Very well, sir." Andy's fingers flew on the laptop.

Jameson let him be. Andy was an expert hacker, easily sneaking into Numen files with human technology, since that's who the Numen learned their electronics from. Heading back to his bedroom, Jameson was glad Miss Sampson would be waiting for him. He had some… emotions…to rid himself of.

Three angels who were good at their jobs would not ruin his plans. He'd waited too long. Suffered even longer. His contact in Numen would deal with the analyst supervisor. As for the other two-winged bitches… There was nowhere they could hide.

CHAPTER 5

*O*dessa chose to walk home. The path from the elaborate marble work of art that was her workplace to her home was mostly quiet, even though the trek to her place took her through the business district. No place in Numen was noisy. The quaint stores in the pristine white marble shop were open during daytime and people meandered back and forth, but the overall atmosphere was relaxed. Congenial. The perfect background distraction to let her mind wander.

There was a lot to think about after dictating more notes on humans that had been seen with the ones she'd been studying at her boss, Cal's, request. She had prepared a detailed report for him, but the male hadn't been in the office today. Unusual for him as he was normally the first to arrive and the last to leave, especially this week. He'd been giving her more watcher's reports and she'd been seeing patterns that she reported back to him. The intuition that made her a good analyst was screaming, but so far, only she and Cal knew there might be trouble.

She trusted him to learn for certain before he acted. Cal

Estevan was meticulous and patient if nothing else. Perhaps she'd talk to him Monday. It was Friday, so why not do something different other than go home to a quiet house to clean some more. Even if Bryant was home, he wouldn't do more than grunt at her and polish his weapons.

When he'd brought all his stuff to officially move in, he'd radiated rage. She'd asked if he was okay. He had looked as if he were going to ask her a question but just shook his head, gave her a curt "fine," and continued ignoring her.

Odessa thought they had made progress. The past week, he seemed less incensed at her presence. She wondered if his animosity would decrease enough that they might hold a real conversation. On a positive note, Odessa had slept better all week than she'd had in years now that he lived under the same roof.

Shaking her head, not daring to get her hopes up, she lifted her face to the sky, grateful for the perpetually gorgeous weather. Until she saw *her*.

Someone so ethereally beautiful shouldn't be that much of a bitch. Persephone Naasim had had it in for Odessa since boarding school, and Persephone was the worst thing that'd happened to Odessa since *that* night. With a mother just as powerful as Odessa's father, Persephone thought she ruled the world. Or at least Numen. And she usually did.

Petite and curvy with obsidian hair, the males trailed after Persephone with tongues hanging, and the females wanted to be her. Both genders wanted the power that came with being the progeny of a powerful senator. What they didn't know was that senators were never home, and work preoccupied them so much that when they *were* home, their mind was at work. At least that's the way it was with Odessa's father. And in the last fourteen years, he'd made sure to not be home as often as he could.

The first day of boarding school, when Odessa entered

Persephone's empire, the girl had recruited Odessa to be one of her groupies. Odessa had tried to fit in, but she was still too traumatized by the home invasion. She'd proven too embarrassing with her nightmares and anxiety attacks that Persephone shunned her.

Boarding school, to use one of her favorite human monikers, sucked ass. Odessa had been glad to graduate early and move on to analyst training.

"Odessa," Persephone called with sugary sweetness, her arms held out for a faux hug and kiss-kiss. "How are you doing, my dear? You don't look a day over thirty."

Odessa refrained from rolling her eyes, not mentioning the fact that, like Persephone, she was only twenty-five.

"I am well. How is your mother?"

Persephone's nostrils flared with hostility. "She's well, also, thank you for asking."

The angel's mother was a gem—for a senator. Odessa held Persephone's mother in high regard; she'd been nothing but genuine with Odessa. Even after Odessa's mother died, when other family friends looked the other way, Senator Naasim had always been someone she could talk to. The senator stopped in to talk, and whenever she'd come to the boarding school to visit Persephone, she'd always check up on Odessa. She suspected that was a major reason why Persephone was such a raging hag to her.

A couple of young angels Odessa recognized as Persephone's simpering groupies appeared as if they'd just happened upon them. Did they run in packs all day looking for some poor soul to humiliate?

Duh. Of course they did. There was a reason why other angels didn't care for the political crowd. Had Odessa been foolish to think life outside of school would be different? Or had it only been practice?

"Tell me again, what duty did you decide on?" Odessa

smiled serenely like her mother had taught her and attempted to sound sincere. She knew Persephone had applied to be an angelic messenger but couldn't perform well enough for even her family's influence to help get her in. She was probably watcher material, but most likely felt it beneath her station to spy all day. The irony was that's what she did all day in Numen.

"Oh, aren't you sweet to ask about me. I should be asking about you and that warrior you got for yourself. How's that working out?" Before Odessa could formulate a response, Persephone displayed her figurative claws and spoke in a loud whisper. "I mean, I heard your sync hasn't even been consummated yet."

Persephone's groupies cleared their throats and glanced away. Even they felt bad for Odessa. She should've never gone looking for Bryant at the barracks. Now everyone knew he avoided her, and the talk turned to speculation about their status as a couple. It was humiliating because the petty angel was right. Bryant hadn't so much as held her hand.

"I can't imagine why my sync life is of any news."

A shadow fell in next to her and when she thought she couldn't be any more humiliated, Bryant rested an arm around her shoulder. No doubt he'd heard it all, and as much as she wanted to lean into his strong embrace, Persephone's gossip hit hard.

"There you are." He lightly kissed her on the forehead. "I've been looking for you."

Was he joking? She gave him a look with that question written all over it.

"Friends of yours?" he inquired innocently.

Odessa looked over at the angelic "it" crowd. Persephone with her short robe and bared shoulder eyed Bryant like she wanted to devour him. He was oblivious, like he assumed no one would want to look at him because of his scars. That made Odessa feel immensely better, even if he was clueless to any female attention because he assumed his scars turned them off.

He didn't understand how intoxicating his masculinity was. His wings were always held tall and flared slightly. When his amber gaze landed on her, she was certain she was the only thing that mattered. So at odds with how he treated her.

Then there was his body—a work of art. In his warrior clothing, the long-sleeved, form-fitting shirt enhanced broad shoulders and pecs carved of stone. Black pants hugged a narrow waist and tapered over a hard butt and thighs that marble statues would envy.

The looks he was so doubtful of? It didn't take long to not notice his scars. When she did, it was only to fantasize about running her fingers over the gentle ridges on his cheek and scalp, maybe use her tongue to…

Bryant lifted an eyebrow and she realized she must be staring at him the way she'd ogle a lollipop. Back to his question. Friends of hers?

"We all went to school together but lost track after graduation." *For good reason.* "Now if you'll excuse me, I'd like to enjoy this beautiful evening." She didn't address anyone in general, just walked away.

Persephone wouldn't be happy by Odessa's departure. The other female was never the one getting dismissed. Her powerful senator parentage made her quite the commodity in social circles. What better way to change policies than to nag the children of senators?

Not Odessa.

Her father was not a well-liked senator and she knew why he'd made the decisions he had. It broke her heart, and as much as she wished he'd throw his wings back and defy their circumstances, she was just as grateful he hadn't. His actions had kept them safe.

Bryant's long strides quickly caught up with her. She should have grabbed his hand when she walked off, made a good show for her old classmates, but Odessa was sick of playing pretend. She'd been doing it for years.

"Want to tell me what that was about?" It was the first sentence he'd spoken to her that wasn't hostile or full of disdain.

"Not really." She repressed the urge to spread her wings and rise to the sky. The extra visibility flying gave her was the main reason she avoided it.

He kept quiet walking next to her. Like the night he'd brought his stuff to her house—their house—she sensed he had a question.

"What?" she snapped.

"What?" He lifted his brows, startled by her abruptness.

"I can tell you want to ask me something. What is it?" Odessa tired of the games angels played. If her mate couldn't be open and honest with her, even if he disliked her and her station in society, then she'd find the nearest cleric to absolve their bond. Like Persephone had pointed out, they hadn't consummated it yet. It'd take nothing but a few divine words and they could part ways.

"I ran into a young senator earlier this week. He inquired about you."

Odessa's eyelids drifted closed for a few steps and she dragged in a calming inhale. How could one walk home become a walk of shame so terribly fast?

"I see. Was it Crestin?" Saying his name brought back all the feelings of clinginess and shame.

"I, uh, didn't get properly introduced."

"Let me save you the trouble, everything he said was likely true."

44

"Which part, you being needy or being great in bed?"

Odessa whipped her head around. "He said that?" she hissed.

Bryant's mouth twitched with a suppressed laugh. Was her personal mortification all it took to lighten him up?

Squaring her shoulders, lifting her downy wings higher, she ignored the last part. "He was my first long-term relationship and, yes, I may have been a little clingy."

More than a little. She had wanted to be around him every minute of every day. It was the first time she'd been on her own, which terrified her just as much as living with a bunch of strangers at school.

"I'm sure he found it inconvenient to have to put in any effort into a relationship he only wanted to use to gain status."

Bryant grunted but didn't say any more. He probably already suspected Crestin's reasons behind his declarations of love for her. Everyone had. Even Odessa knew that Crestin's bid for senator would go over better if he was dating the daughter of one. At the time, she thought it was better than being alone. At least she'd had a reprieve from constant terror.

"I have to work in the field tomorrow." Bryant's accent was soft, not as pronounced as when he was irritated with her. Which seemed to be all the time.

Odessa nodded and peeked at him out of the corner of her eye. He never told her his work schedule. She'd mentioned hers, hoping he would want to adjust his to be with his new mate. But then, she had plans. Like a non-needy female.

They reached the house and he opened the door for her. "Tell me again why you don't have servants?"

Servants were the angels who held no other title, had no duties that'd grant them access to the human realm, and basically just wanted something to do with their lives. Some worked and waited patiently until they were synced and could leave to raise their own families. Some liked the proximity to the upper echelons of Numen society and the latest realm news. It didn't matter the motivation, Odessa didn't want them around.

"I have no need for them," she answered.

Bryant bristled at her lack of elaboration.

Sighing, she headed toward the kitchen. "I'll get some supper ready."

He followed, and they prepped their meal together. If Odessa wanted to delude herself, she'd say this felt right, puttering around the massive kitchen with him, digging food out and grabbing plates. There was no meat in Numen. Agriculture was limited to growing fruits, vegetables, and grains. Livestock in their mystical realm added too many complications with space and feed and…manure. Which was unfortunate. She'd love to whip up a stellar chicken parmesan.

As they sat for their meal and began to eat, Odessa figured she'd throw him a bone and make small talk since he'd been trying earlier.

Bryant was naturally closed off and quiet, but when she asked about his team, his face became more animated and his rough voice was lighter. "There's seven of us—there's always seven warriors in a team."

Ah yes. Humans aren't the only ones to give numbers meaning. The holy trinity meant three must be a good number, or that thirteen was bad luck. So seven, a divine number to go with why they're were called Numen. Because they were the power presiding over the safety of the human race. She smiled at his enthusiasm.

He continued. "They're my family. Jagger, Bronx, and Urban are males I'd lay down my life for and the females are closer than sisters. Harlowe and Sierra are younger than me, along with Jagger and Bronx. Urban and Dionna are close to my age."

Spearing a bean, Odessa thought about what he said. "That's why none have found sync mates yet? They're all pretty young."

"Warriors mate fairly young. Keeps us in the field longer to have the healing aid of a mating bond." Bryant pushed food around his plate before answering her. "Possibly. We've gotten into some dangerous situations, but healing hasn't been a problem. Yet. I'm sure their time will come soon enough." He pushed up and grabbed his dishes to wash them. "Unless we take too many risks, then we get assigned mates so we can heal and be more cautious. Once the children start coming, some warriors retire or become trainers."

Odessa waited until she was done chewing before getting up to help with the dishes. Stepping in next to Bryant, she set down her plates. He turned to get something off the counter. She side-stepped, and he tried to do the same, but they ended up inches away, facing each other.

She was about to say her pardon and sidle out, but his hot look froze her in place.

Good Lord, was he about to kiss her?

Cemented, she waited in breathless anticipation as he dropped his head down. Her eyes fluttered closed right before his lips landed on hers. He was hesitant at first. She didn't get the impression that was normal, but he pressed gently. His arms wrapped around her waist, drawing her close, until she was fully against his hard body.

Holy angel fire, he was delectable. Defined muscle rippled under her hands as she slid them around his shoulders. His kiss deepened and a rumble of approval vibrated through his chest.

His tongue swept into her mouth, weakening her knees. The male could kiss. Molten passion flooded her senses at the feel of him, the taste, all male with hints of the supper they had shared.

Bryant fitted his hands around her waist and lifted her up to sit on the counter where she leaned over him and circled her legs around his back. The movement drew her to the edge of the counter and tugged him closer. The hard length of him straining against his pants made her want to rub against him oh so bad, but her position on the counter made it difficult. What his mouth was doing to her... He skimmed his hands up her rib cage to gently cup her breasts.

She floated her hands up to touch the sharp stubble of his scalp and the warm ridges of his scars. The uneven planes of his skin played under fingers.

He pulled away from her mouth, trailing kisses down her neck, which she bared and arched into his searing mouth. Kisses burned a path down her collarbone, to her chest. Finally, he was heading for the opening of her robe.

"Odessa," he whispered against her skin, "let's consummate our sync."

Oh yes.

Oh, wait. Odessa's eyelids flew open and she pulled back. Bryant brought his head up, his brow creased at her sudden stiffness, his lips parted with panting breath.

"Did you hear what Persephone asked me?" Was that what all this was about? He felt sorry for her and was willing to sleep with her because she'd been embarrassed by a vapid, insulting female who was of no consequence?

He scowled. "Yes, I heard what she said, but—"

Odessa jerked her hands off his head and shoved him. He stumbled back, sporting a confused expression.

"I'm *not* going to be a pity fuck."

"A pity fuck?" He shook his head, his expression lit with shock at her use of profanity. "Where did you learn that term?"

She blew off his question and hopped down from the counter. None of his business. If he had so much as *tried* to get to know her in the last week, maybe she would've told him about how she spent her weekends and about Harper.

She stormed out of the kitchen.

"Odessa!"

"Leave me alone, Bryant," she called over her shoulder. "I might be afraid of the dark. It might have made me desperate enough to sync with a stranger. One that seems to hate me, no less. But I refuse to give up any more of my dignity today."

She was halfway up the opulent staircase by the time he stalked out of the kitchen. Normally, she might have hoped he'd follow her, even beg for forgiveness. Not tonight! Humiliation churned in her gut and her disappointment weighed on her like a mantle of fatigue. She couldn't deal with the aggravating male.

Odessa slammed her door shut and stomped to her nightstand. After digging her phone out from under her unmentionables, she texted the closest thing to a best friend she could claim.

Code Boots On!

Duck yeah!

Before she could text an inquiry as to what that meant, Harper sent a follow-up. Odessa's lips curved into a much-needed smile.

Fucking autocorrect.

CHAPTER 6

*B*ryant tried to unwind by flying back to Odessa's mansion after work.

He didn't know if he'd ever get to a point where he could claim the mansion as his. Since he hadn't sealed his sync yet... He winced at the reminder of the previous night's events.

Pity fuck? How could she think that? But he wasn't stupid, and neither was she. He had felt bad when the spoiled git of a senator verbally debased his mate. Odessa had looked so resigned, so...relatable after her run-in with that vile Persephone. The female had broken many warrior's hearts by stringing them along, then using her birth status to ditch them. Maybe that was why he let his guard down, even though Odessa was clearly hiding something. More than one something, considering her language. Human profanity was not common in those raised in the angelic realm. Where the bloody hell had she picked it up?

Perhaps from that inadequate male, Crestin. Angels like him thought the human realm was their playground and they'd make several trips in their youth to mess about. But

50

Bryant didn't want to dwell on Odessa's time with Crestin—or how good she was in bed with him.

He wanted to growl.

Approaching the mansion, he spotted two male angels standing on the doorstep. They wore the standard long gowns and peered through the stained glass in the ornate door. One was taller but wiry, and the shorter one had to have half the muscle mass of Bryant.

Bryant landed silently behind them. "What do you want?"

The angels started and jumped back from their inspection. They passed each other a worried look before addressing Bryant.

Bryant twitched his wings in irritation.

The smaller of the two spoke first. "Warrior, we are looking for Odessa Montclaire. It seems she is not home and we have an urgent message."

An urgent message for an *analyst*? Or was something wrong with Odessa's family? And why did he want to growl that it was Odessa *Vale*?

"Do you know where we can find her?" the other angel inquired. The tall angel's narrow, dusty wings matched the shade of his hair.

No, Bryant didn't know where Odessa would be if she wasn't home. Yes, he should, because he was her mate.

"You checked her place of work, of course." Bryant couldn't imagine where else she might be, but the truth was, he didn't know her at all. Did she have hobbies? Interests? He'd always assumed the children of pompous senators sat around discussing how amazing they were and plotting about how to interfere with other people's lives. Oddly, he couldn't picture Odessa doing that.

Where could she be?

"We're coworkers of hers and she doesn't normally work weekends," the shorter angel replied.

The tall angel looked to Bryant, who remained impassive, as if that information wasn't a surprise. The male tapped his fingers together while waiting for Bryant to suggest other places to look.

"Why don't you pass the message to me? I'll let Odessa know." Bryant phrased it like a question. It was anything but, which twitched the angel's wings in agitation. "I'm her mate," Bryant added. There was something else going on here. His appearance made others fearful, edgy even, but these males had been anxious before he arrived.

The two visitors exchanged looks and finally the wiry one inclined his head.

"I'm afraid we need to inform Odessa that her supervisor was found deceased today in his home."

Ah. If the males worked with Odessa, no wonder they were upset. "I'll let her know."

"We need her to contact us immediately." The small one opened his mouth like he was going to elaborate, but the other shook his head in warning.

Drawing himself up to his full height, wings splayed, Bryant folded his arms across his chest. "What's going on, gents?" A little intimidation never hurt anyone.

Wiry stuttered his denial. Bryant raised an eyebrow—on the damaged side of his face—until the angel fell silent.

"The thing is," the tall angel began, "the enforcers say he drank the fire."

Bryant inwardly flinched. He knew the kiss of angel fire well, had inhaled the fumes. He sounded like he brushed his vocal cords with sandpaper every morning because of it. Agony was too weak a word to describe his experience with the fire.

"But you don't agree?" he asked. Enforcers were the police force of their kind, and they investigated deaths within the realm. If they said he drank the fire, no one argued, and it wasn't an unusual occurrence.

Numen angels were always given an out from their long immortal lives. Some walked into the fountain of angel fire situated in the middle of the realm. Some kept a vial on hand, for protection, or because they'd been thinking about the end.

"I wouldn't say we disagree," the small one hedged.

These two fit the analyst stereotype of desk-bound, anxiety-ridden intellectuals. It didn't change the fact that they were probably wicked smart. If the angels didn't think this supervisor killed himself, then there was probably a good chance he hadn't.

Bryant carefully rephrased his next question. "Would you agree that someone made him drink it?"

Both males paled and exchanged another wrought look. Murder wasn't common in Numen and the angels residing here often thought themselves above the actions that invited violence. Many forgot how powerful rage, anger, and jealousy could be. Or the need for survival, when one found themselves on the receiving end of such emotions.

"It's just that Cal always took his work home. He was the most dedicated analyst we knew." The wiry angel's gaze darted around, checking for any eavesdroppers, which was absurd in Odessa's neighborhood. Acres and a million trees separated her from the next dwelling. "When we asked the enforcer for Cal's notes to be returned, he said there were none."

"Maybe he didn't take any home because he was planning to end it," Bryant suggested.

The short male bobbed his head. "Exactly what we thought at first. Until we came to break the news to Odessa." His gaze flitted to his buddy's. "Then we remembered seeing him talking with her before he left—the last time we saw him. She was handing over a stack of notes she'd made on her observations and Cal seemed so serious."

"He was always serious," the taller male rushed in, "but this was just...so much more. Cal acted uneasy and dismayed. Something was weighing heavily on him."

An analyst's entire life revolved around looking for threats against their people. If these two nerdy males thought something was wrong...

Where was Odessa?

Bryant's heart threatened to crawl into his throat. "The enforcers haven't talked to Odessa?"

"No, the enforcer on the case talked to Bill and I," answered the short one. "Asked if we had seen her. I'm assuming they already tried stopping by."

Bryant scanned the area. He had thought the action futile when Bill had done it, but now it made sense. Odessa was one of the last to see her boss alive and any material she'd passed on to him was gone. His intuition said she wasn't involved in anything nefarious...yet there was her hateful father and the secrets she hid.

Where was Odessa?

"When you see Odessa, can you ask her to come talk with Davon and I?" Bill lifted a shoulder in resignation, his wings drooping slightly. "Regardless of what's going on, I'm in charge now. She'll need to update me, and...I need to know if I'm in danger."

Bryant needed to know if Odessa was in danger. The thought of one glossy strand of hair on her head being harmed made his wings shake. He might not like her—much —or the family she came from, but he'd rip anyone limb from limb and dip their wings in a batter of angel fire before they touched his mate.

Davon paled and stepped back. Bill lifted his wings, preparing to take flight. Bryant must look murderous, frightening the males, and he sought to calm himself by sucking in a long breath. "I'll find Odessa. Then we'll find out what's going on."

CONCENTRATING, Bryant descended to the human realm. It was a skill he wasn't granted until he'd become a warrior. His parents posed as missionaries on Earth and he'd been at their mercy to travel back and forth, but he'd learned to respect the responsibility of keeping their kind's secret from humans. The consequences were severe and unalterable.

Before he'd dressed for walking among the human realm, he'd folded his wings into his back. Another skill his kind was granted. With his wings morphed, his back looked like any other human's. He'd built his tolerance and could maintain a morph for days with no ill effects other than a mild ache between his shoulder blades.

He descended to a secluded spot in a shopping mall in Dallas, Texas. Never had he been so grateful for his familiarity with the human world. He'd traveled long and far enough that he had many approved places to land when he arrived in the realm.

Bryant strode purposefully through the corridors. Few people milled about as it was near closing time. His footsteps were soundless on the marble floor. A black ball cap with a Cowboys logo was drawn down to conceal his face and scars. He ducked his head and tucked his arms into his brown bomber jacket. Since he was in a shopping mall, he kept it simple in a black T-shirt and jeans and black boots.

He had made a concerning discovery of glitter-laden human clothing while searching Odessa's dresser. Not glitter decorated clothing, but glitter *on* her clothing. Frowning, he had pawed through the drawers and searched pockets for any sign of where she might be. He had even found an undergarment drawer. It had been...an awakening... searching through tiny scraps of vibrantly colored cloth that were considered underwear. Brassieres with dainty, lacy cups and narrow straps. How in the world they were expected to contain Odessa's impressive bust, he had no clue, but he was suddenly, insatiably curious.

Regardless, he had made it through her drawers and finally found a pen with a bank logo on it. Bryant quickly searched bank records, a handy skill he and his team had acquired. Sometimes getting to a possessed human in a place archmasters could be engaged required extensive investigation into a target's life and activities. Walking up to someone in the middle of the grocery store, grabbing their forehead, chanting incantations, and then disappearing into another plane while the body flopped limp to the floor didn't go over well with humans. Or with his boss.

Bryant had found only cash withdrawals and regular deposits from a company called Little Time in Odessa's bank records, and judging from all the glitter he found, it was either a strip club or a craft store. A quick search revealed that it was a children's clothing store.

Relieved, but more than a little perplexed, Bryant had located the mall with the store. All he had to do was take the escalator up to the third level and find out if Odessa was there. He chose to ignore the fact that if they had consummated their sync, he would feel her presence like a beacon anywhere on the earthly realm.

It took only a few seconds after stepping off the elevator to locate the brightly decorated store front of Little Time. It was nearly closing, and only two customers were left in the store, making it easy to find the statuesque brunette he hunted.

Odessa was folding small shirts and tops over a table. Her

bright eyes sparkled as she smiled and laughed with a young woman who was rearranging and sorting clothing across the surface. The other woman was the complete opposite of his mate—petite with shoulder-length curly blonde hair. They must be close. Odessa's face lit up as she chatted, her grin wide and genuine. Bryant's gut tightened. He'd only seen her with a serious demeanor and a face lined with stress and worry. Now her smile went straight through him until he thought he should be striving to be the reason she was happy.

No. He couldn't let his body's reaction to her devastating beauty distract him from finding out what was going on with her and her work.

He ducked his head down, entering the store to pass a mom and her three kids. He usually tried to avoid catching the eye of any kids, but one was always looking at him. He forced a small smile, expecting a terrified look, maybe a shriek of horror, but instead the little imp revealed an impressive grin missing the two top front teeth. Bryant's own smile broadened and the family moved past him out of the store.

Kids. When he expected the worst from them, he got googly eyes or messy smiles.

"Welcome to Little Time. What can I help you fi—"

Bryant raised his head to meet Odessa's gaze. Her mouth hanging open, she stared right back, the purple shirt with a giant rainbow on the front forgotten in her hands.

"Odessa." He didn't mean to sound so irritated. It was like he couldn't just say her name. Some sort of emotion laced that one word whenever it left his lips. Seeing her in a curve-hugging maroon tunic over black leggings and knee-high black boots accentuating her mile-long legs… He had to let some of what he was feeling out or it threatened to congregate in his nether region.

The blonde gasped. "Is that him?" She spun fully around, beaming with approval. "He *is* tall, dark, and brooding, isn't he?" Leaning back against the table, the woman whose name tag read "Harper" shook a finger at him. "Don't think popping up here means she's not going out with me tonight."

Odessa snapped her mouth shut and finished folding the rainbow shirt, an unreadable look on her face. "I'm done in fifteen minutes, Bryant. I can talk after that." When Harper cleared her throat, Odessa added, "But only for a few minutes. Harper and I have plans."

Not the reaction he was expecting. Unsure how to proceed since they had the attention of an avid witness, he'd take that fifteen minutes to figure it out. "I'll be right outside."

WATCHING Bryant's fine form exit the store didn't help Odessa's erratic heartbeat.

I've done nothing wrong. So why did she feel like she was busted? Maybe because Bryant was the first to know of her extracurricular activities. She hadn't intended for her part-time job and human friends to be a secret. Many angels dabbled in the human world. Odessa didn't like anyone to know because then they couldn't threaten the wonderful life she lived on the weekends.

What would Bryant try to do? Her mate that didn't trust her, could barely stand her, had hunted her down. Why? Last night, they had actually talked, then made out in the kitchen. He'd even been willing to sleep with her. Like she had told Harper, who adamantly agreed, she wasn't willing to be a charity case.

"How in the world did you tear yourself away from that man candy last night?"

Odessa peeled her gaze off Bryant's sculpted backside. "Harper! I told you why."

"I don't know, hon. You mentioned he's got that damaged bad boy appeal, but *day-um*." Harper's gaze flicked back out to where the imposing male sat on a bench, arms propped on his knees. His head was down, but turned slightly so he could watch everyone that passed from under the rim of his ball cap.

Odessa couldn't agree more. He'd be a catch—if he wasn't such a prick. "Until he's a decent husband, he's not getting in my pants." Or under her robes.

Harper shot her a proud smile. "Why don't you go chat with your man, 'cause I'm dyin' to find out why he's here. I'll finish closing, then we'll hit the town."

Odessa steeled herself to walk out and face the perpetually irritated male waiting for her. The two of them talking on the bench felt more intimate, though they were both wearing more clothes than they would in Numen.

Heat streamed through his eyes as he took in the heeled boots that made her nearly six feet tall. His gaze burned up her legs and torso to the hair she had left hanging down in waves, curled slightly at the ends. Once his gaze met hers, they had cooled considerably.

"What do you want, Bryant?" From his slight wince, her curtness wasn't missed. But dammit, she was tired of always feeling inadequate around him.

"Is there somewhere private we can talk? About home?"

She'd been looking forward to tonight for weeks and she almost gave it up for him. Now he wanted her time? No. She wasn't that girl anymore, the one Crestin had apparently told him about. "If you want to talk privately, we can wait until tomorrow. I'm going out with people who hang with me because they genuinely like me. I think I deserve that after the week I've had."

Bryant opened his mouth as if to argue, but closed it again, slightly chagrined. "Is it really necessary?"

"Of course it is. What could be so important that we can't talk tomorrow?"

"Cal's dead."

"Cal is— What?" She couldn't do more than stare at Bryant. Had she heard him correctly? Cal was alive and well. She'd just talked to him yesterday.

"Sit."

She plopped down on the bench next to him, nearly on top of him. He slid over an inch, but not too far, and his solid warmth comforted her. Tears welled, but she rapidly blinked them back and looked around. Stores were shutting down for the night, but this still wasn't the place to cry. If she learned one skill in life, it was to hold onto her sorrow for a later time, when she could unleash the flood gates and sob in private.

"How?" Her voice shook.

"That's the bit of it," Bryant said quietly. "Two of your coworkers, Bill and Davon, stopped by to give you the news and I had a chance to talk to them."

Bill and Davon. Competent analysts, compassionate males. They would have shared the news with more caring and less bluntness than Bryant. She tried to be upset, but she was too grateful he'd found her to tell her.

"They don't believe the enforcer's word that your boss killed himself," he said. "And all of the work you gave Cal is missing."

Odessa let that sink in. "Someone killed him?"

"What were you working on that had him troubled?"

Cal was murdered? Her work was missing? It all seemed so preposterous.

Yet fourteen years ago she learned the hard way bad things happened in Numen—to her and to people she cared

60

about. Sometimes they did it to themselves. But Cal hadn't been suicidal. She'd bet all she had on it.

She thought back to her last assignment, the one she hadn't completed. "I was working on a watcher's notes, comparing them to others on duty in the vicinity. I was asked to discern any trends in human behavior that might be aiding the demons. Usually we turn up nothing unusual, you know, beyond the wannabe cult here and there. Most of those are human-based cultures, and don't call on forces outside the human realm, but…"

"You found something."

Odessa lifted a shoulder. She couldn't image her notes getting Cal killed. "It's nothing concrete, just a trend I noticed. I brought it to Cal's attention regardless. He was going to study my work, see if we could make a more definitive observation of the perceived threat and then bring it to the senate."

Bryant's gaze sharpened. "What was it?"

"Hey, you two!" Harper bounced out of the store. Seeing Odessa was clearly distressed, she stopped. "What's wrong?"

"My…" Odessa couldn't tell Harper that her boss had died. She didn't know she worked anywhere else but here. The story she fed her human friends was that she was a rich socialite who worked for fun and got roped into an arranged marriage. Which was almost true.

"Her cousin passed away." Bryant rescued her and Odessa sagged with relief.

Harper rushed over to give Odessa a hug. "I'm so sorry, hon. Were you close?"

Bryant's expression said he'd step in if needed, but he remained quiet. Confidence resonated from him. He must be incredibly adept at dealing with humans.

Odessa swallowed and took a moment before she

answered. "Not terribly, but he was a good guy. I liked him." A tear rolled down her cheek.

Harper stepped back. "'S okay. I understand if you need to get home tonight."

Odessa shook her head. "No. I can't go home." She couldn't hang out in that mansion waiting for something bad to happen—again. Life before Cal's death was nearly unbearable, she couldn't go back now. Bad things were already happening. Was she next? "I mean, there's nothing I can do now anyway. Let's go out."

"Are you sure? Abby's meeting us at the club, so it's not like you're letting me down. It's only a short walk away. I'll be all right."

"I can't go home," Odessa said quietly, aware of Bryant's speculative attention. "I can't go and think of all the horrible things that happen to people I care for. Please, let's just go out and have fun."

"I'll come along," Bryant announced. "I'll make sure she gets home okay."

A refusal formed on Odessa's lips.

Harper spoke, her smile wide and encouraging. "Sure. The more the merrier."

Odessa knew her friend well, and Harper couldn't resist the chance to interrogate the man making her friend miserable.

"Surely, I don't need a babysitter," Odessa said rigidly.

Bryant shrugged and stood up, holding his hand out. "I'm here anyway. Let me help."

Uh-huh. He hadn't done anything out of the goodness of his heart since she'd known him—except try to sleep with her. What was he after now?

Sliding her hand into his, she braced herself against the soothing heat of his skin and how he firmly grasped hers. She could melt into his support too easily. He even held onto her for an extra second after she stood before reluctantly releasing her.

If Odessa wanted to harbor wistful, girly thoughts, she'd think about how if this had been a real relationship, he would've held her hand all the way to the club. Instead, she caught up with Harper and walked next to her out of the mall and down the street to their destination while he followed.

CHAPTER 7

*W*atching Odessa's hips sway under that top as Bryant walked behind them to the club was dangerously mesmerizing. Every time he would scan around them, sensing for demon presence of any kind, monitoring human activity to see if they were being followed, his cursed gaze landed back onto Odessa's derriere. Then they'd drift up to the shiny mane that hung halfway down her back. It made him imagine things. Like how he'd wrap that hair around his fist, bringing her head up for a scorching kiss as he took her from behind. She would be on her hands and knees, or standing—

Gah! He had no business thinking those thoughts about Odessa. Continuing to monitor their environment, he concentrated on what the girls were discussing during the short walk. Odessa was filling Harper in on her deceased "cousin" and how they thought he killed himself and, no, they had no idea why. He wanted to be surprised at how she effortlessly fibbed her way through the human world, but she'd been doing that all along in Numen. After all, no one else seemed to know of her earthly activities and she still hadn't said why she mated him.

Was she behind Cal's demise?

His gut said no. Despite her superficial lifestyle—not fully in the Numen world, not really in the human realm—he didn't get a murderous vibe off her. Logically, it would make no sense for her to turn over notes to get Cal killed. Unless it was a test to see what the analyst would do with such information. And what the devil was the information?

As soon as he could tear Odessa away from her friends without a scene to interrogate her, he'd do so.

Bryant suppressed a groan as they arrived at the club. The place was a bumping throng of bodies where liquid stupidity was dispensed by the shot or pint. He and his team avoided places like these, too many witnesses and camera phones around to take on demons. They had to scout their targets in places like this and it was too tempting to intervene when a poor soul would be coerced into acting undesirably. Bryant hated sitting by to watch a tormented person down shot after shot and disappear into a backroom with one—or more —individuals. Not when it was the furthest thing from normal for that person, or worse, when they wore a wedding ring.

And *those* were the unpossessed. Humans being human. An overtaken soul would be driven to debase themselves or others so badly the soul may willingly give up the body. It was ripe for archmaster possession. The body was nothing more than a puppet and the demon had more use of its power if it wasn't fighting a soul.

Weaving behind the ladies, he wanted to growl at any males that looked Odessa's way. More than a few did. Relief filled Bryant when the ladies made their way to a back booth that was sheltered from the worst of the music. Another young woman with dark hair bundled atop her head waved excitedly from one of the seats.

"We like to be able to chat in between dancing," Odessa shouted into his ear as they slid into a corner booth. She mouthed a quick "sorry" which he shook off before she turned to talk with Harper and the woman that must be Abby.

Great. Dancing.

If Odessa thought he'd sit by as she gyrated with human males, she would learn quickly that he did not play that game. The thought of her writhing and grinding amid a throng of females...not nearly as unappealing. He would tolerate that. Out of duty.

A round of drinks was set in front of them, but Bryant ignored his and not because it was a chick drink. Prickles streamed across his back. He was being watched.

He'd use the drink after all. He brought the straw to his mouth as if he was taking a sip and let his gaze wander. There were a few clusters of men casting quick glances to their group, eyeballing the women. They quickly moved on to the next booth, then the dance floor, looking for lonely groups of ladies to hit on. All other men appeared to be taken. Two men walked in and were scoping out the place for where to sit.

Setting the drink down, Bryant shifted and brought his arm down across the back of the booth behind Odessa. She turned her head slightly to glance at him, then his arm, and went back to chatting with her friends.

It was like he wasn't even there. She must be really pissed at him for last night. Pity fuck. A poor excuse his jacked-up brain gave his hard-up body to get her into bed maybe, but not out of sympathy. She'd just been so vulnerable. After they had gotten home, she had listened attentively as he damn near gushed about his team. The back-to-back instances made him forget she was a senator's daughter, raised in scandal and corruption. And not just any senator's kid, but the power hungry one that had cost him four team members and nearly destroyed his own life as well.

"We're going to dance," Odessa informed him as she was sliding out of the booth. She followed the other ladies to the dance floor, clearly not wanting him to follow.

As if.

A waltz maybe, but not the jerky gyrations with flailing limbs and thrusting hips the youth of today liked to do.

Still, he couldn't wait to see how Odessa's body moved.

Quite well, it turned out. Bryant was riveted. Her arms were in the air, hips swirling and swaying as she dipped and popped that divine figure. Odessa resembled a goddess. The lights touched and caressed her hair and face, giving her an ethereal air.

When the song ended, the girls dissolved in laughter. Bryant snapped to attention. He'd forgotten to inspect the other patrons and evaluate any possible threats.

It had been worth it.

Another fast-paced song began, catching the ladies up in its rhythm. Taking the chance at redemption, Bryant studied the room. The three women were young, attractive, and appeared single. They were earning their fair share of glances. The two men Bryant had observed earlier entering the club had indeed found a seat and were intent on the group. Or rather, Odessa.

Their gaze wasn't leering, hopeful, or enamored. Both men were somber, unsmiling.

Odessa may be in danger after all.

ODESSA BREATHLESSLY CRAWLED BACK into the booth, stopping a little closer to Bryant than she intended. She should scoot away a few inches, but the lure of his body heat eased her frazzled nerves too much.

She turned toward Harper and Abby, diving back into the conversation but Bryant leaned over to whisper in her ear. "Tell them it's time you be going."

The feel of his breath tickling her ear sent shivers down her spine. Ones she couldn't conceal. Did the guy know how potent he was? Even after his asshole move the previous night, then crashing her girls' night, it wouldn't take much for her to change her mind about him.

She glanced at him. His expression was grimmer than usual. "I'm not ready to leave."

His lips flattened and he leaned in again, making her body want to meet him the rest of the way. To smash into him, letting him cover every inch of her possible. "If you don't want your friends caught up in your drama back home, you need to leave now."

His words drenched her stubbornness like a bucket of ice water. If Cal was murdered and her work had made her a target, then her presence endangered those most dear to her. Bryant had come to the club with her and waited until now to mention something. If her warrior mate was concerned, she should be, too.

Odessa faced her friends. "I think it's time I head out. I'm sure it'll be an early morning, you know, with everything going on."

That earned her compassionate hugs and well-wishes from Harper and Abby. After a quick "call me" from Harper, Odessa stiffly followed Bryant out of the club.

Bryant put his arm nonchalantly around her shoulder and spoke quietly. "Let's get to the parking garage before we transcend home."

She curved into him automatically, enjoying how he was tall enough for her to snuggle into his side. He hugged her closer and pressed a light kiss on top of her hair. She brought her head up, startled at his display of affection, but he was surveying the street behind them.

Her heart sank. It was just for show and she was stupid enough to fall for it. Couldn't the guy just like her?

Did she like him? He was surly, argumentative, and despised her birthright. He was also honorable, loyal, and currently trying to protect her. Maybe she liked him a little… His subterfuge stung all the more.

"Did you happen to see the guys sitting across from the bar tonight?" he asked.

Odessa frowned. She had noticed how the two men kept their attention focused on her, but that wasn't unusual in this realm. "I did. I don't know who they are, though."

"I sensed no demon in them. They were focused on you in a way that wasn't romantic. Let's get out of here."

They reached the entrance to the parking garage. A shout stopped them from going inside. Odessa peered in the direction of the noise. One of the men Bryant had asked about were flagging them down.

"Hey! You forgot your purse!"

She didn't have a purse.

Bryant pushed her into the ramp's entrance. She stumbled from the momentum and narrowly missed a knife swinging in her direction. The blade belonged to the second man, who must've run around the back and jumped the ramp's low walls.

Her gasp jerked Bryant's attention off the man outside. He lunged through the doorway, grabbing for the attacker with the knife. Odessa twisted out of the way just as the other man stepped through the door and charged her.

Fear flooded her system. Like most Numen, she didn't know how to fight. She was too scared to run away. What if there were more out there? She'd be safest near her capable warrior.

The human stalked her into a corner, a long, wicked blade in hand. She gulped, looking for something to throw, somewhere to run and hide, but there was nothing. She envisioned her mansion to transcend—to hell with human witnesses—when Bryant tackled the man.

Punches muted by clothing thudded through the parking garage. Bryant's grunts mixed with the attacker's. The human snarled profanity, but Bryant was a silent fighting machine, ducking and hitting with precise efficiency. Odessa squinted through the chaos. Was the other guy coming for her? But the knife wielder lay prone on the floor of the parking garage, the metal blade resting several feet away. A sickening smack ripped her gaze back to the fight. The human was limp on the cement. The two men had been no match for her mate.

Bryant stood still, his chest heaving, his intense gaze sweeping her body. "Are you okay? Did they hurt you?"

Yes. No. Odessa couldn't speak. Her gaze darted between the two men laying still.

"They're just unconscious." His growl dropped low like he was reassuring her.

She nodded numbly. They weren't possessed and killing a human would lead to a senate trial, possibly an excruciating loss of wings. A shudder raced through her at the thought.

"We need to get you back home," he said, misinterpreting her reaction.

Yes, they couldn't hang around unconscious humans. She and Bryant would have to leave soon, before the men awoke or anyone walked in on the scene. But being an analyst was her nature and she had to ask. "Can you see if they have any tattoos?"

Bryant's face scrunched. "What? Why?"

"My work, the data I gave Cal." Impatience spurred her into action. She marched over to the first man that had attacked her and tugged his clothes around to get a look at bare skin. Her nerves were strung tight and she wanted to vomit touching the vile human, but her analyst mind was in overdrive. "See if they have a black rose, or bloody barbed wire inked anywhere, but note any other tattoos. I think there are more symbols than I figured out."

To Bryant's credit, he didn't hesitate—much—and followed Odessa's lead. "This guy's got a black rose on his inner wrist and a dragon on his torso."

"I don't think the dragon means anything, but I'll make note of it." Odessa had to grunt her words. Heaving her load left and right, she pushed and pulled clothing.

Bryant came over and helped move around heavy limp limbs to roll him over. "I need to knock out the cameras before we leave."

Of course, cameras. Bryant encountered this stuff all the time. She usually arrived in an unmonitored corner across from the mall but two people disappearing on camera would attract the wrong attention. Especially after a knife fight.

She was so out of her element.

"There." Bryant pointed to a smudge of black ink. "Black rose on the back of his neck. That it?"

Odessa nodded. Her little isolated office world was no longer. Her research was dangerously real.

Bryant towed her along when he took care of the cameras. She put up no resistance, loathe to be far from his protection. Once the cameras were down, Bryant hooked an arm around her and ascended with her.

JAMESON HADDOCK BROUGHT the cheap whiskey to his lips and grimaced. *Uck*.

Why bother with drivel? It was worth saving pennies for one drop of the quality amber liquid. But he had to blend and this place offered nothing better.

Around him, slot machines pinged and beeped. Ah, the sounds of nature in Las Vegas. Tourists of all shapes and sizes flowed around the bar where Jameson waited for his target. Bawdy laughter sprouted from more than one corner of the giant room and interspersed with tinkling giggles from groups of women strolling by.

What a fucking happy place.

Setting the glass down, he wandered through the casino. He sensed the watcher close by, he just needed to find the subject being catalogued by the Numen. Then he could pinpoint, maybe even visualize, the winged bitch upsetting his meticulous plans.

Ah. Two women walked between slot machines in front of the watcher. Those lovely ladies must be the targets. They looked like his avid follower—skirts as short as their heels were tall, hair as darkly colored as their skin was pale, and of course, the tattoos. Some days he pondered paying a few girls to go blond, even dirty blond, or red. Why did they all assume that since he meddled in the underworld he preferred the goth look?

No wonder Miss Lindy Sampson spun his head so fast the other night. He had strolled through the club on the way to his penthouse, looking for a voluptuous toy for the night. His lips quirked slightly. While Busty was an accurate description, he'd finally gotten her first name. It had even gotten wrenched out of him during one intense orgasm where she'd—

Moving on.

It did no good hunting a watcher sporting an erection.

Besides, he needed to make himself obscure so the two young women didn't recognize him. All of his faithful disciples would know what he looked like if they had visited his club. There, all they saw was a mysterious rich man in an expensive suit. Some lucky doves got to see a little more of him. Occasionally, with one like the carnal Miss Lindy, he might form a fleeting attachment.

There was no way of knowing if the watcher's subjects had ever seen him. Or whether it was enough to recognize him dressed down in jeans and a T-shirt, like an everyday tourist searching for the "what happens" part of what stays in Vegas. Jameson let his hair fall over his forehead to mask his most identifying feature, his unique, dazzling eyes.

There was also no way of knowing if the watcher would recognize him. Her name was Magan, and he didn't recall her from his previous life as an esteemed senator. After disgraced Numen had their wings brutally ripped from their back and were dropped in the human realm to fight for survival like unwanted pets, they were often forgotten. Numen didn't believe in luck, but mentioning a fallen's name was as close as they got to believing in bad luck. As if the very utterance would bring doom on the speaker, or at the very least, remind the naïve idiots that they were fallible.

Jameson's back burned at the reminder of his punishment. The memories this place resurrected were not treasured. After finding himself in Sin City without an identity, much less a cent to his name, he'd used old contacts and resources and clawed his way to the top. All the while plotting his reclamation of power.

The fools. At least his mate had thrown him back to Las Vegas, snidely asking him if his lovers would help him now that he had nothing.

Yes, he was that good and they had. He winced again for

the second time that night. Perhaps not the help he would've preferred, but it had given him the start he needed to thrive.

And thrive he had.

Ducking into a dark corner near the restrooms, he waited as his two disciples passed, laughing animatedly. One of the women had such a short skirt that he could see the tip of a black rose poking out beneath the fabric on one pale thigh. It wasn't completely visible, meaning that when they hit up his club, her skirt would hitch higher. On her friend, the black petals stuck out from between the corset lacing that criss-crossed her back. Which also meant, at his club, she would be shucking her corset only to wear a thin scrap of material over her breasts.

He loved his disciples.

Jameson unfocused his gaze until he could make out the fuzzy image of the watcher trailing behind the two women. Watchers had the same ability as the demonic sylphs. They were like ghosts in the realm. Intangible, invisible, not completely here but present enough to look, listen, and sometimes touch.

Ah, there she was. Being able to see her was a talent that made him the only one able to carry out this mission over any of his human disciples. Watchers had the power to stay in the earthly realm without being seen, no morphing of wings required. They only watched. Humans couldn't see them. But Jameson could.

The ability was a remnant of his former self, a skill that shouldn't remain. After his wings had been wrenched from him, he should've lost all of his angelic abilities. Then one day, he'd been drinking himself into a stupor out of self-pity, letting his body get debased for a few bucks. He'd gotten the thousand-yard stare and noticed a watcher observing his degradation. The watcher probably had orders to report back to Jameson's bitch of an ex-mate and maybe have a good chortle over his demise.

In that moment, Jameson had formed a new identity. He gave a proper show of his misery and when the angel had left, he earned his money and hit the town. Jameson had gone to the most crowded places he could find and relaxed. Eventually, he could make out sylphs, the little demon nuisances that messed with fragile humans, ripening them for possession. From there, he sensed a symaster, riding around on a suburban dad, encouraging his host to gamble away all his money. Symasters were literally like the devil on a shoulder, but they couldn't take full control of a soul. Finally, Jameson had hit jackpot. A possessed soul. An archmaster.

He had confronted the archmaster and made a bargain. With demon weapons and his knowledge of Numen routines and tactics, they could finally make some progress against the arrogant asses behind his fall. And the demons, well, he'd let them think they were going to get whatever they wanted.

Together, they hunted the watcher Jameson had encountered and with the demon's help, tossed him into the Mist and killed him. Then Jameson turned on the archmaster, using the demon's own weapon to destroy him. Demons were sneaky. The archmaster would've tried possessing Jameson next, in hopes of using him against the Numen.

Jameson attempted to use the ascension ability in the watcher's blood to transcend, but it only allowed him to leave the Mist. It was a start. He started negotiating with every demon he could find to gain Daemon steel and Numen blood. From there, he threw a little money around, made some promises about power, and built a human following and earned a new level of respect on the earthly realm, not unlike the kind he had experienced as a senator.

Only better.

He was in charge. Using demons and their ability to possess and utilize human assets to help amass the fortune he dreamed of, build his club, and continue recruiting humans for his grand plan. He provided humans. Demons gave him weapons. Together, they would amass an army and storm the gates of Numen. And then he'd be rid of them, but that was a worry for another day.

Pulling out of the shadows, he followed the women and the watcher out of the casino and into the concrete walkway between the palace of slots and the parking garage. Now was his best chance.

Gliding up unnoticed behind the watcher Magan, he reached under his suit jacket and grabbed the handheld double-bladed scythe he'd stolen off that archmaster many years ago. An otherworldly weapon capable of making the ghostly angel tangible. He could get to her now. Grabbing one of the watcher's wings in one hand, he drew her blood with the scythe. The blood on the metal was the key, like a built-in system to protect their kind. If blood was shed, the Mist automatically let them in to help prevent human detection. His blood was no longer as angelic as it used to be, but the watcher's blood now...

He moved so fast, they disappeared into the hazy realm just as the two women turned around at the whisper of feathers. The watcher's cries were lost in the Mist.

CHAPTER 8

*B*ryant stared at the living room wall, contemplating Odessa's predicament while she rested in her room. When he and Odessa returned after the attack, she had talked for hours about the notes she'd been working on the previous week. At times, his eyes had glazed over from sheer boredom. Give him throwing stars, give him vials of angel fire, make him face an archmaster with nothing but a dull blade. Anything but pile after pile of mundane compilations of human life. How an analyst could sit and comb through them and remain cognizant enough to find historical trends and Daemon interference, he would never understand. He was a man of action.

He had perked up when Odessa mentioned she had started interpreting strange patterns from the watcher's notes. A form of communication that originated in tattoos. The basic symbol being the black rose tattoo Odessa hypothesized meant dedicated servant. Bryant would've been highly dubious if he hadn't seen them inked on both humans himself.

"Where's my daughter?"

Bryant jumped up at a male's voice and spun toward the intruder, dropping to a fighting stance. He regretted throwing on a standard long gown instead of his field clothing.

Kreger Montclaire tramped through the lower level, peeking into rooms. The steady boil of anger Bryant carried with him threatened to bubble over. The male must've landed on the dais and entered like he still owned the place. He'd have to get the locks changed.

"Sleeping." Bryant gave Odessa's father no further information. She had fallen into an exhausted sleep after making sure he'd hang around the mansion until she woke. He had agreed as long as she accompanied him to discuss their dilemma with his team and Director Richter. She had no choice but to accompany him, but she felt powerless enough as it was.

Creases lined the older male's face. He was gaunt, his shoulders stooped, unusual traits in an angel less than several centuries old. The years had not been kind, and for a brief moment, Bryant pitied the senator. All that power didn't equate to happiness. A few years after Bryant's encounter with him, he heard the male's mate had passed—by walking into the fire.

Then there were the male's daughters. Before Odessa had marched into his life, he'd only known that the male had two, one with a hearty reputation around the barracks. Kreger's other daughter was considered a piece of promiscuous bad news. Bryant hadn't cared one way or another but had discouraged gossip regardless. Then there was Odessa, who had willingly mated a warrior she'd never met.

Not many of the senators had happy, serene home lives. Much like what Bryant witnessed of the superrich on Earth —too much time, too little responsibility. Or vice versa. They lacked balance and their children were surrounded by greedy people who did not have their best interests in mind.

Kreger managed to stare down his nose at Bryant despite being shorter. "Go wake her. I must talk with her."

Bryant's fury roiled. The senator was in *his* house now and would *not* be telling him what to do this time. "Pardon me if I don't follow your command, Senator. It didn't work out so well for me or my team last time."

To his surprise, Kreger looked contrite. His brow furrowed and his gaze dropped to the floor. Concern appeared to override any other emotion. But the expression was brief. Kreger straightened, assuming his regal senator air.

"Despite the history between you and I, this is about her."

"Indeed?" Bryant advanced on him, his tone dropping to a menacing level. "Because I've only dealt with you once before, when you ordered my team to their destruction. Then last night Odessa and I were attacked. And here you are."

Kreger's face paled, matching the white streaks at his temples. "Is she all right?"

"She is," Bryant gritted out between clenched teeth. Did the bloke know his daughter was in danger and not mention anything?

"Father?" Odessa sleepily called from the upper level.

The males glanced toward the top of the stairs. Bryant's heart stuttered. Sleep tousled, but alert, Odessa swept down the stairs. She'd been sexy in human garb, but traditional Numen robes allowed her natural elegance and beauty to shine through.

"Odessa!" Kreger rushed to the bottom of the stairs to greet his daughter. "Is everything well?"

"Yes." She met him at the bottom and gave him a perfunc-tory kiss on each cheek, her brows furrowed. Her expression quickly changed to caution. After a quick glance at Bryant, she seemed to choose her words to not alarm her father. "Have you heard?"

The male sighed and stepped back from Odessa. "Come, we have much to discuss."

Without waiting to see if she followed, Kreger strode into the formal office on the first level. Odessa followed and Bryant fell in step behind her. He'd only been in the room twice before. When he checked out the mansion after moving in, and then again to clear the building after they came home early this morning.

Once they were all in the sizable room, Bryant perched on the settee in the corner.

Kreger settled at the opulent desk, like he'd probably done for decades, perhaps centuries before moving out of the mansion. He tossed Bryant a stern look. "Warrior Vale, give us a moment."

Bryant arched a brow. Just as he suspected. Odessa's secrets included her father.

She balanced nervously on the edge of a chair across from the desk. Bryant could only see her profile but had a lovely view of her velvety wings. Were they as soft as they looked? Probably softer. What would they feel like wrapped around him?

Wrong time to fantasize, warrior. He forced himself to concentrate on the perturbed patriarch in the room. "I'll be staying."

The two males glared at each other. Kreger broke first, turning to his daughter. "Have you discussed your past with anyone?"

What an odd question. Kreger had to be privy to the danger posed to Odessa.

She shook her head. "No. Other than my mating, which

was public news, nothing about me has been shared." She fiddled with her hands and shot Bryant an apologetic smile.

"Ah yes. That." Kreger shot him a disapproving look before dismissing him. "Have you heard from Felicia?"

Bryant hadn't met the wayward sister. Was Odessa in contact with her?

Sadness and regret glimmered in Odessa's eyes and her shoulders drooped. "No. I believe she spends most of her time in the human realm these days."

Kreger blew out a heavy breath and nodded. "You've heard what happened to Cal."

Odessa nodded.

Bryant wanted to rip the desk apart and demand answers, frustrated at the tiptoeing around.

"Do you believe he killed himself?" Kreger asked.

"No."

Funny, Odessa had never had a lack of words of what she thought around Bryant.

Enough of this. "Two human men tried to attack Odessa last night." Bryant jabbed his finger toward Odessa. "Targeted *her* specifically, with blades capable of sawing a head off." Numen couldn't recover from decapitation.

Kreger slumped back in his chair, scrubbing his hands over his face. "Whatever research you were doing for Cal, you need to stop."

Odessa opened her mouth to argue but closed it again and remained silent.

Bryant sat forward. "If they're already after her, then they think she knows too much. She'll still be in danger. I need to investigate."

"No."

Bryant shot out of his chair, his wings flared in fury. "Don't forget, Senator. This is *my* house now. *My* mate's life

81

is threatened. You don't get to come in here and throw your commands around."

Kreger followed suit, his own pewter wings flaring with anger. "You forget your station."

"I don't care about your politics," Bryant roared. "This is your daughter!"

"A daughter I can keep safe if she ceases doing what might get her killed!"

"Both of you, sit down." Odessa didn't yell but kept a conversational volume. Both he and Kreger stopped to look at her. "I said sit. Please."

Bryant didn't want to. He wanted to shove Kreger out the window, after tying his wings into knots. Kreger's eyes sparked. The male must be entertaining similar thoughts, but they both grudgingly sat.

"First, I am in the room and this is also *my* house." Her gaze danced back and forth between them, her brilliant blues landing on Bryant. "I'm grateful for your help last night. The way you've been treating me, I wouldn't have been surprised if you felt that my death would give you the freedom you desire."

Why would Odessa think he was better off with her dead? He hadn't wanted to mate her or be forced to sync with anyone. But he protected his people. It was part of his very being.

"Father." She turned to Kreger, who'd been glowering at Bryant. "I listened to you all those years ago and watched our family crumble. Mother killed herself. Felicia is... Felicia. I mated myself to an unknown male who despises me for it and obviously hates you. All because we were going insane and couldn't talk to anyone. I've been driving myself crazy, wondering when it's my turn."

Her turn for what? Kreger's expression turned to shame

and he wouldn't look in Bryant's direction. What had the family been through?

"You tell me to basically quit my job and look the other way when I *know* there's a threat to our people. I'm not staying silent this time." Kreger opened his mouth to argue, but she held up her hand. "He may not like me, but Bryant agreed to help. He already saved me once and...I trust him. I'll have the protection of his team of warriors. You go back to the senate and do what you need to do, but I am not pretending nothing's wrong this time."

This time? "What the hell are you two talking about?"

"It's not just you I'm worried about." Kreger's voice shook, but not with anger or frustration. For the first time, Bryant witnessed the father within the senator. "Don't you think Felecia's been through enough?"

Guilt flared in Odessa's gaze. "Then I need to tell Bryant everything, Father."

Kreger worked his jaw back and forth. An emotional storm raged in his features. "Fine." The struggle in the male was clear. "Vale. Know that the story she tells you happened because I initially resisted giving you the order that left you scarred and killed members of your team. I didn't make the same mistake twice."

Bryant recoiled, shock paralyzing him. Odessa's sharp inhale echoed in the silence left by her father's confession.

"Hate me all you want, but I would do it again to protect my girls." Kreger's gaze lit onto Odessa, warmed slightly, before cutting back to Bryant. "Protect her with your life." He spun out the door and as soon as he was clear, flew away.

Bryant clenched his jaw. The day all those years ago when Kreger had cornered him filled his mind. The memory of the anger, feeling of helplessness...all preceded the worst moments of Bryant's life. "Odessa."

She made a disgruntled noise, standing abruptly, her wings knocking her chair back. "Why do you always say my name like you're disgusted with me? Oo-desssa." She pegged his accent, mocking how he stressed the O and hissed the rest of her name. "Are you going to blame me for what happened to you?"

He couldn't bring himself to say no. Odessa's jaw dropped. She snapped it shut and stormed out.

He jumped up, hot on her tail. "How would I know to blame you or not? You don't tell me anything."

Odessa whirled around so abruptly, she almost bitch-slapped him with her wings. Her cheekbones blushed an angry red, and her chest heaved with indignation. "Would it have mattered? You dumped me as soon as we landed in my foyer. Then you ran off the next morning. We're not even fully synced!"

All his anger toward her father directed itself at her. "Is that what it'll take to get some answers and find out what the hell is going on? Fine! Let's finish mating."

Her eyes widened as the intention of his words registered. Before she could argue, he grabbed her and yanked her close. His lips planted on hers and he backed her into the wall bordering the stairs.

This female! She was so vexing—nothing but trouble, and for much longer than he had realized. He wanted nothing to do with her. *Should* want nothing to do with her. But nothing could pry him away. She melted beneath his hands, her fury pouring out in her kiss. Her molten lips opened for his tongue's entrance.

He dived into the warm depths of her lush mouth. Locating the tie of her gown, he nearly ripped it off before it fell away with his tugs. His erection strained past the part down the middle of his own dressing gown. Desire crowded out any other thoughts, his body finally getting close to what it'd been craving since she'd traipsed into the ballroom.

She reached for the solidness pushed against her belly. They were smashed together. And as much as he wanted to feel those elegant hands wrapped around him, he needed to make her ready for him. Because once he entered her and those long legs were wrapped around his waist, neither of them would want to slow down. He was too close to answering the questions that had plagued his fantasies for days. How she might feel as he stroked her center? Did she get wet at the thought of being with him? How loud she would cry his name as he coaxed the first orgasm out of her?

The sides of her gown parted so only his was keeping their flushed skin from touching. He wanted to drink in her bare body but couldn't take his mouth away from the divine pleasure of kissing her, tasting her passion. He had to feel her. Easing away enough, he cupped her hot center. He groaned. Softer than her wings looked, Odessa was blistering velvet, welcoming his touch. She moaned when he tunneled a finger toward her core.

Wetness coated his fingers. One fantasy answered. He easily found her little nub. She sighed into him and shifted her legs, allowing him greater access.

Oh. Yes.

He wanted lazy, circular strokes, but the lingering rush of anger and adrenaline fueled him. Not enough. Switching to his thumb at her nub, he thrust a finger into the tight wrap of heaven. The clench of her inner muscles, the whimper in her throat… What would she feel like on his cock? She was so tight, so searing hot, the first touch would ignite his shaft.

He should hate the heat. Fear it. But he couldn't get enough.

Anchoring her against the wall, he plundered her mouth like he wanted to plunder her body. He throbbed more painfully the wetter she got. He set a quick rhythm with his hand and kept it, savoring every gasp of pleasure from

Odessa that echoed into his mouth. She pumped her hips against his hand, and her body moved up and down against the wall. Irritated at the fabric keeping his straining cock away from the golden flesh it desired, he ripped his gown open.

Another groan resonated from him when the lovely burn of her skin teased his rigid, pained length. So good. The sounds she made—so erotic. His self-control might shatter and he'd come before he entered her. It'd been several months since he'd had any action, but he was a grown man, helpless against her sensuality and against the tidal wave of emotion that had brought them to this point. Their first time as a synced couple would be angry sex, but damn, it would be hot.

She ripped her mouth away to cry and gasp as she rode his hand. He pumped faster; she moved against him harder. He licked and nibbled his way up and down her neck. She clutched his shoulders.

"Odessa," he breathed into her neck. "Do you like how I say it now?" She clenched and bucked around him when he nibbled on her tender earlobe.

"Oh, Bryant. Don't stop."

"Oh, honey," he growled against her neck, "there's no way I'm fucking stopping."

She strained against the wall, ready to shatter, and he hadn't tasted her breasts yet. They bounced against his chest with her movements, his shaft rubbing against her belly as her hands dug into his shoulders.

She cried his name as her orgasm hit, pulsating around his fingers. It was like a switch flipped in his dick and he couldn't help the orgasm that dominated him, spilling against her belly. Odessa jacked against his hands while tremors racked his body, both of them held up only by the pressure of their bodies against the wall.

He might've come, but he wasn't done. Not even close. With the beautiful angel who had entered his life and plagued his every thought—one release wouldn't be enough. Would never be enough with her.

He continued lazy circles with his thumb. She stiffened before turning liquid and shuddering against him. He lifted his head as her long lashes drifted up, those stunning eyes only making him harder. He moved to position himself at her slick entrance, finally giving both of them what they needed.

There was a brisk pounding. Odessa tensed. He craned his head around to glare at the door.

"*What?*" Bryant snarled all his wrath with that one word. He was so close to the heaven her body promised to give, who *dared* to ruin it?

Muffled shouts informed him of some mess that probably wasn't important enough to interrupt a fully turned-on Numen warrior from claiming his mate.

Odessa released him from her intense grip. Bryant didn't want to move away from her, but she gently nudged him back. He let his hand fall away from her, trying to reconcile with his mind and body why they were not experiencing rapture at the moment.

"It's Bill and Davon." Odessa's voice had a breathless, just-been-sexed quality. A blush stained her cheeks at having to answer the door after what they'd just been doing. And because his pulsating manhood still jutted out proudly.

Grinding his teeth together, he closed and tied her dressing gown first because she was too flustered. He tightened his gown and knotted the damn belt over his dick, so it wouldn't act like a compass announcing to the two analysts which way due sex was.

Odessa stepped toward the door, but he pulled her back. "Let me, just in case."

She bobbed her head, not meeting his gaze. She kept tugging at her gown to straighten it, as if she was afraid the two males would know exactly what they'd been doing.

Stomping toward the door, Bryant dissuaded himself from dismembering each angel and using their limbs to roast s'mores over angel fire. The last time they were here, they'd had important news. Now they either had crucial information, were checking up on Odessa, or wanted to do her harm.

The latter was unlikely. Bryant could read people well after all his years on the job, and Bill and Davon did not scream menace. Even if they were seeped in subterfuge and plotting the downfall of Numen, they were too open to keep anything a secret. Poker faces, those two did not possess.

Bryant jerked the door open. The diminutive males drew back, eyebrows raised. One gasped. He must've made quite the fearsome picture.

"Yes?" He should get a damn medal for managing not to shout.

Bill recovered first. "Warrior Vale, is Odessa well?" His gaze lifted past Bryant's shoulder where Odessa hovered. Relief washed Bill's features. "Oh, thank God. May we come in?"

Bryant stepped back to allow them entrance while he scanned the yard. Were they just here to check on Odessa?

The males rushed to Odessa and embraced her before she ushered them into the main room. She walked behind them, nervously readjusting with her gown's tie. Bryant wondered why she was still doing that, until he remembered the mess he'd left on her satiny skin.

He had the urge to touch her shoulder. But how would he reassure her that no one could see her mate had orgasmed all over belly? He caught her eye. Her cheeks flushed deep red and she looked away.

He was miffed at the interruption. She was fighting

embarrassment. Coupling with his mate shouldn't include this much emotion. He'd have to gain better control of himself in the future. She hadn't told him her family secrets yet, and for a few blissful minutes, nothing in his past or hers had mattered.

CHAPTER 9

*H*ow. Mortifying. *Way to go, Odessa. Hold out. Make him treat you with respect.* In Harper's words —*make him werk for it, gurl.* Instead, she had folded under his lips and let him set her body ablaze with his touch. All in less than three minutes flat.

If the pounding on the door hadn't occurred, she'd be impaled on his impressive manhood, demanding he whisper her name in that growly voice of his that did wicked things to her insides. She tugged at her robe again.

Could her cheeks get any hotter? Probably, because she was remembering the exhilaration of Bryant losing himself against her—doing nothing more than stroking her. She didn't get the impression he was a male who prematurely ended lovemaking sessions. He was too controlled, too intense, too demanding. But she made him lose control...a heady experience. Addicting, even.

The warrior sought to keep his distance from her, but she affected him as much as he did her. She had been tiptoeing around, feeling guilty, like she cornered him into a sync. She desired him, and knowing he felt the same put them on equal footing emotionally, gave her an edge.

She'd composed herself by the time the two males took their seats on the couch, tucking their wings in behind them. Odessa sat in the backless chair, leaving the loveseat—the farthest from her—for Bryant.

He watched her, covertly, under heavy-lidded eyes. His demeanor appeared attentive to Bill, as the tall, thin male chattered on about how worried they were about her. But his whiskey gaze zeroed in on her with an acuity that vibrated to her toes.

"We tried to summon Magan but haven't heard from her," Bill said.

"Who?" Bryant's sharp gaze finally left Odessa.

A cold pit formed in her stomach. "The watcher who requested my workup on her observations."

Bryant's brows drew together. "Do you think something happened to her?"

Davon swallowed nervously. "We asked her manager for Magan's next round of notes. Said we wanted them ready for Odessa on Monday."

"We didn't want to be obvious," Davon added. "If, you know, something is going on." Bill and Davon exchanged a grave look. "He hasn't heard from her since she left last night."

Worry clawed at Odessa's gut. Last night she was attacked. Now Magan was missing?

Bryant didn't look convinced. "Is that unusual for her? It hasn't even been twenty-four hours."

Odessa shook her head. "She follows clubbers and partiers at night and turns in her notes in the morning. She's never late, rushing home to be with her family." Tears threatened to well. "She has children."

"We don't know yet if anything bad has happened." Davon stretched forward to grab Odessa's hand.

"We were attacked last night." Odessa's words caught.

Both males gasped, blurting questions to check if she was all right and asking what happened. Odessa gave them a quick rundown.

"But humans can't hurt Magan. Watchers stay in an incorporeal form when observing." Bill glanced back and forth between Bryant and Odessa, his expression grim.

Odessa was nodding, but noticed Bryant was not.

"They can't, can they?" she asked.

His expression was grim. "Humans? No. But humans aren't the only ones wandering around the earthly realm."

"Demons can't sense watchers unless they're roaming fully formed like other Numen." Bill pondered. "Only other Numen can detect them."

Bryant leveled Bill with an expectant look, like the analyst had answered his own question.

"Other Numen?" Davon's eyes widened. "They would be risking their *wings*."

Bryant stood. "So they say." He paced the living room. "If Magan was targeted in the human realm, any Numen given pass to the realm is suspect. It could be anyone." He gestured to Odessa. "Look at her. She's been traveling there for how long and no one knew."

Odessa pursed her lips, shooting Bryant a scowl. "I work at a children's store. I'm not there to hurt watchers."

"If something happened to Magan… How do we know?" Davon's wings sagged with hopelessness.

"Let's run over what we *do* know." Bryant bowed his head in thought. "Cal was likely murdered, in his home. Odessa was targeted in the earthly realm, by humans. Magan might have been targeted, but it couldn't be by humans or demons —they can't see her."

"The tattoos," Odessa added.

Bill and Davon gave her a questioning look. She explained her findings from Magan's notes and the human men that had attacked her.

"There's a human network working with demons?" Bill's narrow face was pale. "Could they have... Could they have infiltrated our realm and got to Cal?"

Bryant shook his head. "A human would need a damn miracle to get into our realm. Demons physically cannot enter. Any targets in Numen would be dealt with by another angel."

"It's all connected. Someone here is helping the movement down there." Odessa needed to have a long overdue talk with Bryant. Alone. "You guys need to go back to work and pretend you know nothing. Tell whoever asks that you came here to console me about Cal."

"Business as usual," Bryant added. "Tell them Odessa was so distraught, she might not be able to go to work this week."

Both angels readily agreed and Bryant ushered them out with a warning that they interfere no further and watch their backs.

Once the front door shut, Bryant leaned against it. His palms were flat on the door's surface, his corded arms stretched out in front of him, shaved head down.

Should she say something? "I, um... I'm going to go upstairs and freshen up. Then we need to talk."

He bobbed his head in confirmation that he heard her. She left him like that, and would've paid dearly to know what in the world he was thinking about.

IF SHE DIDN'T GET UPSTAIRS FASTER, he might attack her again. The visit from the geek squad should've dampened his libido. Should've, but didn't. He remained hyperaware of his mate, even as he heard about the increased danger to her well-being.

What if the watcher had been killed? And what had Kreger meant that his family tragedy was because he had delayed in ordering Bryant's team to face an impossible task.

Once he heard the door to Odessa's suite close, he shoved off the front door. He needed to think, so he roamed the lower level. For years, he had tried to forget, holding on to his bitterness and resentment toward the senator. Now, he thought back to that meeting with Kreger.

Bryant's team had been hunting an archmaster. A particularly wicked one that had seemed to target angels living in the human realm. That a demon was intelligent enough to plot an attack on angels and not be content wreaking havoc in their possessed human's world had been concerning enough. During the hunt, his team had found three bodies decapitated in the Mist—two watchers and a messenger. Demons weren't supposed to be able to get into the Mist. Had the non-warrior angels tried to take on a demon and brought it into the Mist to kill it themselves and failed miserably? Bryant and his six warriors had doubled their efforts hunting the archmaster. Then they found a headless warrior, missing his vial of angel fire. Bryant had suspected the demon had a grander plan.

He brought the info to Director Richter. The male had presented the unsettling information to the senators. The result was the same as his mate was experiencing—pain and death. There was too much correlation.

"Oh my," said a throaty female behind him. "You're the new male in Odessa's life?"

Who dared intrude now?

He spun toward the intruder, his wings flared for a fight, but he immediately relaxed. The female with a striking resemblance to Odessa reclined on the couch. *For God's sake, can't Odessa's family knock?* He was changing all the locks before sundown.

Felicia's long, shapely legs happened to be in full view since the human hot pink athletic shorts she wore were tailored to extra short. If he was a gambling male, he'd bet the bank that when she stood, the bottom of her ass cheeks peeked out.

Her wings were morphed into her back and from her tight neon apparel, she had come from the human realm. Her hair was as long as Odessa's but several shades lighter, giving it a burnished brass glow. The sisters were tall, statuesque females that radiated life and beauty. But in their eyes, they were worlds apart. Odessa's brilliant teals contained a suppressed zest for life, a sparkle of mirth, and a hint of innocence. Felicia's deep blue orbs were calculating, assessing, and weary. Like she'd been living too hard for too long and searched for a place in her life where she could find some serenity.

Bryant had never ever met her when she was a warrior groupie. Where she went, commotion and drama had followed. Even then, he'd known who she was and to stay away from her. He doubted anything had changed.

"Miss Montclaire," he acknowledged. He wanted to continue his contemplation, dredging every detail up about his past. When Odessa finally spilled what she was hiding, maybe he could put some information together and figure out who was after his mate.

"Aww, you've heard of me?" Felicia sat up straight, her second-skin tank top molding over ample breasts that threatened to spill over the dainty bra attempting to contain them. It must be ninety-five degrees wherever she'd come from. Her gaze drifted up his robed figure, spread over his wings, and glanced over his scars. A look of interest crossed her face. "Call me Felicia. I didn't catch your name, warrior."

"Bryant Vale."

She rose and sauntered toward him. She'd had quite the reputation around the barracks, but he had a sense many tales were made up or exaggerated. Felicia was considered a notable notch on the ol' dressing gown belt. If she turned anyone down, they'd never admit it.

He automatically stepped back. Yes, the female was a devastating beauty and a sexual being. Unlike many other male Numen he heard mentioning her name, he couldn't claim interest in her.

"Vale." She purred his name, slinking closer, playing with her hair, running the tips over the top of her breasts.

Were hips supposed to swing that far from the body? Was she going to dislocate something?

He kept moving back, not trusting what she'd try if he was within arm's reach. What the hell was her agenda? Moving to the backless, single seater chair, he sat down. Taking a page from Odessa's book, he gestured to the loveseat. Two seats, at the farthest points.

"Have a seat while we wait for Odessa to come down."

She seemed undaunted. Adopting a little pout that was meant to be enticing, she passed up the loveseat. She chose the end of the couch closest to him, even if it put her on his scarred side. He didn't feel anything for her, despite her efforts. But damn, if Odessa's bow-shaped lips ever plumped out in a sexy pout like that, he'd be toast.

"Are the rumors true, Vale?" When he gawked at her because he hadn't a clue what she was talking about, she slanted forward. He would have an eyeful of cleavage if he lowered his gaze at all. He looked no lower than her chin. "That you and Ode haven't done the deed?"

"That is no one's business."

"It is if you're leaving your options open." She extended

her legs straight, nearly touching him if he hadn't curled his own legs against the chair.

"I'm mated." *To your sister.*

"You can still back out. Or…expand your selection."

Bryant couldn't believe this female. Or maybe he shouldn't be surprised. Her father was a crooked piece of work. Like father, like daughter. "I'm not that kind of male." The finality of his tone rang through the room.

Instantly, the seductive air was gone, replaced by an assessing look. She sat back and twirled her hair but didn't toy with it at her bosom. Her look had switched from brazen sexpot to calculating mafia boss.

There was more to Felicia than met the eye.

"Yes. I do believe you're not that kind of male. But FYI, if you fuck with her, I will rip your dick off myself."

The hardness in her tone made the visual clear and he flinched. "You barge in here like you're ready to jump in bed with me, and now you're threatening me?"

She crossed one long tawny leg over the other. "I wanted to be sure you were a good male. Not like that slime, Crestin. He was always leering and trying to catch me alone. So I made sure Ode got a look-see." Felicia huffed. "Otherwise, she never would've left his sorry hide."

Should he be impressed, insulted, or grateful Odessa had a rabid sister protecting her?

"You seduced Crestin so I could see?" Odessa's incredulous shout rang out.

Felicia whipped around to find her sister had stepped out of her suite in time to hear everything. Bryant wasn't surprised. He'd heard the door open and sensed his mate when Felicia had been making her revelations.

Felicia recovered smoothly. "Would you have left him otherwise?"

"Our relationship would have taken its natural course to

an end without you sleeping with him." Odessa gripped the railing at the top of the stairs, her knuckles white.

"Uh, one, I didn't sleep with him. Just made a show of how willing he was. And two, the douche was already sniffing around behind your back." Felicia shrugged a fine-boned shoulder. "I had to do something."

"What about Bryant? Are you planning on testing him?" The tightness in Odessa's face piqued Bryant. Felicia's behavior hurt her. But the drama needed to play out, otherwise Bryant would be dealing with sister issues on top of everything else.

"Already did, Ode. I have to admit, I'm surprised. That whole scarred-up thing must really draw the women, but not the kind you're interested in. Am I right, Vale?"

Bryant narrowed his gaze on her. What was she getting at?

"They look at you and think danger, menace—they want the bad boy. But you're tired. Sick of being a random fantasy they can cross off their bucket list. You want someone who'll see the male under those robes, or whatever you wear in the field."

Definitely more to Felicia than he first thought. With a few sentences, she'd flayed him open.

"You synced with my sis, and word is, you hate it. And her. I come in and you don't even look twice, pinging away from me like I have some dreaded disease." Felicia paused. "I don't, by the way. I'd have thought you'd give off some pent-up sexual tension, maybe even hint that you and I could hook up later. But nothing. I'm impressed."

Perhaps she thought her insights would win him over, make him admire how she looked after her baby sister. Instead, his fury grew by the minute. "Do you think you're doing her a favor? You test males because you think you must be more desirable than Odessa?" He didn't bother to cover his scorn. "Any male that could claim Odessa's heart, then betray her, *for anyone*, is a pathetic representative of our gender. And, aye, I've met the sad example that is her ex."

He expected Felicia to become indignant, but she beamed while Odessa's mouth hung open.

"As far as the *rumors*," Bryant was on a roll now, "there'd be no issues, except you both, *and* your father, seem to excel at deceit. So, no. I'm not tying myself permanently to this family until I have the truth."

Odessa's gaze fell on Felicia, who paled considerably.

"You haven't said anything to him?" Felicia's words were barely a whisper.

"I couldn't take the chance, Filly. Your safety is priority over my sync." Odessa cast a guilty glance toward him. "I stumbled onto what appears to be a conspiracy. Then father made an odd comment that what happened to us and the danger to me now are connected."

Felicia gaped at her sister. "Danger? What's happened?"

Good Lord, was everyone going to discuss this while he got no further ahead and no more information? Forcing patience to the forefront, Bryant remained seated, not interrupting until Odessa filled her sister in on the weekend.

"Once I have all the information possible, I can bring it to the director." Bryant threw Odessa a *start talking* look.

Felicia got up, tugging her micro shorts down. "Pardon me if I sit that little talk out. I'm going to head home."

"Filly, wait!" Odessa rushed down the stairs to stop her sister from leaving. "If they are connected, you might be in danger, too. Do you have someone you can stay with?"

Felicia flipped her hair. "I can always find someone to stay with."

"Someone who can protect you?"

She snorted, defiant. "I can protect myself."

Bryant cut in. "From two or three armed Numen?"

She clamped her jaw shut.

"Stay here tonight," Odessa offered. "When we go to Director Richter, maybe he'll have a warrior who can offer protection."

Felicia's gaze flicked up to the left wing of the house that she and Odessa must've slept in when they were children. Her shoulders were rigid and she was shaking her head, about to decline the offer. A less than honorable part of Bryant almost wanted her to so he could have Odessa to himself tonight.

"Bryant's been sleeping on the couch. You can stay with me in the other wing," Odessa urged.

Shite.

Shame swept through Bryant as soon as he had the thought. Felicia's lips curled into a grateful smile, like she wanted nothing more than a girly sleepover with her sister. She probably had as few friends as Odessa. With her reputation, even fewer.

"All right. I'll raid the kitchen and let you..." Felicia swallowed hard and lifted her chin, "While you tell our dirty little secret."

Felicia disappeared into the kitchen as Odessa faintly muttered, "It's not a dirty secret. It was a terrible tragedy."

She sighed and dropped onto the couch. Dark circles lined her ordinarily vibrant eyes. He was used to the stress, but exhaustion still weighed heavy on his wings. She must be stretched thin and ready to topple.

He wanted to ask if she was okay, but she started talking. "I was eleven and Felicia was fifteen." She pointed to the side Felicia hadn't wanted to go to. "That wing was where our rooms were. One night, two males landed on our porch and broke in. Before I could scream, one hit me across the face and said if I made a single noise, Felicia would suffer more."

The solid thump of his heart pounded his ear drums, and

he sensed her story was about to get so much worse.

Odessa's face crumpled, tears spilled onto her cheeks. "I've never told a soul, so— I'm just— This is hard."

"Take your time." He wanted to sit next to her and wrap her in his embrace, surround her in the protection of his wings. But she was an island, needing to let the floodwaters of the past spill over her.

She drew in a shaky breath. "He just straddled me, pinning me to the mattress and tapping my wings with a dagger. I could hear Filly whimpering, crying. I didn't know what was happening to her until… It was so dark."

Shock poured through his body. If the males weren't dead already, Bryant would hunt them down.

"When the male was done with her, they both left, jumping out the window and sailing away. I ran to check on her and call for our parents. Filly never screamed because he'd told her he'd do the same to me if she made any noise. She protected me." Tears spilled over her cheeks. "I-I thought they raped her, but they cut her—" She looked toward the kitchen, her face crumpling. "They mutilated her gorgeous wings. She can't fly. She's always in pain. And she protected me through it all."

Like she had done with Odessa's ex-boyfriend. Protected her at all costs, especially to herself. Felicia made more sense to him.

Odessa's watery gaze met his. "Father said to tell no one, or the males would come back and finish taking her wings. Then start on mine. He said if anyone ever found out, I would pay and Felicia would die. He'd been stressed before the attack, but after… He was different." A small sob escaped. "I guess you and your team paid for our silence. That must be why Father sent you on whatever mission that almost killed you. It was meant to kill you."

Yes, it was. His team was getting too close to someone

and they had used Kreger to take care of the problem they were creating.

This time he did move to the couch to fold her into his embrace. She curved into him, crying softly against his shoulder. Her warmth seeped through his gown, a different kind of intimate than before. Even his body knew she only needed comfort, not proof of how she affected him.

She'd paid for him doing his job. The only Numen powerful enough to order Kreger around were other senators. Even if an angel of lower status blackmailed Kreger, they were still in the realm. The problem originated in Numen. A conspiracy.

"You wanted to know why I chose you to sync with." Her words were muffled against his robe, like she was ashamed by her upcoming admission. "Because I saw your picture and thought I could finally sleep at night with a male like you watching over me. A warrior that wouldn't let the bad guys hurt me if they came back."

He closed his eyes. And he'd assumed the worst of her.

"I'm sorry." She sniffled. "I'm being such a baby. A grown angel afraid of the dark."

"Don't," he growled. When she cowered at his harsh tone, he realized his error. "Don't ever feel bad about your fears."

That was enough to comfort her. He held her while she cried quietly, releasing the pent-up emotion of keeping a significant, terrible secret for so many years.

Bryant considered her situation. She had agreed to mate with him because she feared for herself and had no one to turn to. She trusted him to protect her and it was his innate duty to protect the angels of the realm. He'd help her—and keep his hands off her. When she was safe again, they would annul their sync. She'd be free to pick the life she wanted and not the one she was driven to out of fear.

As much as he wanted her, she wasn't his to have.

CHAPTER 10

*O*dessa couldn't say how she knew a change came over Bryant, but she was ensconced within his embrace, wrapped warmly in his thick wings. But it went from touching consolation to…perfunctory. Like he'd mentally distanced himself from her.

She couldn't fault him after her show of sobbing and sniffling into his strong shoulder, basically confessing that she was the weaker sister. And afraid of being alone. All after her sister had copped to luring her ex into sex—her ex who had already been looking for another bed to warm. If all that didn't scream what a catch Odessa was, she didn't know what else would.

Odessa was never going to get ahead with the warrior. One step forward, two steps back. The idea of a real relationship was getting further and further away.

Her emotions stable, she straightened out of Bryant's warmth and peered into his concerned, shining eyes. Her breath caught. She'd only known him as edgy, irritated, angry, and mostly cranky. This new look into Bryant made her heart stutter. The normal harsh planes of his face had softened; his gaze had warmed. He hadn't shaved lately, and the dark shadow of stubble framed the scarred ridges on his left side.

Odessa traced his scars, her fingers whispering over the raised planes. Could he feel anything? Was there any sensation left in the cindered nerve endings?

He stiffened, and she feared he'd pull away, but she continued and he remained still. Deftly, her fingertips stroked the uneven lines by his mouth, up to his cheek, and feathered along the scarred striations pulling at the corner of his eye.

"Is that why you don't smile?" she murmured, her thumb stroking the injured corner of his mouth.

"What?" He sounded strangled, his body tight next to hers.

"I don't think I've ever seen you smile." She skimmed her thumb away from his lips.

"I can." His breath tickled her. "But that side won't move as much."

"So that's why you don't. But you should."

She continued her perusal, aware she was affecting him, but not knowing how. Finally, she reached his ear, outlining the withered ridges. He flinched, but froze at her censuring expression. His ear deserved the same attention as his face. Much of its shape was retained, though mottled and scarred like the other skin, it definitely had taken the brunt of the angel fire.

From his ear, she flitted her fingers around the back of his head. She searched for how far the ruined skin ran before normal healthy skin dominated, then caressed around to his jawbone and down his neck. Much of the same wrecked skin ran under her touch, though not as severe as his face. Odessa lingered as the base of his throat, admiring the strength in the corded muscles of his neck. They flowed into a wide chest that could only be found on a warrior with hours of training and warring.

Pushing the shoulder of his robe out of the way revealed how shallow his breathing had become. She had a tiger cornered in a cage, one who didn't know whether to bite the hand petting him or bare his belly for her stroking.

She knew what she wanted him to do.

Sliding a hand around the back of his head, she drew downward. The glow of disbelief in his face before her lips touched his almost made her grin.

Odessa took charge of the kiss, licking and tasting. If her sister wasn't in the other room, she might finally have this male.

His wings hugged her closer, then he suddenly drew back.

They'd been having a wonderful connection. She gazed at him through her lashes to cover her confusion.

He tenderly unfolded her from his embrace. Another contradiction to why he'd stopped. Tucking his wings behind him when he stood, he held his hand out to help her rise.

As Harper would say, *WTF?*

"Go upstairs and get into some loose clothing. I'll go in the office and get changed." Before she could question him about his sudden mood swing, he shouted for her sister.

Felicia came out. Her strained, pinched expression broke Odessa's heart. The worst moment in her life had been discussed with a stranger. Odessa's reaction to Bryant's treatment paled in comparison.

To Bryant's credit, he didn't shoot her sister a pitying look, or even worse, avoid looking at her entirely like their father had. He glanced over his shoulder, not turning entirely, and now that they were standing, Odessa knew the discreet reason why.

"We're going to get changed. Can you move the furniture out of the way?"

Stark relief that he hadn't brought up her traumatic past wafted through Filly's features. Then confusion twisted her lips. "Sure?"

"Great. Be right back." He snatched up his duffel on the way to the office.

Odessa exchanged baffled glances with Felicia and went up to her room.

AFTER BRYANT SHUT the office door, he barely prevented himself from collapsing on the marble floor.

No one. *No one* touched his scars. Neither had anyone ever touched the rest of him with the compassion or reverence she had. The way those teal gems had lit with curiosity, learning the contours of a face not even he bothered with.

He'd almost popped off the couch like a hot kernel in scalding oil when she fondled the knob that used to be his ear. He often entertained the notion of getting rid of it all together, but it was still able to offer some protection to his ear canal. And for the removal to be permanent for an appendage like an ear, he'd have to use angel fire.

No deal. The searing, agonizing pain from the first round still sang loudly in his memories.

Then Odessa's elegant fingers had moved down his chest and he was ashamed at his body's response so soon after her confessions. He had just thought about helping her start her life anew, one where her safety wasn't dependent on him. If she touched him like that again, ever *kissed* him like that again, his resolve to not mate her would crumble like a soggy cracker.

Shite, he'd better quit thinking like that. His heart was beating harder in his cock than in his chest. Going through his gear, he dug out some black sweats and a T-shirt. After he dressed, he searched for his inner peace until his body was back under control. When the sisters conversing outside the door broke through his trance, he floated out of his meditation.

"Bryant, the furniture's moved," Odessa called.

"I'm dying to know the type of crazy you're bringing to this place," Felicia added.

Stepping out, all of his serenity almost exploded at the sight of Odessa. He managed to nod his approval at her choice of athletic shorts, longer than her sister's, and sports bra and tank top. She didn't need to bare as much skin as Felicia for her appeal to be undeniable.

Bryant switched his attention to the main room. Felicia had indeed muscled the furniture to the edges, leaving the area rug open. Perfect.

"Great. Felicia, you said you can take care of yourself. I assume that means you know basic self-defense."

He was learning Felicia's personality wasn't one to wilt away, even after the nightmare she'd survived. He had suspected there was more to her, and her extreme measures to protect her sister had issued a strong point, along with her ability—rather, willingness—to shove heavy furniture out of the way. She wasn't an aimless, troubled female. He didn't know how much of her reputation she'd earned or how much was exaggerated—possibly with her help—but she acted deliberately, that was for certain.

Felicia's eyes lit up. "Are we teaching Ode how to fight?"

Odessa glanced between them. "Oh, I couldn't. I mean, I'm not the type to hurt a living creature."

Warriors were rarely bred from the ranks of the elite. Their status in Numen made them too arrogant to take orders from others. They clung to a belief that Numen were too divine for brutality. Many felt too far removed from lowly humans to engage in rough behaviors like fighting. And there were those, like Odessa, who didn't believe humans to be lowly, base creatures, but firmly adhered to no-violence policies.

Bryant would have to change that idea. "To defend yourself, you might need to hurt some creatures."

Felicia nodded emphatically. "And hitting something is an awesome form of stress relief."

"So is a bath."

Felicia shrugged, her wings still morphed into her back. "I don't like my skin getting wrinkled."

Odessa frowned at the room and hugged herself. Bryant feared his attempt was an uphill battle, until she spoke. "You've learned to defend yourself?"

"I've learned more than that, Ode. I've learned not be defenseless or helpless." A hard edge radiated off Felicia. What had the female been up to in the human realm for so many years?

Learning to fight, apparently.

His mate turned to him, her mouth in a resolute line. "Let's get started, then."

THE RESPECT BRYANT had for Director Richter had grown exponentially in the last sixty minutes. An hour ago, Bryant, Odessa, and Felicia had arrived at the director's office. They unloaded their accounts of past trauma and new and old conspiracy, and the male had listened without interruption.

Director Richter sat behind his elaborate oak desk; books and training manuals lined the wall behind him. His wings were relaxed, arms crossed, and his off-white gown moved with muscles continuously tensing and relaxing. He pinned Bryant with a grave stare. "Vale, you're saying that the mission Senator Montclaire sent your team on was intended to kill you all because you got too close to a conspiracy that may originate with one of the senators?"

"Yes, sir. We were on the trail of a powerful archmaster. He seemed more connected than other demons, more deliberate. And he always seemed to know which humans were especially vulnerable and had no watchers monitoring their actions."

The director's features pinched, but he nodded. "Miss Montclaire and Lady Vale, you think you two were attacked to persuade your father to be a corrupt senator's lackey and order Vale's team to be terminated?"

Both sisters agreed. Odessa's small smile appeared cautiously optimistic that the director could and would help them. Felicia's gaze was wary. She must be uncomfortable having another know of her personal trauma.

The director continued, his attention aimed at Odessa. "The notes you gave Cal contained observations of human trends that suggest an organized movement against our realm? Maybe even an organized demonic movement?" When Odessa nodded, he kept going. "You surmised that a black rose tattoo means they are a follower of whomever the leader is. A bloody barbed wire tattoo means they've done more than follow. The hub of activity is the club the missing watcher cited in her report?"

Odessa's smile faded. "Actually, I think a barbed wire tattoo on the right biceps means they've done more than claim devotion. There's disturbing evidence that might suggest they've acted almost like a sylph and helped to create conditions ideal for human possession. It would make sense the bloodied barbs are even more significant. A higher rank, so to speak."

"Any more tattoo messages?"

"I assume there are, but I haven't narrowed them down yet. If we can discover what humans are doing to give them more value to demons, then we'll start seeing more tattoo trends. Right now, I've catalogued every ink symbol Magan reported. There's just nothing else numerous enough to determine a trend."

The director leaned forward, his elbows on the tabletop. "Do you think you could go through your list again and identify more significant symbols now that you know there is indeed a pattern?"

"I could try." Odessa glanced at Bryant in question.

Bryant nodded that he'd be with her. "Sir, I request to be pulled off duty until Odessa's safety is secured. Urban can lead in my place."

"Your team will be reserved for special duty." When Bryant opened his mouth to argue, the director held up his hand. "I can't have them targeted again. Not until we know why a senator would send a team into a trap."

He was crack on. Urban and Dionna needed to be questioned on what they remembered from fourteen years ago when Bryant had earned his scars. The revelations of the past twenty-four hours might shed new light on what had happened. Maybe they could fill in anything Bryant had forgotten or missed while he'd spent months in agonizing recovery. The other four members had replaced the previous team members that had gotten killed, and their ignorance of the situation could be fatal.

"Miss Montclaire will need protection," the director continued. "Vale, who do you think will be best from your team?"

"Oh, dude, that's so okay." Felicia broke in, her brass hair gleaming under the skylight when she shook her head. "I'll just lay low in the human realm."

"Bronx or Dionna would be my choices. The others"— Bryant assessed his mate's sister—"might clash personality-wise."

Odessa's perfect lips twitched like she was trying not to snicker. Her sister had been tenacious, ruthlessly running Odessa through self-defense moves, much more authoritative than Bryant would've been. He had been glad to have her there. Where he would have backed off and let Odessa gather herself, Felicia had been relentless. She hadn't let up until Odessa had executed each move perfectly, without flinching.

"No." Felicia was adamant. "I don't want a warrior getting all up in my business."

The director offered another solution. "We can assign you a female—"

"Even worse."

"Felicia, you have some admirable skills." But she couldn't offer herself enough protection. Maybe giving her some say in the decision would make it easier to swallow. "We don't know who we're up against or what kind of resources they have. You can have your pick from any of my team."

Odessa reached for her sister's hand. "Filly, please."

Felicia grimaced, torn. Odessa's worry was clear. All these years, they'd been trying to protect each other. Bryant hoped Felicia would give Odessa the peace of mind.

"Fine." Felicia's mouth grew wide in a sly grin. "Only if I get Julian Hancock."

Oh, bugger. What had he set poor Jagger up for? "May I ask why?"

"You can ask all you want." She flipped her ponytail. "He'll know why."

CHAPTER 11

*J*ameson had his woman up against the wall, ramming into her, her legs wrapped around his waist. They were just inches away from where they could be seen by Andy in the meeting room, and he liked it like that. So did she. Andy had bad news. All the more reason for Jameson to finish his business with Lindy before he went and got all tensed up.

"You're so big," she breathed in his ear, and he came undone.

Once he finished grunting like a bull into her hair, she lowered her legs to the floor. After she extracted him from her body, she rolled off the condom. He liked that about her. She kept her panties off, let him take her anywhere, and cleaned up after them. He might keep her longer than planned.

She gave him one more scorching look that almost earned her round two, but he couldn't let a female distract him from business. Jameson leaned in, nipping and licking her neck.

"Here." He reached into his wallet and gave Lindy a few

hundred-dollar bills. "Go get something fun for me to rip off tonight."

She palmed the bills then him before walking away. Her hips swayed in a way that dominated his attention. Not that it took much. He loved women's bodies, loved how they gave such pleasure, let him forget...

Zipping himself back into his slacks, he also closed his suit jacket to make sure any wetness on his clothes was covered. He was a walking cloud of sex, but he needed to look professional.

He ran his hand over his slicked back hair, then straightened his tie to finish making himself presentable. When he breezed into the board room, Andy waited with a stack of papers and laptop open in front of him.

Jameson chose his normal chair at the head of the table. "Give me the bad news first."

Andy didn't hesitate. "We failed at getting the analyst."

Jameson's mouth flattened. That was indeed bad news.

"The warrior happened to be with her the night my men tried to kill her."

Ah, fuck. "Did he kill one or both of them?"

"No, sir. Only knocked them out."

Damn. It was worth a shot. An angel could fall for killing a human, even in self-defense if the tribunal decided other actions were warranted. "You took care of them?"

Andy inclined his head. "Naturally. They both overdosed last night in a cheap motel room."

"Perfect."

Andy was worth his weight in gold. He had started as a loyal black rose, an accountant for the club, headhunted because of his shady history allegedly embezzling. He'd advanced to become Jameson's right-hand man. Where others groveled at Jameson's knee, Andy had always seen what needed to be done. The man was efficient and meticulous. He also knew the consequences of reverting to his embezzling ways, or what happened if he otherwise crossed Jameson.

"Any good news?"

"The Numen haven't found the watcher's body yet."

A slow smile spread across Jameson's face. No one knew of his methods, and the less they knew, the better. And the archmaster Jameson currently "partnered" with was more compliant if he didn't know Jameson needed the double scythe to cross into the Mist.

"Have you talked with Gerzon recently?" Andy inquired.

Jameson grunted. Think of the devil and he shall appear. "I try not to. I met with him last week to pay him our agreed upon rate of two vials of angel fire a month for his demon minions protecting the club."

Gerzon was an asshole, even for a demon. His power in the demon world was Jameson's ticket for revenge, and Jameson was Gerzon's ticket into Numen.

Andy shifted in his chair and cleared his throat. "Another demon is interested in partnering with you."

Jameson cocked an eyebrow. "Really?"

Sure, he'd garnered much attention from demons with his activities. But Gerzon was a major power in the underworld, and any demon interested in usurping his authority ended up dead. Gerzon wanted to be the force securing rights to the fountain of angel fire after Jameson ousted the Senate and took his rightful station as ruler of Numen. Of course, no demon would be content with only controlling angel fire. Gerzon would have to meet with a nasty end when Jameson conquered his former realm.

But first, he had to gather enough power to get there.

"An archmaster." Andy peered down at his tablet. "Sandeen."

"Never heard of him."

"I'm having him checked out. I told Gerzon's archmaster servant, Zanda, that he's an archmaster who wants to frequent the club. Should be innocuous enough that she doesn't report him back to Gerzon. She's interrogating some sylphs to get information on him."

"The evil little spirits wet their ethereal little drawers whenever she's near."

"Absolutely. Though it is unnerving that she uses the elderly as her hosts."

Nothing was as disconcerting as a wrinkled old grandma reminiscing about how she was once thrown into the Mist by a warrior she later beheaded. Then cackle with her dentures rattling in her mouth.

"It's ingenious," Jameson said. "They often live alone. No one misses them if they disappear for a few hours. When they can't remember what they did all day, no one blinks an eye."

"I highly doubt they last long after Zanda carts their frail bodies all over town doing her ill-begotten tasks."

"Any progress on weapon smuggling?" Jameson's only Daemon weapon was his double scythe—he wanted more. After his fall from grace, Numen steel seared his skin, branding him as unworthy of touching it.

Good times.

But if one Daemon weapon drenched in Numen blood could help him cross into the Mist and back, it made sense other weapons made with Daemon metal could, too. From the Mist, he could figure out how to cross into Numen entirely. "Gerzon refuses to trade in weapons, only demons for angel fire. I set his lessers up with humans to possess and he gets the angel fire from the warrior kills they log." At least Numen were dying during this deal.

"Thus the reason I think meeting with Sandeen may behoove you. The demons we are using work for Gerzon and would report to him if we used them to target other demons for weapons. But Sandeen may have his own agenda we can capitalize on."

Jameson considered all the angles. After he'd beheaded Magan, he'd drenched himself in her blood and tried to transcend. As a senator, he'd had the ability to move freely between the realms.

For one heart-stopping second, he'd wavered between corporeal and nothingness. He was close, dammit. But it'd do no good to materialize in Numen with one measly weapon. His untrained army couldn't cross into the Mist without special tools.

Maybe this Sandeen would be willing to deal in weapons.

"Oooh, I like this one," the hot blonde whispered when he entered the dressing room.

Sandeen smiled from inside the human host he was inhabiting for a few short hours. When Lindy had reached out to him and said she'd be leaving Jameson Haddock's penthouse and why, he told her he'd meet her in one of the changing rooms of the lingerie shop.

He had watched as she walked in, breezed by stacks of panties to go toward the bustiers and garters. The busy salesclerk helping a bridal party tittering over a set of crotchless panties hadn't noticed Lindy. His target picked an impressive collection to try on and headed to one of the private changing areas in the back, leaving the door unlatched.

"You know you're supposed to keep your underwear on when you try on clothes," he murmured. The sight of her large breasts tucked into a lace bustier and garters lining her long, shapely legs tightened the manhood of the uptight banker he'd possessed. The black fuck-me heels she wore solidified the human's cock. A delicious ache.

Uptight humans were the easiest targets. When Sandeen started using their bodies, he marveled over both their horror and their elation at the activities he made their bodies perform. Most never remembered once Sandeen left them, but some did, seeking to find that special awakening they hadn't found on their own.

Sandeen could empathize. It was part of the reason demons wreaked such havoc when they possessed humans. Life in Daemon was nightmarish at best, so it was the only time they could feel pleasure, freedom, and escape the oppression of living under nothing but cruelty. The opposite of why angels came to Earth to aid the sick, the ragged, the down-trodden. Both beings got a strange rush being close to emotions they never experienced due to their role in creation.

Lindy giggled. "I never wear underwear."

Naturally.

He'd met the buxom bombshell at Jameson's club when he was studying the fallen angel. After taking her home—easiest pick-up of his life—he'd found that while she might be free with her body, she also had a brain. She already had her black rose tattoo and was willing to help Sandeen learn more about Jameson, as long as she rose in power alongside him. How a little human thought she could maintain the upper-hand when it came to demons… If he didn't get killed and officially enter Hell while trying to gain his freedom from Daemon, then he'd deal with her. He wasn't into long-term relationships of any sort.

"Have you found out anything?"

She twirled so her backside ground against him in the small room. "Can you buckle me in?" He gritted his teeth and obliged, tolerating her delay only because her firm ass was divine. And she knew it. "He's keeping me like a pet." This was said with some annoyance. "I mean, he's good in bed, but I'm worth more, you know?"

Oh yeah, he knew—as far as her bedroom prowess went. She leaned forward, putting her hands on the wall, looking back at him invitingly.

"I'll have to take a rain check, Lindy dear. Can't have Haddock getting suspicious."

Lindy wiggled her hips, but he left his zipper firmly latched, as much as he hated to.

He would find a willing partner later. That was why he needed to be able to roam freely with the humans and not be confined inside of them. There was no pleasure in sex in Daemon. Only fornicating for reproduction's sake. And pain's sake. And torture's sake. Inflicting both on others, preferably. They were demons after all.

"Give Haddock time, keep him interested," Sandeen instructed her. "He'll either start to trust you or slip some information accidentally. I have a meeting with him soon, and I doubt he'll be completely forthcoming if he decides to work with me. I'm sure his sidekick is using his Daemon resources to check me out first. If Gerzon tries to kill me, then I'll take that as a rejection."

Lindy sighed and stripped off her lingerie. Watching her get dressed again, he had to adjust himself. *Soon, buddy*. He'd find someone to get off with soon. He caught the wink of light glinting off the wedding ring worn by the man he possessed.

That'd truly be an asshole thing to do—possess a body sworn to another and lead them into blind betrayal. Some demons got off on that, a true test of their power to make the faithful open to possession and lead them to stray. Not Sandeen. He preferred the reluctant deference a soul gave him when he led them down the forbidden path they had already been treading near. This repressed banker with divorce papers sitting on his desk had been ripe for the picking.

Again, he felt the man's avid response to Lindy and wished, not for the first time, that humans could get off more than once before needing a break. With most bodies he inhabited, it was one and done. Some days, he was tempted to inhabit women just so he could experience multiple orgasms in one possession. In Daemon, they could rut for hours, but no peak was attained for either party involved. Not unless one of them was suffering, which was their lot in life for having the misfortune of being born in the realm. Sandeen, always the oddball, never preferred it, seeking mutual pleasure in the human realm.

Lindy blew him an air kiss and strutted out of the changing room. Sandeen planned to wait until the clerk was ringing up Lindy's order before he left. Suddenly, the door swung open and he faced a startled young woman. She was the bride of the group the sales associate had been helping.

"Oh, I'm sorry." She started to turn away, alarmed at having caught a man lurking in the changing area of a lingerie shop.

"No worries. It seems my lady friend has stood me up. We had arranged to meet in here for a little, well…" He shrugged sheepishly. "It doesn't matter."

Managing to adopt a likeable, abashed smile, he caught her eye. The handsomeness of his host kept her from turning away. He knew instantly when she warmed to his hound dog routine. Her gaze swept his expensive suit clad body, interest lighting their depths.

"You're welcome to stay." The banker spoke low, his body primed from hours in the gym and not at home with his soon-to-be ex-wife.

He read her well and knew the ways this could play out.

She could laugh with him, shoot him a smile, and leave. Fast forward years after her wedding, to a night when she'd be out with friends, wondering *what-if*. What if that guy watching her at the bar was interested? What if she was single? Then she'd send her spouse divorce papers, just like the ones sitting on the desk of Sandeen's host.

Or...she could bat her lashes and step inside. One last adventure before she tied the knot. It was her party, after all. Then she'd leave, and the guilt would drag at her until she called the wedding off.

All she had to decide was whether she would experience years of heartache before realizing she wasn't ready to settle down.

Which one would it be?

Her gaze flicked back up to his. Sandeen let his interest shine through, earning him a seductive smile. After a glance back toward her friends to see if they were watching her, she stepped inside.

CHAPTER 12

*I*n the barracks, Bryant located Jagger, pulled him aside to speak in private, and explained the assignment.

The young warrior's face paled, then red crept up his neck until his face flushed with anger. "No."

Bryant silently cursed the situation. If it weren't for Felicia's past, he wouldn't have gone along with her demand. "I wasn't asking."

Julian, or Jagger, as they had come to call him, firmly shook his head. Bryant had guessed there was history between Felicia and his warrior, but she trusted the male.

"Sir, I can't. I might just step aside and let whoever it is rid us of the migraine that is Felicia Montclaire."

Bryant had the urge to grab the young warrior by his shirt and drag him up to his face. Using his scars to intimidate was instinctive at this point. Forcing himself to remain placid, he steeled his resolve. "I know she can be difficult. But you have to trust me when I say she needs our protection and you're the only one she would allow."

"Figures. She couldn't control me once, so she's using you

121

to do it."

"You two were together?" Bryant inquired.

Jagger scoffed. "She wishes. I turned her down, didn't play puppet to her master, but she let the rumors spread that we did. I looked like an ass and my girlfriend, the one I planned to sync with, broke up with me. It was humiliating. And all because a spoiled senator's daughter got rejected."

Bryant suppressed a sigh. Bugger it all. Why couldn't this be easy? Yet Bryant had faith in Jagger that he'd do the right thing—eventually. At least Bryant didn't have to worry about a male guarding Felicia getting distracted by her beauty and sexual nature. But Bryant could see why Felicia had chosen Jagger. It would look like she was trying to have the last laugh, an *in your face* to the young, arrogant warrior. When really, she'd picked the male who wouldn't have ulterior motives where she was concerned.

Bryant wouldn't put it past her to lord the circumstances over Jagger.

It could be a giant mess, but Jagger was a reliable warrior. Bryant would do what he could to mitigate relations. "What happened between you two is in the past and you need to let it stay there."

"The past?" Jagger's wings twitched in agitation. "Not when people see I'm shadowing her every move." He threw his hands up. "They're going to think it was all true."

"You know it's not. She knows it's not. You can't control what others think."

Jagger made a derisive noise. Bryant wished he could tell Jagger the complete truth about why Felicia needed protecting, but he couldn't. He had vowed to tell no one what had happened to her. For now, his team would think she needed protecting because she was Odessa's sister and, therefore, may also become a target.

Jagger's head fell back, his surfer blond hair brushing the

tops of his wings. "There's nothing I can do?" he asked quietly.

This was a big step for Jagger. The hothead kid of two senators had taken a giant step down in social ranking when he chose to become a warrior. He'd been put with Bryant because Bryant was seasoned enough not to care what class Jagger had been born into. Bryant had been veteran enough not to put up with Jagger's righteous attitude or allow him any leeway after learning how and why the young warrior had lost his father.

Jagger had become a stellar fighter, earning his nickname. He was honorable, cultured, but brutal on the battlefield. Bryant just hoped after all that, he didn't lose him to the insanity Felicia could incite in males.

ODESSA WAITED with Felicia in Director Richter's office. Bryant went in search of Julian and after a few moments of awkward silence, the director had stepped out to "check on some things."

"I'm not staying with you guys. Bryant doesn't need to blame me for cockblocking him." Felicia bounced her long leg that was crossed over the other. "Julian can guard me in the human world."

Thanks to time spent with human friends, Odessa knew the term and laughed. "Bryant cockblocks himself better than anyone. You're welcome to stay. We can take the master suite and the warriors can take our old rooms."

Felicia tossed her long ponytail over her shoulder, where it swung freely without her wings to impede it. Odessa suspected that was one of the many reasons she lived among humans. She could keep her wings morphed into her back. She'd get questioned too often in Numen as to why she kept them tucked away. And revealing a less than pristine set of wings? Filly already had a reputation. Without a functional set of wings, she would be shunned, humiliated, and avoided. Well, more than she was now.

"Nah. Julian can go where I go. No need for him to corrupt Bryant where I'm concerned. Your mate seems to not hate me. He even treats me with respect. Julian would encourage him to do otherwise."

Odessa studied her sister and her practiced nonchalance. Felicia cared that Julian thought so little of her. "Bryant seems to not hate me, too. But why would Julian hate you?"

Was the cause rooted in her sister's reputation? Odessa had heard enough angels drop crude comments about Felicia for her benefit. As much as Odessa had wanted to be nasty back, she forced herself to choose the high road—mostly because she had agreed. After catching Filly in bed with Crestin, as much as she loved her sister, she had been disappointed in her. Why hadn't Filly told her that he was planning to stray?

Odessa studied her fingernails. Because she would've been too afraid to be honest with herself and would've stayed by Crestin's side, and she would've inevitably caught him with another female.

"He thinks I'm a worthless whore." Felicia kept her tone light, but it didn't fool Odessa. Filly pretended not to be bothered by the warrior's opinion.

Understanding dawned. Her sister had made it look like she was with Crestin knowing that big-mouthed jerk would tell everyone he'd been with her, regardless of the facts.

"You want everyone to think you're a worthless whore, don't you?"

Her sister made a *puh-lease* face. "Why would I do that?"

More information clicked together. "You can defend yourself. You probably fight really well. Is that what you've been doing on the earthly realm, learning all those moves you taught me?"

Felicia uncrossed her legs and folded her arms. "I just don't want to be caught helpless again."

Odessa lifted her chin, silently challenging her sister. There was more. What was Felicia up to? "And Julian?"

"He's an ass. An arrogant one. Both of his parents were senators, and he thinks I'm not worth his time. Blames me that his little elite girlfriend got all jealous and dumped him."

"You're mad at him because he had a girlfriend and turned you down?" Odessa's respect for Jagger increased a little. She didn't want a male that hated her sister to guard her, but if he had strong morals, then maybe he wasn't a terrible choice.

"Of course not," Filly denied, offended. This was the most time Odessa had spent with her in years. She hadn't known how complex her sister had become. "It was the way he did it. 'As if I'd debase myself with you.' Or my favorite, 'I'd bathe a sword in angel fire and fall on it before being associated with the likes of you.'"

Harsh.

Odessa's heart sank. Maybe Jagger shouldn't be responsible for her sister's safety. "Well, if he talks to you like that again, I'll hold his wings while you kick him in the balls."

Felicia grinned and held out her fist. "That's my blood-thirsty little girl. I knew we made progress with you yesterday."

Odessa bumped knuckles, smiling just as broadly.

"Seriously, though." Felicia grew serious. "I don't want to interfere with you two sealing the deal. Bryant's a good male and you act like yourself around him."

"What's that supposed to mean?" What else would she act like?

Those beautiful deep blue eyes rolled. "You know what

you were like with Crestin. Helpless. Needy. Ring any bells? And who was the male you dated before him?"

Ugh. Odessa's track record with jackasses did not need to get brought up. "Okay, I get it. But Bryant isn't into the sync with me."

"Oh, he's into you."

"The *sync*. He's not into the bond."

"A guy like that, with his scars, probably has some hang-ups." Felicia nudged Odessa's shoulder. "We know about those right?"

Did she ever.

"Do you want to stay synced with him?" Felicia asked.

Odessa's gaze dropped to the floor. With Director Richter's help, and a whole warrior team rotating protection detail around her mansion, she might soon be free of the threat. Did she want to be free of Bryant, too?

"I...don't know. We're kind of stuck at an all-or-nothing point."

"Ah. If you two do the deed, you're stuck together forever. Well, you will have a lot of time to get to know each other in the upcoming weeks. Take advantage of it. Bryant is sister approved, FYI."

"You're awesome, you know that?" Odessa's heart soared. Just days ago, they'd been basically estranged. Now, their camaraderie was much like it'd been before that night, fourteen years ago.

A polite knock barely rattled the office door. Director Richter stepped inside, leaving the door ajar. Bryant and most of his team waited outside.

Five faces full of interest peered over Bryant's shoulder and it was clear which one was Jagger. The tall, formidable male glared at her sister, his jaw so tight he could crack nuts between his teeth, his wings folded together and rigid. All Numen had an innate air of elegance, but the higher class exuded superiority. Jagger had it in spades, along with an intoxicating rebellious cant to his features. Felicia likely wasn't the only female who'd thrown herself at him.

He stood well over six feet tall, and his shaggy sun-bleached hair hung down to his chin instead of being combed back into an austere look fitting his station. The eyes boring a hole into the target of his consternation glowed a soft mint. Normally they probably gave his strong face and powerful size a laid-back quality, but today they were two blazing jade stones.

Filly had been correct. He really disliked her.

"Ladies," the director announced. "Bryant's team has been updated. Bryant will accompany you"—he nodded toward Odessa—"to your office to gather as much information as you can while the others search for the missing watcher." He flicked his gaze to Felicia and his expression turned grim. "Miss Montclaire, we ask that you stay with your guardian until the dust settles on this situation."

Felicia stood. Her shapely legs in the short hot pink shorts caught the attention of the other male members of Bryant's team. Jagger's glare intensified.

"Call me Felicia, please." Her sister sent her trademark dazzling smile the director's way before turning on Jagger. "I need to head to the earthly realm and get my things. Think you can suck those wings in and blend, Julian?"

"Miss Montclaire." His tone was hard, punitive. "We'll be collecting your items and going straight back to Lady Vale's home."

Her sister's answering smile said *we'll see about that.* She strutted toward him and latched onto his arm. When he flinched, she clung to him tighter. "Unless you know where I live, I'll need to descend down there with you."

Odessa could've sworn he growled as Felicia descended with him to the human realm.

CHAPTER 13

"*I*t's gone."

Bryant jerked his attention from the snaked patterns in the rose marble floor in Odessa's office. He'd accompanied Odessa while one of his team, Dionna, was stationed outside the door. Sierra and Urban were looking for Magan, and the rest of his team was stationed at the mansion. His mate frowned from behind her desk, jabbing her finger into the top to press the flat buttons built into the surface. Her forehead creased and her movements increased in agitation.

"What do you mean *gone?*" Bryant was afraid he knew exactly what she meant.

"Like all the work I did last week never happened. In fact, *all* of Magan's notes have disappeared. I've been consolidating and studying her observations from the last few years."

If they needed any more evidence there was a conspiracy, that would do it.

Or it would invalidate any of Odessa's claims there was a conspiracy.

Bryant crossed to stand behind Odessa. Leaning over her, the tips of her wings brushed his belly. He resisted the urge to stroke their downy softness—an intimate gesture, and inappropriate in her office.

How would they feel? Satiny feathers sliding under his fingers... Would they be as soft as her skin?

Odessa slapped the top of her desk in frustration, shaking him out of his reverie. He needed to keep his edge, otherwise he'd have to assign another member of his team to guard Odessa. And...that would bother Bryant. Even if it was one of the females on his team, it should be him. It *needed* to be him.

"Look." She scrolled through all of her documentation from other watchers, but nothing from Magan. They scanned through every file since she'd started as an analyst. The date she landed on was the afternoon before his gala. It was blank.

"That's when Cal requested I take a look at some of Magan's concerns right away. To see if there was anything we needed to warn the senators about. I had to stay late and almost missed your offering." Odessa glanced back at him, a light blush highlighting her cheeks.

"Good thing you didn't have to wait in line." Bryant only meant his words to be humorous, but a little crinkle creased her forehead.

"It's not your scars, you know. It's your don't-fuck-with-me-or-I'll-rip-your-head-off demeanor that scares women off." She turned back to her desk. "At least, the weak ones."

Did she really think so? When he thought about it, he hadn't been a popular catch before his injury. If he had wanted something more with the females he trifled with, they were usually on their way out the door. If Odessa hadn't feared for her life, would she have ever considered him?

"Odessa," he said quietly. A slight shiver traveled through

her wings. "You don't have to be bound to me anymore. I'll still protect you, regardless."

She stilled, her head bowed toward her desk. Would she take him up on his offer? He wanted to reassure her. Tell her it was okay, he would understand. He wasn't good for a refined, elegant beauty like her. She was intelligent, kind, and had her whole life in front of her. He lived for his violent work. When he wasn't hunting and killing demons, he was teaching new warriors how to hunt and kill demons.

How could he come home, drenched in demon blood and venom? Would he give her a peck on the cheek and leave smears of organ remnants on her pristine white robe? Then ask "what's for dinner" while he was cleaning guts and angel fire char off his weapons?

"That's a mighty nice offer. If you want to dissolve our union, then I should have another guard." Her bitterness caught him off guard.

Wasn't he being generous by offering a way out of an arrangement she had felt was her last choice? She would be free to choose another mate, one she wanted, or wait for her destined mate to show up with a matching sync brand.

Another male claiming Odessa made Bryant want to snarl. But, no. She wasn't for Bryant. She was light and beauty. He was harsh and damaged. If Odessa cut ties with him, and he kept his head during the investigation, then maybe Richter would drop his insistence that Bryant sync. Bryant's stomach bottomed out at the thought of settling with another female. Making a home, one where it wasn't Odessa's radiant face greeting him through the door, didn't set well with him.

Eventually, they'd have to talk about their future, her future.

A commotion sounded outside Odessa's office.

"Wait here." Bryant rushed to open the door. An irate

male was on his tiptoes, trying unsuccessfully to intimidate Dionna, who stood at least three inches taller and was packed with considerably more muscle mass.

"I need to talk to her." The male's voice rang with desperation. "I just need to ask her if she knows anything."

Bryant stepped out, pulling the door shut behind him.

Dionna worked to calm the man, holding her hands up and speaking low. If she didn't have the male in a choke hold, then she must not think he was a threat to Odessa.

The harried male turned to him. "Please, is Odessa in there? I need to talk to her."

"About what?" Bryant planted himself in front of the closed door.

The stranger wrung his hands together. "My mate, Magan. I haven't heard from her for days. Something's happened, something bad. I can feel it."

Shite. The male felt what everyone else suspected.

A scream from the office cut through their conversation.

ODESSA'S SHOUT had been repressed for fourteen years. She stared up at her attacker from where she'd landed on the floor after sensing someone behind her and diving over her desk.

With a thump, the guy jumped to the top of her desk and loomed over her. Her scream had given him enough pause as his sinister gaze landed on the door.

The sneer on the male's face was all too familiar. It had been dark that night all those years ago, but she had seen enough of the black-clad figure in the moonlight streaming through her room. The same male from her nightmares was making due on his promise to come back and hurt her if she talked.

A blur sailed over Odessa and tackled the male on the

desk. She was yanked up and backward by a vice grip around each bicep. Another scream almost ripped from her, but it was Dionna yanking her off her feet and dragging her to safety out of the office.

"Bryant," Odessa gasped. She righted herself with Dionna's help and peered through the doorway as Bryant grappled with the attacker. Sharp grunts of pain from both males could be heard. Odessa wished she could be of more help, but Bryant was better off if she stuck close to Dionna.

Dionna edged in front of her and pulled a knife. The female warrior's tarnished pewter wings flared to cast a wall of protection around as much of Odessa as they could reach. Magan's mate Phillip inched next to her to watch the struggle. He didn't seem to be a threat, but Dionna warily eyed both him and the fight in the office.

Odessa strained to get a glimpse of Bryant, but the warrior female was taller than her. Growls of outrage and crashes of furniture emanated from the office, and then...silence.

"Is he all right?" Odessa whispered.

Dionna barely turned her head back to acknowledge she heard the inquiry. Her ink-black gaze riveted around the room; her hand tightened around the knife. "Vale!"

A heartbeat passed.

Then two.

No. Odessa would be able to tell if something was wrong with Bryant. Wouldn't she?

Dionna didn't dart into the office, so Odessa's assailant must've been taken down. Odessa chewed her lip, unsure her assumptions were accurate.

Maybe he'd answer for her instead. "Bryant!"

"It's clear," Bryant rasped.

Relief poured through her. Dionna lowered her weapon.

Odessa surged to move around the solid warrior, but a flap of a wing kept her in place.

"Stay behind me," Dionna commanded. Odessa dared not go against her.

Dionna eased her wall of protection but motioned to Phillip to stay right where he was. Odessa stuck close behind, peeking around as much as possible.

They entered her office and the metallic tang of blood stifled the small space. Her desk was cracked and scattered papers littered the floor. Empty spots dotted her bookshelves and while the fate of the books wasn't a priority, she hoped they weren't destroyed.

Odessa's gaze landed on the crumpled form of her mate on the floor. He was trying to push himself up, but dropped, catching himself with one arm before he face-planted.

"Go to him." Dionna stepped aside so Odessa could rush to Bryant.

She dropped to her knees next to him. He pressed his free hand into his side. Blood oozed between his fingers, and his breathing was labored.

"Go ahead. Heal him," Dionna ordered. "I'll signal for an enforcer."

Dionna crossed to the male Bryant had fought and kicked at him with her booted foot. The male didn't move, a pool of blood spreading from under him. No angel could recover on their own from blood loss that significant. If he didn't have a mate to aid in his healing, he would bleed out and die.

Was it wrong of Odessa to hope for such a thing? One facet of her nightmare would be gone.

Bryant let out a rattling wheeze. He was wrestling to get onto his back, as if he wanted to stretch out on the floor. Odessa helped him shift to sit on his butt. She used her body to support his weight as he reclined back.

The cloth of his black shirt was plastered against his chest and belly. It was soaked, and from Bryant's weakness, most of the blood was his.

He sank into her. She had to brace herself to keep his massive form from toppling to the floor.

Dionna had said to heal him. Yeah, she could do that. She was his mate.

She scanned his form, the paleness of his face. Was the process instinctual? "I don't know how to heal," she finally admitted. The urgency wiped out any embarrassment she'd otherwise feel.

She flinched as a shadow approached on her right. Bryant was weak, deeply injured, but he flipped a blade up, ready to defend her.

Phillip held his hands up. "I can help." He gestured to Odessa's wings. "Wrap them around his body and just think about lending him your strength."

Odessa's nod was shaky, like the rest of her felt. She extended her wings and curled them around Bryant.

She met his half-lidded gaze. Metal clattered when he dropped the knife so he could caress her face. She turned her face into his touch and focused on healing his body.

Did he have more injuries? Any that were also mortal? Did she have to think about them individually or as a whole? For Heaven's sake, why didn't mating a warrior come with a healing manual?

Magan's mate coached her. "Envision skin melding together, the healthy glow of a strong body."

Bryant's hand fell away and he arched, a strangled sound ripping from his throat. Odessa's gut clenched. She was doing it wrong! But Bryant closed his eyes and relaxed with a sigh. Odessa could no longer hold his weight and she lowered him until he was flat on the floor.

For several agonizing seconds, he didn't move. Then his eyelids popped open.

"Dionna," Bryant barked out.

He slowly rolled up, gently moving her wings to the side. His breathing was normal, but the shake in his hands was noticeable, if only to her. She folded her wings back behind her, frowning at his reaction. She didn't expect groveling thanks, or his complete adoration, but something other than him calling for his fellow warrior.

Dionna stood guard over the downed male who had attacked Odessa. "Sir."

"Is he dead?"

"Almost," she replied. "Do you want me to try to save him for interrogation? The enforcers should be here in a moment."

"No," Bryant's reply was clipped.

Dionna only inclined her head.

"That's one of the males from…" Odessa didn't want to continue talking around others. The words choked her, and her lower lip quivered. Bryant caught her meaning.

"Then it's best he's gone for good."

Odessa fought with guilt and utter relief. A portion of the nightmare she had experienced could never come back to harm her. But a life was ending and they were doing nothing about it.

Bryant suppressed a groan as he stood and studied her demolished office. "How did he get in?"

Odessa scrambled up, keeping her expression neutral, unlike her emotions. Adrenaline waned and tremors threatened to take over her body. "All of our offices form a circle with the innermost chamber being our supervisor's. Cal's office is through that panel."

Bryant glanced at the panel that had whispered open and caused the breeze that had alerted Odessa to trouble.

Her mate turned back toward her with an incredulous expression that probably taxed the range of movement of his scars. "You didn't think of telling of us there was another entry point to your office?"

Um…no. The panels melded seamlessly into the walls and only Cal had used them. Her stupidity almost got both her and Bryant killed.

"Cal's dead." She said it like it explained everything. Of course, now she saw how wrong she'd been to assume no one could inhabit a dead man's office. An office that had no less than eleven other entry points.

Dionna stifled a curse and she couldn't blame the female. Though to be fair, they hadn't asked about additional entry points.

"Cal's dead?" Magan's mate paled.

"Has it not been announced?" Odessa asked.

"Not to me!" He gaped at the three of them. "And Magan's missing." His voice cracked. "I've talked to an enforcer both yesterday and today. They mentioned nothing."

Odessa wanted to say something, but she caught the warning in Bryant's look. The less the distraught male knew, the safer he'd be. But there had to be something they could do to help him with his mate.

CHAPTER 14

*J*agger glared furiously at the leggy female leisurely packing her bag. "It's none of your business whether I live alone or not."

Felicia didn't look away from the shirt she was holding up, like she was deciding, *do I take it with? Don't I? Do I take it with? Don't I?* He wanted to scream. Her apartment in the human world was as bright and colorful as the clothing she wore. And, admittedly, nothing he pictured a rich female to settle for. When Felicia had caught him gawking at her eclectic furnishings, she'd jabbered about flea markets and the "steals" she'd found.

"You see, it is. Because we can't stay at Odessa's place. You refuse to stay in the human realm, so..."

"Why can't we stay at Odessa's? Is the mansion too small for your taste?" he asked snidely.

Nonplussed, Felicia chucked the skimpy top and pulled out an even more revealing one to evaluate. Other members of his team might think he'd gotten a pretty sweet gig— watch over the gorgeous daughter of a powerful senator. Emphasis on the watch, Bronx had teased. Not even Jagger could argue with the statement. Her long, curvy figure was on display in the hideously bright human clothing. Anyone would get an eyeful.

But not him. She signified everything he didn't want. He had no patience with liars or with angels possessing few morals. The angels of Numen were tasked with guarding over humans, a prestigious position given to them by the Almighty. He refused to tolerate those who gave little regard to all the good they could do in the world.

"We can't stay with Odessa and Bryant." Felicia tucked the poor excuse of a shirt into her bag and picked up a lacy bra. Jagger seethed at the mischievous glint in her eye and remained impassive to the thought of how the scrap of lace would be tucked in close to those beautiful mounds that revealed themselves all too often in her tank top. "They haven't consummated yet."

"And?" He'd heard that rumor being discussed in hushed tones among the warriors. Unless Odessa was like her sister, and Jagger didn't think she was, he had no idea why Vale would hesitate. Didn't mean there wasn't a reason, and Vale always had a reason.

"Aaannd, they won't if we're hanging around."

Jagger scoffed. "Why? Did you try to sleep with him, too?"

Felicia stiffened, her face drawn tight before she adopted a casual stance. "Don't be silly."

Jagger's jaw went slack. "You did! Have you no *shame*? At least respect your *sister*. Oh, wait, we all know how her last relationship ended."

She rounded on him, the rage of a little sister in her face. "You, of all people, should know not to believe everything you hear. Those little gossipmongers in the clouds go around thinking the wings on their backs mean they don't have to adhere to the rules of common decency."

Jagger was unaffected. "You mean like females who won't

say 'no, I didn't have sex with your boyfriend,' even though the rumor destroyed a relationship? Wouldn't that have been decent?"

"It's not my fault she didn't believe you."

"Uh, yeah, it is!" Jagger sputtered. His face flushed with heat and he clenched his hands to keep from throttling her. "No one believed me!"

No one had believed him. And wasn't that the real issue? No matter what he did, public opinion where he was concerned was at the mercy of his philandering father's actions. Even his mother had glared at him in contempt. Jagger despised Felicia for it.

"Why does it matter if anyone believes you?" Felicia straightened from her luggage and flung her ponytail over a bare shoulder. "You know the truth."

He would've had another angry reply, but he couldn't think of one. "You know what? Just forget about it. Pack your shit, and we're heading back."

"We'll have to go back to your place because I'm not interfering with Odessa's sync."

If he screamed in outrage, how many humans would rush to Felicia's apartment door? "You're *not* staying at my place. Besides, I've been living in the barracks."

"Fine." Felicia upended her luggage back onto her bed. "We'll have to stay here, then."

That spoiled. Little. Brat. If she stayed at his house in Numen, then everyone would think that he was a worthless, weak-willed male like his father. Staying in the human realm with her might invoke the same talk—*if* anyone other than his team found out. No one had to see them in her apartment, and he could unfurl his wings within its walls. He hated having them morphed into his back for so long. It made his shoulder blades ache. Felicia hadn't once let hers out of their morph. How could she stand it?

Still, he didn't like being played, and he didn't like the way this female manipulated him to get her way.

Jagger stalked Felicia until he loomed over her, forcing her to look up at him. Her eyes widened, and her breath hitched.

"You want to play that game?" he asked silkily. "Okay. I will stay here with you, watching *everything* you do. I'll be with you *everywhere* you go. *Every* conversation. *Every* moment. Of *every* day. You wanted me to watch over you. Here I am."

LEO RICHTER RESISTED the urge to flare his wings in irritation. But it was his office, and he refused to allow anyone to see they'd ruffled his feathers. He was the leader of all the Numen warriors. His daily duties, aside from keeping the human realm safe from Daemon influence, was dealing with attitudes from his warriors, who all at one time or another challenged his authority, his decisions, his competence. He'd been director for decades, doing a fine job.

So why in the world did these two enforcers think they could intimidate him?

"It's an enforcer's duty to protect Numen citizens. The protection of the Montclaire sisters will be handed over to us," said the one playing the role of good cop. He was the smaller of the two, obviously used to using his brain more than his brawn. "Vale's team would then be free to continue their duties."

Leo gave a long-suffering mental sigh. "Enforcer Stede, Bryant Vale is Odessa's mate." A snort from the bad cop enforcer tested his self-containment. "*He* has the right to protect her. As for Felicia Montclaire, she personally requested a member of Vale's choir." He held up his hands in a mock helpless gesture, as if to say *whaddaya do, friggin' elite*.

"Can we really trust the duty of protecting Odessa Montclaire to a mate that refuses to fully sync with her?" Enforcer Jackson sneered his question.

"I didn't realize you were on intercourse patrol." Leo smiled at their reaction. Stede sputtered in shock and Jackson's expression flushed a ruddy red. They weren't used to dealing with an angel of equal rank. "What goes on between Bryant and Odessa *Vale* is their business. She wants his protection. He wants to give it. Same with Miss Montclaire and Warrior Hancock." Not nearly, but Jagger would remain loyal even if an enforcer cornered him, trying to get him to admit otherwise.

Stede's shoulders eased as he visibly relaxed, but Leo didn't trust that he relented.

"That still leaves the problem of the rest of your team," Stede said.

Leo raised an eyebrow, waiting for the enforcer's argument. "I don't see how they would be of any concern to the enforcers."

"Because," Stede drawled, "it's leaving one less team out there protecting our realm from Daemon invasion, and *that* is a threat to our citizens. A team of enforcers can watch over her dwelling." Damn. Score one for Stede. "Vale's team will be short two warriors until the threat to Odessa and Felicia is eliminated."

Stede spread his hands as if in offering. "Perhaps they could be tasked to aid the other warrior teams, compensating for the shortage of warriors protecting our realm. Their skills are wasted here in Numen."

Stede thought he was crafty. Warriors often split up on Earth to search and hunt demon possessions. But if Leo pushed too much for having his warriors, and his warriors only, protect Odessa and Felicia, then it'd alert the corrupt senator or senators that he knew something was going on.

"All right," he said reluctantly. "But I'd like to meet with the enforcers assigned to Lady Vale." When Stede opened his mouth to argue, already shaking his head, Leo pressed. "I'm sure she'd like to have some say over who watches her house."

Stede's lips flattened—his hands were tied. The senator's daughter would get her way. Odessa outranked them both, or at least her father did, and it was in both Stede's and Leo's best interest to have fewer people involved. Odessa needed to be comfortable with all the candidates, but more importantly, Vale had to screen them.

"There's also the matter of Vale's team helping the *allegedly* missing watcher's mate search for her." Stede's congenial smile was empty.

Another mental sigh. The watcher's mate had been in contact with the enforcers, making them privy to the business of Vale's team and their plans to search the Mist for her.

"I'm sure your enforcers are fully engaged"—*doubt it*—"in the search for Watcher Magan." Leo used her name on purpose, gauging Stede's reaction—or lack of. "Her mate would like to feel useful. We are only protecting him in the Mist, as that's *our* territory."

Score three for him.

"Perhaps one my enforcers could join in on the search, be kept in the loop."

"Of course. I'll contact them and let them know of your offer," Leo said without hesitation. He didn't promise *when* he'd contact Vale and his team to arrange for an enforcer to join them.

Leo ushered the two males out, commenting that'd he'd have Odessa arrange a time that suited her best to meet with the team of enforcers.

With the way Stede pushed for authority in this matter, even bringing muscle to their meeting, Leo now had an idea who to monitor. Whom did Stede work closely with? It had to be a senator, and one who was growing increasingly nervous the more Vale was involved.

Things were going to get worse before they got better. For many, many years, Leo had protected the realm from outside infiltration. Protecting the realm from corruption might prove to be a harder mission.

CHAPTER 15

Odessa shuddered, wrapping her long robe around herself. Maybe she should have worn human clothing. While she occasionally enjoyed human fashion, she was more comfortable in her robes. Bryant had told her that if they were spending any amount of time in the Mist, it might feel unnaturally chilly.

She hadn't known what he meant then, but it was crystal clear now. It wasn't necessarily a temperature-related coolness, but a chill that settled deep into her bones and filled her with foreboding.

"It's the spirits." Bryant's gravelly voice whispered into her ear, making her shiver again, and not from any spirits.

"I didn't think they lingered in the Mist." Odessa couldn't help but search around her, as if she'd suddenly find apparitions flitting about.

They were following Harlowe, Urban, and Bronx, and Magan's mate, Phillip. Sierra and Dionna stayed behind to watch over her home. To Odessa, it felt like they were wandering in circles in the haze. Everything looked the same. Harlowe's light gray wings blended seamlessly in the like-colored Mist. The endless grass on which they walked, a muted green, was barely discernible underfoot.

"That's what we're taught." Bryant strode next to her like a brick wall, dressed in his black warrior garb. "Warriors learn differently. The human realm has hauntings, likewise not every being that loses its life in the Mist crosses over. In fact, we believe it can be harder to cross over."

"Because no Numen chaperone can sense a spirit that needs escorting to Heaven in the Mist?" Chaperones guided souls to Heaven so they didn't become ghosts haunting old houses and museums—but only in the earthly realm, where no beings had the power to do it themselves.

"Exactly. And no Daemon reaper is allowed here. Since some of the evil creatures destroyed in the Mist don't want to go to Hell, they resist the path. Likewise, some of the good spirits don't want to leave their loved ones behind, even to go to Heaven. There's no guide here to force them, and they remain lost in the Mist."

Odessa frowned. "Will they ever be able to finish the journey?"

Bryant lifted one heavily muscled shoulder, drawing her attention to the harness that held several blades of varying lengths. "We don't know. According to our scholars, it's not possible that spirits are roaming the Mist." His eyes twinkled, giving him a rogue appeal that spiked her pulse. "Yet all the scholars keep declining our offers to bring them here."

Figured. Scholars weren't much different than analysts. Except, while analysts studied current information, comparing them to old trends, looking for new patterns, scholars were educators, studying old text and scripture and assuming they knew everything.

"Your observations of the Mist would turn part of those know-it-alls' world upside down." There was no conscript for the spirits in the Mist and instead of planning and training a new angelic section to deal with the problem, they'd rather maintain status quo than admit they were wrong. In their minds, a team would have been made to patrol the Mist if one was needed; therefore, one must not be needed. "Perhaps I can have a talk with them."

He cocked his head. "You'd do that?"

"Why not?"

He shook his head. "If you get through to them, it would be a large undertaking to learn what abilities are needed to guide spirits along their final path in the Mist. There's also the possibility that in retaliation, they'll put you on the team to clean the Mist. You already have a position. An admirable one." His pride was clear, igniting a comforting glow in her belly. A mighty warrior like him respecting her profession was the highest compliment she'd ever gotten.

"I do. I also have a conscience, and if I can help keep the Mist safe, I will." Odessa hugged her arms tighter around herself. "An eternity here would eventually become a form of Hell."

"Like a purgatory," Bryant agreed.

"Vale." Several yards ahead of them, Harlowe's keen lavender gaze searched their surroundings. "Phillip's bad feeling when it comes to Magan increases closer to the outer edge of the Mist. Should I track it?"

Bryant dipped his head. "Take Urban."

The two warriors jogged away. Both sets of wings were held ready to defend themselves. Harlowe's long dirty-blond braid swung above her wings, and Urban's shoulders were almost as wide as his.

Bryant had a strong team, in body and spirit. Urban was as quiet as Harlowe was outspoken. Odessa's short time around Bronx revealed him to be the jokester of the trio that accompanied them into the Mist. Of course, here, Bronx was watchful, predatory, not at all full of mirth as she'd seen him in the barracks.

"How can she track?" Odessa felt like she had to whisper. "And how can Phillip sense Magan but not find her?"

Bryant spoke just as low. "Phillip and Magan have been synced for many years. He could find her via their bond in Numen or down on Earth, but the Mist warps those senses."

Would Bryant be able to find her anywhere with their bond? She couldn't sense him, and he had only found her in the human realm by snooping. Cold fear had raced through her after their return from the earthly realm when her dresser drawers hung open like they'd been ransacked. But Bryant had admitted how he had tracked her to the store.

To have been a fly on the wall…

"The Mist is a veil between Numen and Earth, but it also acts like its own realm," he continued. "There are ways to tell where beings have traveled, fought, answered the call of nature. Sometimes, an archmaster—even a lesser symaster— can escape and evade us here. We need to be able to track and terminate them." Bryant tipped his head toward the tall, blond warrior. "Harlowe will look for signs of recent disturbance. We don't know how big the Mist is, but we have learned that we tend to travel in the same zone. Like Numen, it's seemingly infinite, but while the borders are hardly tangible, they are impenetrable and not nearly as expansive as a realm."

"She can find tracks in the grass?" Odessa could hardly make out the faint color of green under her slippers, and cool droplets swirled at her ankles with each step. How could Harlowe see anything?

"Footprints last a few hours before the grass rights itself, but blood droplets and where it gets ground down in a fight tamp it down for days. If you look around, you'll see how the Mist has changed where we've walked."

Odessa glanced behind them. There was a faint change in the opaqueness of the gray, as if it did indeed thin from their passing.

This experience was unnerving, and the reason she was here heartbreaking, but learning beyond the little box that was her life was fascinating.

A distant shout from Harlowe reached them. Their group changed direction to follow her voice. As they neared, the Mist parted around where Urban knelt in the grass. His broad frame was hunched over one area while Harlowe crouched and crept along, inspecting a path a few yards away.

Urban glanced up, his coffee-brown stare grave. "There was a fight here. Much of the blood has been absorbed and the ground is returning to normal. I'd guess the fight was quick."

Phillip crossed to Urban, sadness and grief etched into the creases around his eyes. He released a shaky inhale. "Her life ended here. I can feel it."

Urban straightened, murmured something Odessa couldn't hear, but from his folded hands and sympathy-filled gaze, she would guess they were words of condolence. Phillip shuddered a breath, his head bowing as tears flowed freely.

Bryant stood behind the stricken male and set his hand on Phillip's shoulder. Odessa expected him to talk, but the males stood like that for several minutes, her warrior allowing the male time to grieve without being alone. Odessa blinked as tears stung, her heart weeping for the male's loss, for his children's loss. First Cal was taken, now Magan. Could they stop whoever was doing this?

"We'll wait while Urban takes you home," Bryant said.

"Thank you." Phillip used his robe sleeve to wipe at his face. "I'll break the news to Magan's parents before I tell the children. But first, I'll need some time."

Phillip straightened, his wings held as high as his grief allowed them. Before he disappeared with Urban, he spoke to Bryant. "You'll find her body and send her to the angel fire? I can't stand the thought of her rotting away somewhere."

After Bryant's solemn nod, they disappeared. Odessa used her own robe sleeve to clean her face of tears. She wasn't embarrassed by her emotion, but she wanted to be included in the search. Magan died for her work, leaving a family behind. Those sweet children she'd met once when Magan gave her family a tour of the archives.

No way could she return home, even with her fearsome mate by her side, and wait while the others searched for the watcher who was killed for being good at her job.

A whisper of wings signaled Urban's return. He said nothing, but disappeared into the Mist to where Harlowe had gone.

Bryant crouched and inspected the area Urban had been studying. "She was beheaded," he said abruptly.

"How can you tell?" Her gut wrenched. Urban must've known and kept the information to himself. Phillip didn't need to hear more than what his intuition told him.

"Our blades are treated to basically cauterize Daemons when we behead them, otherwise their blood is like acid. Magan's blood is pooled in one spot, as if it emptied rapidly, like when a head is suddenly removed from a body."

"But demons can't cross into the Mist without Numen help. Did she try to fight a demon by herself?" That wasn't like Magan at all. She was a watcher to her core.

"No. I don't sense the fading effects of the incantation we use to bring a demon over."

"Oh." That was bad. Could a demon have killed her? The significance of a demon independently gaining access to the Mist was monumental. If they were in the Mist, it was to be killed. To roam free? It was one step closer to unfettered access to Numen. "What's going on?"

"I don't know," Bryant replied grimly. "Let's find Magan's body and get some answers."

~

"WHAT DO YOU HAVE, HARLOWE?" Bryant held his hand up to signal the rest to stop. The area had to remain pristine for the female warrior to read.

Harlowe squinted through the fog. "Where we stopped is where she was brought into the Mist and killed." She pointed to the larger splotches of fading blood. "But whoever it was carried her body and her head to another location."

Bryant followed her hand to where she pointed to smaller drops. Magan's body must've been slung over one shoulder, her head carried with the other hand. Demons had humanoid forms, but they were draggers, careless of the evidence they left behind.

Bronx crossed his arms over his wide chest, his feet spread shoulder width apart. "If a demon figured out how to cross into the Mist, they couldn't use their host's body. *We* can't even get humans over the barrier. So how did the demon leave? It would've attacked us if it were still here. It couldn't help itself."

"Maybe it was an angel." Urban countered in his usual quiet way. Wider and stockier than Bronx, he was a burly, muscular male with understated intelligence. Not at all like the cocky Bronx.

"Or it was a demon," Bronx reiterated. "If they figured out how to cross here, can we cross into the Gloom?"

Bryant twitched his wings at Bronx's excitement. The Gloom was Daemon's equal to the Mist. Numen couldn't cross on their own. But unlike warrior angels with the Mist, demons didn't try to throw angels into the Gloom for battle. They wanted nothing good to touch their realm, no matter what, and they were only interested in conquering Earth and Numen. Getting into the Gloom was a perfect challenge for a guy like Bronx.

"We don't know for sure a demon came into the Mist unaided." Urban scowled at Harlowe, who had ignored them and crept up to the barrier, searching for the location on the earthly realm the unknown assailant had taken Magan's body. "Perhaps she decided to fight a master on her own."

"Magan wouldn't do that," Odessa broke in. The two burly warriors turned their scowls onto her, but she continued, unfazed. "She wasn't like that, always very proper. Very…watcher-like." Odessa glanced between each of them. She seemed unable to explain further why she knew Magan wouldn't do that.

"Harlowe?" Bryant hoped the female would have more to weigh in with. All warriors are trained to track in the Mist, but Harlowe excelled in her abilities. It was like she had a sixth sense when it came to disturbances in the realm.

"There was no sign of a fight, just a murder. The killer got into this realm with her and took her body back to the human realm. Probably for disposal. I think I've found where." She peered through the veil, walking forward a few steps. The border thinned. "I can't fucking believe it."

Bryant took Odessa's elbow, unwilling to be far from his mate, and led her to where Harlowe was waiting. His mate huddled close to him, enveloping his body in her calming, summer breeze scent. She didn't want to be far from him, either, but that was due to fear. He wouldn't let it go to his head.

Urban reached her first. "Fucking Vegas."

"Las Vegas," Bronx said, a wide smile forming.

The two males had very different views of Sin City.

Odessa squinted through the Mist. "I can see the light from the Strip, but where is this?"

"Looks like it's on the outskirts. Let's cross over and keep searching." Without thinking, Bryant grabbed Odessa's hand and cleared his mind to step out of the Mist. At the borders, all it took was a little concentration to cross the barrier.

She stepped over with him, her warm fingers clinging to his. He didn't sense any danger, but regardless, he didn't let her go. Harlowe, Bronx, and Urban stepped out after him, fanning out to the sides to hunt for clues.

"Oh my…" Odessa scanned their environment.

It was night. Casino lights highlighted the horizon, but where they had entered was surrounded by red dirt and opaque warehouses and…statues. They were on the property of a company that made lawn ornaments, and that didn't bode well.

"Boss," Urban warned, just as Bryant's gaze landed on a particular statue.

Harlowe and Bronx turned simultaneously, drawing short swords into their hands. Urban and Bryant slid out their eight-inch dirks. They circled the two-foot tall statue of a short man wearing a red pointy hat.

Odessa gasped and pressed closer. "What is it?"

"Gargoyle." Bryant kept still, hugging Odessa close as his team slowly circled the lawn ornament while also monitoring their surroundings.

Odessa's brow creased. "It's a lawn gnome."

"Because gargoyle statues aren't as popular anymore." Harlowe paused by each innocuous lawn ornament she passed before moving to another. "So real gargoyles take on cuter images like gnomes, and they can be spread far and wide by adoring landscapers."

Odessa's grip tightened on Bryant, her body curving into him, heating where she touched. As if it wasn't bad enough he had to take his mate out on a mission with him, he had to be so attuned to her presence that he might distract himself by his own arousal.

"Whoever it was fed Magan to a gargoyle?" Odessa's horrified whisper echoed his team's suspicions.

All desire fled, and he didn't reply. They'd find out soon enough.

"Hey." Bronx reached out his sword and gave the gnome's hat a few hard taps. "Shorty."

An image passed over the gnome's face, like a morbid hologram—fangs and red eyes set into a skeletal face.

"I'm talking to you." Bronx clipped the tip of the hat with the sharp edge of his blade, chipping it.

"Stop!" cried a garbled, rough voice.

The little gnome animated, fanning his hat as if the wound burned. Odessa's fingers tightened around Bryant's.

"Look at that." Bronx held his sword at the gnome's throat. "It talks."

"Of course, I talk." The angry gnome was trying to feel his wound with his short little arms. "You chipped me! Now no one will buy me and the company will smash me. I'll have to wait in line for another piece to possess. You know how many gargoyles are waiting to inhabit statues? It's not like they grow on trees."

Bronx's expression remained impassive. He was less than moved by the gargoyle's plight. Bryant stepped forward, shoving Odessa behind him. Reluctantly, he let go of her warm hand and squatted down to put himself at the short statue's level, though with his frame it was impossible as he hovered several inches above the tip of the red hat. He could squat even more, but the still-healing tissue at his side pulled against his movements. For the tenth time, he realized he'd be fully healed if he and Odessa's sync was complete. For the eightieth time, his brain wanted to dwell on what finishing their sync entailed. Now wasn't the time.

"You ate a watcher last weekend." Bryant didn't bother to phrase it as a question and the gnome stilled, narrowing his stony gaze. "Tell me about who brought her to you."

"I don't know what you're talking about." The gargoyle wiped at some stone fragments that had landed on his shoulder.

It'd be comical if Bryant didn't know that the gargoyle would love to feast on his team's remains. They were like the turkey vultures of the demon world. Normally, they subsisted on demon remains in their own realm, concentrating only on their duties as spies in the human world. But they were opportunistic vermin.

Bryant lowered his octave to a more menacing level, letting his accent punctuate each syllable. "You'll have more than a chip in your hat if you don't start talking."

Bronx flicked his blade making the gnome flinch.

"It was a dude. Tall, dark, and handsome, if you're into that stuff." The gnome stopped. Bryant stared him down. He expected more. The statue huffed. "I don't know who he was, just showed up with the watcher's body and told me it was my lucky day." He licked his little lips as if he salivated at the memory.

Disgusting creature.

"Numen or Daemon?"

"Neither."

Bronx scowled. "What do you mean neither? He couldn't have been human."

One pudgy shoulder shrugged. "If it walks like a duck and talks like a duck."

Bryant considered the information. "He stepped out of the Mist carrying the watcher's body and knew how and where to find you?" The gnome nodded. "And then he went where?"

"Just walked off."

"He didn't transcend?"

"Nope."

Bryant lifted his gaze to Bronx, trusting his warrior to read his intentions. Then, as Bryant was rising, Bronx raised his angel-fire–kissed dagger and slammed it into the gnome's chest. He heard a sharp inhale behind him from Odessa. The gnome screamed, the rage resonating through the still night.

Bronx signaled to Urban and Harlowe to search the rest of the grounds for gargoyle-infested statues to destroy.

"You said—" The gnome dropped to the ground, gurgling, writhing in pain, its true form showing through the statue's disguise, all bony wings and sharp fangs.

Bryant leaned in closer. "I made no promises, and I didn't touch your hat. Never"—he poised his own dagger for the decapitating blow—"eat our kind."

He removed the head. The figurine shattered, and the image of the gargoyle dissolved in smoke once its head was removed. A busted, headless statue left behind. Sounds of stone crashing ricocheted through the night as Urban and Harlowe dispatched four more gargoyle gnomes.

He dreaded turning to face Odessa, not wanting to witness her recrimination after watching him lie to and kill a cute little statue. She was gawking at the gnomes' destruction, her jaw hanging open.

"They all had to have taken part in disposing of Magan's body." He offered it as an excuse while convincing himself he shouldn't need to. "An angel is more than one gargoyle's stomach can handle."

Her startled gaze flew to meet his. "No, I know. It just took me off guard." She glanced down at the shattered gnome at his feet and then back to him. "It's so different than learning about it in school. Those creatures actually possess adorable little statues? And can make them move?"

He nodded grimly. "As long as humans give their lawns and buildings ornamentation, gargoyles will inhabit them. They're the watchers of the demon realm."

Odessa shuddered, and he wanted to wrap her in his embrace, wanted her body molded into his again. A male could get used to that.

But he didn't. She didn't need his comfort and it would only make their parting all the more difficult for him. He realized, that he would...dislike...not being able to see and talk to her every day.

"We got 'em all, boss." Urban wiped the dust off his blade before sheathing it.

Bronx and Harlowe had already sheathed their weapons and waited for Bryant's instructions.

"Is there any surveillance we can view before we destroy the last several minutes?"

"No luck," Bronx answered. "It'll look like gnome-hating vandals came through."

Damn. They could've used an ID on the guy that killed Magan. Was he a human working for a nefarious angel? And why? Or was he a human working for a demon?

"The gnome had to have been lying. The guy couldn't have been human."

"He wasn't lying." Bryant had dealt with enough gargoyles to know. The creatures were naturally shifty when talking, a result of being immobilized as a statue for so long. This gnome had delighted in his vague answer. Bryant sifted through possibilities until it settled on one and the impossible became plausible. "Who would know about angels and demons, and be able to find gargoyles? Who would be neither, yet not human, and know *everything* about our worlds?"

Bronx frowned and Urban's brow crinkled just as Harlowe breathed, "Fallen."

"Son of a bitch," Bronx spat out. "A fallen would definitely hold a grudge against Numen. But how did he enter the Mist without his wings?"

"And who would it be?" Urban added. "Most fallen don't survive long without their wings."

"I can search records of fallen in the last century, find out where they were sent to when they were kicked out of Numen." Odessa looked down at her robes, as if thinking about a different outfit. "But first, we should visit that club Magan was watching. Maybe we could find some answers there."

Odessa in a nightclub that could harbor killers? Not just any killers, but angel murderers? No. "You and I can go search records and the others can recon the club."

She shook her head. "I know what to look for. With all my notes lost, it'd be better if I was immersed in the environment. I can recall the details and patterns better."

"No."

The other three warriors fell quiet, watching Odessa and Bryant face-off.

"Bryant."

"No."

She sucked in a breath and held it, like she was at war with her temper. "I don't want to get killed. More so, I don't want any more people to get killed over what I *don't* know. I go to clubs, I know how to act, how to blend in. Harlowe and I could get all gothed up, Sharpie a black rose on ourselves, and just have a look around."

Harlowe nodded. Bryant should refute her idea, but…it sounded like their best option. A good way to get them outed would be for him to go. The scars were too distinctive. He had never hated his scars more than he did now.

He fisted his hands. "I can't go with, I'd stand out too much."

"You'd only be a transcension away," Odessa reassured him. "It'd look more innocuous if two girls went clubbing than if we had an…imposing…guy with. I've been deep in Magan's notes about this place; I know how to make us look."

Say no. Just say no. He couldn't. The leader in him knew it was their best bet, and Odessa would be well protected with Harlowe.

"What's the place called?"

Odessa's brow crinkled as she recalled the detail. She blinked. "Oh my. It should've been obvious from the beginning. Fall from Grace."

CHAPTER 16

*J*ameson reclined in his chair and laced his hands behind his head. He'd taken his suit jacket off and draped it over the seat next to him. While regarding the possessed human in front of him, he briefly wondered if his sweat stains were showing through around his armpits. Perhaps it wasn't as professional as the buttoned-up, suave persona he showed the rest, but he found his casual stance caused demons to lower their guard and underestimate him.

The one called Sandeen possessed the uptight banker. Jameson had yet to find out exactly what the demon was willing to do for him. And what he wanted in return.

"What makes you think I know the answer to your question?" No one did. What the male was asking was impossible. Daemons couldn't walk among humans as themselves. It was a divine gift and only for the ultimate benefit of humans.

"You're Numen, yet you roam the earth, forming alliances with demons. You can reportedly sense angels wandering this plane." Sandeen spread his hands as if it were obvious.

Jameson ignored the skip of his heart when Sandeen

accused him of being fallen. Numen was no longer home. It would be his one day. But it wasn't home. "I'm fallen."

"I've come across fallen in my many years. To put it simply, they were no better than humans. I followed them, studied them. They aged as humans, they had no other sense about the world. Most couldn't even survive here. But you… You fell how many years ago?"

Point made. Jameson had not crossed *any* fallen in his time on Earth. Not knowingly, anyway. He'd had an idea their immortality was lost with their angelic abilities but had no confirmation.

"I'm sure the underworld has some way for you to roam this plane. If angels can fall, can't demons…rise?" Jameson's mouth quirked.

A shadow crossed Sandeen's face. "I'm afraid not. Our Almighty is not as benevolent as yours. We serve our purpose or we are sent to Hell. There is no free pass to be *not evil*. It would upset the balance of the world."

"Why are you interested?"

Sandeen's expression remained impassive.

Eh, worth a shot. Jameson didn't figure he'd tell him, but he was curious. He propped himself on his arms, his elbows on the table. "I'm working with Gerzon."

Sandeen inclined his head. "I have no plans to interfere with Gerzon's claim to the well of angel fire."

How the hell did Sandeen know his deal with Gerzon? Was there a leak in his office?

"Demons like to talk," Sandeen said, as if reading his mind. And damn if he wasn't right. Demon were worse at letting gossip run rampant, and angels were bad enough.

"Then what do you want?"

Sandeen sat forward and mimicked Jameson's position. "I hear you want Daemon steel, more specifically, weapons."

Jameson waited, not acknowledging the statement.

"Are you as picky about divine steel?"

If Sandeen could get his hands on that, Jameson wouldn't complain. The history of their weaponry was clouded in myth, but Jameson wouldn't be surprised if it originated from the same place—or if that place was far below where Numen assumed.

"For every weapon I can get you, I want a vial of your blood."

Jameson blanched. Other than to spill it, angels had no use for blood. Yet Jameson knew well the power of Numen blood on a Daemon weapon. It was part of his key. Jameson's contacts in Numen would provide the entryway.

But he was fallen, and Sandeen knew it. What power would his blood hold? Sandeen must suspect there would be some. As he'd noticed, Jameson was not a normal fallen. He would need to tread carefully, lest he become a pawn for Sandeen.

But dammit, he needed weapons if he was going to advance his plans. Especially with the conniving Gerzon.

"How much blood for your vial?"

Sandeen had his answer ready. "One ounce for every blade I provide."

Sounded fair enough. "What do you plan to do with it?"

"What do you plan to do with the weapons?"

Touché. His blood for a blade. Jameson thought of the scythe he had scored off the archmaster all those years ago. He wouldn't need a whole lot more to fully arm himself and a few trusted allies. As his plans of angelic domination grew, he'd have to share his secret and arm his followers.

All in good time. None of it did any good if he couldn't get beyond the Mist. "We'll start with one transaction and go from there. A trial run."

Sandeen's mouth went flat at the lack of a solid deal. After a second, he nodded.

Jameson reached his hand out to shake. Sandeen leaned forward for a quick clasp to seal the deal. Gerzon would be pissed if he ever found out, possibly withhold the demon servants Jameson was using to hunt angels, and of course, try to kill him. Jameson would have to make sure that did not happen.

"Are you going to partake in the festivities downstairs?" Jameson asked, walking the male to the door of his meeting room.

Sandeen glanced at the suit his host was wearing. "I think I'd stand out."

Jameson waved his hand to ease the male's worries. "Not as much as you'd think. The interests of my clientele are diverse."

Sandeen adjusted his suit jacket and straightened his tie. "Maybe I'll go look around then. It's still early."

Chuckling, Jameson clapped him on the back to see him out the door.

～

"UM, YEAH, HE LIKED IT," Harlowe said as she and Odessa strutted to the entrance of Fall from Grace. The knockout blonde's hips swayed over long legs clad in fishnet stockings.

The five of them had checked into two hotel rooms and had gotten some much-needed rest. She and Harlowe had stayed in one room while the males shared the adjoining room with the door open. Surrounded by four warriors, Odessa had gotten some of the deepest sleep of her life, despite recent events. Then the two females had shopped all day to buy their outfits for the night.

Odessa had a clear picture of how they had needed to look to blend in at the club. Magan's notes had been detailed. But

Odessa wasn't sure how well Harlowe would blend in. Her five-inch black platform heels put her well above six feet tall. If her black-studded midriff-baring halter top and black leather mini skirt didn't attract attention then her face certainly would.

Harlowe was a stunning creature normally. Now with black coal-rimmed eyes and a braid running down each side of her head, and her dirty-blond hair dyed a reverse ombré ending with black tips, she was truly exotic. Her odd-hued eyes looked even more lavender against the black liner and dark red lips.

Odessa was only slightly jealous of the graceful walk Harlowe managed in her shoes. Choosing knee-high black boots with a thick heel, Odessa figured she'd be safer walking through a crowd and not garner even more attention with her already tall height.

While Harlowe went for goth sex kitten, Odessa had chosen goth schoolgirl. She wore a white sleeveless button-up shirt, not buttoned but tied at her waist with a loose black tie around her neck. Tight black shorts she could barely sit in completed her outfit, along with the long fingerless black gloves she wore on each hand.

As for her hair, all she did was darken it a few shades so it was nearly black, and secured it in two ponytails at each side of her head. She rimmed her eyes as dark as Harlowe's and borrowed the same shade of blood-red lipstick.

When she had stepped out of the hotel bathroom and Bryant's gaze swept her body, she couldn't name the emotion darkening his gaze. Passion? Yearning? Anger? Panic? All of them? His jaw tight, he hadn't uttered a word. He had just turned back to Bronx and Urban to finish planning their night while Harlowe got ready.

"I don't think he liked it," Odessa repeated.

Why had she mentioned her insecurity to Harlowe?

Maybe the female would have some insight into Bryant's thoughts since she'd been working with him for so long.

Harlowe's braid jostled as she shook her head. "That was the reaction of a guy who liked it way too much."

"He wouldn't have sent Bronx to scope out the club if he thought I looked like I was capable of doing this."

Harlowe stopped outside of the entrance, which was nothing more than a tin door on a three-story warehouse. The only hint that it wasn't abandoned were the deep thrums of bass that could be both heard and felt from where they stood.

"Bronx can get close like you and I can't, know what I mean?"

Odessa had an idea from the anticipatory gleam in Bronx's eye when Bryant said they should have another warrior on the inside. Harlowe couldn't seduce any information out of anyone because she had to protect Odessa, who was mated and definitely wouldn't be cozying up to anyone. Odessa mentally snorted. She couldn't even do that with her own mate.

"I just don't think he likes me," Odessa muttered, dismayed she said that out loud. Could she sound needier?

"*I* think otherwise." Harlowe raised a black-lined brow. "He probably figures that as soon as you're safe, you'll want to go back to a life that doesn't include him. I don't want to be intrusive, but if the rumors are true about you two not…"

Odessa released a gusty sigh. "It's not for lack of trying on my part." Wow, that came out pathetic.

Harlowe gave her a small smile. "Don't give up on him. Males of any species are pretty thickheaded. Just remember, though, you're playing for keeps. If you really can't envision being his mate, or doing the forever thing, don't string him along. I kind of like you. I'd hate to have to kick your ass for hurting him."

As serious as the warrior was, Odessa smiled anyway. She couldn't see her human friends like she used to, not until the threat following her was terminated. If she could befriend a fierce, closed-off warrior like Harlowe, then things weren't all dismal.

Could she envision being Bryant's mate? He was a stolid male, surly, and looked like he wanted to punch whomever he was talking to. He was also honest, loyal, and a fierce warrior. It was obvious how close his team was and how much they respected their leader. Director Richter definitely held much regard for Bryant as a friend and leader. Whenever Odessa was close to him, it was like her blood was pure ethanol and he was a lighter. She wanted him to come close so he could light her up. She wanted his heat, and she wanted that intensity turned on her.

Following Harlowe through the dank club entrance, Odessa was grateful for the noise and darkness. It masked her flush and rapid heartbeat when she remembered the one time she'd had Bryant's intensity focused solely on her. If only she could have stretched those few minutes into an eternity. Or at least, dear Lord, have kept her coworkers from knocking so she could discover the delicious feeling of being filled by him.

Harlowe turned to say something. Shaking off her rising lust, and regret of a steamy moment cut way too short, she shook her head at her companion. "I'm sorry, what?"

"Don't look twice at him!" Harlowe repeated, trying not to shout.

Odessa nodded. Got it. Don't stare at Bronx, or smile, or totally fuck up and say hi. He was a stranger. Was he here, yet? What would he be wearing? He was too striking not to recognize, but she'd only seen him in the standard long robe or his warrior dress. It'd be hard to skip over him like she didn't know him, but she could do this.

She and Harlowe sported the requisite black rose tattoos. Time to find out what came next. Her rose was drawn in at the top of her breast, barely peeking out of her shirt. Harlowe's was on her upper thigh, obscured slightly by her fishnet hose. Since they weren't real, they thought it best to keep them from being fully visible.

Letting Harlowe take the lead, Odessa trailed behind, gawking at the club. The place was dark, lit with a few strobes from the dance floor and the red lights emanating from the black wrought iron dance cages at each corner. Three cages had a woman, dressed much like Odessa and Harlowe, gyrating to the beat of the music, and a fourth had a man, dancing just as enthusiastically. Despite outside appearances, the inside was modern, open, and spacious. A wall-to-wall window overlooked the bar and dance floor. The window view was of another room in the second level. The interior on the other side was too dark to make out details.

The club's patrons consisted mostly of young women, many dressed like the dancers, but a few slacks and A-line skirts were mixed in. The men varied. Some wore the goth look with long black hair and dark-lined eyes and black clothing. Some were dressed in skinny jeans of varying colors and slim-fitting shirts, some rounded off the look with thick-rimmed glasses. There were even a few men in expensive suits roaming around, eyeing the bared flesh.

Odessa peered into the fringes of the club where booths lined the walls. A threesome was in full swing. Two men and a woman were using all the surfaces for purchase. She quickly glanced away. At the places she'd gone dancing with the girls from work, she'd gotten an eyeful before, but not to the extent of what she had just seen. This was open, blatant.

She feathered a hand over her forehead. Could she do this? Pretend this was her idea of a perfect night out?

Harlowe leaned in. "The girl is possessed. At least one of the males around her is, also."

Odessa resisted the urge to glance back and see if she could figure out which man was hosting a demon. Bryant said they could train her on what to watch for when it came to knowing who, or in the case of gargoyles, what was possessed. Warriors were trained heavily in that skill, analysts weren't. But it didn't mean she couldn't be useful. It was time to prove why she was the best choice to send in and start evaluating ink. She peeked at the woman. Her body blocked much of the male's with her back to the crowd and her legs open toward the wall.

A barbed wire tattoo wrapped around the woman's arm. It was hard to tell in the dark, but the ink was dark, probably black, with a lighter shade on the barbs. Red? Odessa turned her attention to the woman's partners. All the men in the club were harder to search for tattoos and these two were no different. Staring any longer would make others think she was appalled or interested. She needed to blend.

Making their way through the crowd, several barbed wire tattoos caught her eye. Some were decorated with blood on the tips of the barbs and others weren't. They picked seats at the bar. It was the best spot to gather as many observations as they could. Odessa swiveled to face the crowd. Out of the corner of her eye, she spotted Bronx snaking through the crowd.

Wow, talk about blending. Dressed in black jeans and a black shirt that molded over his muscular arms and chest, he had spiked his naturally jet-black hair and drawn a tiny black rose on his earlobe. Between his looks and his swagger, he drew attention from everyone he passed. He paused long enough to strike up a conversation with a petite knockout who had similarly spiked hair. Mere moments later, he took her hand and led her to the outer edges of the dance floor and crowded her into the wall. He planted his hands on each side of her head. From the way the woman snaked her arms around Bronx's perfectly V-tapered back, well—Odessa averted her gaze.

Aside from wanting to be able to look Bronx in the eye after this, their stance reminded her of her own wall episode. When Bronx made his first move, Odessa's first thought had been that she could never do that. Meet a stranger and hook up right away. But that was exactly what she'd done with Bryant—or had tried to do. From the way Bronx was moving, the human woman had already made it farther than Odessa had.

A soft glow from above made her look up. The room on the other side of the window was no longer dark but close, like a hallway light was on. A male faced out, monitoring the crowd. His arms were crossed and his legs spread. Everything about his stance radiated power.

"What do you think of that?" Odessa flicked her gaze up to keep from pointing.

"My guess is it's the owner. I don't see a stairwell or elevator, just the restrooms and a keypad entrance beyond those."

Odessa's heart lurched. That's who they were looking for. Did the shadowed man know who killed Magan? Had he ordered her death?

A deep voice interrupted her musings. "You got a demon in you?"

A burly, bald man was perched on Harlowe's other side. Harlowe tipped her head like she heard the question wrong.

"Want one?" the intoxicated man chortled.

Crude joke aside, relief flooded Odessa. They weren't being asked if they could be possessed.

Harlowe seized the opportunity. "Nice wings."

The man touched the spot where he had a three-inch pair

of torn angel wings inked on his thick neck. During her work, Odessa had noted that this tattoo was particularly uncommon and labeled it as more significant than bloodied barbed wire.

He beamed, his stare glassy. "I earned them the hard way."

"Oh?" Harlowe gave him her full attention.

The man tried to lean into her and almost fell off his stool. He situated himself before speaking. "Yep. I let an archmaster possess me and lured a warrior to me. Boom." The man flared his hand out, his eyes crossing as he stared at his fingers. "When the angel went to grab the demon out of me, there was no resistance."

Harlowe's shoulders tightened. What did that mean? Archmasters waged a constant battle for power against souls. Had this guy somehow opened himself up to possession? Allowed it? And it had gotten the warrior killed?

"The ol' arch jumped out of me, surprising the warrior in the fog, or wherever the hell they disappear to."

That was as bad as Odessa expected.

"Impressive," Harlowe murmured, her gaze speculative. "So, the warrior?"

"Dead."

Ah, now it was clearer. The human helped a demon lay a trap for a warrior. That would explain the increase in warrior deaths. Suddenly, the reality of what Bryant did for a living sank in. If she mated fully with him, she would worry every time he went to work.

What if they had kids? What if a drunk human like this one lured her mate in to his death, leaving her to raise a family alone?

As Odessa's ire toward people like the one hitting on Harlowe grew, her friend gathered information.

"Wouldn't your arch dislike you having so much to drink?"

Oooh, good question. At least the man didn't pose a danger to other warriors if he was incapable of clearing his alcohol-clouded mind.

"He don't bother with me no more." The man's face screwed up and he reached for Harlowe's drink. He downed it in one swallow. "A possession...changes you."

"Really? How?" Harlowe's voice dripped with sympathy, and she angled her body toward him. She put on a good show.

He scrubbed a hand over his face, suddenly somber. "Before you decide to get your wire inked, just think about it for a while. Some things you can't take back."

The man slid off his stool and stumbled away. From the thousand-yard stare, his mind was no longer at the club. Odessa could almost feel sorry for the tortured soul, until she thought of the dead warrior and how it could've been Bryant. Had the warrior had a family?

Odessa turned back to the bar. She had so many questions for Harlowe but couldn't ask them until they left. Maybe she could ask Bryant. Would he be able to tell her?

And why didn't analysts and warriors communicate more? There was so much to the human and demon world that she didn't know but might be the glue to piece the puzzle of her job together.

Harlowe sucked in a hard breath. Odessa glanced at her, then followed her gaze up. The male in the window had been watching them. The burn of his gaze was uncomfortable. Odessa's lungs constricted as he raised his hand, pointed to his eyes, then pointed to them. He was watching them.

Odessa wanted to run. They were in the middle of a crowded club full of devoted Daemon followers. Yet if they revealed themselves as angels or otherworldly in any way, they faced consequences from their own realm.

Harlowe dealt with the stress better. She blew the male a

kiss and tugged Odessa's elbow. Odessa hopped off her stool and they charged toward the back exit. If they could just make it outside and no one was around, they could wink to safety.

"Should we get Bronx?" Odessa called, trying to keep up as Harlowe dragged her.

"He can take care of himself. We'd only single him out if we tried to alert him."

Odessa searched the last place she saw him. The woman unwrapped her legs from around him and Bronx's arm moved like he was closing his zipper. He was murmuring something, stroking her cheek with his other hand while she gazed adoringly at him. Hopefully he wasn't too distracted with his "investigation" and realized he might be in danger.

Harlowe slowed as they neared the back exit, and Odessa's gut clenched when she saw why. They weren't alone. A handsome man in an expensive suit had been leaning against the wall near the door, making out with a girl dressed in a long black dress that hugged the ample curves of her body. Her red lipstick was smeared all over his collar and lips. His tie hung loose, and his suit jacket draped open. But now his gaze was piercing the shadows straight to Harlowe. The warrior dropped to a defensive stance, keeping Odessa blocked.

Harlowe had sensed something about the man, who also seemed to know that they were not just human women out for ladies' night. Odessa evaluated him, at first squinting and then allowing her gaze to unfocus. Just like when she thought she saw a holographic image cross the garden gnome statue, she detected an image over the human's face. It was of a dark-haired male, with obsidian horns coming out of his head to wrap closely around the back. The image was startling, more so because the demon male had well-defined cheekbones, full lips, and piercing blue eyes. He was more striking than his host.

Demons weren't supposed to be good-looking. None of their scholars had taught them that. This wasn't just any demon. He must be an archmaster, and it was highly unlikely he would let them quietly exit while he went back to his debauchery.

"Sander?" the human woman purred, trying to get his attention back to her.

Ignoring her and shoving off the wall, the male stalked toward them, effectively blocking the exit.

"Your human's calling," Harlowe pointed out, almost sounding breathy.

The male stopped, barely turning his head back to the human. When it got to a point he'd have to take his gaze off Harlowe, he stopped and faced the warrior.

"A little far from home?" Like his dual image, the human's voice was echoed by a deeper, richer male's voice.

Was she getting better at recognizing possessions, or was he trying to make it obvious?

"I could ask you the same thing." Harlowe's fingers flexed, like she would've been reaching for a weapon, but she hadn't been allowed to wear any into the club.

The human woman huffed and stomped off, thinking her man was more interested in the tall blonde. She was correct, but not in the way she assumed. At least her absence left them somewhat isolated from other humans. And from the way Harlowe and the archmaster faced off, a fight was imminent.

"Aren't you going to eject me and throw me into the Mist?" Sander, if that was his real name, took off his suit jacket and dropped it to the side. Harlowe watched him closely but waited for the demon to make the first move. The male wasn't armed, either. Both of them had their fists raised, ready to throw a punch.

"Maybe next time, Sandy."

Odessa's mouth went dry. She was a liability. Harlowe wouldn't leave her, and they couldn't disappear into the Mist around witnesses. They'd have to fight the demon to make it out the door and get the hell out of there.

The host's lips curled and revealed the sensual curve of the archmaster's lips in the overlay image. It was just wrong a demon could look so good.

"Shame," he said. "And it's not Sandy, or Sander. Call me Sandeen." He lunged.

Harlowe landed a solid right hook on the male's jaw. He yanked her arm and twisted her around, pinning it behind her back. Harlowe didn't cry out in pain, but snapped her head back—a square hit to his nose. Odessa jumped on him from behind just as his head flew back. It nailed her in the chin. Odessa's teeth rattled with the hit and her grip loosened. He grunted and let go of Harlowe in an attempt to elbow Odessa off of him.

Harlowe spun, her fist heading for Sandeen's face. To keep from impeding Harlowe's hit, Odessa let go and dropped to the ground. But with Odessa's weight off, Sandeen ducked and rammed Harlowe in the belly. Both bodies barreled into the exit, pushing the handle. The metal door swung open. They flew out onto the sidewalk.

Odessa checked behind her to see if anyone was following. Only a few humans had noticed the door open and thought nothing of the couple that exited in a tangle. She dashed outside. The two fighters rolled on the ground. Glimpses of creamy flesh played peekaboo as Harlowe's tiny skirt flapped up while she wrestled. The male's white dress shirt had ripped open and blood ran freely down his chin and chest from his bleeding nose. Harlowe's fists and elbows were a blur, but the male seemed interested in searching Harlowe's body like he was looking for something. Odessa danced back and forth on each boot as she debated how she could be useful.

Harlowe finally dislodged herself and rolled away, popping up into a crouch where Odessa stood.

"What's a warrior doing with no weapons?" The male heaved himself off the pavement. His human host swayed.

"We were just here to party, looking for a good time. But you cut that short." It was a sad attempt at deflecting from their real reason for being there.

Sandeen snorted, then winced and spit a bloody glob to the ground. "Do you expect me to buy that?" He could barely get his host's lips into a cocky grin, but it was portrayed in the image of the real Sandeen. "I could've showed you a good time."

Harlowe had almost backed up to Odessa. Odessa hoped she was correct interpreting Harlowe's intent accurately and reached out to grab hold of Harlowe. She wanted to go together over risking getting caught by herself. One afternoon of practice didn't teach her enough to swat a fly.

Sandeen crouched to attack when he realized they were going to transcend.

"Go!" Odessa told Harlowe. She'd be along for the ride.

He jumped forward to grab onto Harlowe and shuttle along. The exit door clattered open and Bronx barreled out. He shoved Sandeen. The human flew backward, and all three of them disappeared.

CHAPTER 17

*B*ryant paced the sidewalk, his hands folded behind his back. His gaze tracked up and down the street. Urban stood impassively by the outer wall of an empty building, a former brewery. This part of town was perfect to wait in. Nearly abandoned, any others cruising the streets wouldn't think anything of him and Urban loitering in dark clothing. Cops weren't interested in coming here if they didn't have to.

It was an ideal neighborhood for a club like Fall from Grace in that there were many isolated spots to do business in—human or otherwise.

The other male hadn't spoken all night. He was used to Urban's quiet nature, but tonight it grated on him. Couldn't he help pass the time while Odessa was in a club that might have patrons hunting her?

On the flip side, if Urban had been hitting him up with idle conversation, Bryant might have decked the bloke.

A faint sizzle in the air prepped him for the incoming arrival.

Three bodies appeared in front of him and Bryant went

175

straight to Odessa. Her face was pale and she was breathing hard.

"We need to go," Harlowe announced.

"What the fuck was that about?" Bronx demanded.

"We gotta go. Now," Harlowe urged.

"You okay?" Bryant ignored the other two, waiting for Odessa's breathing to calm down.

She nodded weakly, her eyes darting around like she expected the shadows to come alive. Shouts rang through the night from the direction of the club.

"Guys!" Harlowe pitch rose.

Bryant finally took his gaze off Odessa to address Harlowe. "Hotel or Odessa's mansion?"

"Mansion. We need to get out of this realm."

"Let's go."

Instead of just grabbing onto Odessa to make sure she transcended back to her home with him, he curled his arm around her waist. She let him carry her back to the mansion.

After they arrived on her doorstep, he waited, sensing the others arrive around him, standing in the same positions they had on the street. Odessa's head rested on his shoulder and he was content to hold her.

"What the fuck was that about?" Bronx repeated as they piled into her living room.

"*That* was an archmaster," Harlowe said.

Odessa lifted her head. "I could see him. Is that normal, or was he allowing it?"

"He was allowing it," Harlowe nearly growled.

"Do they all look…" Odessa's forehead creased, like she didn't know how to finish her sentence, "Like that? That…good?"

Bryant's brows shot up. What?

"Not usually. Archmasters are our size and look more humanoid than symasters. They all have horns and black

176

wings, but usually they look…" Now Harlowe seemed uncomfortable. "Worse."

"The demon was good-looking," Bronx agreed. "I only caught a glimpse, but I don't think he was even covered in fur."

Bryant was stuck on his mate thinking a demon was hot. As if he didn't have enough stacked against him.

"DEFINITELY NO FUR or cloven hooves on him." Harlowe gave a sharp shake of her head. "He figured out I was a warrior, but he wasn't armed, just a customer. I don't think they ever suspected the angels would find their club."

"Magan did." Odessa straightened and Bryant missed her warmth. "She and Cal were killed because they knew about the club and what might be happening there."

"Then they thought their contacts in Numen were keeping their secret safe. Maybe they don't know Odessa's still alive." Bryant finally realized he still had his arm around Odessa when he instinctively went to pull her in closer. He dropped it to his side. She didn't need him hanging on her to protect her.

Odessa frowned. He doubted it was because he took his arm away. The fight must be bothering her.

"I agree, Harlowe," Bronx said. "They had bouncers, but none of them were possessed. Everyone there was looking to have a good time—a real good time. I think the tactical decisions on who to target and what they're after are made somewhere else."

"Yes," Odessa said. She chewed briefly on her lower lip as her brow furrowed. "It's a place for that guy we saw, and whoever works for him, to see who they are going to use for their dirty work, but most importantly—who'll get possessed. Those people want to be watched by him, but he's really observing them. It's like a warped job interview."

"What guy?" Bronx asked.

Harlowe rolled her eyes. "You were busy."

A smug grin lit his face. "All in a day's work. I got her to talk. She said she's waiting for a demon to possess her so she can earn her wings. They're trying to hunt chaperones."

"Shiiiit." Urban exhaled. The first thing he'd said in hours and it hit the mark.

"*Hunt* chaperones?" Bryant asked.

Harlowe nodded toward Odessa. "The guy we got talking said he helped an archmaster kill a warrior. No resistance when we use our power to free a soul."

"What's that mean, exactly?" Odessa asked.

Bryant reeled over the revelations. "When a human is possessed, their soul puts up a natural resistance. Only an archmaster can destroy a soul and take over the body completely, otherwise a part of the host's mind is always working. Ripping a demon out of their host involves untangling them from the soul. Warriors learn how to do it in training, but it takes considerable divine power, and we do it while prepping to ascend to the Mist. If the host is willing and is taught how to let go, it'd be like playing tug of war and the other side suddenly dropped the rope."

"The warrior after the archmaster would've stumbled into the Mist with the demon, who then had the advantage." Harlowe shook her head, unsettled.

Urban spoke to Bryant. "The leader must be a fallen. How else would a host know to do that?"

Bryant was thinking the same thing. "Tell me what you saw."

Bronx and Harlowe filled him in on their respective conversations, including the man in the upper level who had watched the crowd and sensed their angelic presence.

Bryant turned to Odessa. "Were you able to recall many of your notes?" He wanted to hear how Odessa put the information together. Her mind didn't work like a warrior's.

Odessa went to the couch and sat down, those ridiculously sexy shorts riding up even higher on her mile-long legs. She looked like she wanted to untie her boots and kick them off, but she sat back instead, taking off her tie. Which only drew more attention to her bust-line and nicely rounded cleavage visible above the last button.

"I got more clarification on the tattoos. Like I thought, a black rose is a follower. They watch for potential candidates, look for the characteristics that make a person open to possession, maybe shake up their life a little. They function like sylphs in that manner. If the follower wants to play host to a demon, they get tatted with a barbed wire tattoo, usually around the left arm. I assume that once they've played house with a demon, they ink the blood on. The guy that hit on Harlowe confirmed that the torn wings mean he helped destroy an angel. I'm not sure that there are any more."

Bryant thought for a moment, trying to keep from looking at Odessa stretching her long legs and arching her back like she was stretching cramped muscles. Morphing wings so they weren't visible to humans was taxing, and she'd spent the day shopping and the night was getting late. She must not be used to having them tucked in so long. Warriors hunted a possession for days at a time, so he was more accustomed to the discomfort. He barely noticed it until several days had gone by.

He worked over the details of the night. "We know they're hunting warriors and watchers who threaten their existence. We need to know why they're hunting a chaperone? To keep the soul of a deceased human from reaching the divine realm? Or is it the angel they're after? The leader has contacts in all three realms. What their overall goal is, we don't know yet."

He studied his team. Harlowe and Bronx were pumped full of adrenaline after their little fight and couldn't stand still. Shifting from foot to foot, they each periodically rolled their shoulders, their gazes alert. Urban had energy yet to burn because he was Urban. He was like a ticking time bomb waiting to go off, quiet for hours and an explosion of energy when necessary.

"Urban, you fill in Sierra and Dionna. Dionna can stay to guard the mansion. Sierra can use her contacts to search for information about the owner of the club. After Odessa gets some rest, I'll take her to start looking into records of the fallen."

His mate rewarded him with a grateful smile. "I'm going to go clean up. When you're done here, can I talk to you?"

Odessa stood, bid the others good night, and ascended the stairs without glancing in his direction. He could tell himself it was because she was knackered, but he couldn't escape the feeling he'd done something wrong.

ODESSA HAD no idea if Bryant was going to come up to talk with her or not. She had many questions banging around in her head. It was time to get answers.

Unbuttoning her shirt, she shed the flimsy material and shook her wings free.

Ahhh. How did Felicia do it with her wings morphed the entire time down on Earth? Odessa knew why, just not *how*. She unbuttoned her shorts. It felt like she had been fending off the wedgie from hell all night. It was time to get those things off.

Oh, damn, the boots.

Sighing, she left her shorts in place and decided to tackle the boots after she cleaned her face.

On her way to the bathroom, she grabbed a tee to throw on. After shrugging into it and settling the special slits over her wings, she tackled the thick liner around her eyes, first smearing it until she resembled a raccoon before it finally wiped off. Her skin glowed a healthy pink thanks to several minutes of scrubbing.

She released her hair from its ties and bent over, letting it hang down to the floor. After a good shake, she straightened up and flipped her head back.

Nice. Pressure off her head, pressure off her back. Time to get the pressure off her feet.

She went out to her main bedroom and stopped when Bryant entered. He'd also let his magnificent wings out of their morph. Normally lending him a commanding presence to his profile, his wings were lowered, and he stumbled to a stop and closed the door behind him.

"Oh." She pressed her hand against the thrill that zinged through her belly. "Hi."

Bryant's gaze fell on her and his nostrils flared. How must she look? Makeup-free face, wild and dark hair, pale pink tee, short and tight black shorts, and knee-high laced boots.

A hot mess.

She expected him to go for the door, saying he'd return when she was ready. But his gaze roamed down her body and landed on her boots. The amber depths blazed with pent-up emotion.

Her breath caught. *Is this it?* If they moved forward and had sex, they would be bound together for eternity. Did he want that? From the looks of him, he wanted her.

"I was just checking that you were all right." He sounded forced, strangled.

How would she sound when she answered him? Breathy? Needy?

"Yes. I was just going to take these boots off. They hurt my feet."

When he didn't move other than to give a slight nod of his head, she crossed to the settee on the far side of her room and sat. She stretched a leg out to untie her boots. They came just over the knee, the tie at an easy spot for her to work on, but it was like her fingers weren't connected to her mind. She fumbled at the laces. The imposing male in the room with his wings nearly quivering with repressed desire distracted her.

She sensed him drift closer before she saw him. Her fingers uselessly picked at the knot.

"I just can't seem to get this." She laughed nervously.

He squatted down in front of her and put one knee on the floor so he straddled her foot.

"Let me help." He focused on the flimsy strings.

She gave up on the ties and held her breath, trying not to remember how capable the talented fingers were that were unlacing her boots.

He deftly picked at the bindings and when they were loose enough, he lifted her foot and slid the boot off. Cool air flowed over her skin. She sighed in relief.

Bryant shifted the other knee to the floor and worked on the second boot. Same held breath, same mesmerized gaze, she tried not to move as he loosened the ties and slid it off.

After dropping the boot to the side and giving her bare legs one last scorching look, he glanced up.

"I got the feeling I upset you earlier." His words were like a caress, his slight accent making her shiver, a movement that didn't go unnoticed.

And he'd come to find out why? Her heart melted. "No, but I think we should talk."

"About what?"

"Us."

He shuttered his gaze. She feared she'd lost him and the raw honesty she'd seen. She cupped his face before he closed himself off. She expected him to pull back, instead his eyelids floated shut and he leaned in to her touch.

"Do you want to stay synced with me?" She was afraid of his answer.

He opened his eyes, and she was pinned with amber fire. "The decision isn't mine alone. What do you want, Odessa?"

She loved how he said her name. "I asked you first. Do you want me?"

Hot hands landed on her thighs, and she almost gasped at how much she needed him to touch her, caress her. She wanted to feel more of him on her naked skin. He rubbed small circles with his palms, the vibrations settling into her core.

"I want you more than I've wanted anything. Looking at you all day, not being able to be with you…it's painful. You ask me if I want eternity with you, and the answer right now is that I'd agree to anything to lay with you."

She had wanted honesty, she got it.

"What do you want, Odessa?"

She stroked his cheeks with her thumbs before dropping her hands to his strong shoulders and savoring the slide of the smooth fabric of his black shirt under her fingertips.

"When that guy told us about killing the warrior, it hit me. That's what you do." He stopped massaging her thighs, waiting for her to continue. "You put yourself in danger every day for our kind."

"Yes," he said softly. "It's who I am, and I won't change that."

"I like how you stand up for what you believe in and protect what's yours." Unlike her father. "I realized that we're wasting time. You could be killed, I could be killed. What are we doing tiptoeing around each other?"

He was rigid, his muscles tight, like a coiled snake, ready to strike. Calloused hands slid farther up her legs, over her shorts, and to the buckle.

"Be very sure, Odessa. We've already synced. If you say yes, there's no going back. You are mine."

"And you're mine," she whispered. Oh God, was this going to happen?

He hooked his finger over her waistband. "It won't matter if you're a higher class than me. It won't matter what your father does. I won't quit being a warrior. But I won't live in the barracks. I will be here with you, in your bed."

Finally.

Odessa realized she spoke that word out loud when he bracketed her hips to drag her shorts down. Arching back, she gave him the room to do so. They were so snug, sticking to her skin, he tore at the seams, ripping them off her.

"I hope you didn't want to keep these. But those fucking boots are going to stay."

He really *had* liked how she'd looked. Odessa bit her lip. What would be his next move?

He lifted her shirt and removed it. She was naked before him.

"Odessa," he rasped. "I can't believe how beautiful you are." He cupped her breasts as if weighing them in each hand. "Perfection."

Splaying his hands across her ribs, he ran them down her belly, his avid stare soaking in every visible inch of skin. She wanted to see him, wanted every bit of skin on his body for her perusal, but the way he was making her feel…intoxicating. She wanted more.

He didn't stop, skimming his hands past her belly button and down to stroke her core, but he didn't linger. He lifted and pushed her thighs until she was bared to him, her slick pink folds greeting him, waiting for him.

"You're so beautiful, so wet for me."

He languidly stroked his thumb between her crease.

Odessa moaned and arched into his touch. Reclining, she settled into her soft wings, allowing him complete control over her center.

"I've got to taste you." He dipped his head toward her.

She exhaled a gasp as soon as his silken tongue found her sweet spot. A low growl of approval resonated from his chest and he licked the length of her slit, dipping his tongue into her. Her hips undulated in response. Only one word rimmed inside her skull.

More.

"My word, you're like honey." Increasing the pressure, he flicked his tongue against her clit, changing pace, building the intensity.

She spread her hands out over his scalp, loving how each small muscle flexed as he worked his tongue against her. He wrung gasps from her. She was trying not to shout, aware they still had company downstairs, but when he inserted one long finger, she almost cried out.

She clamped down on her bottom lip. He thrust and set a steady pace. She moved with him, seeking the release her body so desperately needed.

"Do you want this, Odessa? Do you want me?"

Still biting her lip, she wanted to snarl at him to keep going. When she saw the stark reality of his question in his whiskey pools, she knew he meant more than just climaxing.

Before she could pant her yes, he dipped his head back down, attacking her nub, smoothly sliding his finger in and out. She was lost.

Her release hit like a lightning bolt slamming through her body. The rush of energy was so strong, she feared her heart would stop. She wanted to scream, to shout his name, wail into the night, but the sound froze in her throat. Flinging her head back against the cushions, she rode the wave of her orgasm, barely keeping her fingernails from scoring Bryant's skull.

He kissed her drenched skin and removed his hand before raising his head. She wanted to fall into a boneless heap, but she wanted Bryant more. He crouched back on his heels, watching her as if awaiting her reaction to what they'd just done, expecting it to be negative.

"I want to see your body," she said.

With measured movements, he unbuckled his shoulder holsters. He was shrugging out of them when there was a pounding at the door. Odessa jerked upright and Bryant froze.

"Vale?" Dionna hollered

"What the fuck?" Bryant hissed.

Odessa gulped, afraid the warrior might open the door and walk in even though it was her private quarters and this male was her mate.

"Vale!" Dionna tried again.

"What?" His anger at being interrupted poured into that one word.

"Director Richter's here and he needs to talk to you."

Bryant dropped his chin to his chest. Was he counting?

Odessa uttered her thought out loud. "It must be important."

His gaze snapped to hers, and except for a brief flare of uncertainty, he calmed his expression. He was back to being the cool-headed team leader. Did he think she wanted him to go?

"I'll wait here for you," she offered. "For when you're done."

The flush of heat in his gaze mixed with relief. Instead of

leaving, he held out his hand. She accepted it, liking how he was still very aware of her body.

"Crawl into bed and cover up before I open the door."

She did as he asked, not bothering to put on anything before she burrowed between the covers. He tucked her in. Repressed heat touched with tenderness wavered in his expression. Odessa was struck by the intimacy of the moment. He had just been as close as a mate could get, settled between her legs, but drawing the covers up around her was...sweet.

He'd been gruff, cranky, obstinate, bossy, serious, angry, passionate, but not tender. It wasn't that she hadn't thought him capable, she hadn't expected to experience it.

Enjoying the view of his tall, powerful body striding toward the door, she gave him a little wave when he looked back before he left.

Alone once again in her room, she could hardly wait for him to return so they could seal their sync once and for all.

CHAPTER 18

*J*ameson glared at the senator. "I thought you said you had your end contained."

After texting his Numen contact a big *WTF*, the senator had agreed to meet him in their prearranged spot. An off-the-beaten-track area of the desert where they were safe from prying eyes of all kinds.

"There've been some complications. It's getting taken care of," Beto Kenton replied smoothly, his slate-gray wings held high and proud like most obnoxious elite angels.

The distinguished male had perfectly coiffed yellow-blond hair and an oval, angular face with deep-set sharp blue eyes. At first glance, he looked like a Numen whose calculating ambition could be easily dismissed.

"Warriors were in my club." Jameson loomed over the senator. His plans had nearly dissolved, and after all he'd suffered. "Good thing there was only one archmaster in attendance, and that he's a colleague of sorts. Otherwise, I'd have one very important demon thinking I'd turned traitor."

Gerzon would rip him apart. Jameson's followers might

188

be loyal, but the real test would be when they witnessed the slaughter of their own as Gerzon and his devoted mowed them down to get to him.

Instead, Jameson had convinced Sandeen any Numen interference would be quickly dealt with. The male had nursed his busted nose, mostly concerned with a delay in his research and whether his host could still get it up. That right there was a good reason why Jameson didn't trust him. Any being with the ability to wield power should do so. Sandeen talked like a shrewd, dynamic male—at times. Mostly, he acted unaffected and patient. Why wasn't he satisfied with anything less than overtaking a realm?

Senator Kenton's gaze darkened. "They will be dealt with."

"It's not just a few warriors we're talking about here," Jameson gritted out. "They work in teams—you know that. Can you deal with seven warriors without drawing attention?"

The senator raised himself to his full height, which was still inches shorter than Jameson. "I did last time, didn't I, when Gerzon had a team of warriors trailing him?"

"And if I recall correctly, half that warrior team is still around, still causing me trouble."

"I told you they would be dealt with. This kind of work takes finesse. An entire team of warriors *and* a senator's daughter being terminated will raise eyebrows. I have a plan to make it look like an accident, but it will take time."

Time? He knew all about *time*. These plans had been in progress for decades, and he was reaching the boiling point. It was still early yet, his power tenuous, but he was so close he could taste sweet victory. In the quiet moments before he drifted off to sleep, he imagined marching into the realm, over revered Numen soil, and looking the smug senators in the eyes that had determined he was no longer worthy of his wings. Then, with the power of the Daemon legions at his back, he'd slaughter every last one of them before turning on his hateful, spiteful mate that had spearheaded his exile. Chanel. The angel that had seized his ascension ability, and especially the angel that had severed his wings from his back, would pay. Each angel that heard his screams that day would suffer the same pain.

If the incompetent fool before him didn't ruin everything.

Kenton was Jameson's eyes and ears in Numen and that was the *only* thing keeping him alive now. The double scythe damn near vibrated against Jameson's chest as if it had a natural affinity for angelic blood and it wanted that blood spilled.

Senator Kenton's arrogance and superiority complex led him to Jameson, seeking to use him as a means to overthrow the Numen government. Jameson long suspected the senator had observed his demise those long years after he'd lost his wings. And when Jameson had started to thrive, he'd stepped in. The senator didn't want to protect humans, he wanted to use them to rely on their kind for survival and to worship the Numen as the senator thought just.

What he didn't realize was that his time was severely limited once Jameson breached his former realm. Once the senator's use was fulfilled, he would meet the same fate as Jameson's punishers.

BRYANT'S MIND wanted to wander back to his time with Odessa, but the task at hand was too important. Director Richter had shown up, interrupting the most decadent experience Bryant had ever had, and filled him in on the bad news. Enforcers wanted to infringe on his duty to protect Odessa.

"I don't trust them," he had stated plainly to his boss.

"I don't either, Vale," the director had agreed. "That's why I want you and Odessa to interview each enforcer and select for yourselves which ones you want protecting the mansion."

Both Bryant and Director Richter agreed that at least two of Bryant's team should hang around, and no enforcer would be allowed inside the mansion. Odessa didn't need to be bothered with interviewing strangers tonight, not after he'd had her laid out and vulnerable just minutes ago. The thought threatened to make him hard again. It had been no small battle calming his body down after he had to leave a beautiful female who seemed to openly desire *him*, and not just the experience of being with a battle-hardened soldier.

Since it was late, the director had agreed to let Bryant conduct the interviews and then, if she wished, Odessa could cross-examine them in the morning when she was rested.

He was on his sixth candidate. They needed at least three, and Bryant was severely critical and highly suspicious. So far two enforcers had been rookies just out of training, one had been too interested in Odessa, and one he almost drop-kicked back to the precinct for not taking this assignment seriously. Only one had passed his rigorous interview so far.

Bryant was beyond impatient to get back up to his mate and finish what they'd started, but he needed to make sure she was protected by nothing but the best. Director Richter stood next to him out on Odessa's lawn because Bryant refused to allow a single enforcer through the doors of the mansion. The dark of night was lit only by the faint glow of moonlight and a scattering of the fireflies that constantly roamed the realm.

Candidate six was wrapping up a spiel on the best form of hand-to-hand combat when Bryant cut him off.

"You're dismissed."

The enforcer stopped and looked to Director Richter.

The director pinched the bridge of his nose. "Thank you for your time."

The enforcer stalked off the lawn and took flight.

"For Heaven's sake, Vale. What was wrong with that one?" Fatigue weighed on his boss.

"He was arrogant. I don't trust him."

"If arrogance was used to rule out every candidate, then your entire team wouldn't qualify. I don't want to rush you, but you need to make your choice before Stede interferes."

The guy was right, but Bryant didn't like it. He trusted his team, and no one but them, with Odessa's safety.

"Fine," he growled. "That guy will do." But he wasn't chasing him down. "Bring on the next one."

The seventh candidate was a female with a short pixie cut and the build of the gymnasts he used to see on cereal boxes decades ago. Maybe humans still did that, but he quit eating his Wheaties when it got to be too much of a pain in the ass to hide his face in the grocery store.

She was professional, and even though she was young, she still had years of experience policing their realm.

"You start the next shift, Tosca." The tiny enforcer bobbed her head at Bryant's orders. "One of my warriors will be on hand until all of you have worked at least two full shifts." Bryant knew Stede wouldn't like it, but it was an innocuous request and Stede's refusal would raise too many questions.

After getting the first enforcer settled into his shift with Dionna and giving the director his good-nights, Bryant practically sprinted through the door and bounded up the stairs. His shaft was back to full and throbbing by the time he strode into Odessa's suite.

A small, round orb like a snow globe cast a gentle yellow glow near the four-poster bed. He suspected Odessa made sure to never sleep in the dark after her attack, especially if she was alone.

The soft sounds of steady breathing told Bryant that he would not be finishing what he'd started earlier with her. She was fast asleep, curled up on her side under the blankets he had tucked her into himself.

Damn.

He walked quietly to the bed to gaze down at his mate. To make sure she was all right. That was as good an excuse as any. Her curtain of hair fell over her face and draped across her bare shoulder.

The sight was a punch to the gut. She was still nude and had awaited his return before she drifted off to sleep after a long, trying day.

She had waited for him.

He took advantage of the precious moment to look her over. So young. She was twenty-five, with a birthday coming up. He would have to remember that and get her something special.

Then the awful truth clawed its way to the forefront of his conscious. He might look no more than five years older, but he had decades on her. He had lived and experienced a different life. He'd always known exactly what he was meant for. She'd known violence and fear in her short time, and she'd sought him out for her own well-being. Desperation and terror had driven her to his side. To him, and a face that was even more fearsome than her nightmares.

He had been right to keep his distance and allow her the chance to think clearly instead of feeling obligated to him.

He dropped his head and closed his eyes. She was lovely, intelligent, and fiercely loyal. She should be allowed to be all that—with a mate that was destined for her and could be there for her. Not one who left her waiting alone in bed. He couldn't give her anything other than long, violent work days where she'd fear for his life. More violence and fear.

Bryant allowed himself one long sigh, one moment to regret what he could never have. Then he left the room and headed down to the couch that had been his bed every night he'd slept in the mansion.

CHAPTER 19

*O*dessa stretched, her arms reaching out to each side. Her body felt relaxed, pleased, yet still wanting.

She frowned. Daylight streamed through her windows. And her bed was empty. She sat up and looked around the room and over to the settee. Empty.

Had Bryant come back, grabbed some shut-eye, and left again already?

Had he come back at all?

Holding the sheets up to her chest even though no one was around to see her, she thought for a few minutes. What were all the reasons Bryant could be absent?

Climbing out of bed, Odessa went to her closet. She would give him the benefit of the doubt. Maybe he was called away again. Except, the room felt...bare, like he'd never been back. There was no use torturing herself with questions of whether he stayed away of his own freewill, or if it was out of his control.

Odessa scanned her closet. Should she wear a white robe today, or a white robe?

There. A white robe.

She almost had the robe swung around to shrug into when she spotted a yellow sundress. It was the type that could be stepped into and tied around the neck. She usually never wore human clothing in Numen, but the dress had caught her eye because few human fashions could be worn easily with a set of wings. Most had to be adapted. And yellow went well with her coloring, so no matter what was going on with Bryant, she was going to feel spectacular.

She selected the dress and went to the bathroom to wash up and secure her hair into a ponytail. Then she stepped into the dress, tied it, and gave herself a good look.

Nice. The vibrant dress set off her eyes. Her darker hair was only temporary, but the shade was complemented by the color of her clothing. In fact, the dress was so bright, her wings didn't look washed out next to it. She gave them a little ruffle. Damn, she felt good.

Time to find her mate.

Odessa hopped down the stairs when she saw a familiar form sleeping on the couch. She stopped midway.

What. The. Fuck?

Descending slower this time, she frowned at Bryant. Her footsteps must've been enough to wake him. He righted himself and did a double take, but as soon as heat flared in his gaze, it was squashed.

"I'll go clean up," he said, folding the blanket. "You go ahead and grab some breakfast. We need to head to the archives and research fallen angels to see if we can narrow down any suspects."

Okaaay? He stood, still wearing the same clothes he'd worn last night. Clothing she remembered clearly. The same shirt she had felt between her thighs, the one she'd grabbed onto when he was making her come harder than she had ever experienced.

She was speechless. He didn't give her a second glance as

he walked out of the room, but headed to the downstairs bathroom he'd always used.

Hurt gnawed at her chest, and anger made her wings quiver. She didn't know why he had gotten called away, but he'd chosen to not come back to her. He acted like it hadn't happened.

She stormed into the kitchen. Hot tears spilled down her cheeks. She hastily swiped at them. She was the needy girlfriend all over again. Why did she fall for males incapable of the same level of feelings she was?

She wasn't going to be that person again, begging for a male's attention. If she was scared, she would learn to fight. Felicia would help her. If she was lonely, she'd get a damn cat. If she had to sleep with a light on every night for the rest of her long life, so be it.

Asshat.

The word made Odessa think of Harper and the tears flowed faster. She missed her human friends, but even a "men suck" text to Harper would be too risky. Odessa couldn't put someone else's life in danger.

Okay, step one to not being that girl was to make breakfast. She sniffled and wiped her cheeks off. What did she have to eat? Closing drawers quickly became slamming. Instead of letting a cabinet door drift shut, she shoved it. The satisfying whack was a balm to her rage.

How dare he do that to her? She deserved a motherfucking reason why he didn't want her anymore.

Calm down. There would be no begging for a reason, no simpering for his attention.

And he could make his own damn breakfast.

Just as Bryant drifted into the kitchen, she marched past him on the way out. He barely looked at her and that dumped gasoline on her raging fire.

How could life turn so quickly? She had just been a

normal analyst who went to work and came home. Her only claim to anything remotely wild was her job at the children's clothing store and dancing with friends on the weekends. To go from that to being hunted and her entire realm in danger, and being part of a select few that knew about any of it, was surreal. Before she thought her life was dedicated to helping her people. Now their safety depended on her. Her and that maddening male in the kitchen.

As if summoned, Bryant exited, munching on an apple. Odessa wished she had her own apple so she could lob it at his head. It wasn't fair how good he looked, various blades strapped over his form-fitting black shirt and wrapped around his tapered waist. The black tactical pants warriors favored in the field molded against his hips and butt, teasing a girl's eye all along his legs. Even more unfair was his casual stance, managing to exude power and masculinity while nonchalantly chewing on a damn apple.

"You ever been in the archives?" he asked around his mouthful.

"I'm an analyst, of course I have," she snapped.

He flinched at the anger she threw into her words. "I've only ever been to the main vestibule, not inside the actual record rooms. Since we want to get in and out without notice, we'll need to land nearby and sneak as close to the entrance where the records of the fallen are kept."

"Do you think you can tolerate me being there with you?" She was being petty, but dammit, she was upset.

A fleeting look of regret moved over his face. "Look, Odessa—"

"No. I don't want to hear it. The sooner we figure this out the sooner you can be done with me."

He opened his mouth to say something, but Odessa marched outside. His heavy steps followed her. She did as he said, leading the creep toward a concealed door in the arching archive building that favored human Renaissance architecture—or vice versa, since the archives were ancient.

The eight-foot wooden panel door opened at her touch. It wouldn't have budged for Bryant's. That gave her a little satisfaction. He needed her in some way.

Once inside, she dropped her hand and stepped away. The path to the archives was empty, the space quiet. She stepped lightly so her sandals wouldn't slap on the ground. Earlier, Bryant's footsteps had rattled the mansion, but he was nothing but stealth here. Arching ceilings were just tall enough an angel would have to fly to touch it, but the walls were narrow enough, they could never adequately spread their wings to do so.

Light filtered in from ceiling panels, natural resources used to spare angelic energy.

A lone door at the end of a long hallway beckoned her. They entered and Bryant softly clicked the door behind them.

"This is the hall with the history compiled by analysts," she explained to Bryant about the large circular room lined with scrolls of various ages. "We toured here to see how recordings used to be kept. Some analysts are dedicated to the preservation of these scrolls, even converting them to electronic form."

"How exciting," Bryant said dryly.

"It would be fascinating." Odessa sniffed. He might not think much of her position, but their people's history intrigued her. Archiving would be a good career, but she enjoyed how her current assignment paired their history with modern events.

"I prefer to preserve our history by making sure we have a future."

"And you say the elite are obnoxious," Odessa mumbled. If he heard her, he made no comment.

She walked around to figure out where they should start looking for records of fallen angels. He followed her lead, as she wandered from hall to hall, hunting for where the scrolls or cartridges of exiled Numen were kept. Before they entered a new section of the archives, Bryant went first. She assumed he was making sure they were alone and that no others had decided to come down for a peek into history.

"Shouldn't we have told Dionna where we are?" Odessa asked after the first time Bryant had rushed to inspect a room before she entered.

"It's not like I had time before you hauled us out of the mansion."

Yeah, well, okay. He had a point.

"Besides," he continued, "Director Richter was getting pressured from the enforcers to turn over your protection detail to them."

"Why?"

"Their story is because it's their jurisdiction. Our feeling is it's because whoever is behind your attack wants to be able to get in close enough to kill you. It'd be easier with their own people in charge of your protection."

Her hand touched where her heart wanted to thump out of her chest. There was no reason to worry. They had to get through Bryant.

She willed herself to calm and strolled around the current archival room they were in. Almost a narrow tunnel, it held the archives of messaging between Numen and Heaven. A long table piled high with forgotten scrolls took up the surface. The archives weren't a high-traffic spot so the caretakers only arrived occasionally to tidy up.

"So then what?" She didn't like the feeling of dread over the thought that Bryant and his team wouldn't be around for her. She didn't think she took them for granted, but getting to the bottom of the mystery would be more difficult if they had to sidestep around enforcers all day.

"I interviewed several enforcers last night. You should meet them eventually, give your stamp of approval. Until we know how far the corruption goes, I'm okay with none of them knowing we're gone yet. Dionna will take care of things and cover for us, if need be. She'll be pissed when she finds out I didn't tell her."

Odessa wasn't going to ask the questions that had been nagging her all morning, but it wasn't unreasonable to want an answer as to why he brushed off what they'd done together. "Why didn't you come back last night?"

Bryant sighed and rubbed the back of his neck. His expression was resigned. "I did come back, but you were asleep. And that was for the best. What we did was a mistake."

He had come back? *Mistake?* "What do you mean?"

He shrugged and looked away. "You're young, you're in danger. I'm helping you. I don't want you to feel beholden to me. I'll help you, Odessa. That won't change whether you sleep with me or not."

"Don't give me that you're trying to do the right thing bullshit."

His brows popped. "It's not bullshit. You need to be able to make the decision of being mated with a clear head. You deserve the opportunity to mate with the right angel."

The simmering anger Odessa had harbored toward Bryant all morning peaked. "Quit with the young excuse. I grew up way before my time. After the attack, my mother didn't care enough about her daughters to face life and stay strong for us. She chose to walk into the fire instead. Just left a note. 'Sorry,' it said." She flung her hands out. "Sorry? My father sent me and Filly off to boarding school. Pretended as if we didn't exist, using the guise that he was protecting us by keeping his distance. My sister's a mess and I have no idea what's going on with her life. The last fourteen years hasn't been a fairy tale."

"Exactly." He leaned in, his body language earnest. "You deserve to live a happy life. You can't do that if you're tied to me only because of what's going on."

"I've been alone, begging for any scrap of affection anyone would give me, while fearing too much attention would only bring me harm. Yes, my decision may have originated in fear of being alone. But when I walked into your sync gala, I was committed to you. My decision was made. *You* turned me away. Then again after my father's visit, and again last night. That's three times now." Her body shook holding back the rage. He was spurning her because he thought it was in her *best interest*? "My mind's made up. It's you who's tiptoeing around, using any excuse you can to break our sync. Don't put it on me."

Sparks glinted in his gaze. He crowded close, his size more welcome than intimidating. "I'm thinking only of you. I want what's best for you."

Odessa leaned into him, getting up in his face. "I say again, *bullshit*. You don't want me—that's fine. But be a man and cut it off. We don't need the sync to keep going on this investigation." A new thought dawned on her. "Unless you only want us synced so I can heal you."

"Of course not!" he shouted. "Have you looked at yourself? You're bloody gorgeous. You don't need to be synced with a wreck like me. I work. That's it. I don't play house."

"Did I ask you to quit working?" she yelled back at him. "Do you think I'm going to sit at home and wait only for your return? Sorry, I've done that with Crestin and I didn't enjoy it. All it got me was an asshole that was willing to sleep with my sister and, apparently, anyone else. Have I seemed repulsed by your appearance?" Her wings flared wider as she spoke. "I don't know if you realize this, but you're hot, scars and all. And unlike whatever partners you've been with since your injuries, I'm interested in you because you're an honorable pain in the ass that dedicates his life to those he cares for and isn't ashamed about it. Even if you act like a dick sometimes."

Tension radiated off Bryant. Her words unsettled him. They disrupted her inner peace, too. All of her anger at Bryant, her frustration over the situation she found herself in, swirled inside, seeking an exit.

"You still don't get it, Odessa," he growled low, his accent thick. The timbre shot straight to her center. "I keep telling you that once we do this, there's no going back. No chance of annulment. You are mine, and you will regret it."

She threw her hands up. "Then make sure I don't regret it. Is it that hard to think you could make someone happy just by being yourself?"

"I can make you happy." He moved forward, backing her up against the wall, her wings flattened against the shelves of scrolls. "I can make you scream with pleasure. I can make you shout with ecstasy. Is that going to be enough when we're not in bed? What are you going to do when you find out the only things I'm good at is being a warrior and making you come?"

His words…were turning her on. Savagely. He was trying to scare her, trying to scare himself. She knew what he was doing, even through her lust-induced haze.

He pressed against her, his wings held up so high, they blocked the natural light from the skylight. The only things he was good at? Two could play that game. "What are you going to do when you find out my hair gets all over the bathroom? Or when I talk incessantly about comparing the patriarchal family structure in developed nations to modern

Numen familial organization? Because as an analyst, I love that shit."

He pushed harder against her, his arousal digging into her abdomen. "I could listen to you spout nonsense all day. Your voice makes me hard, and that brain of yours," he rasped, "so bloody sexy."

Her breath hitched. His gaze was on her lips. Was he going to kiss her? She wanted him to. Badly. They hadn't resolved anything—if possible, they only broached more issues. But she had wanted him since she'd first seen his picture. He frustrated her and enraged her. He also made her feel safe, worthwhile, and cherished. She had few people in her life that made her feel that way.

She didn't have to wait long. He captured her lips. She clutched his shoulder holsters as he greedily plundered her mouth. Every swipe of his tongue, she latched on, teeth bumping, lips crushing.

When he lifted the hem of her dress, she wedged her hands in between them to yank at the clasp of his pants and tug down his zipper.

A deep groan vibrated through his chest into hers. Her dress went higher, and his zipper went lower. She managed to pull out his thick length, relishing the steely heat of him in her palm before he lifted her up and wedged himself between her legs.

She wrapped her arms around his shoulders and adjusted herself until the broad tip of him prodded her entrance. She was slick and ready for him, and after their last two times together, she didn't want to chance any delays.

He gazed into her eyes, waiting for her to give a signal for him to stop. She rocked her hips, encouraging him. He eased her down his long length. *Yes.* She filled deliciously with his width, stretching to accommodate his size.

Bryant leaned his forehead down on hers, rocking gently,

letting her get used to him. He grabbed her around the hips, and she wrapped her legs around him. He dropped his head farther, to nibble along her neck as his thrusts increased in speed and urgency.

Letting go of his shoulders, she flung her arms wide, past her wings, clamping her hands on the edges of the shelves. Bryant licked and nibbled at her neck, sending shockwaves of pleasure through her body.

She tightened around him, hugging him deep inside, resisting each slide out, wanting to keep him close.

He moaned against her neck. "If you don't want this, say it now."

Her answer was tightening her legs to take more of him in. She was so close to an explosion, and she wanted to lose herself with him. He groaned again and pumped into her, his hands digging into her flesh.

Rearing his head back, the cords stood out in his neck as his face pulled tight. Her name was like a devotion on his lips as he released inside of her.

Warmth spread through her, her knuckles white with the force of her grip on the shelves. His climax spurred her own.

"Bryant!" Stars exploded in her vision. A deep sensation of bonding settled over her. A reassuring glow of comfort and warmth signaled her soul intertwined with his. They were still tangled together with her wrapped around him. Two halves part of a perfect whole.

They quivered together as the finishing aftershocks faded. Odessa peeled her hands off the shelving. Scrolls littered the floor. She twined her arms around Bryant's shoulders, burying her face into his neck. She loosened her legs slightly; the impressions of his tactical belt probably marked her thighs.

Bryant turned his face into her hair. "Are you all right?" His spoke so soft, affectionate, she smiled into his neck.

"I'm awesome. You?"

"I'm not done yet."

She smiled wider, biting her lip. "I noticed."

"But we have work to do, and I couldn't stand it if anyone walked in and caught us."

After the ruckus they just made, anyone in the archives may indeed come searching.

He gently cupped her chin, lifting her face up, searching it intently. "You sure you're all right?"

She let her smile shine again. "I'm fine. Really."

He looked around them, at the mess on the floor. "This isn't where our first time should've been."

"Are you kidding? It was fabulous. Think of the story we can tell."

He gave her a stern look, as if it was no one's business where they got it on. Of course not. But...the archives!

Bryant pulled out of her, as hard as he was when they had started. He helped her settle her feet back on the floor and drape her dress down. With more than a little difficulty, he tucked himself back in his pants. She straightened her dress, and he stopped, his body rigid. With visible restraint, he stepped back and pivoted to the side.

"I don't stand a chance against you and that damn dress," he mumbled before he headed to the door.

The dress had been the right choice. Same with her decision to forgo underwear.

"So I was thinking," she said, following him, "that the way we deal with fallen is to forget about them. It's almost as if speaking of them brings bad fortune. I doubt their records would be given their own room. The way we angels obsessively keep records, I know they have to be down here, in a dedicated area. They would probably be stuck in a nook or shelf that's, like, an afterthought."

He stared at her with the same gleam he'd had when he

looked at her dress. "Makes sense. If you had to come and throw something down here, where would you go?"

Odessa mentally ran through all the different areas she could remember in the archives. They'd already gone through the main ones, so what records area would have spare room?

"Land records. Not much changes here, and we often live in the same homes for centuries. I bet there's room for a shelf of non-land related stuff."

"We'll head there." Bryant crossed to the door but stopped and held up a hand for Odessa to be silent.

She could hear angels speaking—and they were getting closer.

A male's voice drifted through the door. "I'm telling you, I heard shouting from over here."

Odessa's eyes widened.

"Is this like your office?" Bryant whispered.

Why would the archives be like her— Oh! The hidden panel door. They each skimmed the room, hands out, feeling for a wall that could double as an entrance.

The handle on the door jiggled turned downward.

A breeze lifted her hair. "Odessa," Bryant hissed. He had a narrow panel cracked. She scurried toward him. He nudged her inside the dark office and slipped in after her but didn't rush to shut the panel. It whisked closed as the main door swung open.

Bryant grabbed her hand, but they remained still. Her heart was racing at almost getting caught, but Bryant's grip was firm, his breathing measured. She attempted to follow suit.

A male and a female murmured on the other side.

"Ugh, this room needs a cleaning," the female said.

"Agreed," the male replied. "We must've heard the scrolls clatter on the floor. Some of these shelves need repair."

"I shall leave a note for the cleaner."

The door opened and closed again.

"Think you can find the land record room from here?" Bryant released her hand to tap a light sconce on the wall, feeding it only enough energy for dull illumination.

She glanced around the empty office. The archivists must've abandoned this space, but like Cal's office, it was surrounded by several doors.

"No luck on labels." Bryant went to each door, one by one, and listened. Odessa did the same and the ones they didn't hear anything in, they investigated. One panel opened into a sparse, tiny room.

"This is it," Odessa said. "It has to be."

She charged in, her hip bumping a rolling cart partially filled with scrolls. Her free arm cartwheeled as the cart rolled away, but it wasn't helping. Her balance was gone, and the wheel's faint squeaks were heading toward a shelf. They didn't need to attract any more attention.

Bryant yanked her into his chest before that could happen and with her hugged to him, he caught the cart with a boot.

"Sorry." Her words were muffled because she was content to stay draped against his hard body.

He chuckled and she sucked in an awed breath. He was smiling. The grin was lopsided, his injured side not rising as high as the other. Only the eye on his uninjured side had the tell-tale crinkle of a good laugh.

He immediately dropped his grin, his face settling back into the stern facade he usually wore.

Odessa reached up to caress the damage on his left side. "Is that why you don't laugh much, or are you a tough crowd?"

He softened under her touch. "A little of both I guess."

"Well, I'll have to learn your sense of humor. I like your smile."

His brows drew together as if he didn't understand what she'd said. "We'd better start our search in case those angels come this way."

Okay, she'd give him that one. She'd made more progress with him today than she thought possible only hours ago. Hell, only minutes ago.

Switching her attention to the shelves, she nodded. Just as she'd guessed. The shelves were only half full, but there wasn't a section that looked haphazard.

"What are these?" Bryant stood over the cart. He snatched one, undid the tie, and rolled it open. "I knew this guy."

Odessa peered at the scroll. In loopy calligraphy was a name and date, followed by a section that highlighted in detail all crimes committed, and ended with what the angel had to say for himself.

"He was a warrior, exiled when I was in training," Bryant elaborated. "An archmaster was hunting Numen families that lived in the human realm. This warrior killed at least three of the demon's hosts trying to stop him."

That sounded bad, but... "Aren't the human hosts usually dead after an archmaster possession?"

Bryant shook his head. "Their soul is corrupted, but it's not up to us whether they can be saved or not. The host can die from what the demon did to it during possession and drop dead as soon as the archmaster quits using them like a puppet." Bryant turned grim. "That's a game many archmasters like to play. Ultimately, it's our job to try to save the human life, not write it off as a lost cause, or sacrifice it to do our job."

Odessa shivered. The stories she'd heard whispered in corners her entire life were real. She'd known, but it was different being confronted with the evidence of lives destroyed. "He was exiled for killing humans. Do you think he could be a suspect?"

"If he's still alive. Many fallen succumb after a few decades among the humans. They can't handle the pressure and have no sense of the danger humans face each day."

She couldn't imagine losing everything and having to start over in a new place with nothing. Numen were a coddled and spoiled race. They had a task to carry out for the Almighty looking after His creations. Many thought themselves better than humans, more advanced, more civilized. In some ways they were. But humans had many obstacles and hardships to overcome, many experiences Numen would never find themselves facing.

Bryant set the scroll on an empty shelf. "We'll put our strong suspect pile here. Any we know for sure are deceased or incapable, we'll stack on the neighboring shelf. Then we'll take the suspect pile back your place." A mirthful glint flickered across his face. "Since my team is freed up from protecting the mansion, we can all fan out and search for the fallen."

CHAPTER 20

*T*hey quickly searched through scrolls. Bryant could barely concentrate. His body was still humming from the quick coupling with Odessa. That feeling when he came inside of her, when their bond solidified…bloody epic. He had just climaxed, but he was ready to go again. The archives weren't the place, though. He couldn't tolerate the idea of someone else witnessing Odessa's passion. That was for him alone.

He still couldn't believe she'd goaded him into taking her. She hadn't realized how little it would take for him to ignore his resistance. Anticipating her regret, he anxiously waited for her to realize her grave mistake. It would come soon.

Yes, he could pleasure her, keep her satisfied in bed. She was a passionate female, expressive in her desire. His confidence nose-dived when it came to keeping her happy on a daily basis. As an adult, he'd only ever lived in the barracks with his fellow warriors. Hell, he'd never had a steady girlfriend, never kept a relationship past the first couple of encounters. And that was before he'd become disfigured. After that, he was fortunate to find a willing body when his natural sex drive became too distracting. None had been Numen females, either. From the averted gaze and changed paths when they saw him in the vicinity, he hadn't bothered trying, keeping to the human realm to sate his body's needs.

Odessa read through scrolls, using her training to skim pertinent information and make instant decisions. He was grateful she was the one with him, trusting her instincts with the scrolls over anyone else he could think of. No wonder Cal had gone to her when the watcher showed some concern with her observations. Bryant had no doubt Odessa hadn't chosen to be an analyst to stay isolated and hidden from her greatest fear. Her talent was unmistakable.

As they worked for the next few hours, Bryant wondered if Dionna had found them missing yet. Maybe she had already switched with another member of his team. He hoped she warned them to leave him and Odessa alone. Or was Enforcer Stede trying to start some shit and banging the mansion door down? Either way, his team would take care of it.

"I think that's it." Odessa brushed off her hands. The lower the layers of scrolls, the more dust they'd had.

Although they had looked through all the names, their priority was the most recent fallen. They'd likely still be alive, hold a grudge, and still know the angels in power. No fallen would be ruled out, but it was a place to start.

Still...Bryant stared at the empty bin.

"What's wrong?" Odessa asked.

"I can't say why, but I feel like we missed something."

"Do you think there are more stored somewhere else?" He appreciated how she didn't brush off what his gut was telling him.

"No, this seemed about right. There's only been about three to five fallen a century." He glowered at the empty bin longer but couldn't come up with a reason for what his intuition told him. "I'll put everything back, if you'll gather up the eight we're going to start searching for."

He put the other scrolls back, attempting to get them close to the disorder they had been in before. Anyone coming to add another name to the pile or enter more land records into the room wouldn't know the bin had been tampered with.

Odessa gathered up the leftover scrolls. When they were ready, he asked Odessa where the best place in the house would be to hide them.

He had already come to the conclusion himself but didn't want to force her. He could tell when she came to the same decision he had. Color leeched from her face and she swallowed.

"My old room," she said, reluctantly. "Anyone who gets in the mansion might search the office and my suite first."

"Have you been in there since...?"

Odessa averted her gaze, her hands twisting together. "No. I tried when I moved back, but I couldn't get past opening the door to the wing."

"There's nothing to be embarrassed about. It was a traumatic experience for a child, and you've had to hold onto it as an adult." He laid a reassuring hand on her arm and was rewarded with a grateful smile. "We'll fly to your suite's dais first. I'll check in with my team, then I'll walk with you to your old room."

They managed to skirt the halls, spying and listening to avoid others. As soon as they hit an exit, they stepped out and took flight. Anyone that saw them would only see a couple out and about together. Once they landed on the perch outside of her room, he went to the door and listened. "It's quiet. I'll be right back."

"Okay. I'm going to find a bag or something to put these in."

Before he left, he checked on her one last time. She was heading to her closet, most likely to rummage around for a container. She caught his eye and sent him a smile that she'd be okay. He forced himself to return the gesture. She had said she wanted him to smile more, but it was like molding stiff wax. He couldn't help how he looked so he might as well let her get used to it. The compulsion to please her wasn't helping, either.

~

THERE IT IS! Odessa pulled out the pink drawstring backpack with neon yellow piping she'd bought when she first started working in the store. Dumping the scrolls into the bag, she pulled the strings tight and perched on the edge of the bed waiting for Bryant to get back. Her fingers played with the piping, memories of learning to work among humans cascading through her mind. At the store, she could forget she lived a life in fear. She could forget how alone she felt. She could live.

Her stomach fluttered. She wasn't alone anymore. She had a male, a partner who was determined to eradicate her fear, make her safe.

That male. She still couldn't believe he was hers. After waking up this morning, she was sure Bryant couldn't wait to go his separate way.

Now he was hers. She was his.

The sex… Delicious. He'd taken her hard and fast. It was exactly what she had needed. He'd been coiled to detonate if he didn't get into her. He made her feel desired. Wanted. Needed. Emotions that had been lacking her entire adult life.

She was sitting in her delayed afterglow when Bryant cautiously walked in. She knew what he was concerned about. He was willing to accompany her into a place where a nightmare had occurred. A nightmare that had followed her like a second shadow, threatening to get much worse if she told anyone. A nightmare that eventually claimed her mother, almost took her sister away, and destroyed her relationship with her father.

Going into her old room was the last thing she wanted to do. At least it had been, before she met Bryant. With him, her old room and what had happened to her family was something she could face. No longer would an empty space hold her hostage.

"Ready?" he asked.

"Not yet." She left the bag on the floor and stood. Untying her dress behind her neck, she let it drop to the ground.

Bryant's breath *whooshed* out as she stood naked before him.

"I want to be with you first. Then we'll go to my old room." She waited. The next move was his.

He unstrapped his shoulder harness and tactical belt and dropped each of them on the floor. "The rest of my team will be here in two hours."

"Then my old room can wait. We have to show them the scrolls anyway, right?" She might not be begging, but she sounded breathless, needy.

He stalked toward her, drawing his shirt over his head and letting it drift to the floor.

It was her turn to stare. The body of her mate. Mouth. Watering. Her fingers twitched to run over the ridges and planes of his stomach. His arms were corded, rippling with sinewy muscle.

She licked her lower lip. The intensity of his gaze burned along her breasts and her belly. He kicked his boots off, snapped open his pants. He came to a stop before her and kicked those off, too.

She stroked along his shoulders, the ripple of the scars on

his torso tickling her palms. Fully dressed, he cut a fine figure. But naked... "You are stunning."

His wings were folded behind him, betraying the sexual tension he was holding in.

"Odessa." He dropped his head and ran his tongue along her lips. She opened for him, tasting him. She wanted more.

Grabbing his thick shaft in one hand, she dropped to her knees and cupped his heavy sac in the other.

"I want to taste you this time."

His look was fire. This was freeing. It was power. She didn't beg, didn't plead. They both wanted to be here because they were mates. For once, she felt like herself in a relationship. And she wanted to pleasure him for him, not to keep him around, not to perform tricks to keep his interest. For him. And for her.

She maintained eye contact as she massaged his balls. Slowly, she licked him from tip to base and back up again.

He swayed, resting his hands on her shoulders, his grip pulsing like he didn't want to squeeze her. She allowed herself a smug smile before flicking her tongue across his wide tip and swirling it around the ridge.

He groaned and circled his hips as if trying to keep up with her movements. She opened her mouth wide and sucked him inside as far as she could.

"Odessa."

She worked his length, keeping her attention on his balls at the same time. They drew up tight, his release near.

Odessa licked and sucked. Bryant's head fell back as she kept him helpless against the pleasure. He tunneled his hands in her hair as much as he could around her ponytail. He didn't jerk on her head, didn't try to control her movements, just held her like he couldn't believe she was doing this for him.

She increased her rhythm, and his hips bucked faster. His

release jerked up his shaft, and he tried to pull away. She was going to get all of him. Firming her grip on his balls, she gave them a slight squeeze.

He roared. Hot jets released into her mouth, but she didn't let up. She worked him until he was spent, and then gave him one last lick.

He shuddered, swaying again. "You're amazing. You didn't have to do that."

She cocked her head at him. Her lips must be puffy and red and damp from his release. And the way he couldn't take his gaze off them? Euphoric.

"I wanted to." For once, that had been her only motivation.

Uncertainty flickered through his gaze before it turned predatory. "You know what I want to do?" he growled, helping her to her feet.

A delighted gasp escaped her. She couldn't wait to find out.

Instead of talking, he showed her. Flipping her back on the bed, she landed with her wings splayed. Bryant came down, not quite on top of her, moving down her body.

"I constantly dream of these long legs wrapped around my neck."

"They were not too long ago, if I remember correctly."

His heavy-lidded stare hovered inches above her sex. "Too long ago. I think I could have you for breakfast, lunch, and dinner."

With that, he opened her legs wider and dropped a kiss on the feverish skin of her sex. "You're wet."

"Because of you," she gasped.

He parted her folds and tongued her clit, not letting up, not pausing. She was about to career over the edge when he backed off.

"What are you doing?" Why didn't he let her finish?

"Playing." He spoke the word against her sensitized clit. She bucked her pelvis off the bed. He chuckled and lapped at her, driving her to the brink before once again backing off.

"Bryant," she cried. "Let me come." Damn, she said she wouldn't beg, but he was driving her crazy.

Her feet were on his shoulders. She clawed at the bedspread and arched her hips into him, searching for the finish she was looking for.

He replaced his tongue with his thumb and inserted two fingers inside of her. She gasped again before moaning her approval. Thumbing her nub while hitting her most sensitive inner spot, he raised up to watch her fly apart.

"Bry-ant!" Her knees had moved farther up with him, opening her even more. Her climax hit.

She cried and shook the entire time she rode her orgasm. He watched her and it was like giving him his own private show.

"You. Are. Stunning." He repeated her words back to her.

Odessa barely had to time to recover when he grabbed her knees, stretching her wide. He looked down to watch himself impale her while her tight channel still quivered.

She only had time to grab onto his shoulders before he started a ruthless pace, pumping hard. With pewter wings flared wide to keep his balance, he watched himself move in and out.

The pressure built again, and she wasn't sure she could take another powerful release so soon. But she trusted Bryant with her body.

His thrusts increased in force, and he grunted each time he pounded into her. "You. Are. Mine." It was like he needed to prove it to himself.

"Yes!" Her nails dug into his shoulders as she crested another impossibly strong orgasm.

He pushed against her knees as he thrust, once, twice,

before watching himself, driven into her up to his balls, release within her thoroughly pleasured body.

When her vision cleared, he was sagging over her, spent.

"Oh no, I scratched you." Mortified, she couldn't ignore the score marks from her fingernails running down his shoulders to his well-defined pecs.

He shrugged. "Don't feel 'em."

She smiled lazily at him and opened her arms for him to fall into. After a moment of indecision, he pulled out and collapsed to her side, folding one wing behind him and intimately draping his other over her.

Snuggling in, she inhaled his scent deep into her lungs. It was mixed with hers, and it felt right.

"We still have time before the others get here," he said.

She turned her head to the side, giving him an incredulous look. "You're ready to go again?"

"With you? Yes."

~

BRYANT CLEARED his throat to get started. All of his team was here, except Jagger, who was with Felicia at her apartment. Something tickled his mind when he thought of Jagger, but it was like a thought he couldn't complete. He gave himself a mental shake. Maybe he should check in on his warrior when they went searching for fallen. The poor bastard might have the hardest assignment of them all.

Odessa hadn't come into the office yet. He'd kept them both too late. It seemed he couldn't get enough of her delectable body, and she met him every step of the way. He had cleaned up quickly, dressing to blend in with humans, and let her have more time to prepare herself for the meeting.

God help him if she wore that dress again. He'd forever

have the image of it drifting down her body seared into his mind.

Finding his team quiet and waiting for him to speak, he realized he'd gotten himself distracted again thinking about his mate's divine curves.

"All right, let's get started."

"I just want to say, boss," Bronx interrupted, "that I'm happy for you."

Harlowe and Dionna nodded, and Sierra and Urban squinted at him as if they were looking for a change. Then they nodded their heads like they'd found the answer.

"Nice," Urban added.

And bugger if it wasn't uncomfortable standing in a room where a bunch of people knew he'd just gotten laid like it was tattooed across his arse. Did he look happier? More relaxed? Glow? They worked so closely together his team just knew.

Bryant felt like he had to say something about it. "She's stuck with me now." Damn if his guilt at trapping her into their sync didn't hover in his statement.

"She's not stuck anywhere," Harlowe said. "She's always been into you. It's not like she hasn't been obvious about it."

Bryant frowned. "What do you mean?"

"Dude." Bronx shook his head. "When she strode into the gala, *like a boss,* and claimed you? Or when she marched into the barracks demanding to know where you were?"

Harlowe chimed in. "You should've heard her when she thought you didn't like her goth getup."

Didn't like it? He'd fucking loved it. Not as much as that sundress...

"Or when she was frantic because she thought she couldn't heal you?" Dionna added.

All the instances his team listed Bryant attributed to Odessa needing him around, wanting his protection. He just couldn't imagine her not regretting her decision when she was finally free of her past.

"I may have missed a lot," Sierra said. "But even I knew she was into you."

"Sorry I'm late." Odessa rushed in.

The drawstring bag was slung over her shoulder and tucked under a wing. Her hair was out of its ponytail. It hadn't been secured well after he'd gotten done with her. The long, glorious locks hung in a loose knot at the back of her head. Her wings were morphed in and she wore blue jeans, a tee, and slip-on shoes. She would blend in beautifully on Earth in their search for fallen.

Blend might be optimistic. No matter what Odessa wore, she would turn heads.

"I was just going to tell them about the plan," he informed her.

She settled next to him with a hesitant smile, blushing, and handed over the bag. He resisted wrapping an arm around her while he filled in the rest of his team about how they were going to split up and search.

"We're sticking to the fallen from the last two centuries. The scrolls say where they were dumped in the human realm, usually in a populated city to attract as little notice as possible. If they perished, their bodies would just be another John Doe. The city is often one they had ties to as an angel. It's the only courtesy shown to them."

Bryant dug out the scrolls.

"I'll go with Odessa. We'll search for two fallen and then check in with her sister." He handed three scrolls to Urban and Dionna, and three to Bronx and Harlowe. "Sierra, you can run the information to us when you have leads. Everyone have their phones?"

They used regular cell phones to communicate when they were split up. It sure beat the days of having to arrange regular shuttles to continually exchange information.

They all nodded. Good. They were almost ready.

"Sierra, what'd you find out on the club owner?"

His tech-savvy warrior straightened, her no-nonsense expression in place. She was the shortest one of the bunch, but for some reason she always reminded him of Harlowe. She was also blond, but kept her hair short and spiky. Her eyes were cornflower blue and she was curvier than Harlowe's more athletic build. Maybe it was their facial structure—heart-shaped faces with full lower lips and high cheekbones.

"His name is Jameson Haddock and there's not much information on him. Nothing that stands out anyway. He has a clean record, and he runs his club legally. I found no history on him other than he had ties to a prominent crime boss in Vegas. Jameson worked for him until he had enough money to purchase his own property and turn it into Fall from Grace. Doesn't seem like he was mentored into the mob way of life, though."

"None of our fallen trace back to Las Vegas, but maybe we'll find out he's one of them. What happened to the guy this Haddock used to work for?"

Sierra shook her head, telling him there was no lead there. "He's dead. Died in his sleep of a heart attack. I couldn't find anything that said he left his money to Haddock, but there is a sizable chunk I couldn't trace anywhere. Either Haddock is truly legit, or he's good enough to keep us off his trail."

"He knew what we were," Odessa spoke up.

"It's possible we stood out or they know their regulars. Maybe someone saw our tattoos and could tell they were fake?" Harlowe didn't sound like she believed it, either.

"He's definitely involved." Bryant knew his intuition

wasn't the only one screaming at him about this Haddock. "We'll find our fallen, then concentrate on the owner."

He waited for his team to descend in case they had any more questions, before turning to Odessa. "Ever been to London?"

CHAPTER 21

*S*andeen's skin still crawled. He was roaming the Gloom, looking for a suitable human body to "borrow" for a few days. After that blond Amazon warrior beat the shit out of his host, he'd popped back to Daemon to recharge his abilities.

He spent as little time as possible in his home world. It wasn't Hell, but that didn't mean it was a friendly place. Numen thought they all ran amuck, wreaking havoc, fighting, and fornicating.

Wrong. Those were hobbies. His kind was more cultured and organized than Numen gave them credit for. To the Numen's defense, no angelic species were able to enter Daemon any more than Daemons could enter Numen. Actually, less so. An angelic creature tainting their realm would cause chaos with creatures suspicious of good deeds being done under the table.

Numen were charged with protecting the human species so they could live long, full lives and enter Heaven. Likewise, Daemon were charged with orchestrating their downfall, paving the way for more souls to get assigned to Hell. And just like Numen, they had a hierarchal society. Maybe with a bit more devastation, humiliation, and, of course, fornication.

Sandeen's sire was one of the most devious demons, over-seeing legions of archmasters. Zadren was sadistic, manipulative, and irreprehensible—a male any son should be proud to call sire. Maybe at one time Sandeen had idolized him, had wanted to learn from the evil master of masters and dominate this realm. Then his sire had killed his puppy.

Never touch another male's dog.

Sandeen had rescued the wolf pup, Hound, from the Gloom when he'd been accidentally dumped there on the coattails of a demon crossing back from the human realm. He'd had big plans to create his own brand of hellhound. The pup had been trained to do tricks and worked his way up to more protective maneuvers. Hound had been an avid learner, intelligent and instinctive. Sandeen planned to try to mate him with another ferocious canine breed. Hell, maybe even one of the more attractive gargoyles.

His plans had come to an abrupt end when his sire dropped by for his annual this-is-how-to-take-over-the-realm lesson. Zadren dropped in on Sandeen, who was fornicating with one of the more humanoid archmasters. His father had thrown the female out the window and started berating Sandeen for his lack of ambition.

Sandeen never won a fight against his sire, so he had learned to take a more logical route. He attempted to elaborate on his plans of forming a new breed of Daemon, a loyal, personal army. Zadren, as always, had thought it was another reason for Sandeen to be weak, an epic fail of a son. Hound had heard them arguing and broke through the door.

Zadren had grabbed Hound by the throat but hadn't killed him. Digging his claws into the raging wolf's neck, he delighted in watching Sandeen's anguish and despair over watching his only friend perish. Then he'd thrown Hound to the floor and stomped on him, flinging Sandeen easily off as he'd tried to intervene.

Sandeen had retracted from Daemon life that day, seeking instead to find an escape in the human world. It was very undemonlike of him to want to avoid pain and despair. Sure, he got the occasional thrill out of it. But he felt like there was more to his long life. He was addicted to the feelings ordinarily forbidden in his realm—enthusiasm, excitement, adventure.

He could crush a million more human souls than he'd already had. Nothing would change. It wouldn't equal being able to walk freely in a realm where he didn't have to worry about recovering from constant familial maiming.

Once he solved the problem of being able to roam among humans in his own body, then he could tackle conquering his own little corner of the world. He could be like one of the ancient pharaohs with harems feeding him clusters of grapes.

Until then, he was back to wandering the Gloom, spying on various humans. Unlike the Mist, the Gloom overlaid the human world. He wasn't a ghost, but an observer.

It was a good way to pass time. He was mostly recovered from his latest bashing. Or attempt at. His sire liked to pair him against some of his finest archmasters, for shits and giggles.

Sandeen cracked his neck. He had been beaten, but not beat. Many demons assumed that just because he didn't get off on killing and destruction, he was weak. He might even aid them in thinking that by nearly throwing his fights.

Wandering through a casino, Sandeen stayed away from the locales on the Strip. Too many out-of-towners. He didn't need anyone to come looking for his host, so he was searching for long-term possession. He liked to stay in the realm and get some work done.

This casino brokered a little too much in the older crowd. He didn't care to inhabit a body plagued with high cholesterol and arthritis, but maybe Sandeen could kill two birds with one stone. As he drifted through the Gloom, he could make out Numen, performing their divine duties of human protection.

And there was one now. Not a warrior, but Sandeen could sense a small blade tucked into the waistband of the male's pants. How the male got his hands on Daemon steel was probably an interesting story Sandeen didn't care about.

He focused on the Numen. Older, possibly centuries old, and the way he was eyeballing the blue-haired ladies punching their slot buttons, he was looking to get physical. His natural angelic charisma was drawing a fair amount of attention.

An idea formed.

He kept following the older angel, watched as he sat and struck up a conversation with an attractive older woman who must have worshipped the sun in her younger days from the thick, dried skin that was deeply creased. They talked and laughed, her deep smoker's rattle cackling at the male's jokes.

Fascinated, Sandeen watched as the angel and the woman wandered through the casino into the adjoining hotel. He could've drawn farther back into the Gloom and wait it out, but he wouldn't be a proper demon if he didn't practice his voyeuristic skills. Who was he if he didn't use his ability to remain in the Gloom while spying on people? Not many of his kind had the same finesse.

Whaddya know? The angel had a hotel room ready that he brought the woman to. Oh yeah, it might give him nightmares to watch an old angel do the horizontal, but Sandeen was going to stick this out.

Some of the male's moves made even Sandeen raise his

eyebrows. Kinky angels. The woman seemed to enjoy it. Sandeen waited, hoping his gamble paid off, that the angel would drift off while the woman snoozed.

Their races were similar in their increased sex drive and stamina. Sandeen hoped the male would take advantage of a willing female and keep her around as long as possible. Sometimes it was an arduous task to find a new partner, starting a new hunt with each new host. Not that many demons had enough patience to find willing partners. Ever the black sheep, Sandeen preferred to demonstrate his superiority over the female's body by eventually getting her to turn over complete control to him for hours on end. Or prove what he was made of in two minutes or less, whatever the situation called for.

To Sandeen's relief, after an hour making the woman scream in passion until her voice broke, the male laid down next to her, eventually falling asleep.

Concentrating hard, Sandeen targeted the woman. After her exertion, she'd be weakened, both physically, and perhaps mentally. After what Sandeen had just seen, her mental guards *should* be weakened.

She resisted. Most did. But she was tired, broke, and had let a man she just met have his way with her. And God help her, she hoped he'd do it again. Sandeen shuddered and ignored her pleas to her lord. He shushed her soul's worries. His intent wasn't a targeted evil at the woman. He just wanted to use her for a little errand.

With a deep breath, her body gave in and he entered, molding himself into her petite form. It wasn't the first time he'd inhabited a woman, sometimes the circumstances called for it. Each time was a bit disconcerting. The emotional roller coaster, the extra flesh in places he wasn't accustomed to, and not enough flesh in places he was. Remembering to sit down to pee was the hardest adjustment.

Rolling deftly out of bed, he grabbed the lamp from the nightstand. The angel woke at the movement.

Time to move.

Sandeen grabbed the bedside lamp and swung. The base whacked the side of the male's head. He went limp and Sandeen found the discarded pile of the angel's clothing and sifted through them.

Ultimate score.

Not one, but two blades. One a small weapon resembling a switchblade. That one would go to Jameson. The other, a four-inch curved blade. It was small but wicked and effective. That one he would keep for himself. He had a few ideas regarding Numen weaponry and Jameson's blood and couldn't wait to test them. Like Jameson, Sandeen suspected there were other uses for them since their gear could cross through all the realms.

He worked on dressing his host's body but gave up after fumbling with the bra. How did they get their arms to bend back like that? His host was old enough that her breasts hung low and flat. He'd just cross his arms or something. Once he was presentable, he tucked the weapon under his shirt and left.

He'd need to find a new host, definitely a dude, but not until he got far away from here. Then he could make an exchange with Jameson—the blade for some blood—and get to experimenting.

～

"THIS IS WHERE THEY DROP THEM?" Odessa wrapped her sweater tighter around herself, looking around at the dismal setting.

It was chilly in the evenings in London at this time of year. Bryant had planted them as close as he could to the area

229

where the fallen had been dumped. Then, using his knowledge of London's transit system, he got them even closer. They walked the rest of the way, which helped keep her warm.

Bryant was wearing the same clothes as when he had found her at the store, and somehow managed to look even better. The brim of his ball cap was pulled down. He must walk like that whenever he was in the human realm.

"If he spent a lot of time here, yeah. This bloke was a warrior that set off an explosion when confronting a possession. He didn't do his homework, went in for the kill, but the demon had been waiting for him. The fallen lost his wings about five years ago."

Odessa shuddered, and it wasn't from the cold. "That could happen to any of you."

"No, it couldn't." Bryant said it with such confidence it didn't sound arrogant. "If a warrior does the proper investigation and recon, they know exactly when to confront the demon and where to do it."

Bryant's statement brought up a question Odessa'd had since she'd known him. After his chilly treatment of her, she hadn't dared ask. Maybe their relationship was at a place where he'd open up to her.

Might as well try.

"Bryant, why did you have a sync gala?"

"The director was going to take me off duty otherwise."

Odessa gave him a sharp look. Yeah, he'd told her that before. "Why?"

Bryant's lips thinned. "Because I probably would've been another scroll in the bucket. I was getting careless, cutting corners, putting humans at risk."

Odessa wanted to ask why again, but waited.

"I was…angry." He shrugged. "About everything."

Odessa's heart wrenched. "Losing your mate?"

"Yes. No. I don't know. It's weird, I guess. I didn't know her, but her death was my fault." He adjusted his cap and shoved his hand into his coat pocket. Talking about this was uncomfortable. "I know it was an accident and all that nonsense, but she stopped dead on a busy street when she saw my face."

"She lived on Earth, Bryant. It's not like in Numen, where we all look like we're on covers of humans' magazines. Earth has variety. People are different, scarred, missing limbs, unable to use limbs. Humans don't heal completely. They have acne scars, pierced everything, bad hair days. She wouldn't have still lived on Earth if she didn't see the beauty in that. Maybe she stopped because she didn't want to leave. Maybe she stopped because she wasn't ready to commit to a mate for centuries. Maybe she was scared she wasn't strong enough to heal you. You don't know why she did what she did."

Bryant considered her words for a moment, but resolutely shook his head. "She acted the same as everyone in Numen."

Odessa didn't want to let him get away with thinking the worst, but she didn't have much for rebuttal. They could be a vain race.

"Perhaps those people are acting more like my father when he sent me and Felicia off to school. He moved out of the mansion when mother…"—dammit they were being honest here—"killed herself."

How liberating. Their people said "walked into the fire." That made it sound so serene, so brave. In her mother's case, it wasn't. She had run from her problems and never returned. Perhaps Bryant's first destined mate had done the same thing. Perhaps not, but he couldn't take the blame any more than Odessa could.

She feathered her fingers over the scars on his cheeks.

"They don't like being confronted with evidence that we have vulnerabilities and bad things can happen to us, so they choose to look the other way. I finally had to realize I had done nothing wrong. The problem was with my parents and how they chose to help me and Felicia, which was by not helping us. Just like there's nothing wrong with how you look. The issue is with the asshats that turn the other way."

His mouth twitched. "Asshats?"

"I learned a few things at the children's store."

Humor lit his face.

His phone vibrated. End of conversation, but at least she'd said her part.

He checked the screen. "Sierra sent a picture of the fallen we're looking for. He must've gotten into some trouble because he's in the human system. She found his name, Gregor Franklin, in a London Police database. Fallen don't tend to change their name, it's the only thing they have left."

"Is the address close by?"

Bryant punched it into the map app. "A few blocks away."

He clasped her hand, and they headed in the direction the map showed. She wanted to smile to herself. He didn't seem to notice that he'd automatically reached for her. Bryant Vale wasn't a male predisposed to PDAs, and while he tried to maintain his distance around her, he couldn't stop himself. Odessa rather liked that. Especially since he hadn't lost the undercurrent of tension, like he was waiting on her eventual rejection of him. She would have to prove that, like him, she couldn't help herself, either. And if she could, she wouldn't want to.

A square brick building was where the pin on the app had pointed them.

"A homeless shelter." An angel living among the humans with no home. Her kind helped people like this; they didn't become them. Logically, she understood that the angel had lost his wings for a reason, but it was just so…final. Devastating.

Bryant studied their surroundings before entering. Odessa expected a dark, dingy corridor lined with hopeless mounds of sleeping homeless, but the place had a softly lit, clean entry. A young woman and male, close to Odessa's age, chatted idly in an office close to the front door.

They stopped when they noticed Bryant and Odessa. The woman smiled politely. "How can I help you?"

Bryant took the lead, flashing the picture on his phone. "We're looking for my uncle. Last heard he might be here."

The woman peered at the picture. "Looks like Frankie, yeah?" she asked her coworker.

The guy took his turn studying the picture. "That must be an old picture, but I'd say that's Frankie."

"Is he here?" Bryant asked.

The two workers exchanged a look. The woman cleared her throat. "I'm sorry to tell you, he passed away several months ago. Died of exposure."

"Tragedy." Bryant's response was brusque, with a touch of sadness. "I thought I'd try to help him one more time, but I'm too late."

The male stood to shake his hand. "It's still nice to see the poor bloke had someone who cared. He seemed so lost and alone."

They were here because they cared all right—cared to make sure the fallen wasn't planning to amass an army for attack. "Frankie" made a mistake, and it cost him everyone and everything. Guilt ate at Odessa. Frankie wasn't the fallen they were looking for. He'd suffered and died.

Bryant thanked the employees for their help, commented on the importance of their work, and towed her out of the building. Once they were back out in the chilly night air, he led her back in the direction they had come.

"The next one was also dropped in London, so hopefully we don't need to go far."

Bryant wasn't going to dwell on the tragic end to Mr. Franklin. Odessa wouldn't forget the fallen, but she had to move on.

If only it were that easy.

The street they were on was quiet, only a few people littering the sidewalk. They'd gone about a block when he steered her into a hidden nook between two buildings.

"What's wrong?" he asked.

She was surprised he'd noticed her mood. "It's just that... That poor warrior..."

"A lot of fallen give up. Some can't take not living as an angel. Many can't figure out how to gather resources and survive down here. Maybe a demon saw he was a weak target. To them a fallen Numen is better than no Numen."

"What would you do if you fell?" The possibility was real. Her kind fell. Bryant had admitted how close he'd been to making a fatal mistake that could've cost him his wings.

Bryant responded with a question. "What would *you* do if I fell?"

Odessa blinked. Bryant was too good to fall. "Find you and beat you for messing up and leaving me."

He chuckled. She got to see his smile again, no matter how limited it was.

He cupped her face, his thumb stroking her cheek. "You surprise the hell out of me, Odessa."

She turned her face into his hand, enjoying the touch of his skin. He brought his lips to hers for a tender kiss she eagerly returned.

The kiss was deepening when they heard a shout from across the street. "Crikey, get a room!"

Bryant broke the kiss and glanced at the shouter. It originated from a group of young males laughing and weaving down the sidewalk away from them.

He pulled his phone out. "I'm going to update Sierra."

He wrapped his free arm around her while he sent the message. She assumed it was so they couldn't be seen so easily by the next group of passersby. They may not be as harmless as the last. But she hoped it was because he wanted to hold her close.

When he was done, he looked around. The street was empty.

"Come on. I have a place to wait." He whisked them away.

CHAPTER 22

*L*anding on the deck of a darkened flat, Bryant waited for Odessa's questions.

She spun slowly around, taking in the small unit containing well-used, mismatched furniture. Nearly the whole apartment could be viewed in a full turn, from the tiny galley kitchen to the bedroom that barely held more than a queen mattress.

"Yours?" she asked.

"My parents keep it for me so I always have an empty place to descend to in an emergency. The landing is narrow and not good for relaxing, but it's perfect for a Numen." He shrugged out of his coat and held his hand out for her sweater. He hoped she wouldn't mind staying here while they waited for information about where to go next. His place wasn't a mansion. "When I'm forced to take vacation, I stay here."

Odessa cast a knowing look his way and handed over her sweater. The tee underneath plastered against her breasts. He could barely look away.

"Not for sex." He interpreted her expression, and she

lifted a brow. "It wouldn't do me any good if a woman came searching for me and saw me wandering around with my wings hanging out."

Odessa gave a theatrical gasp. "Bryant Vale leaves his wings hanging out on Earth?"

He scowled at her, dangerously close to cracking another smile. He seemed to be doing that a lot around her without even trying.

"Go ahead and bust your own set out if you need to. The blinds are drawn and we're five stories up anyway." He checked his phone. "Sierra said she needs a little time to research the next fallen, but she's onto something."

"Have the others made any progress yet?" Odessa asked, going to the kitchen cabinets.

She must be searching for food. He should've taken her someplace better.

"Nothing yet. We lucked out."

He winced at how callous his words sounded. The incident had shaken Odessa up. Bryant knew the drill. If a warrior was smart, they had a fallback plan. Demons could be tricky and goad warriors into acts that cost them their wings. The longer an angel was a warrior, the more they thought they were indestructible. Arrogance had cost more than one. No, if he fell, he had his flat and some money stashed away. He wouldn't be Frankie.

Opening the fridge, Odessa looked inside. She peered at the containers. "When was the last time you were here?"

"Before the gala. Why?"

"I think you need to do a clean sweep in the fridge. There's some pretty fuzzy food."

Ah, damn. His parents checked on the place, but he stocked it with food. With Odessa, he didn't know how often he'd come back.

He'd missed his tiny flat. The barracks had been adequate,

and he'd been around his team, but this was the only home he'd had for years. It saddened him to think he'd hardly ever hang out here again.

"I like it here," she announced, as if she'd read his mind.

Closing the fridge door after she pulled out a couple bottles of water and set them on the counter. Her attention turned back to the cupboards until she found a box of unopened crackers.

"You like London?" he asked for clarification.

Odessa sat on the sofa and dished out the spread like it was a romantic dinner. Crackers and water. He should have more to offer her.

"Both. I'd love to see London during the day, but I like this place." She waved around the small flat. "I didn't catch the view when we landed."

Since they both still had their wings morphed, Bryant opened the drapes. "It's spectacular."

With an excited inhale, Odessa jumped up and ran to stand next to him. "Oh, it's beautiful. Just like all the stars we see at home, but lower."

He might not have much to give, but he could give her this. Pinpricks of glow coming through the window danced over her face.

She smiled over at him and his heart stuttered. Breathtaking.

"Let's have our crackers and get some rest."

His cock twitched in response, because her sexy smile suggested there'd be more to their rest than sleeping.

Hell, yes. He needed to rest.

BRYANT'S PHONE RANG, waking him to the pleasant feeling of a lush bottom snuggled into his side. He grabbed his cell off the end table and sat up so he could sound more businesslike. Not like he'd just been thoroughly sexed by the most beautiful creature he'd ever laid eyes on.

"Hey, boss," Sierra greeted. "I figured this deserved a call."

"Tell me what you've got." Bryant put the phone on speaker so Odessa, who had woken from his movement, could hear, too.

Sierra cleared her throat. He could picture her in the little apartment she kept in Manhattan, with her booted feet propped up on her desk, her cargo pants untucked. Her face would be lit by the three large monitors she liked to do her hacking on, and a Bluetooth would be secured in her ear. She was a talented computer expert. Bryant didn't always share the extent of her abilities with Director Richter.

"I could find nothing of Junie Perez. I mean, nothing since her fall eleven years ago. But check it. Her mate, Mathias Perez, has a house not far from where she was dumped."

Interesting. Bryant had a few questions but knew better than to interrupt Sierra. It usually earned him a caustic remark.

"Did he have the place before or after she lost her wings?" Sierra echoed his unspoken question. "Before. Get this. He's a chaperone, yet he had money saved up and claimed they were going to buy a house before she lost her wings. He said they were going to do missionary work on their downtime. But *after* she fell, he purchased it anyway."

Junie Perez had been an excellent warrior, but she fell into a trap a savvy archmaster had set for her. She sprung the trap, which killed the demon's host and his entire family. Her fall had hit all the warriors hard, reminding them that even good angels could make irrevocable mistakes.

"I'll send you the addy and an image straight off Google maps. Dude's still a chaperone. Once you think about it, it can be a work-from-home job. He doesn't need to be in Numen to get the message a soul needs transport. His records say he was too distraught after losing his mate, he had to create some distance from the home they had made together."

Losing wings severed the mating bond. Odessa still had one out if she needed to cut ties with him. He'd sacrifice his wings for her. He wouldn't make her stay with him if she was miserable.

"Thanks, Sierra." Disconnecting, he said, "We need to rent a car."

~

ODESSA SPOTTED the little cottage at the edge of small village outside of London.

"This is the place." Bryant found a spot to park.

Sierra's directions had been exceptional, and they'd driven right to it. It wasn't her first car ride, but Odessa hadn't realized how...sexy...it could be to ride in a car with a male that could handle it. Like, really handle it. He was comfortable driving on the left side of the road. She wondered if, since he'd grown up here, he did as well driving on the right, or if he was ambidextrous that way.

Odessa mentally snorted. It was Bryant. Of course he was confident driving anything, anywhere.

Even though they were going on a hunch, Odessa was afraid of what they might find. After Frankie, an empty, depressed cottage would bother her more. She hadn't expected good news from investigating fallen, but the sadness piled up.

Urban and Harlowe reported the two fallen from their search hadn't survived. The third fallen they were searching for had three jobs trying to afford an apartment in the city he was dumped in. Bronx and Dionna had only found one of theirs—a former analyst, to Odessa's surprise. She had fallen because she'd purposely dictated a watcher's notes incorrectly out of jealousy. It had caused several human injuries. That fallen had bought a black-market ID, got herself a decent job, and was living a good life—in the state pen, for embezzlement. The two warriors were searching for their second fallen but suspected he had met with a similar life.

"If she's here, are you going to turn her mate in?" Odessa asked.

Bryant didn't answer her question, but his mouth flattened. She knew the answer. Her kind was forbidden from aiding a fallen and Mathias giving his former mate a home would be a grievous violation.

She was about to push him for a reason why, the couple probably wasn't hurting anyone, when he said, "Bugger all, there's kids."

Odessa whipped her head around to look. Two young kids ran into the front yard to play. She was terrible at guessing children's ages, but from her time working in the kiddy store, she would estimate them be about five and eight years old.

"Did he re-mate?" She should be relieved that Bryant wouldn't have to report Mathias. But to move on after losing a mate? She heard it happened. Did he have to do it near the city his fallen mate had been dumped?

A woman with long, black hair strode out of the cottage. She headed down the walk, gesturing for the kids to follow her. The woman was identical to the picture Sierra had sent of Junie Perez. A male followed behind, Mathias Perez, and the family held hands toward the market uptown.

Odessa and Bryant were both stunned into silence.

"That's one badass male," Odessa said in stark appreciation. "Matthias Perez is secretly raising a family with his fallen mate."

"Those kids can't be hers." Bryant's finger flew as he punched in information to send to Sierra.

"I've heard fallen can't reproduce, but is there anyone that actually tracks that?"

"I've got Sierra on it. The kids don't really look like them, but that doesn't always mean anything."

"Perhaps they adopted." Numen had the means to forge human paperwork.

They sat for several minutes in their shock. The family meandered back to their cottage, their errand done, happy and laughing, swinging kids around.

Odessa asked her question again. "Are you going to report them?"

Bryant's phone vibrated, saving him from having to answer again. "She found info with their names. They go to school and everything. Her thought is they were taken off the street, unofficially adopted by the Perezes. She suspects Junie would've stayed away for a while, years maybe, to make sure anyone checking in on Mathias would think he was doing exactly what he said. She might've lived in the shelters, with Mathias's help."

Bryant put his phone away. "I have to tell Director Richter," he finally admitted.

Odessa's heart sank. She couldn't stand to see the beautiful family ripped apart in any way. Not any more than they had been.

"But," he continued, "while this is going on, he might have to set the case aside. You know, then it might get shuffled under other work, and who knows, forgotten for a while."

Hope rose. "The director would do that?"

"My gut tells me she's not 'the tall, dark, handsome type' the gnome described, so he might. He's not heartless."

Bryant's thoughtful tone didn't inspire the most confidence. The director was far from heartless, but he was all about duty.

"It's an excellent plan," she uttered quietly. "One mistake ruined her life, but she rebuilt it."

"A smart warrior would. I have my plan. If I fall, I'll be fine. I have my flat. And you'd be able to move on and wait for your destined mate."

He said it so definitively, Odessa was taken aback. "I've only known you for a few weeks, but I know I couldn't just *move on.*"

"Odessa—" Bryant started in a placating tone.

"No, don't start that with me. I believe in us. You don't seem to." Her anger and irritation rose at his hard-headedness. "Unlike a destined mate, I got to chose you. We knew each other better when we sealed our bond than most synced couples do. And I've seen plenty of synced couples living in misery with their mates. Couples that quit trying. Several societies in the human world use arranged marriages, and many of them are successful. I like you. A lot. I don't know what else to do to get that through to you."

All she could do was watch his profile, and since they were in a car in England, it was his scarred side she stared at. For a while during their drive, he had hunched over the wheel and tipped his head in an attempt to get his cap to shadow his face. Eventually, he had lost his self-consciousness. At the moment, he seemed to be making a point presenting her with what he considered his worst side.

"When you don't need my protection anymore, you might very well think differently," he finally said. "And it's okay. You never have to be stuck with me."

Odessa opened her mouth to say something, then clamped down. He was so. Damn. Frustrating. "How about this? You wait until I don't need your protection before you decide how I'll feel. Give me a chance to show you."

He remained maddingly calm as he stared straight ahead. "What if that's not until years from now?"

"Then I guess we'll have a lot of sex until then."

Bryant let out a startled sound like a cough. "Shite, Odessa. You're never what I expect."

"Good. Now, should we return this rental and go to the U.S. to see my sister?"

CHAPTER 23

*B*ryant held Odessa's hand as the cab pulled up to Felicia's apartment. The sun was high in the sky and the temperature approached three digits. By the time they'd gotten the rental car back, it was evening and the sun was sinking low in the sky. Here in Atlanta, sunshine was going full force. They had arrived at a place Bryant used when he had to travel here. All warriors had a spot in most large cities. Then they'd flagged a car.

He and Odessa spilled out and entered the building with the code Sierra had given them. Once they reached Felicia's place, Bryant rapped on the door and called, "It's me."

The door swung open to a glowering warrior. He looked just as pissed as he did when Bryant last saw him.

"Jagger," Bryant greeted.

"Boss." He sounded just as upset.

Odessa had messaged her sister, letting them know when they'd be arriving. Felicia was nowhere to be seen. Loud music boomed from behind a closed door down the hallway along with random sounds, like muffled hits.

"Is Filly in here?" Odessa headed in the direction of the music.

"Yep." Jagger didn't look in the direction of the noise. "She holes up in there for a good few hours at a time. Best part of my day."

Bryant lifted an eyebrow toward the male. "What's she doing in there?"

"Hitting shit. Thinks she's some kind of fighter." Jagger made a *pffft* sound. "Whatever."

"Have you ever seen her in there? Ever sparred with her?"

"Nope." He brushed his blond hair off his forehead and reclined back against the sofa.

"You should. Find out what she really does know." Felicia wasn't wasting time in her workout hole, not from the way she handled herself training Odessa.

Jagger's mouth twisted like he couldn't believe Felicia would know anything. "She might *think* she knows a lot."

"And it's your job as her guardian to know what skills she does and doesn't have."

A chagrined look crossed the male's face. He knew what he should be doing and knew his feelings toward Felicia were clouding his judgment.

"Got it, boss."

A spark of doubt niggled at Bryant. Was Jagger the best choice for this assignment?

"'Sup, bro?" Felicia strode down the hallway, Odessa trailing her.

Bryant inclined his head in greeting to his newest family member. Felicia was glowing with perspiration and wearing only a purple sports bra and neon yellow running shorts. Her brassy locks were secured in a sloppy twist behind her head. He glanced at Jagger, but the male was glaring out the window.

Things were going to get worse between the pair before

they got better. Jagger didn't like it, but he'd do his job. But would he do it well enough?

"Have you had any problems here? Suspicious activity?" Bryant's gaze vacillated between the both of them.

Felicia shook her head and wandered into the kitchen for some water. Odessa crossed to his side.

"Not a thing," Jagger replied.

Felicia called from the kitchen. "No one knows about this place. Except for you guys."

"What about your dad?" Bryant asked. He despised the male, but he didn't believe Kreger would intentionally hurt his family. Yet, it was still a potential security leak if someone was watching Senator Montclaire to get to his daughters.

"Father can suck it."

That was a no.

Jagger snorted and shook his head. He made no effort to hide his derision for the way Felicia talked about her dad. Bryant understood why she wouldn't want to tell anyone about her traumatic past, but he wished she would confide in Jagger. Maybe he'd be less of an asshole.

Odessa spoke up before her sister confronted Jagger about his attitude. "We think we might be closer to finding out who the one in this realm is, the one responsible for amassing a human following for Daemon possession."

Jagger sat forward, his hands folded over his knees. Felicia came out from around the bar that separated the kitchen from the living area and leaned against the wall, sipping from her glass. Bryant filled them in on the watcher's death and the fate of her body. He told them about the club, and how they researched the archives for the fallen who was responsible for Magan's death. During his speech, Jagger grew still, his face tight.

When he was finished, there was silence. Even Felicia watched Jagger closely.

"So...who's the poor bastard that had to find my father?" Jagger's question landed like a bomb between all of them.

Odessa frowned and she glanced at Bryant. Felicia paused with her glass halfway to her mouth.

Son.

Of a.

Bitch.

His gut had *told* him something was wrong, something was missing. How did he not notice? One of his own team had a father who fell—and whose name wasn't in the bin.

Jagger's father fell decades ago, and he'd diligently worked on separating himself from that scandalous part of his life. All of them had—for Jagger's sake. Fallen were never spoken about, and it was encouraged they be forgotten all together. Association of any sort could result in their own loss of wings.

The answer was in front of their noses, and they'd all looked beyond it—a consequence of their upbringing. Fallen are forgotten. Or his team had assumed Bryant was either discreetly handling the check on Jagger's father—or that Jagger was already in the know and they were fine looking the other way.

Bryant ran a hand over his scalp. "No wonder all of us hit dead ends." The remaining fallen his team had tracked down had all either expired, or were barely scraping by. "Fuck."

Jagger stood slowly. "You don't think my father had anything to do with the murder, do you?"

Bryant faced his teammate. Disbelief was etched in Jagger's features. The warrior didn't think his father capable, but then, he had a skewed opinion of the man he'd grown up adoring. Disbelief wasn't the only emotion warring in Jagger's expression. Anger that they would think of accusing his father, and horrified that it might very well be true.

"His scroll was missing." That by itself was telling. Why

was it gone? Had it been destroyed? And by whom? Bryant didn't think Jagger was involved. His reaction was too visceral, too hurt.

Jagger abruptly sat back down. "He was a liar and a cheat. Being a murderer wouldn't be a stretch." His tone was morose, withdrawn.

"What was your father's name?" Odessa asked gently.

"James Hancock."

Bryant and Odessa exchanged a look. Fuck. It was bad enough they had a fallen that had figured out how to enter the Mist and kill Numen. He might be the earthly mastermind behind the whole thing.

"What?" Jagger asked, catching the exchange.

"The club owner's name is Jameson Haddock. It's…very similar," Odessa said softly. Jagger realized the rest on his own. His father was working with demons.

The play of emotions across the young warrior's face made Bryant want to hunt Jameson Haddock down just for destroying his son all over again. No kid should have to live through that mess once. Jagger was facing it twice. Only, if Jameson was behind all this, his fate would be permanent.

Bryant squatted down next to him. "Do you want to come with us and search for him?"

The warrior had to watch a parent lose his wings and then grow up under that shadow. No one spoke of his father, probably not even his mother. For years, Numen had probably avoided Jagger, like falling might rub off on them. The warrior had thought he reached a point where it was all left behind. He had earned respect of his own, only to find out his father fell to become a murderer of their kind.

The muscle in Jagger's jaw flexed. It was a chance to see his dad, a chance to right the wrong his father had done. Bryant knew Jagger. In his mind, it would also prove undeniably that he came from regrettable parentage.

"No." Jagger inhaled sharply, his nostrils flaring. "I can't chance taking Felicia near him." He added in a hard tone, "Knowing how they both are."

Odessa gasped.

Shock crossed Felicia's face before it clouded with pain and anger. "You think I would throw myself at your father?"

She slammed her glass down on the bar and stormed to her room. Odessa chased after her, throwing a heated look back at Jagger.

Jagger ground his jaw, his gaze on the floor in front of him.

Bryant tried to control his disappointment in Jagger. The male was hurting, furious, and he'd lashed out at Felicia for it. "I get you're going through some shit right now. Just know, you have *no* idea what that female has been through. Be a better male than your father and treat her with some respect."

Jagger's angry gaze met his with a dirty glare. "It's hard when neither one deserves any respect."

Bryant got it. He did. His first few minutes after meeting Felicia gave him insight on how she'd lived her life. He also knew about the attack and what she suffered, Jagger didn't.

"Have you ever done anything stupid and at the time, you had a damn good reason?"

"What my father did wasn't naïve stupidity."

"I'm not talking about James Hancock. He was old enough to know better and held a position in government that made it unforgivable. Felicia was a troubled young girl when you knew her last. She lied, yes. But I doubt she's the only one that's lied when it comes to her." Bryant let him think about that.

Jagger's pale brows drew together. "Are you saying you believe the rumors regarding her aren't true?"

Well...probably not all of them. "I'm saying it's possible

some of them may be nothing more than boastful locker room talk."

Jagger sighed and ran a hand through his hair, swiping it off his forehead. "Fine. I'll be nice…er."

Nicer. That was better than calling her a slut that would sleep with the plotting, murdering father of her guardian.

"I'll keep you updated on what we find out. I need to get Odessa and find this Jameson Haddock."

SANDEEN WANDERED along the Strip in Las Vegas, a curved Daemon blade tucked into his side. Jameson had been only slightly pleased with the tiny little blade Sandeen had handed him. Then Sandeen had held out an empty vial that would hold a good few milliliters of Jameson's fallen blood.

Something told Sandeen that Jameson wasn't an ordinary fallen. He might not have his wings, but he wasn't merely fallen. He hoped his blood would still contain some of the properties that made Numen special.

Jameson's lips had thinned, but he had used the Daemon blade to nick his wrist. He allowed several drops to fill the vial, his bright chartreuse eyes challenging.

"Are you going to drink it?" Jameson had asked accusingly.

Sandeen had shrugged ominously. The question hadn't offend him like it was meant to.

Angels might not drink blood, but for demons, it meant the fight was over. Or just beginning.

For the first test, Sandeen had kept it simple and polished his new curved blade with Jameson's blood. The test would be to find a way to slice a possessed host, or even better, an angel. A Numen wouldn't go running to his father and tattle that Sandeen was hunting his own. Any angel he took on, he'd have to kill, and he'd need to do it sparingly. It wouldn't do to have Numen completely on guard—more than they were when it came to his kind.

Still, Sandeen was determined to find out what a little Haddock blood could do. Looking up, he spotted the perfect scenario.

Ah, so sweet.

A tourist, an overweight middle-aged balding man, who had come to participate in the kinds of activities that would stay in Vegas, had unwittingly opened himself to an archmaster. The master was careening down the Strip, looking for a good time while he had the power to hold the man's body at will.

The demon was terribly oblivious to the warrior trailing him, diligent in his pursuit. Sandeen didn't recognize the warrior, but he recognized the type. Gritty, determined, willing to go to any lengths to succeed. Sandeen would bet—and did often—that the warrior would be daring enough to grab the demon out of the human's body in a dark corner, parking garage, or bathroom. Places that were usually too public and too risky.

It'd be a great setup for Sandeen's experiment.

The warrior was intent on his prey, unaware of the good-looking thirtyish-year-old man with a solid build that Sandeen was inhabiting. After Sandeen had secured his weapons and a place to reside while he carried out his earthly duties, he had gone to a local gym. He needed a new body, a younger one.

There were a lot of defeated souls in a gym. Men and women who realized they couldn't beat time. They clung to their youth, regretting the damage they had done to their bodies back when they thought they knew all the answers. Men and women bombarded by media and the image of a perfect body since their young, nubile minds could watch TV or read a magazine. Those individuals were almost panicked in their efforts, their inner dialogue rough and harsh toward themselves.

Then there were the vain spirits that swaggered around like they owned the place. They defined today's image of perfection. Those people thought others must be running, stepping, yoga-ing their way to look just like them. It was an environment rich with youth, desperation, nasty thoughts, and, more importantly for Sandeen, beautiful people that got laid.

He had taken over a human's body after the man had lured a fortyish married woman into the sauna. Sandeen waited patiently in the Gloom until the man was distracted, then he thrust the soul aside and captured the body to finish the ride. Then he walked away from the woman and found his new body's locker. He grabbed a shower, threw on the man's jeans and shirt, and pocketed the wallet to go hit the Strip.

The paunchy, possessed male the warrior was following dived into an obnoxiously loud casino. The dude would be better off finding whatever he was looking for out on the street—drugs, private strip shows, fetish clubs. But after they entered, the guy made a beeline for the bathroom.

Fucking perfect.

The warrior was going to make his move. Probably follow the guy into a stall and slam him out of the human into the Mist. Sandeen had to catch up to them before that happened.

The warrior disappeared into the bathroom, Sandeen trotted to catch up. The warrior's snarl of "get the fuck out" carried through the door as a couple of frightened men rushed out. Sandeen burst through the door in time to see the warrior catching the stall door before it shut behind the possessed guy. The warrior glanced back to see who had entered, then looked away. Just as quickly he was spinning around again, sensing Sandeen's presence in the host.

Sandeen rushed him, grateful the bathroom stalls were empty and no one was at the urinals. The possessed human shoved his stall door closed, bumping the unsuspecting warrior, who was intent on Sandeen.

An anonymous slaying would be better, but this would have to do. With a grim smile, Sandeen palmed his blade and struck. The warrior jumped back, hissing at the sting of the blade on his upper arm and drawing his own weapon. He lunged forward, his lips moving as he was saying the incantation to remove a demon from a host and toss his ass into the Mist.

Oh shit.

If Sandeen was thrown into the Mist, he'd lose his body, and he didn't know if he could get back. He had no doubt he would win in a fight. But the complications it would create were undesirable.

Unfortunately, the archmaster peeked out to check what was going on. Seeing Sandeen had taken the focus off him, he ran out, shoving Sandeen into the warrior. The angel blade tumbled from Sandeen's hand.

Fuck me. Sandeen was jerked out of his host. Stumbling into the coolness of the Mist, he quickly righted himself. He was in his own body, so he flared his deadly black wings and faced the warrior.

The warrior's lip curled and he spit on the ground. Sandeen didn't care to kill angels, a feeling in itself that could destroy him in Daemon. It was just that he usually had other things he wanted to do than the stark murdering of creatures. But this angel was different. Sandeen would almost wager there were a few deeds under the angel's wings that perhaps his superiors would find interesting. Thinking of Jameson and his contact in Numen, Sandeen amended his previous thought. Perhaps the angel's superiors were taking advantage of it.

Baring his fangs in a hiss, Sandeen wished he still had the blade tucked in his palm. He dove at the warrior the same time the warrior lunged for him. They met in a clash of wings. Sandeen sliced the face of the warrior with his claws, earning him a satisfying grunt of pain.

They grappled, punching and kneeing, and in Sandeen's case, biting, each other. In the mess of limbs and protecting his organs, Sandeen knocked the long knives out the warrior's hands, but not before losing some hunks of flesh from his forearms and feathers from his wings. Sandeen cracked the male on the side of the head with a wing. The warrior staggered to the side. Sandeen grabbed his wings, yanking him around in a stronghold to twist and break as many bones as he could.

A cry of anguish ripped from the warrior and he fell to his knees. Sandeen expected him to ascend. Was the pain too debilitating?

Sandeen kicked him in the kidneys, making him face-plant into the ground. The warrior scrambled for one of his blades that lay nearby and rolled, wincing as he crushed his damaged wings. Sandeen landed on top of the male to wrestle the weapon away. Playing dirty, he used his weight to put more pressure on the warrior's wings, knowing it was excruciating.

"I—" The warrior gasped, confusion rippling over his features. "Can't. Ascend."

Noted.

They played a grim tug of war over the knife. The warrior's strength was dwindling while Sandeen still had plenty left in the tank.

Thank you, Dad, for all the practice, he thought wryly.

Getting the blade free, he drew it swiftly across the

warrior's throat. He grabbed the vial of angel fire out of the male's waistband, and jumped up. That fact that warriors carried the fire on them was a testament to their skill. Pouring the contents out and risking getting a drop on their skin could mean it spreading and taking off a hand. Yet they used it on every demon they vanquished. Repeatedly exposing themselves to its devastation.

Popping the top and tipping it over on the warrior, he stepped back to watch the effects. Instant disintegration. At least neither race suffered under its full effects. Partial effects, now that was a different story. Numen and Daemon alike couldn't heal from angel fire wounds.

With the warrior vanquished, Sandeen thought back to the fight. Why didn't the warrior ascend, even if he moved only a few feet away? The nuances of Numen travel weren't well known by his own kind, but this male was a warrior. They were masters of ascension, using the skill in fights and not just traveling realm to realm.

But the warrior made it sound like he couldn't at all. From his wounds? No, it couldn't have been. Sandeen had damaged enough Numen wings to know they could still transcend, even all busted up. The only difference? The angel had been scored with fallen blood.

Hmmm.

Sandeen had no wish to spend any more time in the Mist, so he wandered to the edge. He was still by the bathroom his disoriented former host was in, though it was harder to see than if he'd been in the Gloom. But Sandeen could make out his host standing at the sink, water dripping from his face as he peered into the mirror. No doubt trying to figure out how the hell he ended up in a casino bathroom. The human had found the knife but left it laying on the side of the sink.

Sandeen smirked. Confused and disbelieving and previously inhabited.

Perfect.

The fight with the warrior had been brutal, but not enough to drain Sandeen. If he had a body to possess right away, he was a powerful enough archmaster to leave the Mist without piggybacking on an angel.

He picked up the other weapon the angel had dropped during their battle and compared them. Two dirks, identical, except one was coated in the angel's cooling blood and the other was stained with Sandeen's blood, an obsidian feather still stuck to the hilt.

Stepping forward, he prepared to invade the human's body again. A curious thing happened instead. Instead of dematerializing and shoving his host's soul aside, he stepped right out of the Mist.

The human's pupils constricted at the dark, horned form standing behind him. Sandeen thought it was an illusion, but even he could see himself in the mirror. Blood ran from his mouth and dripped down his black, battered wings.

Fuuuuck.

Just. Fuck.

The man opened his mouth, sucking in a gusty breath to scream. Sandeen punched his hand out and nailed him behind the head. The human fell forward over the sink and slid to the floor, unconscious.

Sandeen looked around. The bathroom was still empty, but voices carried through the door. Glancing down, the hand he punched the man with no longer held a blade. The metal had gotten left in the Mist. In his other hand hung the blade with angel's blood coating it.

His kind had been fighting angels in the Mist for centuries. They'd been coated in each other's blood and stolen the weapons. Why was this different?

Because he had a fallen's blood. The Mist wanted him out

257

and far away from Numen. And the blood had circumvented his need for a host to do it.

A slow smile spread across his face, baring his fangs. He snatched up the curved blade the human had set on the counter and secured both weapons in his waistband. Hefting the unconscious man, Sandeen carried him into the handicapped stall.

He barely got them both into the stall before someone came into the bathroom. He kept his wings tucked in as he bent low so they couldn't be seen above the stall. Humans seeing a demon walking around would bring more than a little attention—even in Vegas. He didn't need questions from any race regarding how the hell that could happen. After securing the door, he lifted his host onto the toilet.

Snickers filtered in from outside the door. "Hey, guys, I know a good club you can do that in instead of the shitter."

Sandeen realized how it must look. Sounds of muffled exertion, one set of designer shoes pointing one way, a set of shitkickers pointing back.

"Thanks. I know the place you're talking about." Sandeen even sounded like himself. Not like a host, because he was in his own body. On Earth. Whoa.

He couldn't roam with horns and a set of wings. Or fangs. Not yet. Shit, how did angels do that morphing thing? Would it work on horns? He also needed to get back to his hidey hole and stash his weapons.

With a resigned sigh, he took out his weapons and tucked them into the human's clothing. He made sure the guy was steady, slumped back against the flushing tower, his head leaning against the wall. It wouldn't do to get into the body only to slide to the floor. Some do-gooder might try to help him and find the guy strapped down with knives. Already without the angel blood-coated weapon on his body, the

Gloom was calling, his hold on this realm growing tenuous. He allowed it, closing his eyes and concentrating on his host.

When next he opened them, he was in his host, sitting on the toilet, staring at the stall walls. Despite a pounding headache, he grinned.

He had a hell of a trade for Jameson's blood.

CHAPTER 24

"There are possessed everywhere," Harlowe reported. The rest of Bryant's team, minus Sierra and Jagger, were at the same meeting spot as the last time they infiltrated Fall from Grace. It was far enough from the club to keep from being detected, but close enough to spy on.

After his talk with Jagger, they hadn't wasted any time. As soon as the eight fallen were accounted for, Bryant called them here. It was evening in Las Vegas, but he and Odessa had been awake for over twenty-four hours. They were still in the same clothing, but this needed to be done.

Bronx nodded next to Harlowe. "We must've made Haddock sweat. Sylphs are ghosting all over. Symaster victims are littering the street and loitering in front of the club, wondering how they got on this side of town."

Damn. Bryant should've expected as much.

They needed to confirm that Jameson Haddock was a fallen angel and Jagger's father. Those were the two most burning questions. A few others were how the hell a fallen had killed a watcher, in the Mist no less? Then got her body *out* of the veil to feed to gargoyles. Another biggie...how *the fuck* could a fallen detect Numen or Daemon?

They couldn't get close to the club. Jameson knew what Harlowe and Odessa looked like, possibly even Bronx. With sylphs surrounding the club, it'd be impossible to be on the same block and remain undetected.

"What about if we materialize at the alley door?" Odessa ventured.

Bryant's first response was no. Hell no. "After your encounter with the archmaster, I'm sure it's being monitored." And Odessa wasn't going near that building.

"But there's a roof," Harlowe said. "We could climb up to the neighboring building's roof and jump over."

"We won't know what we'd encounter up there." Bryant didn't want Harlowe's idea to work, but it was looking like their only option. This club was where Jameson lived and worked.

"Two of us can go. Trouble starts and we can reach the roof or jump out of a window. There's only possessed humans and sylphs around. We won't have to hide to shuttle out of there."

Bronx rubbed the back of his neck and spoke to Bryant. "So you and Harlowe go in? Me, Urban, and Dionna standing by. You get into trouble, we'll charge in?"

No. "Dionna, stay by Odessa."

"I should go with," Odessa said. Bryant was shaking his head when she continued. "Like before, I might have different insight into anything we find, or—or where to find it. Watchers observe a lot of things, like where humans hide stuff."

They weren't finding just anything. They were determined to find the fallen himself. Bryant wanted to coddle Odessa. Bringing her to find a man that might be a fallen capable of murdering angels went against all of his protective instincts.

Yet...having Odessa's insight to the conversation would be invaluable. He and Harlowe could do just fine, but as his mate had proven over and over, her analytical mind could see layers that weren't obvious to others.

And maybe he didn't want to leave her in a sylph-infested neighborhood without him by her side.

"We need to arm Odessa better before we go in." Bryant and Odessa hadn't had any more time to work on her self-defense skills. He couldn't send her in relying on only them to help her if they came to blows.

Urban and Dionna gave up their smaller, easier-to-handle blades to his mate. Now was one of the times Bryant wished they could use guns. Odessa wouldn't need to get close to anyone to hurt them. Angels worked their own metal and it ascended easy enough, but gunpowder had proved too volatile to carry through the realms. It was difficult to remain inconspicuous among humans when a gun was fired, not to mention the increase in collateral damage. Didn't mean demons couldn't use hosts to get guns and fire at warriors. Many weren't skilled in their use and preferred to use more devious, underhanded methods, but violence and death prevailed.

"I think we're as ready as we'll ever be," Odessa announced. She finished arranging her clothing so the hilts weren't easily visible above the waistband of her jeans.

Bryant knew they were there. He could almost feel the soft skin the metal was resting against; so warm, so smooth. Before he could think too much harder about it and create a hell of a distraction for himself, he took Odessa's hand and nodded at Harlowe.

The trip was brief, but for Bryant, it was too quick. He wanted it over with, but bringing Odessa closer to danger instead of farther away gnawed at his conscience. They crept to the edge of the roof.

"We can shuttle over easier than jumping," Harlowe whispered.

The distance was ten feet, but the scuffle of their footwear on the rooftop might draw attention. He nodded and pointed to an exhaust stack they could materialize next to.

The roof was empty. Jameson was only worried about the club being infiltrated, not the other levels of the building.

Harlowe pried open the door to the stairwell. The creaks the hinges made were as loud as a fog horn, but no creatures heard. They filtered into the dank space and crept down the stairs.

"The space the window overlooks takes up part of the second level," Odessa murmured. They trailed down the stairs, their eyes growing accustomed to the dark, and came upon a locked door.

Harlowe squatted, digging in a kit on her shoulder holster. Bryant shone his phone light on the doorknob as she picked it open.

"Any electronic security?" he asked. The club itself had minimal cameras, as though Jameson preferred his eyes and ears to mill among his customers. But then, if he was James Hancock and fell because he exposed their kind to humans, he probably shunned video evidence of his supernatural activities.

"No. Jameson is surprisingly old school."

Inching the door open, Harlowe peeked inside.

Muted music of the nightclub vibrated in the walls. The place was dark. They filed out, sticking close to the walls. He kept a grip on Odessa's hand.

"Over there," she hissed.

He glanced over his shoulder. A sizable, empty room had

an entire wall made out of glass. That must be the overlook. The area was dimly lit from another hallway that angled in the opposite direction.

This spot was just for watching the happenings in the bar and on the dance floor. Partiers would know he was there, but be unable to clearly identify him, heightening the mystery. Hearing no movement, the three of them drifted toward the room.

They had just stepped clear of the passageway when a door opened in other the hallway. They all spun toward the sound. Bryant stepped in front of Odessa.

"Come. I'll show you the updates," a cultured male said.

Bryant bristled. The male sounded just like all the senators he'd ever dealt with.

As the two shadows approached, another male said, "Somehow, I don't think that we'll get that far."

The males entered the viewing room and stopped. One male was as tall as Bryant, with shoulder-length dark hair pulled back at the base of his head. He wore an excellently tailored suit, and arrogance poured off of him. His expression changed from surprise to that of a wolf guarding his kill.

The other male was a possessed human, a handsome young man who could blend in anywhere. Bryant envisioned the archmaster inhabiting the body, like a wicked holographic image. Both the demon and the host wore a huge grin, only Bryant could see the fangs of the master over the teeth of the human.

The male was aiming his smile toward Harlowe. "We meet again."

She didn't return the grin. "Sandy, isn't it?"

The host shrugged. "Close enough."

"To what do I owe the pleasure of your visit?" The tall man smiled congenially at Harlowe; his resemblance to Jagger was in the way he held his chin high and his shoulders back. Jagger got his light coloring from his mother. "Was your first visit here so memorable you had to come again? And so soon?"

The man didn't panic, scream, or brandish a weapon. He'd just found three Numen in his personal space and he rolled with it.

"Jameson Haddock?" Bryant asked. The man dipped his head. "Or should I should I call you James Hancock?"

Jameson's features pinched, and for the first time his smile faltered. "You must have me confused with another. I am fallen, yes. Is that why you're here? To make sure I'm receiving no aid from former loved ones?" His expression hardened. "I assure you, all who knew me in my former life have shunned me."

Aw, poor guy. Bryant's sympathy for Jameson didn't exist. "Have you seen a friend of ours? A watcher named Magan?"

The sly bastard didn't react. He creased his brows in mock confusion. "No other Numen have approached me since I fell. Part of the deal, and all that."

"You would've approached her," Harlowe said, frustration in her tone. "And killed her."

Jameson's mouth curved like a Cheshire cat. "Now my dear...warriors, I assume? My wings have disappeared; therefore, I would not be able to see a watcher if she came up and bopped me in the nose."

The archmaster was content to watch the interplay. Out of the two, Bryant wasn't sure which was more dangerous.

"Want me to test that?" Harlowe snarled.

Jameson threw back his head and laughed. The demon next to him continued to grin.

"You knew what we were when we were here," Odessa pointed out.

Jameson's sharp gaze landed on Odessa, trying to see her clearly around Bryant. "My lovely lady, you and your friend made a stunning presence. I was only acknowledging you, even thinking of heading down to buy you both a drink."

He was smooth.

Bryant wanted to keep the male talking and get his attention off Odessa. "Your clientele seems very fond of black rose tattoos."

The grin faded.

"My guests like all kinds of ink. It goes with the theme."

"Do your guests like being possessed?"

Jameson took a placating breath. "As you can see, I no longer have wings. Therefore, it is no longer my issue whether or not humans are possessed." He spread his hands. "I wouldn't know anymore, now would I?"

Harlowe jutted her chin toward the human. "But you're buds with Sandy, here?"

"There's no such sanctions against demons revealing themselves to me." Jameson rolled one shoulder and straightened his tie. "Demons are under no such restriction regarding contact with me. Sometimes I find their company...refreshing."

Bryant suppressed a growl. They would get no answers, other than the club's owner was indeed Jameson Haddock, formerly known as James Hancock. If he and Harlowe hurt Jameson, and he wasn't guilty of Magan's murder, their wings might be on the line—although fallen were a gray area. It was possible the human host could get injured if Harlowe yanked Sandy into the Mist. Plus, he still had Odessa to protect.

"What are you up to, Hancock?" he asked.

Jameson's face clouded over. "It's Haddock. I'm surviving. Quite well, I might add."

"I can see that." How was he doing so well?

He'd get no answers there, either. They'd have to gather evidence to present to the senate, who could then order

Jameson's eradication. Would it be enough to get the hit called off of Odessa and her sister?

"Someone wants my mate dead." Bryant tried a different approach. "Her boss was already a victim and your club seems to be a common factor in each instance."

Astonishment crossed Jameson's flawless face. "I can't imagine such a thing. And in Numen, no less." A faint smile ghosted his lips as he eyed Odessa. She stiffened.

Either the male was a good guesser, or he knew Odessa was the analyst being hunted prior to their arrival.

"Indeed," Bryant replied smoothly. "We have some concern that her sister is in danger as well."

Jameson cocked an eyebrow.

The info surprised him. Interesting.

"We have them both under protection," Bryant continued. He had one last way to confirm this was James Hancock. "Warriors of my own team, as a matter of fact. You may know one. We call him Jagger." There was no change in the male's humoring expression, so Bryant pushed on. "It'd be in your best interest if there was no threat to my family. Their protectors would die for them, and I have no plans to see that happen to Jagger— Oh, I'm sorry. You may know him as Julian."

Color leeched from Jameson's face as Jagger's real name registered. All the pieces connected. Jameson Haddock was indeed Jagger's father.

Jameson spoke evenly, but murder rippled under his expression. "I'd hate to see that as well."

"Well," Bryant said, reaching back for Odessa's hand. "We'd better be going. No worries, we'll come out the way we came. No one will know you had Numen visitors."

"Wait." Jameson took a step forward but stopped when a six-inch blade appeared in Harlowe's hand. "Julian? He's well?"

"He's a fine *warrior*." Bryant stressed the last word out of spite. Jameson might be fallen, but he'd been a senator for centuries. His son becoming a warrior would be a slap in the face, no matter how fine an angel he was.

Jameson blinked, stunned. Bryant might even feel a little guilty about using Jagger to get to the fallen angel, but it was for Odessa and Felicia's benefit. If Jameson was behind any of the attacks, he'd be less likely to encourage they keep going if it put his son in danger.

CHAPTER 25

"*I*'ve heard a disturbing rumor."

The voice that came from the host sitting in front of Jameson in his meeting room should've been that of a normal human man. Not when Gerzon let his guttural grunt bleed through just like his features. He was accustomed to Sandeen using that trick. He assumed it was because it bothered the males. They felt like they were hiding behind an inferior bag of skin.

Gerzon's true form was not as pleasing to the eye as Sandeen's. Where Sandeen could be mistaken for an angel except for the ink-black wings, short horns, and fangs, Gerzon could not. His eyes were reptilian, for one, his horns much more prominent, for another, jutting out from his head like two engorged phalluses. Jameson wasn't clear since the image overlay was faint, but Gerzon's wings looked like they were covered in scales instead of feathers. Quite the contrast from the paunchy older man Gerzon wore like an ill-fitting suit. When Gerzon was done, he'd go back to his realm, removing his energy from the body and leaving it wherever it fell.

"What rumor would that be?" Jameson asked, not liking where this was going.

He was recovering from the angels' visit *in his home*. He'd had Odessa Montclaire, rather Lady Vale, in his vicinity and could do nothing. Killing her might not solve the problem of his secret plans getting out. Her mate and his entire team knew about him, but it'd make Jameson feel better since she was the one that started this headache in the first place. As soon as they had left, Gerzon had called Andy, demanding to meet with him.

Jameson managed to maintain his composure and hustled Sandeen out. The other male had acted amused, like Numen dropping in on him and announcing they knew exactly who he was and what he was up to was no big deal. And it might not be to Sandeen. That archmaster had his own master plan.

Gerzon's visits were always trying. Negotiating with a demon was an exercise in patience and fortitude. Today, it was even more annoying. He wanted to sit and ruminate over the information Sandeen had traded with him.

The handy tidbit of using his blood to keep angels from transcending to Numen, or shuttling anywhere else in the human realm, did no good until he could coat some weapons with it. And find an angel to use them on.

He'd had three right in front of him. Jameson kept his hands from clenching.

"The *rumor*," Gerzon snapped, "is that you needed extra protection for the club because some angels showed up. They're on to you."

Dammit. Unfortunately, he needed Gerzon's assistance. He couldn't take on the angelic race with nothing but a scythe covered in his blood. He couldn't protect his club with humans because they couldn't sense angels. He needed at least sylphs. He'd ordered Zanda to up demon protection around the club, thinking he had more time before Gerzon came slithering by.

"Gerzon." Jameson relied on his years of politics. "You didn't expect to not run into a few snags, did you? It was just a couple of female Numen looking for a good time at the wrong club."

The host's lip curled as Gerzon growled. "You asked for more protection around the club. Said there was fighting and you couldn't have police involved."

"Basically. An archmaster participating in my club's… offerings…sensed them, otherwise I wouldn't have known," Jameson lied effortlessly. "I needed more sylphs patrolling the area. The symasters are for if we run into trouble. I would take an archmaster if you're offering." Jameson knew he wouldn't. Gerzon was too greedy for power.

"You mean when the two angels go back to Numen and tell the warriors there's a demon-infested club in Las Vegas?"

"I have someone taking care of them. My main goal is to get more demons protecting the club, not just participating in its festivities."

Gerzon regarded Jameson. The demon knew he was hiding something but was probably deciding if it was that important to him.

"Who was the archmaster?" Gerzon finally asked.

"He left pretty quickly. My assistant didn't catch his name. He was sampling my guests and was upset when the angels interrupted an entrée."

Gerzon grunted at Jameson's response.

"I invite you to do the same," Jameson offered, rising, prompting Gerzon to as well. "However, I encourage you to remember that we don't need police presence, so keep the violence down."

Baring his teeth, Gerzon let his image fade away so

Jameson saw nothing more than the pathetic-looking man. "I always find someone who enjoys it."

Riiiight. Jameson smiled and clapped Gerzon on the back, then showed him out. When Andy heard the door shut, he came out to check on Jameson.

"Have you any orders for me, sir?"

Still facing the door with one hand on the knob, Jameson nodded. "Call Kenton. Tell him we need to meet."

Did that traitor plan to take out his son? What the fuck did Bryant Vale call Julian? Jagger?

Had the boy changed his name after— Jameson forced the thought out of his head. What was done was done.

"Right away, sir?"

Jameson smoothed his hands down his suit jacket. "No. Tomorrow." He had to let his feelings out first. Treacherous emotions. They made it hard to get work done.

"Very well, sir." His diminutive assistant promptly went back into his office to complete his task.

Jameson strode down the hall to where his apartment was. Not even Andy was allowed in it. Just his flavor of the week, although Lindy had claimed more than a week and Jameson was in no hurry to see her go. He'd be done with her eventually, but for now he found her skills useful.

Lindy was wandering around his place getting ready. He'd promised her a dinner out. He intended to keep his word.

Eventually.

She glanced toward him, wearing nothing but a lace Wonderbra and matching boy shorts. Stopping in front of the table, she smiled at him. "Oh, hey. I was just picking out a dress for tonight."

Need pounded through Jameson, matching his anger at the turn of events. Fuck Odessa and her stupid analyst brain; fuck Bryant Vale and his righteous duty; fuck Gerzon and his demon manipulation; fuck Sandeen because the male was crafty; and fuck Kenton for hiding the fact that Julian was part of the problem that would be "taken care of." And fuck that watcher who had people she'd never met looking into her death. His own family knew where to find him and hadn't even tried.

"Bend over," Jameson snarled, ripping open the fly of his pants.

"Is this how you usually feel after a fight?" Odessa ran up the stairs. Bryant struggled to keep up.

His team was catching up on some rest before they reconvened to figure out their next move. Bryant had to meet with Director Richter first, after he got Odessa settled. She entered her room and turned to talk to him while walking backward.

"How do you feel?" he asked warily.

"Like I have all this energy." She held her hands up as if sparks were going to fly from her fingers. "And nothing to do with it."

"It's just adrenaline. We planned for a fight, but all we got was a conversation that went nowhere."

"What do you do with it?" She was shifting from foot to foot.

"Each warrior is different in how they process after an encounter. Some workout, some spar, some…" Have sex. Some warriors went out for a good fuck, and he used to be one of those—ages ago.

Odessa fingered the collar of her shirt, eyeing him like he was a triple scoop chocolate cone and she'd been eating nothing but broccoli and diet pills for weeks.

Aww hell. He couldn't have sex with her now. She was

hyped up on adrenaline and he didn't want her to feel taken advantage of.

"I need to meet with the director." It sounded lame. Even to his own ears.

She gazed at him from under hooded lids. "Now?"

Yes.

He couldn't get the word out. It was in his mind. Say yes. Just say it. He had a duty. Duty first.

The way she was looking at him... He'd never had anyone look at him like that. Not even before the injury. He had seen it in other couples, even among humans, but never directed his way. It gave him hope. Was there a chance Odessa would want him after she didn't need him?

"Bryant." She stalked close to him. Standing on her tiptoes, she licked the rim of his twisted ear. He had thought all the nerve endings destroyed, but whatever was left, her hot tongue hit.

He was hard as a rock and aching for his mate. If she felt the same way, he couldn't leave her to suffer.

The director would have to wait.

JAMESON IGNORED the rest of the restaurant on his date with Lindy. Her red lips closed around her wineglass as her gaze drank him in. She crinkled her nose. She wasn't a wine girl, but she wanted the whole fancy package tonight and after what Jameson had done to her body, he provided.

Swirling the wine, she watched the blood-red liquid circulate. "Are you going to tell me what earlier was about?"

Jameson stared at her cherry-red lips. That color still lined his cock after the limo ride on the way to the restaurant.

She gave her head a quick shake. "I didn't mean to pry. I'm sorry."

Lindy seemed slightly embarrassed and he realized how she must feel, like nothing but a piece of ass. Normally, that wouldn't bother him. It's what women to him usually were. He enjoyed them, and liked to make them feel good, but their overall well-being was never his priority.

Once again, Lindy didn't fit his usual type.

"I'm divorced." It was the only term she would under-stand, but what he went through was so much more. "My family quit speaking to me."

She raised an eyebrow but said nothing.

"Earlier, someone gave me some information about my son." Jameson took a drink of his wine. Lindy was right. It was atrocious, just like its price. He much rather preferred his whiskey if he was going to pay that much. "I didn't know how to deal with it."

Her eyes warmed. "He's doing well?" She sounded appre-hensive, like she worried the answer would be no, or he'd quit talking, or both.

"Yes. Rather well. His career choice isn't what I'd expected."

"He's grown?"

Ah yes. Jameson looked like he was in his early thirties and while she might know some of his world, she didn't comprehend it.

"I'm older than I look," he said with a little smile.

The waiter arrived with their first course. He set the plates up with a flourish and stood back awaiting their approval. Jameson nodded at him and watched Lindy's reac-tion with amusement.

"Two shrimp?" She was looking around her plate. "That's it?"

He laughed, and it felt good. When he first saw Lindy

partying at Fall from Grace, he thought she looked refined, classy. Perhaps, compared to the rest of his clientele. He was learning that she lived life the way she had sex—full throttle with a sizable appetite. He enjoyed that.

At that thought, Jameson frowned at his own meager portions. What kind of red-blooded male ate that small of a steak? And what the hell was he thinking keeping Lindy around? The last time he grew something that resembled feelings for a woman, he'd lost his wings.

"It's what you wanted," he snapped at her.

Her shoulders dropped along with her gaze. She picked up her fork to dig at the food artfully arranged on her plate.

"Look, I didn't mean—" Was he apologizing now? To a human? "I've had some shit happen at work and it's making me edgy."

There. An explanation but not an apology.

"It's all right. Is there anything I can do to help? I do have a black rose."

He considered her for a minute before he tackled his two-bite steak. "What brought you to my club in the first place?"

She pondered his question. "I guess, I wanted more. More than an adventure— I wanted to feel like I'm doing something." She shrugged and stared at her plate. "I get tired of being a woman who likes sex but is seen as nothing more than a walking vagina. I meant it when I said I could help."

Most women who visited his club liked to walk on the wild side. Once they experienced Fall from Grace, they either ran the other way and cleaned up their life, or they wanted more and got recruited. Aside from the rare devil worshipper, it was a slow process as they eased the humans into service. Lindy was...not totally good but not evil. A little wicked like him—perhaps why he was drawn to her.

Yet he couldn't see her outright killing any beings. He didn't want her to earn the bloodied barbed wire. He wanted no possessed bodies in his bed, and an archmaster could destroy her.

No, he couldn't use her in those ways. She had a brain, she had looks, and she supported his plan. He could keep her in his home, providing for his body, *and* utilize her full package.

Yes, he might have some other uses for her.

CHAPTER 26

*B*ryant finished updating his boss on everything. The director leaned back in his chair, blew out a gusty exhale, and stared at the ceiling. His steel-hued wings rested on either side of his elbows on his chair's armrest.

"So a fallen, Jagger's father, is organizing humans to host demons and support them in hunting angels." Director Richter squinted at Bryant. "He's likely working with someone high-ranking in the senate, but we don't know who and we don't know why. We know Jameson Haddock has Daemon alliances, but we don't know who and we don't know why."

"Correct."

"And now that Haddock knows we know about him, he's surrounded his club, and likely himself, with sylphs and possessed humans for protection."

"That about covers it."

Director Richter sighed and was quiet for a few moments. "Keep Jagger with Felicia. We can't be sure she won't be targeted since they, whoever 'they' are, have used her before to get to her father."

Bryant nodded. "It will also keep Jagger from having a conflict of interest when it comes to dealing with his father."

The director's face was grim. "We need to have a talk with Odessa's father. He's got to be able to provide us with the name of the corrupt senator, maybe even have insight as to why. What benefit is there to have a bunch of humans worshipping demons?"

"For Haddock? Revenge." Bryant put himself in Haddock's shoes. "To survive and be able to amass an army must be intoxicating. A big 'fuck you' to the angels that took his wings."

The director snorted. "If he would've kept it in his pants, or at least kept his mouth shut and not told his mistress he was an angel, then he'd still have his wings."

"I doubt he sees it that way."

"Those types of males never do. Righteous bastards." The director pinned Bryant with a sharp look. "How are things with you and Odessa?"

Bryant resisted squirming in his seat like a five-year-old. "Good. For now."

The male Bryant respected most in the realm frowned.

Dammit. He should've kept his mouth shut, but his feelings and worries about his lovely mate had been eating at him. It wasn't like he'd had time to head to London and have a sit down with his dad for some guy talk. He couldn't go to his team because he was their fearless leader. Telling the director about what'd been weighing heavily on his mind as far as Odessa went suddenly seemed appealing.

"Our sync has been finalized." The director's brows shot up. "We get along okay. Well, actually, really well."

Bryant waited and the other male kept watching him, waiting to see what the problem was. It was obvious to Bryant. Couldn't Director Richter see?

"I'm just worried about after we neutralize the threat to

her and her family. She won't need around the clock protection. She'll be free."

The director waited a couple of seconds, his brow furrowed. "And?"

"And she'll be free to realize that syncing with me was something she felt cornered into doing."

Director Richter tilted his head back in an *ah-ha* movement. "I see. Has she given you any indication she regrets her decision?"

"No." If she had, it'd be easier once the hammer dropped.

"The delay between the sync ceremony and the…sealing… Your resistance or hers?"

"Mine, sir."

"When you two finally… She knew you'd stick around even without a fully sealed bond, correct?"

"Yes." Why was it so hard for people to understand? "I'm talking about after all this is done, when she realizes she doesn't need me in her life anymore but is synced with me forever."

"Vale, you're mixing up normal issues with issues about your looks."

"What?"

"Most mates worry their mate will come to resent them. An eternity together is a long time. Because of your history, you're obsessing about it and you blame your looks." Director Richter rested his elbows on his desk. "Most warriors think I left the field because Millie didn't want to spend her life worrying about me. She saved my life, fully syncing with me when I landed on her doorstep. My wings were nearly falling off and I was bleeding out of a nasty head wound."

That was totally what Bryant thought, but from the male's voice, maybe not?

"But that makes no damn sense, does it?" the director asked.

Actually, it did.

He continued. "I mean, there was only one director position and hundreds of warriors. How many of those warriors are mated and still out in the field? I've been in this chair for decades and no one's walked in demanding to take it. What happened was that Millie helped me to see my worth. I was a good warrior, but I could be a damn good leader. Maybe Odessa can help you see your worth past your injuries, past your abilities as a fighter. *She* obviously sees the worthy male under all that negative attitude."

Bryant considered the director's words. What would Odessa think he was worth? He was a warrior. He'd reached his potential already.

"Once you see your value as a male and as a mate," the director obviously wasn't done, "then you can see why it's worth it to you to spend your time making sure Odessa would never consider the possibility of *not* being mated to you. It's called romancing. Some humans are quite good at it, actually."

Bryant opened his mouth to speak, then shut it again. Romancing? How did he begin to research that?

Director Richter spoke before Bryant could think of a rebuttal. "Convince yourself *you* are the best mate for Odessa, then set about proving it to her for the rest of your life."

Odessa had said much the same.

What if...what if he *was* good enough for her? What if he could make her happy enough to not regret her decision? Each time he'd gotten close to pondering the same thing, he'd backed off. There'd always been a good reason. She'd had no choice. She was stuck. He had nothing more to offer her.

But those thoughts weren't as quick to pile on. What if?

The director moved the subject along before it became uncomfortable for either one of them. "I've been keeping Stede off your back. He's been wanting his team to have access to Odessa's mansion, but I'm waving your mate card around. It's your home now, too."

Bryant barked a laugh. "My home is a mansion. Never thought I'd see the day." He didn't think it even felt like home to Odessa.

"I'll surreptitiously let Senator Montclaire know we need to talk to him," the director continued. "We need to find out who is in charge, both up here and in Daemon, and then find out why. At this point, even if we could take out Haddock, they'd just replace him with another."

"We need proof, or if we touch Haddock, whoever his senator friend is could find a loophole and take our wings."

The director's mouth tightened. "All right, you figure your next move with your team, and I'll work on Odessa's father. First, I need to get word to all team leaders. We're being hunted."

They'd lost another warrior under suspicious circumstances. The theory was he'd been consumed by his own vial of fire, but the possession he was hunting wasn't capable of winning a fight. The warrior's team was adamant that nothing else would've stopped the warrior from doing his job and reporting back. The leader had described him as a fully trained warrior who was known to get almost brutal in his dealings on both realms.

There was no sign of the demon, either. It'd managed to find a way out of the Mist before it could be hunted down. The loss disturbed Bryant only because it was sign that demons were becoming more organized and more skilled.

SIERRA GLARED at the male talking to her. How he'd tracked her to the IT headquarters she'd set up, she didn't know. But here he was, in the glow of her monitors, on the verge of making a threat.

"Here's the thing." Enforcer Stede smiled darkly and steepled his fingers. "If you don't, we might"—he gave a nonchalant shrug—"I don't know... Tell your leader what you really are. Or at the very least, who you really are."

Sierra's blood iced. He couldn't know. No one knew. No one but her dad and mom. Well, there was... She shook off the thought. Impossible.

"Bullshit." He was bluffing. He had to be. There was no way the male could know her past.

The smile on the sick bastard's face was nauseating. "Is it? I'm sure at least your sister would like to know."

Oh. Hell. Her sister would indeed find it interesting that she wasn't an only child. Sierra had grown up blissfully unaware until her sister was born. As for *what* she was—she was Numen, dammit. Her wings were a dark, murky gray. They were *not* black.

"And what is it you want me to do?" Sierra studied the asshole in front of her.

He was a high-ranking enforcer, and she didn't like him. Those two details were the most concrete. He was average height, still several inches taller than her, slightly bigger than average build, but his demeanor all but yelled what a class A dick he was. And somehow, he found the place she kept on Earth where she housed all her gadgets.

"Nothing much," he replied. "The next time your team gathers at Odessa Vale's place, I need you to make sure Director Richter arrives, too."

His demand made her sick. "Why?"

He separated his hands in a shrug and put them back together in steeple formation, holding eye contact.

"Are you going to hurt my team and the director?"

His gaze glinted with steel. "Little *angel*, you have a hell of a secret. If you don't want anyone to find out, you'll do as I say."

Sierra sighed. If it was any other reason, she could've told Stede to go fuck himself. But turns out, she was a fucking coward. "What am I supposed to tell him?"

Stede stood up, smoothing his shirt and slacks. "Whatever works."

"And my sister?"

Stede's steady stare captured her. "Keep her out of the way if you don't want to see her hurt."

He strode out, leaving her alone in her computer den. He could come back anytime. It was a helluva situation she found herself in.

$\approx$

"WHO ARE WE WAITING FOR?" Bryant entered the living area in the mansion.

"Jagger is with Felicia," Dionna reported. "I left a message on Sierra's phone. Bronx is out talking"—Dionna gave the last word air quotes—"with Tosca."

Harlowe chuckled. "He's been trying to get to her since she arrived. I give her one week before she gives in."

"Two," Urban interjected.

Harlowe shook her head, blond braid swinging. "One. She's resisting out of pride, but Bronx is good."

"Perhaps he's using it as a tactic to check up on the enforcers?" Odessa suggested.

"Odessa," Harlowe sighed, "you're too nice."

Bryant smiled to himself. His mate saw the best in his team. And she was right. Bronx used his charm and exotic looks to get a lot of information. If it got him a lot of sex, then bonus. He wasn't above using any skill available to him to get the job done. Using Tosca to find out what the enforcers were doing was right up Bronx's alley.

"All right, we'll get started." Bryant motioned to his team to have a seat. "This is more of a brainstorming session anyway."

Odessa perched beside him. Urban and Harlowe took the couch while Dionna took post across the room by the kitchen entrance.

"We need the archmaster and the senator helping Haddock."

Odessa stuck her hands in her robe pockets. "It'd sure be useful to build our own human army to spy on him since we can't get close to the club without them knowing."

"Wouldn't it be cool?" Harlowe agreed. "Too bad we'd get kicked out of the realm for telling humans about us."

"Unless we use some that already know," Urban suggested. The others stared at him.

Harlowe frowned at her teammate and asked what they all wondered. "Who would that be?"

He lifted a heavily muscled shoulder. "Not everyone that goes to Fall from Grace becomes a follower. Some of them have to know and it must scare the hell out of them. I mean, what do they do about the ones that don't get tattooed?"

"We could ask around other nightclubs in Vegas, try to find someone who's gone there. Haddock's spreading the word somehow." Bryant pointed at Harlowe and Urban. "You two and Bronx can start on that tonight. Let's get him in here."

"I'll go grab him." Harlowe started for the door. "I keep getting texts from Sierra. I should check 'em out." As she disappeared around the corner and opened the door, she said, "Oh hey, director. Vale's in the main room."

The director rushed around the corner, his features steeped in concern. "Is everything okay?"

"Yeah, why wouldn't it be?" Bryant asked.

"Sierra contacted me. Said she's worried her system has been hacked. She couldn't get ahold of any of you."

Bryant was about to suggest Dionna fly to Sierra's house when a crash echoed from the wing that used to be Odessa's. All the warriors jerked to their feet, weapons already in hand.

A dark form, clothed entirely in black, including a mask, wings morphed into his back, burst out of the bedroom door on the second level. From each hand he lobbed throwing knives. Several small blades were strapped to his chest, and his hands were a blur as he launched one after the other.

Bryant and the others scattered. He wrapped his arm around Odessa as tight as a vice and rolled over the back of the sofa. She yelped but didn't resist as they spilled over the edge.

The director grunted. A black handle stuck out of his white robe. A bloom of red stained his gown.

Director Richter scurried next to the wall, getting out of the line of fire. "Get her out of here!"

Bryant tugged Odessa toward the office when another disguised male darted out of her old room. He held a canister in each hand.

Terror punched into him. He recognized what the canisters held. "Fire!"

The male tossed both containers of angel fire. One canister blasted by the front door, blocking the fastest exit. Dionna's shouted a warning from where she was crouched by a pillar. Angel fire blew out and wicked up the pillars.

The other canister landed in the main room, inches from Urban's feet. He'd taken cover behind the lounge chair.

Diving over the sofa, an explosion of flames followed his booted feet.

Bryant released Odessa enough to drag Urban toward him and away from the flames.

"Here!" He kept yelling to get his team's attention. The other men had cut off the front door and second level exits. "The office!"

Flames spread, their peaks reaching higher by the second. Dionna lobbed daggers at the second level and sprinted by the base of the stairs toward Bryant. He caught her and whipped her through the office door.

He fisted Urban's shirt and shoved Odessa's hand into his. "Get her out of here."

"Bryant," she cried, but Urban overpowered her. Dionna flung open the office window. Bronx was on the other side, reaching through to help her out. Urban and Odessa followed.

His scars were growing tight. The front door was encased in flames, and the main room was getting covered, the substance devouring everything in its path. Glass shattered in the room affected by the fires. The small vials each warrior carried was enough to destroy up to three demons. The mansion was attacked with two canisters. There would be nothing left.

The director. Had he gotten out?

Groaning of rock scraping against rock preceded heavy thuds that shook the entire structure. Leaving the brief reprieve of the office, he threw an arm over his face and edged along the wall to search the living area and the entrance.

His eyes dried and burned. Breathing was painful, and the memories that rose threatened to drop him to his knees. But it was what had happened to him that propelled him forward. No one else needed to suffer the agony of angel fire.

The director's dark hair was a stark contrast to the white floor. He was prone, a large pile of rubble had pinned him to the ground.

"Director! I'm coming." Hearing those words had saved his sanity before. Would they be enough to help the director?

Bryant shaded himself against the blinding white, yellow, and orange flames. The fire ate away the banister and the landing. Bryant edged through a narrow margin of floor that remained unmarred.

Marble shattered around him, as if it was getting smashed to bits. Essentially, it was. As the fire decimated a marble stone pillar, the others came crashing down on top of it. The roof would come down soon.

He squinted to where he had last seen the director. When he finally found the male sprawled on the marble floor, he feared he was too late. The fire was burning a path up the director's body from his feet where the engulfed pillar had pinned him.

Bryant deftly stepped where no angel fire touched and made it to the director's side.

He had passed out. It was for the best. The agony was more than a person should ever tolerate.

Director Richter was face down, the fire around him quickly closing in. Bryant's escape path was disappearing. Angel fire burned clean, but the combustion of the materials it destroyed clogged the air. The heat was worse than being in an oven.

He had to work quickly or the fire would claim both of them. Anchoring his hands around the director's shoulders, he tugged and yanked until the director body's inched away from the pillar.

Straining, he roared into one last effort to free his friend. It worked. He dragged the male by his shoulders and ran for their lives, keeping the smoldering angel fire away from his own body.

Without letting go of the director, he dove through the office window, smashing half the frame as they tumbled out. He laid the director on the lawn. The male gasped awake, his mouth stretching to scream. His mouth was stuck open, but terror raged in his eyes.

Bryant had to get him to his mate. Digging his hands under Richter's shoulders, he launched into the air, spreading his wings out wide. He only hoped he could fly to the director's mate in time for him to be healed.

CHAPTER 27

O dessa wrung her hands. She couldn't leave and follow Bryant, but she wanted to scream at Dionna to hurry up with the others. Finally, Dionna turned to her and Urban. "Check on Vale and report back about Director Richter."

"I'm coming with you." Odessa stuck close to Urban as they flew to a tidy little house on the edge of the warrior's section of Numen. Her relief at Bryant diving out of the window died when she viewed the battered baggage he carried. When Bryant had taken flight, Dionna had barked orders to the rest of the team.

Urban didn't bother knocking. The stench of burning flesh lingered on the landing. They barreled into the house.

A slight female with long pale hair and wings almost as pale was in the foyer. She spared them a glance from where she was crouched over two forms. Odessa approached, her hand flying to her mouth. The director's legs were ravaged from the fire.

Bryant was rolling the director over. "We have to let the fire burn itself out."

Millie stopped short of them, taking in the damage. "Wh-what if it doesn't stop?"

Odessa's heart wrenched. The angel was facing the loss of her mate.

Bryant wrestled the knife out of the director's shoulder and applied pressure. It had been shoved in nearly past the hilt.

It was the most helpless Odessa had ever felt. They all had to feel the same, doing nothing but watching the flame creep past the director's shins, ash dusting the now sooty floor. Ever so slowly, embers sizzled up the director's knees, eating away flesh and bone. It wasn't until the joints were each gone that the bright red glow died.

Silent tears streamed down Millie's face. Bryant motioned for her to approach. She dropped to her knees as soon as she reached his side and covered her mate with her pale wings. Only the knife wound could be healed. The director's legs were gone. They would not regenerate.

Millie sat back, sniffling, her hands stroking the director's hair. He remained unconscious, blissfully unaware at the damage that had been done. "Can you help me get him upstairs to the bed?"

Urban rushed over to help Bryant, his face bleak. They each took a side, gently lifting him and they gingerly carried the director up the stairs. Millie led them all to the bedroom.

After he was settled on the simple bed in the plain but homey room, Millie perched on the bed, holding her mate's hand. Her gaze roamed his body, disbelief mixed with sorrow when they touched upon his mangled legs.

"Lady Richter," Bryant spoke gently. "Has anyone you don't absolutely trust ever been to your home?"

Her eyes watery, she shook her head. "No. We don't get many visitors. Leo works so much and I..." She shrugged. "I'm gone a lot."

From what Odessa had understood, Millicent Richter had been from an elite family but accepted Leo Richter's sync offer. If she hadn't, the director surely would have died from his wounds. Odessa didn't know what Millie did now. If the director was gone a lot, certainly the angel had to do something all day. The couple didn't have any children yet.

Bryant's gaze narrowed on her, targeting the hesitation. "Someone targeted us, ma'am. Is there anything we should know?"

Millie blinked. "It's nothing that would put us in danger. I've been working as a chaperone."

Her words stunned the warriors. Odessa couldn't see why, other than they had sorely underestimated their boss's mate. Chaperones were not faint of heart. They escorted worthy souls to the pearly gates of Heaven, often witnessing tragic, sometimes brutal deaths. No wonder Millie had been so stoic through her mate's injuries. It would be a long road ahead for them.

"I need to go back and check on the mansion." Bryant's gaze flicked from Odessa to Urban, then back to Millie. "Can this warrior and Odessa stay with you? No one knows we're here, so I think we're safe for a while, and I'd feel better if you and the director had extra protection."

"Of course. Help yourselves to anything in the kitchen." A subtle message that Millie wanted to be alone with her healing mate.

They left as quietly as they could. Odessa followed them back down the stairs, to where they had watched the director's legs burn away.

"Urban, can you give us a moment?" Odessa asked.

The warrior looked to Bryant for a nod before he did as Odessa requested.

"Look, Odessa—" Bryant tensed, as if prepared for her resistance at him leaving her there.

Yes, Odessa wanted to argue, wanted to stay close to Bryant and go see the damage to her home. She understood his caution about bringing her back there. What she wanted more was Bryant's comfort.

Throwing her arms around him, she buried her face in his shoulder. He smelled of smoke and the unique gaseous odor she attributed to angel fire. His arms twined around her. If she could melt herself into him, she would.

"I thought I was going to lose you when you didn't leave the first time," she whispered out of respect for the director and his mate.

He buried his nose into her hair. She was a mess, but she was alive.

"I'm sorry I made you worry," he said.

She searched his face. It was a loaded statement.

She brushed her fingers over his scars. His skin was still hot and red, but no fire had touched him. "I don't like it, but it's who you are. I wouldn't have been able to live with doing nothing for the director any more than you."

His expression didn't lighten, but he hugged her tighter.

"I have to go and find out what's going on." He dropped a kiss on the corner of her mouth and left.

Odessa stood by herself for a few minutes, letting everything sink in. Her home was likely gone. Was she upset about it? Relieved? It had no sentimental value, other than the memories she had made there with Bryant.

She was almost killed. Again. Only now her mate and his entire team were in danger. She dug her phone out from her robe pocket and texted Felicia a "Hey, how ya doin'?" She left out the "our childhood home is burning to the ground" part until she could speak to her personally.

Then there was the director's devastating injury. Odessa had just met Millie, didn't know Leo Richter well, but she wanted to be there for them and help them any way she could.

Glancing back up the stairs, she would wait. Millie needed time alone with her mate until he healed enough to wake. Then she would be the one to tell him the news.

Odessa let out a heavy exhale and dropped her head, closing her eyes for a minute. Never did she image how one assignment at work would change her life so drastically.

"I COULDN'T DESCEND," the director said woodenly from his bed.

"That's understandable." Hang on. "When did you try to descend?"

Two days had passed since the fire. These were the first words the male had said to Bryant since he'd been allowed in the bedroom. Millie announced when he'd come to, but the dark circles under her eyes and the way she'd sigh and trail off told Bryant a lot about the director's condition.

His boss had only looked at him when he had first entered the bedroom, but after that he stared at the ceiling. Millie said that was status quo. When he woke, writhing in pain, she had broken the news to him. She said he had looked down at what was left of his legs and flopped back. He mostly slept and barely tolerated the cooling packs she would put on each stump. Where his skin wasn't blackened, it was a fiery red. The angel's natural healing response slowed from the extent of the injuries. His body was going wild trying to correct the wrong the fire had caused. The director would be inflamed for weeks.

Bryant's eye twitched and the skin on his injured side tightened. He hoped the director maintained his sanity through it all.

"I. Couldn't. Transport," the director repeated. "When we got outside. I didn't want Millie to see... I didn't want her to..." He turned his face away to stare at the wall opposite Bryant.

The male was going to run away? To another realm? He would've let himself die over letting his mate see him hurt? It wasn't for Bryant to understand. He clung to the descending detail. "I understand. As for the descension, with the extent of your injury—"

"It wasn't the injury. There's no way I would've put this"—his lip curled—"on Millie's shoulders."

"How is that possible?" Bryant didn't want to argue with the male, but it had been a tumultuous time for both of them.

"Did anyone else get hit by the flying knives?"

"No. I don't think they were aiming for us as much as distracting us. They escaped as soon as they started the fire."

The director's mouth tightened. "Then I would assume Jameson Haddock or his demon helpers found a way to keep us from ascension. It's tied to the knives. It's the only thing I can think of. It's the only thing I've been thinking about."

Bryant released a hiss of air. So much for the director being out of his mind from his injuries. He hadn't been able to descend, and he'd been the only one hit with a dagger. No one else had reported an issue with their ability.

Bryant nodded. "I'll get the one we dug out of you tested for anything unusual. Sierra, Bronx, and Harlowe sifted through the remains of the mansion. We'll test any others that were missed by the fire."

He needed to get what was left of his gear and any of Odessa's belongings they had been able to recover.

The next subject was necessary, but one he dreaded. "I need to report to the senate. I've already held them off, saying I had to talk to you first."

Millie had deftly turned away senators pounding on her

door, demanding a report on what happened. But Senator Montclaire had been strangely absent. Bryant hated him just for how that made Odessa feel.

The director didn't flinch. Perhaps he appreciated the reprieve from the senate hounding him while he recovered. "Tell them everything, but leave out that you know there's a traitor."

"Yes, sir. Stede also found me when we were searching the rubble. Said his enforcers were ready to guard your home and Millie, and wherever Odessa made her home next."

His leader sneered at that. "What did you say?"

"I told him to fuck off. I don't trust him or any of his enforcers after the mansion was so thoroughly decimated."

"Good."

Bryant shrugged. "Word has spread through the warriors that they are being targeted and to be on heightened alert when they're out hunting. I'm waiting for you to tell them the rest. After that, I suspect the direct danger to Odessa, Felicia, and Millie will be decreased. Haddock's grand plan won't be a secret anymore and all of Numen will know."

"Loved ones that threaten the identity of the traitor in the senate will be used against us."

Bryant inclined his head, fully agreeing. He was all in the hunt for Haddock, his demon helpers, and anyone who has given their alliance to them.

"Vale."

"Sir?" Bryant didn't like the director's tone.

Before the director could say anything, there was a tap on the door.

Director Richter kept staring at the ceiling. Bryant turned to see Millie poking her head in.

Her voice was calm, her gaze was anything but. "Bryant, can I speak with you?"

He stood. His boss showed no interest in whatever the

problem was. That bothered Bryant more than seeing his damaged body.

"I'll come back after I talk with the senate."

Director Richter uttered nothing as Bryant left. Odessa was at the bottom of the stairs, wringing her hands.

"What's going on?" Bryant asked quietly. He didn't want Director Richter to hear anything and get upset. If anything could get to the male right now.

"Stede." Millie's face was drawn. "He's looking for you. Insisted on coming in here. I told him over my dead body, and I meant it."

Bryant's brows shot up. Over the last two days, he'd learned he'd severely underestimated Millicent Richter. She appeared weak and mousy, when in actuality, it was quiet confidence.

Odessa's wrought look broke for a quick smile. "She told him more than that, and not as pleasantly." The grin faded. "He's got other enforcers with him and insisted I come out while waiting for you."

Bryant clenched his jaw. He had enough going on, he didn't need Stede interfering. Like buying fresh clothes for one. He and Odessa had been washing and wearing what they'd been in the night of the fire. There'd been no time for shopping in the aftermath, and Bryant didn't want to let Odessa out of his sight.

He yanked open the door. Stede waited with three other enforcers. Bryant recognized them as ones he'd interviewed for mansion guarding duty. Three he had rejected. For good reason.

"What?" Bryant growled, letting his rough voice express his full irritation.

"Warrior Vale," Stede announced. "You are under arrest for the murder of Kreger Montclaire."

Shock and disbelief rocked Bryant. His next thought was for his mate.

Odessa stepped up beside him in the doorway, nearly pushing him out of the way. "Excuse me?"

Stede turned his ruthless gaze on her. "Your father was found this morning, decapitated."

Odessa gasped and stumbled back. One hand went to her gut, the other at her mouth. Her gaze was horrified, but wary, like she hoped Stede was lying.

"Is this how you break the news to his daughter? Have you no compassion?" Bryant abandoned the door and gathered her in his arms. Her body shook, and small strangled noises were wrung from her as she fought sobs.

"It is when she's also a suspect." A smug glint entered Stede's gaze.

"What are you talking about?" Then Stede's first words after he'd opened the door sank in.

"Warrior Vale, the murder weapon has been traced back to you."

CHAPTER 28

*O*dessa's heart hurt. Her eyes were red and puffy. She had snot caked all over her sleeve. Looking around the cell, despair washed over her once again.

Stede had dragged them to the holding cells. She was thrown into a small cell and Bryant was sent…somewhere else. She wasn't allowed to know.

Odessa huffed. She refused to give the enforcers any fodder for thinking she was guilty. It was best to ride this out. How bad could it be? Of course, Bryant hadn't killed her father. Of course, she had nothing to do with it, either.

Tears welled and she started weeping again.

She hadn't been close with him since the first attack. Before that, though, they'd been a happy family. The past weeks' events had shown her that while she hadn't agreed with what he'd done, he'd done it to protect her and Felicia.

"Ode?" Felicia was on the other side of the cell, dressed down in black yoga pants and a neon-yellow running shirt. Her sister was pale but not nearly as distraught as Odessa. She couldn't blame her.

"What are you doing here?" Odessa hissed. "Where's Jagger?"

Felicia waved her off. "He's waiting with the guards, comparing dick sizes or something."

"It was no comparison," Jagger said. Filly stiffened and shot him a glare. He was unaffected. "We have five minutes."

"Did they let you see Father?" Please say no. It was a stupid fantasy, but the lack of confirmation let Odessa think it could all be a dream.

Her sister's mouth flattened and she nodded. "It was him."

Sniffling, Odessa tried not to break down again. "It's a lie. I didn't kill him. Neither did Bryant"

"Duh."

She glared up at her sister. It wasn't worth asking her how she could be so callous. She had every reason to be cold regarding him.

Jagger spoke next. "Their goal is Bryant's wings. They've gotten the director out of the way. With Bryant out of the way, they can get to his team and to you two."

Odessa drew in a shaky breath. Not his wings. "What do we do?"

"The senate still hasn't heard the whole story. One of us needs to get into one of their sessions and tell them." He scowled again at Felicia. He probably wanted to be the one to do it, but he couldn't ditch her sister. "It'd help if we could prove who killed your father. Or even how they got the weapon."

"All of Bryant's gear was in the house. He kept his stuff downstairs since that's where he'd been sleeping."

Felicia crossed her arms. "Anyone could have sifted through the rubble and found a knife."

"They can't prove Bryant did it," Odessa pointed out.

"Doesn't matter," Jagger said. "Numen don't practice

human law. If Stede can convince the senate Vale's guilty, that's all they need. They'll take his wings."

"Where's the big guy at?" Felicia asked looking around.

"They're keeping him somewhere else. An isolated cell."

Jagger shook his head, his blond hair flying. "They're after his wings. They won't waste time before trying him for the murder."

Odessa grabbed the bars, wishing her rage and fear equaled strength and she could just pry them open. "I need to get to him."

"Anything we do is going to make it worse," Jagger said grimly.

"Let me go to the house Father lived in," Felicia said. "It's close enough to the senate's headquarters. Maybe we can find out what's going on."

"You've been to his place?" She'd been under the impression they'd had nothing to do with each other.

"It's where I last talked to him. We had *words*." Felicia didn't elaborate beyond that, but from the glint of pain in her eyes, her talk with Father was not him telling her how much he loved her and how he'd failed her. "But I didn't kill him."

Jameson stepped forward, but refrained from touching Felicia. "We'd better go. At least it won't look as suspicious if we're snooping around the senate's campus."

"Find him." Odessa was two heartbeats away from panicking.

Her sister and Jagger disappeared. She looked around. Dammit. A full-on panic attack would do no good in this place.

So now what?

BRYANT'S shirtless torso stretched over the post. His hands were tied to a bolt in the floor, his feet bound in the same chains behind them—also secured to the floor. Dread gripped him.

What the hell had he gotten himself into?

Winger stood over him, waiting for the final announcement. Nobody knew his real name. He was the angel who took wings from those doomed to fall. The male was massive. He had to be. Once he took hold of an angel's wings, there was no wrestling away. The only thing that came next was the slice of the blade. And it kept coming until the wings were severed.

His fucking wings.

Bryant had tuned out the hushed conversations of the senators long ago. All he thought about was his wings. An extremity he never gave much thought to. Took them for granted, really. Sure, he liked to fly—barely did it. They were good in a fight, had saved many a blade from entering his heart. It burned like a motherfucker when they got sliced, though. Like a foot-long paper cut.

The asshole pressing for his de-winging was a senator called Kenton. Bryant had never crossed paths with him. In the hour he'd been in this position while the blowhards debated the fate of his wings, it was clear the senator didn't like him. The guy was gunning for his feathers. With Stede's help.

Stede painted a convincing picture, all right. Years of resentment due to blaming Senator Montclaire for his team's demise. Senator Montclaire trying to save Odessa from him. That was the first Bryant had heard. Stede was lying. Even the mansion's tragedy was laid at his feet.

The only thing Bryant was grateful for in all this was that Odessa was not implicated as being responsible for her father's death. Stede had tried, but Senator Naasim shot him down. She'd known the Montclaire sisters their whole lives and she wouldn't see them dragged into this. Bryant had always liked that one. She was centuries old but looked like she was sixty in human years. Her mate was still a warrior. They'd probably live forever and kick ass and take names the whole time.

To his surprise, even Odessa's ex, Crestin, had spoken in her defense. Bryant still hated him. Just a little less now.

"It's time to make the official proclamation," Senator Kenton intoned. "I hereby decree, Bryant Vale, fallen."

Gasps echoed off the marble walls of the circular auditorium.

"Ready for this?" Winger spoke so low, only Bryant could hear.

To answer, Bryant laid his head down and prayed.

~

A ROAR RIPPED through the air. Odessa ran for her life.

No, not her life. Bryant's.

Felicia and Jagger had discovered Bryant was being tried and came back as Odessa was being released. She'd been found innocent.

All three of them flew to the senate auditorium and landed as close as they could to the entrance and Odessa sprinted the rest of the way. The others were close behind.

Guards stepped in front of the door. Another bellow echoed from within the chamber. Adrenaline laced Odessa's blood. She punched the guard on her right, ignored the agony in her hand, and dodged the one on her left. She spun around them. Surprise made them slow, so by the time Odessa had the door open, Jagger and Felicia had engaged them.

"No!" The vision that greeted her drove her to her knees.

Bryant was chained down. His chest and stomach draped over a large wooden stump. His bloodied hunk of wings hung from a scowling, menacing male.

The one called Winger dropped Bryant's pewter wings. They landed with sickening thump, feathers crooked and splayed, blood splattered across the floor.

He flipped a metal latch. A metal clang rang through the open auditorium as the chains holding Bryant released.

His groan spurred her on. She popped up and raced through senator seating.

Winger's spotted her and his forehead furrowed. "You know the rules."

Bryant would never be dead to her. She'd never forget him. She sped toward her mate. The bloody pits in his back threatened to either make her sick or attack Winger with all her rage. Rage was winning. She'd turn that knife of his on him.

Bryant shifted to gaze at her. He was gray and shaking, his breathing raspy. The muscles of his strong body rippled as waves of pain crashed over him. His warning expression made Odessa slow. Only slightly.

He shook his head. Was he ashamed to be seen by her? Did he expect her not to care? Or was he afraid she'd risk her own future by not disowning him?

Winger bent down and yanked Bryant's arm.

"Stop!" she screamed. She was almost there.

They disappeared.

Odessa pulled to a stop in front of Bryant's limp wings. She searched the sky for them, but Winger had transported away.

"He was innocent! You fools!" she shrieked to the silent auditorium. She glared at the audience. Her brain registered no familiar faces even though she knew everyone in the room.

Dropping to her knees, she sunk shaking hands into the warm feathers. Burning tears streaked down her cheeks. Bryant's deep gray wings were soft under her fingers. So soft. She remembered how they had felt when he draped them over her during sleep. How they looked when he held them high.

Footsteps rushed from behind her.

"Oh my God, Ode." Felicia stopped next to her, but Odessa couldn't look up. She didn't want to hear it. She wanted nothing to do with these people.

There was only one place she wanted to be. Odessa stormed back out the way she came. No one stopped her. Once outside, she descended.

~

CALCUTTA.

"Yep," Winger answered. "It's Kolkata now."

Bryant hadn't realized he said it out loud. He sagged on all fours on the ground, not bothering to look around. He recognized the sights and smells.

His back. Huuuurt.

"What happened to dropping me in London?" It'd be a miracle if Winger understood him. His normally gravelly voice was thick with pain.

"Senator Kenton gave me instructions before your hearing."

"It wasn't exactly a hearing. It was a witch hunt."

"We expected no less," Winger agreed.

Yeah. It went exactly as they had thought. Until the last ten seconds.

"Odessa." Bryant groaned her name. How the hell had she gotten there? If she left the enforcer's prison, they could still try to punish her.

"Don't know, man." Winger dropped his hold on Bryant. "Made it look believable, though."

"Whaddya mean, believable?" Bryant staggered under his own weight. "It was real."

"Yeah. It was." Winger wasn't a male of many words. But he was a good angel, despite his job. "Remember what I told you?"

"Yeah," Bryant answered, fighting to a standing position. "You remember the address?"

"Yep. You got twenty-four hours."

"I'm in fucking Calcutta."

"Kolkata," Winger corrected. Bryant shot him a dirty look. The male shrugged. "I have a lot of downtime. I travel."

Bryant tried standing in a position that didn't aggravate the molten volcanoes burning in his back. Nothing helped. "You have a way out of here for me then?"

"Nope." Winger turned his attention toward Bryant. "I'm sure you'll figure something out. See you in twenty-three hours."

The executioner of the senate left in a blink.

Bryant slowly turned in a full circle, leaving a swirl of blood droplets on the ground. At least Winger had dropped him in a private section of the city. A rundown, gritty area, but Bryant would make it work.

Maybe.

What was he going to do? His fallback plan was set in London. Not fucking India.

All right. First things first. He needed a towel and a shirt.

Bryant had spent at least two hours looking for a kind soul that was willing to let him make an international call. His scarred appearance and lurching form made humans rush in the other direction. He couldn't see his back, but he was sure blood from his injury was seeping into his shirt.

Twenty-one hours left. To get halfway around the world.

Keeping to the shadows, Bryant staggered until he found what he was looking for.

A dude on a phone.

It wasn't a good idea to start off a fall by committing a crime. Not when he wanted to get his wings back.

Twenty-one hours.

Bryant hung out, watching people pass. He bided his time, waiting for the right target.

More than luck was on his side when a young man stepped into the shadows. He was frantically typing into his phone. Bryant glided up behind him and knocked him out. The phone dropped and clattered on the ground.

Bryant lunged for it. Swearing, he picked it up.

Score, it wasn't a smart phone.

It took a lot of calling around, more than a few informational calls, until he was finally connected with his target.

"Hello?"

"Matthias Perez?"

"Yeah?"

"You're going to help me, and I'll tell you why." Bryant filled in the astounded angel on how he knew about him and Junie, and exactly what he needed. He couldn't call his parents, or they'd pay for being in contact with him. "You're a chaperone. Get here."

"It doesn't work like that."

"People die everywhere. Get here."

"It doesn't work like that," Matthias repeated.

"You wanna be hanging out, wingless, with me? I doubt the senate will be kind to you, or your mate."

"Okay. Fine. Fuck." Matthias inhaled deeply. "Give me a meeting point and I'll get there."

Bryant rattled off an address he passed a few streets back. After he hung up, he dropped the phone to the ground by the human. He pitied the man's cellphone bill.

CHAPTER 29

The sheets smelled like him.

Odessa was curled on Bryant's bed in his London flat. She'd been here with Bryant only days ago, after the fire. It felt like years.

She didn't know how much time had passed since she witnessed Bryant's life get taken away. Her only solace was that he wasn't dead.

And that he had a backup plan.

He loved this flat. He loved London. He'd be back. She'd pull a Matthias Perez and keep her mate.

Only he wasn't back yet. Oh God, what if he bled out before he could get here?

Odessa sat up. Maybe she should go look for him.

She laid back down. It was a ridiculous idea. They could've dropped him anywhere in the city.

She sat back up. What if they didn't take him to London? It would be cruel to take Bryant anywhere else, but the senate hadn't been kind when they had ordered his wrongful punishment.

Odessa stood to go to the window, but remembered her wings were still out. It felt a little insulting, waiting for Bryant with her wings on display.

Oh no. If Bryant even had a key to this place, he wouldn't have it on him.

Heading to the door, she stopped when she heard huffing and scraping on the other side. Odessa was frozen in place, trying to figure out her next move. She'd taken on two guards already today. Sort of. Jagger and Felicia finished what she'd started.

Okay, she'd messed with two guards already, she could take on whomever was outside the door.

To prevent changing her mind, she marched to the door and whipped it open.

A battered Bryant fell over the threshold.

Startled, she caught him against her and stumbled backward. The door swung closed behind him.

He straightened and his own bewildered expression changed to one Odessa could only explain as guarded hope.

"What are you doing here?"

"Waiting for you." Odessa took the chance to look him over.

Poor guy. He was haggard and exhausted, but he still stood strong. There was visible tightness in his shoulders from the pain radiating through his back.

"It could get you in trouble." He was still looking at her funny.

"I don't care. It worked for Matthias and Junie Perez, we can make it work for us. Come on." She turned to head to the bathroom. "Let's get you cleaned up. Maybe my healing abilities will still work on you."

"Odessa." He hadn't moved.

"What's wrong?"

"I need to tell you something."

"Okay." She resumed her path to the bathroom. Grabbing washcloths and towels, she called back to him. "We can talk while we get you taken care of."

While she was running water to warm it for the cloths, he shuffled into the bathroom. His expression had changed to a baffled concern.

"What's wrong?" she asked again.

He gave his head a shake. "Hopefully nothing."

The sound of the front door bursting open had both of them charging out of the bathroom to see who it was.

A male boomed. "I can't find your girl. They say she descended as soon as I left with you. Oh—"

Winger pulled up short. He had changed clothes since Odessa had last seen him. She was relieved he was no longer covered in Bryant's blood. The large male was carrying an enormous duffel bag.

He dropped the duffel and eyed her. "Well, I guess that solves one problem."

Odessa wanted to be angry. She felt like she should be angry, but she was confused as hell.

"What are you doing here?" she asked Winger. Then she looked at Bryant, who didn't appear surprised. "You were expecting him?"

"Y'all are going to have to chitchat later, because the sooner we do this the better. If I'd known she'd be here already, I'd have come earlier."

"I just got here," Bryant answered.

Winger grinned. "That was cutting it close. How'd you manage it?"

Bryant shrugged and winced. Odessa finally looked at his back. Dots of blood covered the back of his shirt and lumps that must be some form of padding gave him a hunchback appearance. He needed to get his wounds tended.

Winger gestured to the open space in the main room.

311

"Looks like the best spot to try this." He picked up the duffel and headed to where he'd pointed.

"Try what?" Odessa had so many questions.

"Try? You're not sure if this'll work?" Bryant followed Winger. Odessa followed Bryant.

"I told you." Winger drug an end table into the middle of the floor and set the duffel beside it. "It's only a suspicion. A strong one, but it's not like it's ever been done before. The senate isn't full of angels that say 'whoops, we shouldn't have done that.'"

Odessa stopped, put her hands on her hips, and flared her wings out. "What are you two talking about?"

Bryant exhaled, still glaring at Winger. "I'm sorry. I couldn't get to you to tell you. And I thought you'd still be in the holding cell by the time Winger went looking for you."

Winger snorted. "Made it look totally believable, though."

Bryant rounded back on him. "It *was* totally believable. You cut my bloody wings off."

The other angel held up his hands in a placating manner. "I get it. It's a sore subject."

Odessa was about to blow, anger overtaking confusion. Bryant turned back to her.

"I knew my wings were goners. Stede would make sure I looked guilty. My only goal was to get you cleared. Then Winger found me."

Odessa's gaze flicked back to the burly angel.

He stood proud, his chest puffed out. "If I take a pair of wings, I make damn sure the angel deserves it."

"I told him everything. I hadn't gotten to talk to the senate yet, and I wanted to make a deal with Winger but he had a better idea."

"Y'all needed to know who the dirty senators are. The ones gunning for Bryant's wings would be the best clue."

It seemed a bit drastic. Odessa waited for the rest of the story. There was still Winger's presence and the duffel bag, but nothing changed that Bryant had been found guilty of murder and his wings had been cut off.

"Winger also told me a tidbit about the wings." Bryant gestured to Winger to finish the story.

Winger leaned down to unzip the bag. Odessa gasped. Pewter colored feathers popped out of the opening in the bag.

"I'm under strict orders to keep each set of wings for a full twenty-four hours. No one's ever really said why, but I've gleaned enough to suspect"—he pinned Bryant with a hard look—"strongly, that it's a preventative measure, a grace period. In case a de-winging was ever deemed a mistake."

Odessa couldn't believe it. "Do you just pop them back in?"

The male chuckled. "Nah. I assume we use the mate's healing ability. If there's no mate, I bet it's like a warrior. A sync brand would appear if the fallen is destined to be saved."

Falling was an angel's biggest fear. To know that it was reversible, to an extent, would radically change how it was viewed. Or not. Twenty-four hours wasn't much time.

Her heart launched into her throat. "How long has it been?"

"Twenty-three hours and ten minutes," Winger answered.

She rushed past Bryant to stand by Winger. "We need to hurry. What do we need to do?"

Winger raised a sardonic eyebrow and glanced at Bryant.

Bryant shuffled forward, pain shining in his eyes with each step. "Are you sure, Odessa?"

Of course, she was. Then she saw past the pain, past the concern, to the insecurity underneath it all.

"You didn't know if I'd agree to help you get your wings

back." Odessa was crushed. How could he think she was that shallow? She—

"I wanted you to have a choice. We have our list of suspects—for certain Senator Kenton. The investigation could go on without me. I'd be fine here." He stepped closer to her, but stopped. "I didn't mean to worry you. Honestly. You weren't supposed to see any of that. After Winger dropped me"—he glared at the angel—"in fucking Calcutta—"

"Kolkata," Winger interrupted. "I had to make it look real."

"He was going to get you and tell you our plan. See if you were…" Bryant drifted off.

"See if I was willing to save you?" Odessa asked, bitterness lacing her tone.

"But you were here already." His brows drew down. "Did you really plan on living here in secret?"

"Yes," Odessa snapped the word out. "Because I love you. There. There's my choice. What's yours?"

"Make it quick, 'cause time's running out." Winger could talk all he wanted, but Odessa was intent on Bryant and he was focused on her.

"You love me?" Bryant echoed.

Odessa gave him a look like *duh*.

He shuffled the rest of the way to her. "I've been too afraid to acknowledge my feelings for you. If I did, and you didn't return them, I'd be destroyed. Wings or not. I love you, Odessa."

Happiness and relief filled her. She would've been okay if he cared for her, if she was important to him. But love was divine.

Bryant reached for her face, she leaned in for a kiss when Winger's throat clearing interrupted them.

"Tick-tock, people."

Odessa broke away but didn't miss the promise to pick up where they'd left off in Bryant's gaze. "What do you need us to do?"

"Bryant, stretch across the table. I'll plop your wings back in and Odessa will do her healing mojo."

Bryant got into position, Odessa knelt next to him.

Winger dragged the wings out of the duffel and gave them a little shake. "I hosed them off. Hope that didn't mess anything up."

"It'll be a miracle if this works anyway," Bryant grumbled, draped over the table.

She gently lifted his shirt and pried away the blood-soaked rags. "You were a miracle for me when I needed one."

A choking sound could be heard from Winger. "Can you two hit pause on the lovey-dovey until I'm gone?"

"You don't want to hear how I didn't know I had a favorite color until I looked into Odessa's eyes?"

A warm glow filled Odessa. She knew Bryant was teasing Winger, but there was truth in his words.

"God, no. I might take my own wings." Winger hefted Bryant's pair. He leveled them over the holes in Bryant's back and placed them in.

Bryant jerked, his body going taunt. Right now, there was no healing. Just an object getting shoved into his wounds.

Odessa flared her wings over Bryant and leaned in. She concentrated on the ripped flesh in his back.

For a few terrifying seconds, nothing happened. She squeezed her eyes shut and thought about how much this male meant to her.

A deep moan emanated from her mate. "It feels like my back's covered in angel fire."

Did that mean it was working? She concentrated harder.

"Think about his wings." Winger spoke in her ear. He was standing over them, holding Bryant's wings in place.

"Think about repairing his tissue, healing his wings back in place."

Odessa did as instructed. She envisioned Bryant's back like a well gone dry. As his wings were poured in, his skin and bones, and tendons took them in, greedy for the substance. She pictured the wound closing around the base of each appendage, sealing stronger than before. Finally, she thought of what Bryant looked like, wings proudly flared—breathtaking. Her heart skipped a beat.

A deep groan vibrated through his body. Odessa opened her eyes and leaned back.

She watched as Winger tentatively let go of Bryant's wings.

Another rough sound came from Bryant. "If it worked, I might need a wing sling for a while."

A wide grin spread across Winger's face. "Congrats, dude. You're the first angel in history to be re-winged."

Odessa spread her fingers over the feathers, smoothing them under her hand. She couldn't believe it. "We did it," she breathed.

"You did it." Bryant shifted to look at her. Love poured through his gaze. "Have I mentioned how in love I am with you?"

"On that note." Winger grabbed his duffel and shook his wings out. "I'm outta here. Rest up for a day and I'll talk to Senator Naasim. Come find me and we'll take down Stede and Senator Kenton."

Winger stepped out on the deck and disappeared.

Odessa continued to stroke Bryant's feathers. He grabbed her hand and they both stood.

"I need a shower." He led her to the bathroom.

Odessa gave him a stern look and tried to break away. "You go clean up. I want you to rest."

The look he turned on her was pure fire. "I don't need my wings for what I have planned."

Her breath hitched. She tugged on the belt to her robe and it fell open.

An ardent smile spread across his face. "Now that is a sight worth falling for."

CHAPTER 30

*B*ryant glanced between Senator Naasim and Director Richter. Or rather, former Director Richter.

"You're in charge now." Leo Richter made a disgusted noise. "I can't. I can't even fucking walk. How can I lead the warriors?"

"You can still get around. Your wings—"

The bitter male interrupted with a disgusted sound. "They're no good indoors. Fucking wings. Why wasn't it those that burned? Then maybe Millie wouldn't have to care for me like a baby."

The director's reaction took Bryant by surprise. He couldn't blame the guy, he was still in a bad place after his injuries. But Bryant was damn glad he had his wings.

He was more than a little concerned about Richter. The male wasn't merely his boss, he was a friend. Bryant had lost enough friends to angel fire, damn if he'd let Leo give up on life.

"Look, sir. I realize you've got some shit going on. I'll give you time to work that out, but don't think for one minute,

318

I'm staying in the director's chair. The fire took your legs away. It didn't take your brain."

He stood up because he anticipated the male to either get very angry or very morose. The answer was definitely angry.

Taking a gamble, he decided to plant a seed in the director's mind, using the male's own words on him. Ones he heard himself not too long ago.

"You can still live a fulfilling life, even without legs. Many humans are good at it." Staying would be pointless. Richter had his mind set. For now. Bryant turned to the stately senator who'd been watching the exchange. "I'll be back after we get shit with the senate straightened out. Ma'am?"

Senator Naasim adopted a demure smile, nodded toward Richter, then followed Bryant out of the room.

"I must say Warrior Vale, you are an excellent choice for Odessa."

Damn right. "Why do you say that?"

"You don't desert the people in your life. You care deeply and are an honorable male." She sighed heavily. "I wish I could say the same about her parents, unfortunately... She and Felicia were both abandoned." Senator Naasim shook her head, her silver hair glinting in the light. "I knew something must've happened for the Montclaires to change like that. If only Kreger had said something."

"I agree." Bryant descended the stairs next to her. "But if I were to put myself in his shoes, he didn't know who he could trust. He was doing the only thing he knew to keep them safe."

"True. I assume you told Winger to approach me because I advocated for Odessa during your trial."

"Yes, ma'am."

"Good choice. Let us grab Odessa and transcend ourselves to the auditorium. The other senators probably have their robes in a bunch since I'm late for session."

They collected his mate and arrived in front of the doors of the auditorium. The two guards looked back and forth between Bryant and Odessa, unsure of what to do.

Bryant twitched his wings in irritation. It was highly satisfying to see their disbelief. Even more satisfying when they eyed Odessa warily, afraid she'd strike again.

"Move," Senator Naasim commanded with so much authority, Bryant almost sidled away.

A blink of uncertainty and then the two males shifted out of her way.

Bryant opened the doors for the two females to enter.

Chatter ceased as soon as Bryant entered. The shock was palatable. He could feel their gazes move from him, to his wings, to Odessa, back to his wings. Out of the corner of his eye, he could see Winger off to his right with a shit-eating grin.

"What's the meaning of this?" Senator Kenton sputtered from the middle.

Senator Naasim strode toward him. "Senator Kenton, it seems you've been keeping a secret from us." The male's face turned gray. Senator Naasim walked around where he stood so she could address the crowd. "It would seem Odessa Vale uncovered a conspiracy in the human realm. A plan between the fallen James Hancock and *a senator* to ally with demons and find a way to cross the Mist to Numen. Care to add to their findings?"

Gasps and chattering surrounded Bryant. He doubted any of them would have believed him if he brought the news to them at his hearing. Confronted with a fallen who'd gotten his wings back, they were more inclined to listen.

"That's preposterous," Senator Kenton sputtered.

"Is it?" A female senator stood. She was older than Bryant, but in human years, only looked to be in her thirties. "My mate was a cheater and liar who put our realm at risk. Why would he change among the humans?"

Chanel Hancock gazed imperiously around the crowd. Her hair was a darker blond than Jagger's, and her eyes were a golden brown.

"He goes by Jameson Haddock," Bryant spoke up. The crowd quieted again. "He's amassing a human following. Humans that are willing to host demons and hunt angels roaming the earth. Once a watcher became suspicious, she brought her concerns to Odessa's supervisor. You remember, the one they say died of suicide? No Numen is safe."

Senator Kenton snorted in derision. "And you say it was all a part of a big, bad plot between me and Haddock."

Bryant glared at the male. "Funny how you adapted to his new name so quickly." Kenton's face went from gray to angry red. "Cal Estevan gave Odessa the assignment. She gave him her findings. The next day, he was dead. That night, humans attacked Odessa. The watcher, Magan, was hunted and killed"—Bryant paused for dramatic effect—"by Haddock."

Voices rose, none believed him.

Figured.

Bryant shouted over the noise. "My team has verified this." Silence fell again. "We've also confirmed that Haddock has discovered a way to inhibit ascension. We need to move on this situation. Now."

Senator Naasim spoke up. "In light of this news, I move that we approve Director Richter's recommendation that Bryant Vale fills his position as Warrior Director. I also move that we have a hearing, immediately, for Senator Kenton."

"This is nonsense," Kenton shouted. "This male *killed* one of ours."

"Nope, sorry." Bryant flared his wings out, making more than just Senator Kenton jump. "Someone stole one of my weapons from the rubble of the mansion."

"My father's last words to Bryant were instructions to watch over me." Odessa had everyone's avid attention. "Fourteen years ago, my family was attacked. My father was told it would happen again." Her accusatory gaze landed on Senator Kenton. "He was ordered by someone in this room to send Bryant's team on a fool's errand. You see, fourteen years ago, his team of warriors were chasing an archmaster that was hunting angels. We think it may be the same archmaster working for Haddock and Kenton."

"This is ridiculous," Senator Kenton scoffed. "We need to call in the enforcers."

"Yes, let's call them in," Senator Naasim agreed. "Especially Enforcer Stede. He should have a hearing, too."

A frail senator sitting in the front row stood. Bryant had heard of Senator Thomas, the oldest senator serving Numen, but he'd never seen him.

From the way the crowd quieted, even Senators Kenton and Naasim, the male commanded a large amount of respect.

"I move," Senator Thomas said, "to hold Senator Kenton and Enforcer Stede until we've heard the full story from Warrior Vale." He made a motion with his hand.

Bryant jerked around when he sensed movement, but it was just Winger descending through the senator's seating. He was heading straight for Senator Kenton.

Alarm filled the senator's face. He charged for the exit, catching everyone by surprise. Once he cleared the doorway, he disappeared.

"Coward," Bryant heard from the crowd.

"Go find Stede," Senator Naasim commanded Winger.

Winger inclined his head. "Ma'am." The angel strode out of the auditorium.

Stede would be gone. Bryant planned to comb through the intentions of every angel residing in Numen. He'd make sure this realm was safe from traitorous motivations.

That is if he became the director, if the senate believed him.

Senator Thomas hushed the crowd again. "I move to find out what Director Vale has to say and how he plans to keep this realm safe."

～

JAMESON HADDOCK STEPPED out of his Maserati. The phone call he'd gotten summoning him to the desert meeting spot was more than foreboding. Now he was cranky because his car was all dusty.

The two angels anxiously awaited his arrival surrounded by an air of complete arrogance. Idiots. White robes in red dirt.

Why would Stede be here? Jameson had never liked the male and was glad he usually went through Andy.

"Gentlemen." Jameson leaned against his car and crossed his arms.

"We have a problem, Haddock." Senator Kenton ran a hand through his hair. "Do you know anything about fallen getting their wings back?"

Jameson raised a brow. Don't they think he'd have a set if it were possible?

"Something about a mate being able to heal them?"

Jameson barked out a laugh. "I don't think my dear Chanel would've been so willing to oblige. I take it your plan to de-wing Vale…"

Kenton emphatically shook his head. "We thought we succeeded. Convinced the senate he killed his mate's father. I stood five yards away as his wings were hacked off. Then the next day, he shows up with his mate and starts naming me as your Numen accomplice. They were going to hold me and Stede, to be put through a hearing ordered by that old bastard Thomas."

Stede scowled, his gaze jumping between them. Jameson watched the two males calmly.

Fools, the both of them. "They were going to hold you for a hearing, to determine if you were guilty, and you what? Disappeared? Confirmed your guilt by running?"

The two males looked at each other.

Stede spoke up first. "We couldn't risk losing our wings. Once Winger got ahold of us, we would've been done."

Ah yes, Winger. Jameson's back throbbed. He remembered well the rise of panic, the mad attempts to run, to descend, to somehow get away, but the executioner's hold was absolute, holding him firmly in place for each slice of the blade.

"You still had a chance to spin a story to defend yourselves. Now you're fugitives." Jameson was tempted to hop back in his car and drive the fuck off.

"We had good reason for leaving," Kenton said with his senator cockiness.

Jameson hated him all the more for it.

"And you want what from me?" Maybe Jameson could get some joy out of this. The human realm was now his domain. "I don't know if you realize this, but without access to the happenings in Numen, you're worthless to me."

"We can still get into Numen, and you can't," Stede pointed out.

Touché, jackass. Jameson could only make it as far as the Mist. "Can you get a demon army into Numen?"

"Not yet, but I have something on one of Vale's team. She's proven very helpful in order to keep her secret." Stede was steady, calm. Kenton was ruffled, ready to run circles like an angel on fire.

Stede was the steady one. A big-picture guy. As an enforcer he had to answer to every single senator. But if

Jameson succeeded, every single senator would answer to Stede.

"Interesting," Jameson said. "What have you got on her?"

Stede smiled and Jameson could see the psychopath beneath. "You can see why I don't want to share."

Calm, conniving Stede. Jameson needed to get him alone. They could work well together.

"I assume you're looking for some help hiding?"

"Not me," Stede said adamantly. "I have a place to go."

The way he said it almost made Jameson feel bad for whomever Stede planned to hang out with. Jameson would hide the senator. Right where he could distract the warriors so they'd back off his club.

"I'll need clothes and money. And two demon guards you can trust." Kenton had some balls, Jameson would give him that. "I want to be kept apprised of your progress. We still have contacts in Numen we can get updates from."

One, demons and trust don't go together. Two, he'd be kept apprised enough so Jameson could lay a wide trail of breadcrumbs. Let the warriors deal with the senator. He'd served his purpose. The Numen knew about Jameson and his plan. He had to switch to evasive tactics and step up his game.

"Stede, you'll be in touch with Andy once you get settled?"

From the gleam in Stede's gaze, he interpreted his tone correctly. The enforcer also thought Kenton had reached his expiration date. The angel nodded and transcended.

Jameson eyed Kenton. He remembered when he first ran into the male after his fall. "I wanted to kill you when I first saw you in Fall from Grace. It's a shame you could no longer frequent there after we partnered up."

Kenton narrowed his eyes on him like a hubris-filled bird of prey. "What are you getting at?"

"I know you had to go to other places to find partners to

suit your particular...tastes. Do you have a paramour who could shelter you?"

Frowning, Kenton studied the dirt. Jameson waited patiently. The angel's penchant for whips, chains, and pain wouldn't go over well with most Numen females. Or males, for that matter. It was what opened the door for an alliance between Jameson and Kenton.

"I'd need money," Kenton finally said.

"What's a few dollars among partners?"

Jameson could recruit a couple of hosts to watch Kenton. Kenton could distract himself with his human toys. The warriors should have no trouble finding him. Meanwhile, Jameson could keep working on Gerzon to up his demonic contribution to Jameson's plans. The demon might be interested in some potion that prevented Numen from traveling between realms.

Yes, Kenton thought they'd taken a severe hit, almost had their plans derailed. But to Jameson, things were looking up.

CHAPTER 31

"*H*ey." Odessa smiled as she let herself through the door.

"Hey, yourself." Bryant pushed back from his desk to greet his mate.

God, she was beautiful. Her hair hung free around her shoulders, a lush frame for her work-of-art face. She wore a maxi dress that teased him about the treasures lying underneath.

He'd hardly seen her in the last week. Since the senate hearing, he'd been steeped in paperwork and planted in meetings. What a fucking headache. How'd Richter survive this?

His appointment had created waves, but Senator Thomas and Senator Naasim were strong supporters to have on his side. They strongly encouraged the senate to back his position as Warrior Director. He was even asked for a recommendation to take Stede's place, who—shocker—had turned up missing.

Tosca's appointment to Stede's position had made almost as many waves as his. She didn't put up with any shit from

MARIE JOHNSTON

her fellow enforcers and her intense scrutiny was on each one. Starting with the ones that had worked closely with Stede.

"I brought lunch." She held up a bag from one of his favorite pubs in London. "Don't worry," she rushed on. "I didn't go there alone. Jagger and Felicia came with me."

Bryant smiled. It was something he did easily around her now. Odessa had spent much of the last week at Felicia's place where Jagger and her sister kept working on her self-defense skills. Odessa's presence helped the other two fight less between themselves.

When she wasn't in Atlanta, she stopped by to help Millie. The two had become fast friends, sharing the same privileged background and both being mated to warriors. Bryant needed to get over there and check on Leo. And remind him he was still a warrior and make sure he at least got his ass out of bed.

"It smells great." He wanted to lean in to kiss her. Hug her in tight. That would only be the beginning. He wanted to do so much more, but it wouldn't be very director-like. Well... he wasn't very director-like, anyway.

"Come." She smiled. "Let's eat."

They sat at the round table in his office where he usually held smaller meetings. She talked about her day while he ate and enjoyed the pleasing cadence of her voice. These moments were too precious to be interrupted. If anyone knocked on the door, he'd tell them to fuck off.

"That was super greasy. And delicious." She pushed her wrappers to the side and set her elbow on the table. She leaned into her hand. "How's it been going?"

"I spoke with Chanel Hancock today." Bryant suppressed a shudder. A chilling female to say the least. "She told me what Haddock was like when they were mated."

"Is she as cold and unfeeling as Jagger?"

328

He couldn't help but smirk. His mate was definitely on Team Felicia.

"Jagger feels, then shoves it down and gets angry. His mother is stone cold. She's willing to help us. I think she despises her ex-mate even more since finding out he's thrived among the humans."

"Yes, Jagger's still a little angry about being on Felicia duty. She refuses to reside up here, so Dionna ordered him to stay with Filly."

Bryant wanted to stomp his foot and pout like a five-year-old. Dionna had his old job. He'd freaking loved his job. But he loved his mate and his realm more; they came first.

"Yeah, she's a solid leader. Always has been. She could've had her own team long ago, but always turned it down."

"Hmm, wonder why." Odessa swiveled in her chair to face him. "How are the others?"

"Sierra's running intel for Harlowe, Bronx, and Urban, who are in the field hunting down the senator and Stede. I put another team on surveillance of Fall from Grace. We'll get Jameson Haddock, but Kenton and Stede are higher priority since they can still transcend into Numen. How's your sister?"

Odessa's forehead furrowed. "Good, I guess."

Bryant waited. There was more.

"I think…" She frowned. "I strongly suspect that all her training is more than to keep from ever feeling weak and being a victim again. I think she's going to hunt down the male that brutalized her."

He couldn't blame Felicia. Honestly, he didn't want to stop her, but he didn't want to see her hurt.

"Until we know for sure…" He shrugged. "She has me and you backing her actions, if she chooses to follow through."

His mate looked relieved. "So…" Odessa began to twirl

patterns on his thigh. He swelled uncomfortably behind the fly of his pants. "Your door is locked, right?"

"Yes," he growled, dragging her onto his lap. He buried his nose in her neck. "It's been too long."

"It's been since yesterday." The breathy quality in her words hardened him even more.

"Right. Too long."

"Are we going to christen your office?" she purred, rocking into him.

He felt like he was going to explode. He needed to get in her.

"We're going to break in this chair. Then the table. Then my desk."

Odessa giggled and reached between them to undo his pants. "That's how dedicated we are to your new position."

She freed him and he rejoiced in the feeling of his length cradled in her warm hands.

He cupped her face. "I love you, Odessa. I couldn't do this job without you. You make it worthwhile."

A sweet smile rewarded his words. "Bryant Vale. I didn't have to wait for a destined sync mate, because I was meant to be with you. If I have to bring you lunch every day to sneak a few moments here and there, it's okay. You're worth it."

He brought his lips to hers. She lifted herself up until her robe was out of the way, and gifted him with the sweet ecstasy of her wet heat sliding down his shaft.

She was right. Everything he'd been through had brought him to her, drew her to him. He thought of the time not so long ago when he was in this office. Leo Richter had been right. He *had* needed to sync.

. . .

I'D LOVE to know what you thought of Angel Fire. Please consider leaving a review. Thank you so much!

FOR NEW RELEASE UPDATES, chapter sneak peeks, and exclusive quarterly short stories, sign up for Marie's newsletter and receive download links for the book that started it all, *Fever Claim*, and three short stories of characters from the series.

ABOUT THE AUTHOR

Marie Johnston lives in the upper-Midwest with her husband, four kids, and an old cat. Deciding to trade in her lab coat for a laptop, she's writing down all the tales she's been making up in her head for years. An avid reader of paranormal romance, these are the stories hanging out and waiting to be told between the demands of work, home, and the endless chauffeuring that comes with children.

mariejohnstonwriter.com

instagram.com/mariejohnstonwriter

ALSO BY MARIE JOHNSTON

New Vampire Disorder:
Demetrius (Book1)
Rourke (Book 2)
Bishop (Book 3)
Stryke (Book 4)
Creed (Book 5)
Bastian (Book 6)
The Seer (Novella 7)
Demon Q (Book 8)

Angel Fire:
Angel Fire, book 1
Wicked Fire, book 2 (coming soon)

Printed in Great Britain
by Amazon